Four Great Plays
of Henrik Ibsen

FOUR GREAT PLAYS

A DOLL'S HOUSE, THE WILD DUCK,
HEDDA GABLER,
THE MASTER BUILDER

Henrik Ibsen

Supplementary material written by Alyssa Harad
Series edited by Cynthia Brantley Johnson

POCKET BOOKS
NEW YORK LONDON TORONTO SYDNEY

POCKET BOOKS, a division of Simon & Schuster, Inc.
1230 Avenue of the Americas, New York, NY 10020

This book is a work of fiction. Names, characters, places and incidents are products of the author's imagination or are used fictitiously. Any resemblance to actual events or locales or persons, living or dead, is entirely coincidental.

Supplementary materials copyright © 2005 by Simon & Schuster, Inc.

ISBN-13: 978-0-1-4165-0038-4
ISBN-10:   1-4165-0038-3

First Pocket Books paperback edition August 2005

10 9 8 7 6 5 4 3 2

POCKET and colophon are registered trademarks of Simon & Schuster, Inc.

Cover art by Mark Hess

Manufactured in the United States of America

For information regarding special discounts for bulk purchases, please contact Simon & Schuster Special Sales at 1-800-456-6798 or business@simonandschuster.com.

CONTENTS

INTRODUCTION   *vii*

CHRONOLOGY OF HENRIK IBSEN'S
   LIFE AND WORK   *xv*

HISTORICAL CONTEXT OF IBSEN'S PLAYS   *xvii*

A DOLL'S HOUSE   *1*

THE WILD DUCK   *89*

HEDDA GABLER   *207*

THE MASTER BUILDER   *305*

NOTES   *399*

INTERPRETIVE NOTES   *404*

CRITICAL EXCERPTS   *413*

QUESTIONS FOR DISCUSSION   *423*

SUGGESTIONS FOR THE
   INTERESTED READER   *425*

INTRODUCTION

IBSEN'S PLAYS:
THE SHOCK OF THE MODERN

Each of the plays in this volume arrived onstage to loud cries of derision and bafflement. In some cases they were deemed downright dangerous, incurring the wrath of the censors and the morals police. In others, they were satirized into submission: one London response to the erotic violence of *Hedda Gabler* was a racy burlesque titled "Go A Hedda." After watching *The Master Builder,* some reviewers decided, charitably enough, that Ibsen's characters, and the author himself, must simply be insane. As one critic wrote, unconsciously echoing *Hedda Gabler*'s Judge Brack, there could be no other explanation, since "people simply don't *do* such things." At the same time, Ibsen won fervent admirers who were willing to risk their money, reputations, and professional lives to translate and produce his works. Some of these included writers who would themselves become famous, notorious, or both, including August Strindberg, Henry James, George Bernard Shaw, and James Joyce.

What was all the fuss about? How did this cantankerous man, writing in a language understood by a tiny minority of the world's people, accused of madness, immorality, and worse, come to conquer the international theater?

When Ibsen began writing his realist tragedies, the theater world was almost wholly given over to lavish commercial entertainment. Spectacle and titillation were the rule of the day. Ibsen offered nothing to his audience in terms of sex and violence that they had not already seen magnified, dusted with sequins, and performed to a hit tune. What they had never seen was people dressed more or less like themselves, sitting in tastefully furnished drawing rooms more or less like their own, using everyday language filled with awkward silences, saying and doing the socially unthinkable, right there on the stage in front of them.

The effect was electrifying because, of course, people *did* do (or dream, or fantasize) "such things"; they simply never talked about them—at times not even to themselves. Ibsen proffered nothing less than the middle-class social unconscious, decades before Freud arrived to diagnose its dark workings. *A Doll's House* presented audiences with the repression and power struggles inherent in a seemingly happy marriage and presented the idea that a woman might choose to leave her husband and children rather than destroy herself (still a radical idea for today's Hollywood). In *Hedda Gabler*, audiences faced the deadly consequences of thwarted female power and intelligence. In *The Wild Duck*, they saw a child's life sacrificed to selfish adult illusions. And in *The Master Builder*, they watched as bitter ambition and visionary dreams combined to destroy not one but several lives. It is no wonder that they struggled to assimilate Ibsen's alien forms and ideas, and that the playwright developed a persistent reputation for grim truth telling.

But for Ibsen's fans, his plays acted as a tonic shock, a jolt that freed them from the enervating oppression of Victorian hypocrisies. They welcomed the sophistication of his spare modern forms, and the new rough poetry of his characters' speech. They saw not only the tragedy, but also the ironic comedy of his plays. They strove to emulate his courageous truth telling and to pass that truth on to others.

Today, Ibsen's plays still have the power to shock. In spite of the huge changes wrought by feminism and other social movements, many of his themes are dismayingly relevant. But most of all, his characters remain modern, living beings—puzzling, exasperating, even repellent, but always fascinatingly human.

The Life and Work of Henrik Ibsen

Henrik Ibsen was born on March 20, 1828, in Skien, Norway. His father was a charming but reckless merchant who mismanaged the family into bankruptcy by the time Ibsen was seven. After his father's failure, Ibsen's mother, a frail, loving woman, withdrew into a fantasy land peopled by her collection of dolls. Ibsen too grew up withdrawn, preferring books to other children. He would later draw on memories of his childhood, including the family attic where he hid away to read, to create *The Wild Duck*.

At sixteen, Ibsen left Skien to work as an apothecary's apprentice in the seacoast town of Grimstad. While there, he had an affair with Else Sophie Birkedalen, a housemaid (also from a formerly middle-class background) ten years his senior. In 1846 she gave birth to their illegitimate son. Ibsen suffered great social humiliation from the episode and paid child support his entire life, even through his own frequent poverty.

In spite of these hardships, Ibsen found his vocation early. By 1851 he had completed his university work and written several pieces, including two verse plays. He was appointed resident playwright and stage manager at the Norwegian Theater in Bergen, where he learned the business of theater from the ground up for the next six years.

In 1857 Ibsen moved to Norway's capital, Christiania (now Oslo), to become the artistic director of the Norwegian

Theater. There he continued to write and produce his plays with increasing success. He also met and married Susannah Thoresen, his helpmeet, debate partner, and muse. Though Ibsen had a series of platonic affairs with young women as he grew older, Susannah remained his romantic and philosophical ideal. Remote, intelligent, queenly, and "pure," Susannah was Ibsen's "eagle," other women merely twittering songbirds. Nevertheless, Susannah sacrificed all semblance of normal family and married life for Ibsen's art and subsequent fame—even her intimate life and habits were displayed and distorted upon the stage.

Ibsen's son Sigurd, his only child with Susannah, was born in 1859. In 1862 his play *Love's Comedy* was published in a journal, causing the first of many Ibsen scandals. The Norwegian Theater refused to produce it. Shortly thereafter, the theater went bankrupt and was thrown into poverty. For the next two years Ibsen traveled Norway on a government grant to collect folktales.

In 1864, incensed by Norway's refusal to assist Denmark in the Dano-Prussian War, Ibsen moved with his family to Rome, beginning his self-imposed twenty-seven-year exile. Two years later, ironically, he achieved widespread Scandinavian acclaim for his great verse drama *Brand* and was awarded a lifetime writing grant from the state. The following year he published the great *Peer Gynt*.

Over the next ten years, Ibsen's work, friends, and ideas gradually shifted to encompass the perspectives that would enable the great twelve-play realist cycle from which this collection is drawn. Beginning with 1877's *The Pillars of Society*, Ibsen produced a play nearly every other year, each another blow in his struggle to create dramas that would bring the intensities, hypocrisies, tragedies, and power struggles of middle-class life to the stage. The intense controversies that greeted so many of his works were matched by the fervent admiration of his many followers.

In 1891, homesick for the northern seascapes of his youth, Ibsen returned to Norway, where he was greeted as a national hero. (Susannah, who suffered greatly from rheumatism, remained, for the most part, in Italy.) There, following the strict timetable and habits that had long supported his tremendous productivity, Ibsen became a kind of tourist attraction, surrounded on all sides by camera-bearing admirers every time he took his daily walk.

In 1900, one year after the publication of *When We Dead Awaken*, Ibsen suffered the first of two debilitating strokes. Unable to write, he declined for the next six years, finally dying in 1906. Ibsen was an iconoclast to the last breath: his final words were "To the contrary."

Historical and Literary Context of Ibsen's Plays

Late Victorianism and the Rise of the Middle Class

Ibsen found his subject matter in the hidden lives of the rising middle class. The new technologies and urban growth brought on by the Industrial Revolution had resulted in a greatly expanded middle class by the late Victorian age. Previously, social trends had been dictated by the tastes of the nobility, who were, in turn, imitated by the masses. Now, the middle class began to set the pace. Even though it was Queen Victoria of England who gave her name and oppressive moral codes to the age, it was the newly expanded middle class that allowed these codes to flourish. The exaltation of what are still called "traditional family values," including piety, purity, the strict enforcement of separate spheres of influence for men and women (home for women, business and politics for men), and a taboo on sex and the body supported the still fragile identities of the middle class. For underneath the elaborate repressive social manners of the late Victorians seethed a populace shocked and dazzled by the huge changes—in science, technology, religion, politics, and social mores—that had transformed their lives. Their anxieties ranged from doubts about the nature of man and the existence of God, to an obsession with purity and hygiene spurred by the huge growth of cities, fear of the urban poor, and, as the century drew to a close, concerns about the "New Woman" and her increasingly vocal demands for political, economic, and sexual freedom. Ibsen's plays went straight to the heart of these anxieties and exposed the illusions and hypocrisies his audiences held so dear.

Late Victorian Entertainments, the Well-Made Play, and Norwegian Nationalism

With so much change afoot, it is unsurprising that the new middle class preferred its entertainments to be either moral or inconsequential. Didactic literature meant to train children and adults in the proper way to behave flourished, as did all manner of home entertainments that allowed the middle class to escape the bewildering world of their dirty, slum-ridden cities.

In the mid-Victorian age, the theater had fallen into disrepute and been replaced by that enchanting new literary genre, the novel. But by the late Victorian age, the respectable middle class had been wooed back to the theater by pleasant entertainments like Gilbert and Sullivan's musicals, and the so-called well-made plays patterned after French playwright Eugène Scribe's template. These fashionable, lavishly produced, technically adroit, but insubstantial comedies and melodramas were the Hollywood films of their day. They provided thrills, chills, spills, and happy endings (or a good moral cry). Though they often dabbled in immorality—adultery was a common subject—transgressors were always punished, villains and heroes were easily identified, and the more dangerous subjects were set safely in ancient history.

When Ibsen began to write his plays, governments or private interests oversaw most theaters and closely monitored their profits and morality. His rise to prominence required the bravery and hard work of investors, actors, and producers who were willing to open small private theaters to produce his daring work. But Ibsen got his first toehold in the theater world as a result of a small but growing movement in Norway that sought to replace the well-made plays imported from France, England, and Denmark with a truly Norwegian theater. The Norwegian Theater at Bergen, where Ibsen first worked as a playwright, had been founded by the eccentric musician and Norwegian nationalist Ole Bull, and Ibsen's early verse dramas deliberately drew on the myths and folklore of his native land.

Realism and Ibsen's Modern Legacy

Ibsen is largely regarded as the founder of social realism in drama. Many critics have pointed out that the dramatic crises of Ibsen's plots owe something to the well-made plays his work rebuked, and that they also bear the marks of the folklore, mysticism, and myths that populate his early works. However, Ibsen's close attention to the contemporary details of middle-class life, his complex characters, the spareness of his language (and, in production, his reliance on meaningful silences), and his scrutiny of the modern-day myths and hypocrisies that inform his characters' lives all place him squarely in the camp of realism. Like the novelist Henry James, who was so influenced by Ibsen that he tried his hand (unsuccessfully) at drama, Ibsen attempted to present a contemporary reality heightened only to make its conflicts clearer. In his lifetime, Ibsen inspired many playwrights and novelists, including George Bernard Shaw, Oscar Wilde, James Joyce, and fellow Scandinavian August Strindberg. Contemporary drama as we know it is thoroughly indebted to Ibsen's radical vision and renewal of the modern play.

CHRONOLOGY OF HENRIK IBSEN'S LIFE AND WORK

1828: Born on March 20 in Skien, Norway.
1835: Family moves to smaller home due to father's financial troubles and debt.
1843: Ibsen leaves home to work as an apothecary's apprentice in Grimstad.
1846: Fathers illegitimate son with apothecary's maid. He will pay child support his entire life.
1849: Writes first play, *Catiline*.
1851: Appointed resident playwright and stage manager at Norwegian Theater in Bergen where he will work in every aspect of theater for next six years.
1856: *The Feast at Solhoug* performed—Ibsen's first commercial success.
1857: Ibsen appointed artistic director, Norwegian Theater in Christiania. *Olaf Liljekrans* performed.
1858: Marries Susannah Thoresen. *The Vikings at Helgeland* performed.
1859: Son Sigurd born. Poems "On the Heights" and "In the Picture Gallery" published.
1862: Publishes *Love's Comedy*. Ensuing scandal scares Norwegian Theater out of producing play. Norwegian

Theater goes bankrupt and closes. Jobless and in debt, Ibsen obtains government grant to collect folktales.

1864: In January, *The Pretenders* performed at Christiania Theater—a success. In April, Ibsen moves to Rome and begins twenty-seven-year self-imposed exile from Norway.

1866: In March, *Brand* published to great Scandinavian acclaim. Awarded lifetime government grant to write.

1867: *Peer Gynt* published.

1868: Moves to Dresden, lives there through 1875.

1869: *The League of Youth* published. Befriends Danish critic Georg Brandes.

1871: *Poems* published.

1873: *Emperor and Galilean* published.

1877: *The Pillars of Society* published, the first of Ibsen's twelve prose realist plays.

1879: *A Doll's House* published. The ensuing scandal gradually spreads throughout Europe and America.

1881: *Ghosts* published, causing an even bigger scandal than *A Doll's House*.

1882: *An Enemy of the People* published.

1884: *The Wild Duck* published.

1886: *Rosmersholm* published.

1888: *The Lady from the Sea* published.

1889: *Hedda Gabler* published.

1891: Ibsen returns to Norway and great acclaim.

1892: *The Master Builder* published.

1894: *Little Eyolf* published.

1896: *John Gabriel Borkman* published.

1898: Seventieth birthday celebrated with international good wishes.

1899: *When We Dead Awaken* published.

1900: Suffers a debilitating stroke.

1906: Ibsen dies May 23.

HISTORICAL CONTEXT
OF IBSEN'S PLAYS

1828: Russian author Leo Tolstoy born.

1831: German dramatist Johann Wolfgang von Goethe publishes *Faust*.

1837: Queen Victoria ascends the throne of England.

1848: Karl Marx and Friedrich Engels publish *The Communist Manifesto*. Sparked by events in France, a series of revolutions sweep through Europe.

1855: Norwegian telegraphic networks installed over the next fifteen years.

1857: Gustave Flaubert publishes *Madame Bovary*.

1859: Charles Darwin's *Origin of Species* published. Its impact is felt over the next few decades. Eugène Scribe major propagator of the "well-made play," dies.

1864: Dano-Prussian War. Tolstoy's *War and Peace* published over next five years.

1865–90: Ten million immigrants arrive in the United States, primarily from Germany, Ireland, and Scandinavia.

1867: Marx publishes *Das Kapital*.

1869: John Stuart Mill publishes *The Subjection of Women*.

1870–71: Franco-Prussian War. Revolt and subjugation in

Paris. Friedrich Nietzsche publishes *The Birth of Tragedy*. Second wave of Industrial Revolution begins.

1872–90: Danish critic Georg Brandes publishes *Main Currents in Nineteenth-Century Literature*.

1872–1905: Oskar II ascends throne of Swedish-Norwegian union.

1874: First Impressionist exhibit in Paris.

1879: Thomas Edison produces incandescent lightbulb.

1881: Henry James publishes *Portrait of a Lady*.

1882: James Joyce born. G. B. Shaw's first play, *Widower's Houses*, published.

1883: Friedrich Nietzsche's *Thus Spake Zarathustra* published.

1895: Oscar Wilde's *The Importance of Being Earnest* produced. Oscar Wilde imprisoned for homosexuality.

1900: Sigmund Freud's *The Interpretation of Dreams* published.

A Doll's House[1]

CHARACTERS

TORVALD HELMER
NORA, his wife
DR. RANK
MRS. LINDE
NILS KROGSTAD
HELMER's three young children
ANNE, their nurse
A HOUSEMAID
A PORTER

The action takes place in HELMER's house.

ACT ONE

———————————❧———————————

A room furnished comfortably and tastefully but not extravagantly. At the back a door to the right leads to the entrance hall; another to the left leads to HELMER's *study. Between the doors stands a piano. In the middle of the left-hand wall is a door and beyond a window. Near the window are a round table, armchairs and a small sofa. In the right-hand wall, at the farther end, another door; and on the same side, nearer the footlights, a stove, two easy chairs and a rocking chair; between the stove and the door a small table. Engravings on the walls; a cabinet with china and other small objects; a small bookcase with well-bound books. The floors are carpeted, and a fire burns in the stove. It is winter.*

A bell rings in the hall; shortly afterward the door is heard to open. Enter NORA *humming a tune and in high spirits. She is in outdoor dress and carries a number of parcels; these she lays on the table to the right. She leaves the outer door open after her, and through it is seen a* PORTER *who is carrying a Christmas tree and a basket, which he gives to the* MAID *who has opened the door.*

NORA: Hide the Christmas tree carefully, Helen. Be sure the children do not see it till this evening, when it is dressed. (*To the* PORTER, *taking out her purse.*) How much?

PORTER: Sixpence.

NORA: There is a shilling. No, keep the change. (*The* PORTER *thanks her and goes out.* NORA *shuts the door. She is laughing to herself as she takes off her hat and coat. She takes a packet of macaroons from her pocket and eats one or two, then goes cautiously to her husband's door and listens.*): Yes, he is in. (*Still humming, she goes to the table on the right.*)

HELMER (*calls out from his room*): Is that my little lark twittering out there?

NORA (*busy opening some of the parcels*): Yes, it is!

HELMER: Is it my little squirrel bustling about?

NORA: Yes!

HELMER: When did my squirrel come home?

NORA: Just now. (*Puts the bag of macaroons into her pocket and wipes her mouth.*) Come in here, Torvald, and see what I have bought.

HELMER: Don't disturb me. (*A little later he opens the door and looks into the room, pen in hand.*) Bought, did you say? All these things? Has my little spendthrift been wasting money again?

NORA: Yes, but, Torvald, this year we really can let ourselves go a little. This is the first Christmas that we have not needed to economize.

HELMER: Still, you know, we can't spend money recklessly.

NORA: Yes, Torvald, we may be a wee bit more reckless now, mayn't we? Just a tiny wee bit! You are going to have a big salary and earn lots and lots of money.

HELMER: Yes, after the new year; but then it will be a whole quarter before the salary is due.

NORA: Pooh! We can borrow till then.

HELMER: Nora! (*Goes up to her and takes her playfully by the ear.*) The same little featherhead! Suppose, now, that I borrowed fifty pounds today and you spent it all in the

Christmas week and then on New Year's Eve a slate fell on my head and killed me and—

NORA (*putting her hands over his mouth*): Oh! don't say such horrid things.

HELMER: Still, suppose that happened,—what then?

NORA: If that were to happen, I don't suppose I should care whether I owed money or not.

HELMER: Yes, but what about the people who had lent it?

NORA: They? Who would bother about them? I should not know who they were.

HELMER: That is like a woman! But seriously, Nora, you know what I think about that. No debt, no borrowing. There can be no freedom or beauty about a home life that depends on borrowing and debt. We two have kept bravely on the straight road so far, and we will go on the same way for the short time longer that there need be any struggle.

NORA (*moving toward the stove*): As you please, Torvald.

HELMER (*following her*): Come, come, my little skylark must not droop her wings. What is this! Is my little squirrel out of temper? (*Taking out his purse.*) Nora, what do you think I have got here?

NORA (*turning round quickly*): Money!

HELMER: There you are. (*Gives her some money.*) Do you think I don't know what a lot is wanted for housekeeping at Christmas time?

NORA (*counting*): Ten shillings—a pound—two pounds! Thank you, thank you, Torvald; that will keep me going for a long time.

HELMER: Indeed it must.

NORA: Yes, yes, it will. But come here and let me show you what I have bought. And all so cheap! Look, here is a new suit for Ivar and a sword, and a horse and a trumpet for Bob, and a doll and dolly's bedstead for Emmy—they are very plain, but anyway she will soon break them in pieces. And here are dress lengths and handkerchiefs for the maids; old Anne ought really to have something better.

HELMER: And what is in this parcel?

NORA (*crying out*): No, no! You mustn't see that till this evening.

HELMER: Very well. But now tell me, you extravagant little person, what would you like for yourself?

NORA: For myself? Oh, I am sure I don't want anything.

HELMER: Yes, but you must. Tell me something reasonable that you would particularly like to have.

NORA: No, I really can't think of anything—unless, Torvald—

HELMER: Well?

NORA (*playing with his coat buttons and without raising her eyes to his*): If you really want to give me something, you might—you might—

HELMER: Well, out with it!

NORA (*speaking quickly*): You might give me money, Torvald. Only just as much as you can afford; and then one of these days I will buy something with it.

HELMER: But, Nora—

NORA: Oh, do! dear Torvald; please, please do! Then I will wrap it up in beautiful gilt paper and hang it on the Christmas tree. Wouldn't that be fun?

HELMER: What are little people called that are always wasting money?

NORA: Spendthrifts—I know. Let us do as I suggest, Torvald, and then I shall have time to think what I am most in want of. That is a very sensible plan, isn't it?

HELMER (*smiling*): Indeed it is—that is to say, if you were really to save out of the money I give you and then really buy something for yourself. But if you spend it all on the housekeeping and any number of unnecessary things, then I merely have to pay up again.

NORA: Oh, but, Torvald—

HELMER: You can't deny it, my dear little Nora. (*Puts his arm around her waist.*) It's a sweet little spendthrift, but she uses up a deal of money. One would hardly believe how expensive such little persons are!

NORA: It's a shame to say that. I do really save all I can.

HELMER (*laughing*): That's very true—all you can. But you can't save anything!

NORA (*smiling quietly and happily*): You haven't any idea how many expenses we skylarks and squirrels have, Torvald.

HELMER: You are an odd little soul. Very like your father. You always find some new way of wheedling money out of me, and as soon as you have got it it seems to melt in your hands. You never know where it has gone. Still, one must take you as you are. It is in the blood; for indeed it is true that you can inherit these things, Nora.

NORA: Ah, I wish I had inherited many of Papa's qualities.

HELMER: And I would not wish you to be anything but just what you are, my sweet little skylark. But, do you know, it strikes me that you are looking rather—what shall I say— rather uneasy today.

NORA: Do I?

HELMER: You do, really. Look straight at me.

NORA (*looks at him*): Well?

HELMER (*wagging his finger at her*): Hasn't Miss Sweet Tooth been breaking rules in town today?

NORA: No; what makes you think that?

HELMER: Hasn't she paid a visit to the confectioner's?

NORA: No, I assure you, Torvald—

HELMER: Not been nibbling sweets?

NORA: No, certainly not.

HELMER: Not even taken a bite at a macaroon or two?

NORA: No, Torvald, I assure you, really—

HELMER: There, there, of course I was only joking.

NORA (*going to the table on the right*): I should not think of going against your wishes.

HELMER: No, I am sure of that; besides, you gave me your word. (*Going up to her.*) Keep your little Christmas secrets to yourself, my darling. They will all be revealed tonight when the Christmas tree is lit, no doubt.

NORA: Did you remember to invite Dr. Rank?

HELMER: No. But there is no need; as a matter of course he

will come to dinner with us. However, I will ask him when he comes in this morning. I have ordered some good wine. Nora, you can't think how I am looking forward to this evening.

NORA: So am I! And how the children will enjoy themselves, Torvald!

HELMER: It is splendid to feel that one has a perfectly safe appointment and a big enough income. It's delightful to think of, isn't it?

NORA: It's wonderful!

HELMER: Do you remember last Christmas? For a full three weeks before hand you shut yourself up every evening till long after midnight, making ornaments for the Christmas tree and all the other fine things that were to be a surprise to us. It was the dullest three weeks I ever spent!

NORA: I didn't find it dull.

HELMER (*smiling*): But there was precious little result, Nora.

NORA: Oh, you shouldn't tease me about that again. How could I help the cat's going in and tearing everything to pieces?

HELMER: Of course you couldn't, poor little girl. You had the best of intentions to please us all, and that's the main thing. But it is a good thing that our hard times are over.

NORA: Yes, it is really wonderful.

HELMER: This time I needn't sit here and be dull all alone and you needn't ruin your dear eyes and your pretty little hands—

NORA (*clapping her hands*): No, Torvald, I needn't any longer, need I! It's wonderfully lovely to hear you say so! (*Taking his arm.*) Now I will tell you how I have been thinking we ought to arrange things, Torvald. As soon as Christmas is over— (*A bell rings in the hall.*) There's the bell. (*She tidies the room a little.*) There's someone at the door. What a nuisance!

HELMER: If it is a caller, remember I am not at home.

MAID (*in the doorway*): A lady to see you, ma'am—a stranger.

NORA: Ask her to come in.

MAID *(to* HELMER*)*: The doctor came at the same time, sir.

HELMER: Did he go straight into my room?

MAID: Yes sir.

HELMER *goes into his room. The* MAID *ushers in* MRS. LINDE, *who is in traveling dress, and shuts the door.*

MRS. LINDE *(in a dejected and timid voice)*: How do you do, Nora?

NORA *(doubtfully)*: How do you do—

MRS. LINDE: You don't recognize me, I suppose.

NORA: No, I don't know—yes, to be sure, I seem to— *(Suddenly.)* Yes! Christine! Is it really you?

MRS. LINDE: Yes, it is I.

NORA: Christine! To think of my not recognizing you! And yet how could I? *(In a gentle voice.)* How you have altered, Christine!

MRS. LINDE: Yes, I have indeed. In nine, ten long years—

NORA: Is it so long since we met? I suppose it is. The last eight years have been a happy time for me, I can tell you. And so now you have come into the town and have taken this long journey in winter—that was plucky of you.

MRS. LINDE: I arrived by steamer[2] this morning.

NORA: To have some fun at Christmas time, of course. How delightful! We will have such fun together! But take off your things. You are not cold, I hope. *(Helps her.)* Now we will sit down by the stove and be cozy. No, take this arm-chair; I will sit here in the rocking chair. *(Takes her hands.)* Now you look like your old self again; it was only the first moment— You are a little paler, Christine, and perhaps a little thinner.

MRS. LINDE: And much, much older, Nora.

NORA: Perhaps a little older; very, very little; certainly not much. *(Stops suddenly and speaks seriously.)* What a thoughtless creature I am, chattering away like this. My poor, dear Christine, do forgive me.

MRS. LINDE: What do you mean, Nora?

NORA (*gently*): Poor Christine, you are a widow.

MRS. LINDE: Yes; it is three years ago now.

NORA: Yes, I knew; I saw it in the papers. I assure you, Christine, I meant ever so often to write to you at the time, but I always put it off and something always prevented me.

MRS. LINDE: I quite understand, dear.

NORA: It was very bad of me, Christine. Poor thing, how you must have suffered. And he left you nothing?

MRS. LINDE: No.

NORA: And no children?

MRS. LINDE: No.

NORA: Nothing at all, then?

MRS. LINDE: Not even any sorrow or grief to live upon.

NORA (*looking incredulously at her*): But, Christine, is that possible?

MRS. LINDE (*smiles sadly and strokes her hair*): It sometimes happens, Nora.

NORA: So you are quite alone. How dreadfully sad that must be. I have three lovely children. You can't see them just now, for they are out with their nurse. But now you must tell me all about it.

MRS. LINDE: No, no; I want to hear about you.

NORA: No, you must begin. I mustn't be selfish today; today I must only think of your affairs. But there is one thing I must tell you. Do you know we have just had a great piece of good luck?

MRS. LINDE: No, what is it?

NORA: Just fancy, my husband has been made manager of the bank!

MRS. LINDE: Your husband? What good luck!

NORA: Yes, tremendous! A barrister's profession is such an uncertain thing, especially if he won't undertake unsavory cases; and naturally Torvald has never been willing to do that, and I quite agree with him. You may imagine how pleased we are! He is to take up his work in the bank at the new year, and then he will have a big salary and lots

of commissions. For the future we can live quite differently—we can do just as we like. I feel so relieved and so
happy, Christine! It will be splendid to have heaps of
money and not need to have any anxiety, won't it?

MRS. LINDE: Yes, anyhow I think it would be delightful to
have what one needs.

NORA: No, not only what one needs but heaps and heaps of
money.

MRS. LINDE (smiling): Nora, Nora, haven't you learned sense
yet? In our schooldays you were a great spendthrift.

NORA (laughing): Yes, that is what Torvald says now. (Wags
her finger at her.) But "Nora, Nora" is not so silly as you
think. We have not been in a position for me to waste
money. We have both had to work.

MRS. LINDE: You too?

NORA: Yes; odds and ends, needlework, crochet work, embroidery and that kind of thing. (Dropping her voice.) And
other things as well. You know Torvald left his office when
we were married? There was no prospect of promotion
there, and he had to try and earn more than before. But
during the first year he overworked himself dreadfully.
You see, he had to make money every way he could; and
he worked early and late; but he couldn't stand it and fell
dreadfully ill, and the doctors said it was necessary for him
to go south.

MRS. LINDE: You spent a whole year in Italy, didn't you?

NORA: Yes. It was no easy matter to get away, I can tell you. It
was just after Ivar was born, but naturally we had to go. It
was a wonderfully beautiful journey, and it saved Torvald's
life. But it cost a tremendous lot of money, Christine.

MRS. LINDE: So I should think.

NORA: It cost about two hundred and fifty pounds. That's a
lot; isn't it?

MRS. LINDE: Yes, and in emergencies like that it is lucky to
have the money.

NORA: I ought to tell you that we had it from Papa.

MRS. LINDE: Oh, I see. It was just about that time that he died, wasn't it?

NORA: Yes; and, just think of it, I couldn't go and nurse him. I was expecting little Ivar's birth every day and I had my poor sick Torvald to look after. My dear, kind father—I never saw him again, Christine. That was the saddest time I have known since our marriage.

MRS. LINDE: I know how fond you were of him. And then you went off to Italy?

NORA: Yes; you see, we had money then, and the doctors insisted on our going, so we started a month later.

MRS. LINDE: And your husband came back quite well?

NORA: As sound as a bell!

MRS. LINDE: But—the doctor?

NORA: What doctor?

MRS. LINDE: I thought your maid said the gentleman who arrived here just as I did was the doctor.

NORA: Yes, that was Dr. Rank, but he doesn't come here professionally. He is our greatest friend and comes in at least once every day. No, Torvald has not had an hour's illness since then, and our children are strong and healthy and so am I. *(Jumps up and claps her hands.)* Christine! Christine! It's good to be alive and happy! But how horrid of me; I am talking of nothing but my own affairs. *(Sits on a stool near her and rests her arms on her knees.)* You mustn't be angry with me. Tell me, is it really true that you did not love your husband? Why did you marry him?

MRS. LINDE: My mother was alive then and was bedridden and helpless, and I had to provide for my two younger brothers; so I did not think I was justified in refusing his offer.

NORA: No, perhaps you were quite right. He was rich at that time, then?

MRS. LINDE: I believe he was quite well off. But his business was a precarious one, and when he died it all went to pieces and there was nothing left.

NORA: And then?

MRS. LINDE: Well, I had to turn my hand to anything I could find—first a small shop, then a small school and so on. The last three years have seemed like one long working day, with no rest. Now it is at an end, Nora. My poor mother needs me no more, for she is gone; and the boys do not need me either; they have got situations and can shift for themselves.

NORA: What a relief you must feel it.

MRS. LINDE: No indeed; I only feel my life unspeakably empty. No one to live for anymore. (*Gets up restlessly.*) That was why I could not stand the life in my little backwater any longer. I hope it may be easier here to find something which will busy me and occupy my thoughts. If only I could have the good luck to get some regular work—office work of some kind—

NORA: But, Christine, that is so frightfully tiring, and you look tired out now. You had far better go away to some watering place.

MRS. LINDE (*walking to the window*): I have no father to give me money for a journey, Nora.

NORA (*rising*): Oh, don't be angry with me.

MRS. LINDE (*going up to her*): It is you that must not be angry with me, dear. The worst of a position like mine is that it makes one so bitter. No one to work for and yet obliged to be always on the lookout for chances. One must live, and so one becomes selfish. When you told me of the happy turn your fortunes have taken—you will hardly believe it—I was delighted not so much on your account as on my own.

NORA: How do you mean? Oh, I understand. You mean that perhaps Torvald could get you something to do.

MRS. LINDE: Yes, that was what I was thinking of.

NORA: He must, Christine. Just leave it to me; I will broach the subject very cleverly—I will think of something that will please him very much. It will make me so happy to be of some use to you.

MRS. LINDE: How kind you are, Nora, to be so anxious to help me! It is doubly kind in you, for you know so little of the burdens and troubles of life.

NORA: I? I know so little of them?

MRS. LINDE (*smiling*): My dear! Small household cares and that sort of thing! You are a child, Nora.

NORA (*tosses her head and crosses the stage*): You ought not to be so superior.

MRS. LINDE: No?

NORA: You are just like the others. They all think that I am incapable of anything really serious—

MRS. LINDE: Come, come.

NORA: —that I have gone through nothing in this world of cares.

MRS. LINDE: But, my dear Nora, you have just told me all your troubles.

NORA: Pooh!—those were trifles. (*Lowering her voice.*) I have not told you the important thing.

MRS. LINDE: The important thing? What do you mean?

NORA: You look down upon me altogether, Christine—but you ought not to. You are proud, aren't you, of having worked so hard and so long for your mother?

MRS. LINDE: Indeed, I don't look down on anyone. But it is true that I am both proud and glad to think that I was privileged to make the end of my mother's life almost free from care.

NORA: And you are proud to think of what you have done for your brothers.

MRS. LINDE: I think I have the right to be.

NORA: I think so too. But now listen to this; I too have something to be proud and glad of.

MRS. LINDE: I have no doubt you have. But what do you refer to?

NORA: Speak low. Suppose Torvald were to hear! He mustn't on any account—no one in the world must know, Christine, except you.

MRS. LINDE: But what is it?

NORA: Come here. *(Pulls her down on the sofa beside her.)* Now I will show you that I too have something to be proud and glad of. It was I who saved Torvald's life.

MRS. LINDE: "Saved"? How?

NORA: I told you about our trip to Italy. Torvald would never have recovered if he had not gone there.

MRS. LINDE: Yes, but your father gave you the necessary funds.

NORA *(smiling)*: Yes, that is what Torvald and the others think, but—

MRS. LINDE: But—

NORA: Papa didn't give us a shilling. It was I who procured the money.

MRS. LINDE: You? All that large sum?

NORA: Two hundred and fifty pounds. What do you think of that?

MRS. LINDE: But, Nora, how could you possibly do it? Did you win a prize in the lottery?

NORA *(contemptuously)*: In the lottery? There would have been no credit in that.

MRS. LINDE: But where did you get it from, then?

NORA *(humming and smiling with an air of mystery)*: Hm, hm! Aha!

MRS. LINDE: Because you couldn't have borrowed it.

NORA: Couldn't I? Why not?

MRS. LINDE: No, a wife cannot borrow without her husband's consent.

NORA *(tossing her head)*: Oh, if it is a wife who has any head for business—a wife who has the wit to be a little bit clever—

MRS. LINDE: I don't understand it at all, Nora.

NORA: There is no need you should. I never said I had borrowed the money. I may have got it some other way. *(Lies back on the sofa.)* Perhaps I got it from some other admirers. When anyone is as attractive as I am—

MRS. LINDE: You are a mad creature.

NORA: Now you know you're full of curiosity, Christine.

MRS. LINDE: Listen to me, Nora dear. Haven't you been a little bit imprudent?

NORA *(sits up straight)*: Is it imprudent to save your
husband's life?

MRS. LINDE: It seems to me imprudent, without his knowledge, to—

NORA: But it was absolutely necessary that he should not
know! My goodness, can't you understand that? It was
necessary he should have no idea what a dangerous condition he was in. It was to me that the doctors came and said
that his life was in danger and that the only thing to save
him was to live in the south. Do you suppose I didn't try,
first of all, to get what I wanted as if it were for myself? I
told him how much I should love to travel abroad like
other young wives; I tried tears and entreaties with him; I
told him that he ought to remember the condition I was in
and that he ought to be kind and indulgent to me; I even
hinted that he might raise a loan. That nearly made him
angry, Christine. He said I was thoughtless and that it was
his duty as my husband not to indulge me in my whims
and caprices—as I believe he called them. Very well, I
thought, you must be saved—and that was how I came to
devise a way out of the difficulty.

MRS. LINDE: And did your husband never get to know from
your father that the money had not come from him?

NORA: No, never. Papa died just at that time. I had meant
to let him into the secret and beg him never to reveal it.
But he was so ill then—alas, there never was any need to
tell him.

MRS. LINDE: And since then have you never told your secret
to your husband?

NORA: Good heavens, no! How could you think so? A man
who has such strong opinions about these things! And
besides, how painful and humiliating it would be for Torvald, with his manly independence, to know that he owed
me anything! It would upset our mutual relations alto-

gether; our beautiful happy home would no longer be
what it is now.

MRS. LINDE: Do you mean never to tell him about it?

NORA (*meditatively and with a half-smile*): Yes—someday,
perhaps, after many years, when I am no longer as nice
looking as I am now. Don't laugh at me! I mean, of course,
when Torvald is no longer as devoted to me as he is now;
when my dancing and dressing-up and reciting have
palled on him; then it may be a good thing to have something in reserve— (*Breaking off.*) What nonsense! That
time will never come. Now what do you think of my great
secret, Christine? Do you still think I am of no use? I can
tell you, too, that this affair has caused me a lot of worry. It
has been by no means easy for me to meet my engage-
ments punctually. I may tell you that there is something
that is called, in business, quarterly interest and another
thing called payment in installments, and it is always so
dreadfully difficult to manage them. I have had to save a
little here and there, where I could, you understand. I
have not been able to put aside much from my housekeeping money, for Torvald must have a good table. I
couldn't let my children be shabbily dressed; I have felt
obliged to use up all he gave me for them, the sweet little
darlings!

MRS. LINDE: So it has all had to come out of your own neces-
saries of life, poor Nora?

NORA: Of course. Besides, I was the one responsible for it.
Whenever Torvald has given me money for new dresses
and such things I have never spent more than half of it; I
have always bought the simplest and cheapest things.
Thank heaven any clothes look well on me, and so Torvald
has never noticed it. But it was often very hard on me, Christine—because it is delightful to be really well dressed,
isn't it?

MRS. LINDE: Quite so.

NORA: Well, then I have found other ways of earning money.

Last winter I was lucky enough to get a lot of copying to do, so I locked myself up and sat writing every evening until quite late at night. Many a time I was desperately tired, but all the same it was a tremendous pleasure to sit there working and earning money. It was like being a man.

MRS. LINDE: How much have you been able to pay off in that way?

NORA: I can't tell you exactly. You see, it is very difficult to keep an account of a business matter of that kind. I only know that I have paid every penny that I could scrape together. Many a time I was at my wits' end. (*Smiles.*) Then I used to sit here and imagine that a rich old gentleman had fallen in love with me—

MRS. LINDE: What! Who was it?

NORA: Be quiet!—that he had died and that when his will was opened it contained, written in big letters, the instruction: "The lovely Mrs. Nora Helmer is to have all I possess paid over to her at once in cash."

MRS. LINDE: But, my dear Nora—who could the man be?

NORA: Good gracious, can't you understand? There was no old gentleman at all; it was only something that I used to sit here and imagine, when I couldn't think of any way of procuring money. But it's all the same now; the tiresome old person can stay where he is as far as I am concerned; I don't care about him or his will either, for I am free from care now. (*Jumps up.*) My goodness, it's delightful to think of, Christine! Free from care! To be able to be free from care, quite free from care; to be able to play and romp with the children; to be able to keep the house beautifully and have everything just as Torvald likes it! And, think of it, soon the spring will come and the big blue sky! Perhaps we shall be able to take a little trip—perhaps I shall see the sea again! Oh, it's a wonderful thing to be alive and be happy. (*A bell is heard in the hall.*)

MRS. LINDE (*rising*): There is the bell; perhaps I had better go.

NORA: No, don't go; no one will come in here; it is sure to be for Torvald.

SERVANT (*at the hall door*): Excuse me, ma'am—there is a gentleman to see the master, and as the doctor is with him—

NORA: Who is it?

KROGSTAD (*at the door*): It is I, Mrs. Helmer. (MRS. LINDE *starts, trembles and turns to the window.*)

NORA (*takes a step toward him and speaks in a strained, low voice*): You? What is it? What do you want to see my husband about?

KROGSTAD: Bank business—in a way. I have a small post in the bank, and I hear your husband is to be our chief now.

NORA: Then it is—

KROGSTAD: Nothing but dry business matters, Mrs. Helmer; absolutely nothing else.

NORA: Be so good as to go into the study then. (*She bows indifferently to him and shuts the door into the hall, then comes back and makes up the fire in the stove.*)

MRS. LINDE: Nora—who was that man?

NORA: A lawyer of the name of Krogstad.

MRS. LINDE: Then it really was he.

NORA: Do you know the man?

MRS. LINDE: I used to—many years ago. At one time he was a solicitor's clerk in our town.

NORA: Yes, he was.

MRS. LINDE: He is greatly altered.

NORA: He made a very unhappy marriage.

MRS. LINDE: He is a widower now, isn't he?

NORA: With several children. There now, it is burning up. (*Shuts the door of the stove and moves the rocking chair aside.*)

MRS. LINDE: They say he carries on various kinds of business.

NORA: Really! Perhaps he does; I don't know anything about it. But don't let us think of business; it is so tiresome.

DR. RANK (*comes out of* HELMER's *study. Before he shuts the door he calls to him):* No, my dear fellow, I won't disturb you; I would rather go in to your wife for a little while. (*Shuts the door and sees* MRS. LINDE.) I beg your pardon; I am afraid I am disturbing you too.

NORA: No, not at all. (*Introducing him.*) Dr. Rank, Mrs. Linde.

RANK: I have often heard Mrs. Linde's name mentioned here. I think I passed you on the stairs when I arrived, Mrs. Linde?

MRS. LINDE: Yes, I go up very slowly; I can't manage stairs well.

RANK: Ah! Some slight internal weakness?

MRS. LINDE: No, the fact is I have been overworking myself.

RANK: Nothing more than that? Then I suppose you have come to town to amuse yourself with our entertainments?

MRS. LINDE: I have come to look for work.

RANK: Is that a good cure for overwork?

MRS. LINDE: One must live, Dr. Rank.

RANK: Yes, the general opinion seems to be that it is necessary.

NORA: Look here, Dr. Rank—you know you want to live.

RANK: Certainly. However wretched I may feel, I want to prolong the agony as long as possible. All my patients are like that. And so are those who are morally diseased; one of them, and a bad case too, is at this very moment with Helmer—

MRS. LINDE (*sadly*): Ah!

NORA: Whom do you mean?

RANK: A lawyer of the name of Krogstad, a fellow you don't know at all. He suffers from a diseased moral character, Mrs. Helmer, but even he began talking of its being highly important that he should live.

NORA: Did he? What did he want to speak to Torvald about?

RANK: I have no idea; I only heard that it was something about the bank.

NORA: I didn't know this—what's his name?—Krogstad had anything to do with the bank.

RANK: Yes, he has some sort of appointment there. (*To* MRS. LINDE.) I don't know whether you find also in your part of the world that there are certain people who go zealously snuffing about to smell out moral corruption and, as soon as they have found some, put the person concerned into some lucrative position where they can keep their eye on him. Healthy natures are left out in the cold.

MRS. LINDE: Still I think the sick are those who most need taking care of.

RANK (*shrugging his shoulders*): Yes, there you are. That is the sentiment that is turning society into a sick house.

NORA, *who has been absorbed in her thoughts, breaks out into smothered laughter and claps her hands.*

RANK: Why do you laugh at that? Have you any notion what society really is?

NORA: What do I care about tiresome society? I am laughing at something quite different, something extremely amusing. Tell me, Dr. Rank, are all the people who are employed in the bank dependent on Torvald now?

RANK: Is that what you find so extremely amusing?

NORA (*smiling and humming*): That's my affair! (*Walking about the room.*) It's perfectly glorious to think that we have—that Torvald has so much power over so many people. (*Takes the packet from her pocket.*) Dr. Rank, what do you say to a macaroon?

RANK: What, macaroons? I thought they were forbidden here.

NORA: Yes, but these are some Christine gave me.

MRS. LINDE: What! I?

NORA: Oh well, don't be alarmed! You couldn't know that Torvald had forbidden them. I must tell you that he is afraid they will spoil my teeth. But, bah!—once in a way— That's so, isn't it, Dr. Rank? By your leave! (*Puts a macaroon into his mouth.*) You must have one too, Christine. And I shall have one, just a little one—or at most two. (*Walking about.*) I am tremendously happy.

There is just one thing in the world now that I should dearly love to do.

RANK: Well, what is that?

NORA: It's something I should dearly love to say if Torvald could hear me.

RANK: Well, why can't you say it?

NORA: No, I daren't; it's so shocking.

MRS. LINDE: Shocking?

RANK: Well, I should not advise you to say it. Still, with us you might. What is it you would so much like to say if Torvald could hear you?

NORA: I should just love to say— Well, I'm damned!

RANK: Are you mad?

MRS. LINDE: Nora dear!

RANK: Say it, here he is!

NORA (*hiding the packet*): Hush! Hush! Hush!

HELMER *comes out of his room with his coat over his arm and his hat in his hand.*

NORA: Well, Torvald dear, have you got rid of him?

HELMER: Yes, he has just gone.

NORA: Let me introduce you—this is Christine, who has come to town.

HELMER: Christine? Excuse me, but I don't know—

NORA: Mrs. Linde, dear; Christine Linde.

HELMER: Of course. A school friend of my wife's, I presume?

MRS. LINDE: Yes, we have known each other since then.

NORA: And just think, she has taken a long journey in order to see you.

HELMER: What do you mean?

MRS. LINDE: No, really, I—

NORA: Christine is tremendously clever at bookkeeping, and she is frightfully anxious to work under some clever man, so as to perfect herself—

HELMER: Very sensible, Mrs. Linde.

NORA: And when she heard you had been appointed man-

ager of the bank—the news was telegraphed, you know—
she traveled here as quick as she could. Torvald, I am sure
you will be able to do something for Christine, for my
sake, won't you?

HELMER: Well, it is not altogether impossible. I presume you
are a widow, Mrs. Linde?

MRS. LINDE: Yes.

HELMER: And have had some experience of bookkeeping?

MRS. LINDE: Yes, a fair amount.

HELMER: Ah well, it's very likely I may be able to find something for you.

NORA (*clapping her hands*): What did I tell you?

HELMER: You have just come at a fortunate moment, Mrs.
Linde.

MRS. LINDE: How am I to thank you?

HELMER: There is no need. (*Puts on his coat.*) But today you
must excuse me—

RANK: Wait a minute; I will come with you. (*Brings his fur
coat from the hall and warms it at the fire.*)

NORA: Don't be long away, Torvald dear.

HELMER: About an hour, not more.

NORA: Are you going too, Christine?

MRS. LINDE (*putting on her cloak*): Yes, I must go and look
for a room.

HELMER: Oh well, then, we can walk down the street together.

NORA (*helping her*): What a pity it is we are so short of space
here; I am afraid it is impossible for us—

MRS. LINDE: Please don't think of it! Good-bye, Nora dear,
and many thanks.

NORA: Good-bye for the present. Of course you will come
back this evening. And you too, Dr. Rank. What do you
say? If you are well enough? Oh, you must be! Wrap yourself up well. (*They go to the door all talking together. Children's voices are heard on the staircase.*)

NORA: There they are. There they are! (*She runs to open the door. The* NURSE *comes in with the children.*) Come in! Come in! (*Stoops and kisses them.*) Oh, you sweet blessings! Look at them, Christine! Aren't they darlings?

RANK: Don't let us stand here in the draft.

HELMER: Come along, Mrs. Linde; the place will only be bearable for a mother now!

RANK, HELMER *and* MRS. LINDE *go downstairs. The* NURSE *comes forward with the children;* NORA *shuts the hall door.*

NORA: How fresh and well you look! Such red cheeks!—like apples and roses. (*The children all talk at once while she speaks to them.*) Have you had great fun? That's splendid! What, you pulled both Emmy and Bob along on the sledge? Both at once? That *was* good. You are a clever boy, Ivar. Let me take her for a little, Anne. My sweet little baby doll! (*Takes the baby from the* NURSE *and dances it up and down.*) Yes, yes, Mother will dance with Bob too. What! Have you been snowballing? I wish I had been there too! No, no, I will take their things off, Anne; please let me do it, it is such fun. Go in now, you look half frozen. There is some hot coffee for you on the stove.

The NURSE *goes into the room on the left.* NORA *takes off the children's things and throws them about while they all talk to her at once.*

NORA: *Really!* Did a big dog run after you? But it didn't bite you? No, dogs don't bite nice little dolly children. You mustn't look at the parcels, Ivar. What are they? Ah, I daresay you would like to know. No, no—it's something nasty! Come, let us have a game! What shall we play at? Hide and seek? Yes, we'll play hide and seek. Bob shall hide first. Must I hide? Very well, I'll hide first. (*She and the children laugh and shout and romp in and out of the room; at last* NORA *hides under the table; the children rush in and look for her but do not see her; they hear her smothered laughter, run to the table, lift up the cloth and find her. Shouts of laughter. She crawls forward and pretends to frighten them. Fresh laughter. Meanwhile there has been a knock at the hall door but none of them has noticed it. The door is half opened and* KROGSTAD *appears. He waits a little; the game goes on.)*

KROGSTAD: Excuse me, Mrs. Helmer.

NORA *(with a stifled cry turns round and gets up onto her knees)*: Ah! What do you want?

KROGSTAD: Excuse me, the outer door was ajar; I suppose someone forgot to shut it.

NORA *(rising)*: My husband is out, Mr. Krogstad.

KROGSTAD: I know that.

NORA: What do you want here then?

KROGSTAD: A word with you.

NORA: With me? *(To the children, gently.)* Go in to Nurse. What? No, the strange man won't do Mother any harm. When he has gone we will have another game. *(She takes the children into the room on the left and shuts the door after them.)* You want to speak to me?

KROGSTAD: Yes, I do.

NORA: Today? It is not the first of the month yet.

KROGSTAD: No, it is Christmas Eve, and it will depend on yourself what sort of a Christmas you will spend.

NORA: What do you want? Today it is absolutely impossible for me—

KROGSTAD: We won't talk about that till later on. This is something different. I presume you can give me a moment?

NORA: Yes—yes, I can—although—

KROGSTAD: Good. I was in Olsen's Restaurant and saw your husband going down the street—

NORA: Yes?

KROGSTAD: With a lady.

NORA: What then?

KROGSTAD: May I make so bold as to ask if it was a Mrs. Linde?

NORA: It was.

KROGSTAD: Just arrived in town?

NORA: Yes, today.

KROGSTAD: She is a great friend of yours, isn't she?

NORA: She is. But I don't see—

KROGSTAD: I knew her too, once upon a time.

NORA: I am aware of that.

KROGSTAD: Are you? So you know all about it; I thought as much. Then I can ask you, without beating about the bush—is Mrs. Linde to have an appointment in the bank?

NORA: What right have you to question me, Mr. Krogstad? You, one of my husband's subordinates! But since you ask, you shall know. Yes, Mrs. Linde *is* to have an appointment. And it was I who pleaded her cause, Mr. Krogstad, let me tell you that.

KROGSTAD: I was right in what I thought then.

NORA (*walking up and down the stage*): Sometimes one has a tiny little bit of influence, I should hope. Because one is a woman it does not necessarily follow that— When anyone is in a subordinate position, Mr. Krogstad, they should really be careful to avoid offending anyone who—who—

KROGSTAD: Who has influence?

NORA: Exactly.

KROGSTAD (*changing his tone*): Mrs. Helmer, you will be so good as to use your influence on my behalf.

NORA: What? What do you mean?

KROGSTAD: You will be so kind as to see that I am allowed to keep my subordinate position in the bank.

NORA: What do you mean by that? Who proposes to take your post away from you?

KROGSTAD: Oh, there is no necessity to keep up the pretense of ignorance. I can quite understand that your friend is not very anxious to expose herself to the chance of rubbing shoulders with me, and I quite understand, too, whom I have to thank for being turned off.

NORA: But I assure you—

KROGSTAD: Very likely; but, to come to the point, the time

has come when I should advise you to use your influence to prevent that.

NORA: But, Mr. Krogstad, I *have* no influence.

KROGSTAD: Haven't you? I thought you said yourself just now—

NORA: Naturally I did not mean you to put that construction on it. I! What should make you think I have any influence of that kind with my husband?

KROGSTAD: Oh, I have known your husband from our student days. I don't suppose he is any more unassailable than other husbands.

NORA: If you speak slightingly of my husband, I shall turn you out of the house.

KROGSTAD: You are bold, Mrs. Helmer.

NORA: I am not afraid of you any longer. As soon as the New Year comes I shall in a very short time be free of the whole thing.

KROGSTAD (*controlling himself*): Listen to me, Mrs. Helmer. If necessary, I am prepared to fight for my small post in the bank as if I were fighting for my life.

NORA: So it seems.

KROGSTAD: It is not only for the sake of the money; indeed, that weighs least with me in the matter. There is another reason—well, I may as well tell you. My position is this. I daresay you know, like everybody else, that once, many years ago, I was guilty of an indiscretion.

NORA: I think I have heard something of the kind.

KROGSTAD: The matter never came into court, but every way seemed to be closed to me after that. So I took to the business that you know of. I had to do something; and, honestly, I don't think I've been one of the worst. But now I must cut myself free from all that. My sons are growing up; for their sake I must try and win back as much respect as I can in the town. This post in the bank was like the first step up for me—and now your husband is going to kick me downstairs again into the mud.

NORA: But you must believe me, Mr. Krogstad; it is not in my power to help you at all.

KROGSTAD: Then it is because you haven't the will, but I have means to compel you.

NORA: You don't mean that you will tell my husband that I owe you money?

KROGSTAD: Hm! Suppose I were to tell him?

NORA: It would be perfectly infamous of you. (*Sobbing.*) To think of his learning my secret, which has been my joy and pride, in such an ugly, clumsy way—that he should learn it from you! And it would put me in a horribly disagreeable position.

KROGSTAD: Only disagreeable?

NORA (*impetuously*): Well, do it then!—and it will be the worse for you. My husband will see for himself what a blackguard you are, and you certainly won't keep your post then.

KROGSTAD: I asked you if it was only a disagreeable scene at home that you were afraid of?

NORA: If my husband does get to know of it, of course he will at once pay you what is still owing, and we shall have nothing more to do with you.

KROGSTAD (*coming a step nearer*): Listen to me, Mrs. Helmer. Either you have a very bad memory or you know very little of business. I shall be obliged to remind you of a few details.

NORA: What do you mean?

KROGSTAD: When your husband was ill you came to me to borrow two hundred and fifty pounds.

NORA: I didn't know anyone else to go to.

KROGSTAD: I promised to get you that amount—

NORA: Yes, and you did so.

KROGSTAD: I promised to get you that amount on certain conditions. Your mind was so taken up with your husband's illness and you were so anxious to get the money for your journey that you seem to have paid no attention to the conditions of our bargain. Therefore it will not be amiss if I remind you of them. Now I promised to get the money on the security of a bond which I drew up.

NORA: Yes, and which I signed.

KROGSTAD: Good. But below your signature there were a few lines constituting your father a surety for the money; those lines your father should have signed.

NORA: Should? He did sign them.

KROGSTAD: I had left the date blank; that is to say your father should himself have inserted the date on which he signed the paper. Do you remember that?

NORA: Yes, I think I remember.

KROGSTAD: Then I gave you the bond to send by post to your father. Is that not so?

NORA: Yes.

KROGSTAD: And you naturally did so at once, because five or six days afterward you brought me the bond with your father's signature. And then I gave you the money.

NORA: Well, haven't I been paying it off regularly?

KROGSTAD: Fairly so, yes. But—to come back to the matter in hand—that must have been a very trying time for you, Mrs. Helmer?

NORA: It was, indeed.

KROGSTAD: Your father was very ill, wasn't he?

NORA: He was very near his end.

KROGSTAD: And died soon afterward?

NORA: Yes.

KROGSTAD: Tell me, Mrs. Helmer, can you by any chance remember what day your father died?—on what day of the month, I mean.

NORA: Papa died on the twenty-ninth of September.

KROGSTAD: That is correct; I have ascertained it for myself. And, as that is so, there is a discrepancy (*taking a paper from his pocket*) which I cannot account for.

NORA: What discrepancy? I don't know—

KROGSTAD: The discrepancy consists, Mrs. Helmer, in the fact that your father signed this bond three days after his death.

NORA: What do you mean? I don't understand.

KROGSTAD: Your father died on the twenty-ninth of September. But look here; your father has dated his signature the second of October. It is a discrepancy, isn't it? (NORA *is silent.*) Can you explain it to me? (NORA *is still silent.*) It is a remarkable thing, too, that the words "second of October," as well as the year, are not written in your father's handwriting but in one that I think I know. Well, of course it can be explained; your father may have forgotten to date his signature and someone else may have dated it haphazard before they knew of his death. There is no harm in that. It all depends on the signature of the name, and *that* is genuine, I suppose, Mrs. Helmer? It was your father himself who signed his name here?

NORA (*after a short pause, throws her head up and looks defiantly at him*): No, it was not. It was I that wrote Papa's name.

KROGSTAD: Are you aware that is a dangerous confession?

NORA: In what way? You shall have your money soon.

KROGSTAD: Let me ask you a question: why did you not send the paper to your father?

NORA: It was impossible; Papa was so ill. If I had asked him for his signature, I should have had to tell him what the money was to be used for; and when he was so ill himself I couldn't tell him that my husband's life was in danger—it was impossible.

KROGSTAD: It would have been better for you if you had given up your trip abroad.

NORA: No, that was impossible. That trip was to save my husband's life; I couldn't give that up.

KROGSTAD: But did it never occur to you that you were committing a fraud on me?

NORA: I couldn't take that into account; I didn't trouble myself about you at all. I couldn't bear you because you put so many heartless difficulties in my way although you knew what a dangerous condition my husband was in.

KROGSTAD: Mrs. Helmer, you evidently do not realize clearly

what it is that you have been guilty of. But I can assure you that my one false step, which lost me all my reputation, was nothing more or nothing worse than what you have done.

NORA: You? Do you ask me to believe that you were brave enough to run a risk to save your wife's life?

KROGSTAD: The law cares nothing about motives.

NORA: Then it must be a very foolish law.

KROGSTAD: Foolish or not, it is the law by which you will be judged if I produce this paper in court.

NORA: I don't believe it. Is a daughter not to be allowed to spare her dying father anxiety and care? Is a wife not to be allowed to save her husband's life? I don't know much about law, but I am certain that there must be laws permitting such things as that. Have you no knowledge of such laws—you who are a lawyer? You must be a very poor lawyer, Mr. Krogstad.

KROGSTAD: Maybe. But matters of business—such business as you and I have had together—do you think I don't understand that? Very well. Do as you please. But let me tell you this—if I lose my position a second time, you shall lose yours with me. (*He bows and goes out through the hall.*)

NORA (*appears buried in thought for a short time, then tosses her head*): Nonsense! Trying to frighten me like that! I am not so silly as he thinks. (*Begins to busy herself putting the children's things in order.*) And yet— No, it's impossible! I did it for love's sake.

THE CHILDREN (*in the doorway on the left*): Mother, the stranger man has gone out through the gate.

NORA: Yes, dears, I know. But don't tell anyone about the stranger man. Do you hear? Not even Papa.

CHILDREN: No, Mother; but will you come and play again?

NORA: No, no—not now.

CHILDREN: But, Mother, you promised us.

NORA: Yes, but I can't now. Run away in; I have such a lot to do. Run away in, my sweet little darlings. (*She gets them into the room by degrees and shuts the door on them, then sits down on the sofa, takes up a piece of needlework and sews a few stitches but soon stops.)* No! *(Throws down the work, gets up, goes to the hall door and calls out.)* Helen! bring the tree in. *(Goes to the table on the left, opens a drawer and stops again.)* No, no! It is quite impossible!

MAID *(coming in with the tree)*: Where shall I put it, ma'am?

NORA: Here, in the middle of the floor.

MAID: Shall I get you anything else?

NORA: No, thank you. I have all I want.

Exit MAID.

NORA *(begins dressing the tree)*: A candle here—and flowers here— The horrible man! It's all nonsense—there's nothing wrong. The tree shall be splendid! I will do everything I can think of to please you, Torvald! I will sing for you, dance for you— (HELMER *comes in with some papers under his arm.)* Oh, are you back already?

HELMER: Yes. Has anyone been here?

NORA: Here? No.

HELMER: That is strange. I saw Krogstad going out of the gate.

NORA: Did you? Oh yes, I forgot, Krogstad was here for a moment.

HELMER: Nora, I can see from your manner that he has been here begging you to say a good word for him.

NORA: Yes.

HELMER: And you were to appear to do it of your own accord; you were to conceal from me the fact of his having been here; didn't he beg that of you too?

NORA: Yes, Torvald, but—

HELMER: Nora, Nora, and you would be a party to that sort of thing? To have any talk with a man like that and give him any sort of promise? And to tell me a lie into the bargain?

NORA: A lie?

HELMER: Didn't you tell me no one had been here? *(Shakes his finger at her.)* My little songbird must never do that again. A songbird must have a clean beak to chirp with—

no false notes! *(Puts his arm around her waist.)* That is so, isn't it? Yes, I am sure it is. *(Lets her go.)* We will say no more about it. *(Sits down by the stove.)* How warm and snug it is here! *(Turns over his papers.)*

NORA *(after a short pause during which she busies herself with the Christmas tree)*: Torvald!

HELMER: Yes.

NORA: I am looking forward tremendously to the fancy-dress ball at the Stenborgs' the day after tomorrow.

HELMER: And I am tremendously curious to see what you are going to surprise me with.

NORA: It was very silly of me to want to do that.

HELMER: What do you mean?

NORA: I can't hit upon anything that will do; everything I think of seems so silly and insignificant.

HELMER: Does my little Nora acknowledge that at last?

NORA *(standing behind his chair with her arms on the back of it)*: Are you very busy, Torvald?

HELMER: Well—

NORA: What are all those papers?

HELMER: Bank business.

NORA: Already?

HELMER: I have got authority from the retiring manager to undertake the necessary changes in the staff and in the re-arrangement of the work, and I must make use of the Christmas week for that, so as to have everything in order for the new year.

NORA: Then that was why this poor Krogstad—

HELMER: Hm!

NORA *(leans against the back of his chair and strokes his hair)*: If you hadn't been so busy, I should have asked you a tremendously big favor, Torvald.

HELMER: What is that? Tell me.

NORA: There is no one has such good taste as you. And I do so want to look nice at the fancy-dress ball. Torvald, couldn't you take me in hand and decide what I shall go as and what sort of a dress I shall wear?

HELMER: Aha! So my obstinate little woman is obliged to get someone to come to her rescue?

NORA: Yes, Torvald, I can't get along a bit without your help.

HELMER: Very well, I will think it over; we shall manage to hit upon something.

NORA: That is nice of you. *(Goes to the Christmas tree. A short pause.)* How pretty the red flowers look! But tell me, was it really something very bad that this Krogstad was guilty of?

HELMER: He forged someone's name. Have you any idea what that means?

NORA: Isn't it possible that he was driven to do it by necessity?

HELMER: Yes; or, as in so many cases, by imprudence. I am not so heartless as to condemn a man altogether because of a single false step of that kind.

NORA: No, you wouldn't, would you, Torvald?

HELMER: Many a man has been able to retrieve his character if he has openly confessed his fault and taken his punishment.

NORA: Punishment?

HELMER: But Krogstad did nothing of that sort; he got himself out of it by a cunning trick, and that is why he has gone under altogether.

NORA: But do you think it would—

HELMER: Just think how a guilty man like that has to lie and play the hypocrite with everyone, how he has to wear a mask in the presence of those near and dear to him, even before his own wife and children. And about the children—that is the most terrible part of it all, Nora.

NORA: How?

HELMER: Because such an atmosphere of lies infects and poisons the whole life of a home. Each breath the children take in such a house is full of the germs of evil.

NORA *(coming nearer him)*: Are you sure of that?

HELMER: My dear, I have often seen it in the course of my

life as a lawyer. Almost everyone who has gone to the bad early in life has had a deceitful mother.

NORA: Why do you only say—mother?

HELMER: It seems most commonly to be the mother's influence, though naturally a bad father's would have the same result. Every lawyer is familiar with the fact. This Krogstad, now, has been persistently poisoning his own children with lies and dissimulation; that is why I say he has lost all moral character. (*Holds out his hands to her.*) That is why my sweet little Nora must promise me not to plead his cause. Give me your hand on it. Come, come, what is this? Give me your hand. There now, that's settled. I assure you it would be quite impossible for me to work with him; I literally feel physically ill when I am in the company of such people.

NORA (*takes her hand out of his and goes to the opposite side of the Christmas tree*): How hot it is in here, and I have such a lot to do.

HELMER (*getting up and putting his papers in order*): Yes, and I must try and read through some of these before dinner, and I must think about your costume too. And it is just possible I may have something ready in gold paper to hang up on the tree. (*Puts his hand on her head.*) My precious little singing bird! (*He goes into his room and shuts the door after him.*)

NORA (*after a pause, whispers*): No, no—it isn't true. It's impossible; it must be impossible.

The NURSE *opens the door on the left.*

NURSE: The little ones are begging so hard to be allowed to come in to Mamma.

NORA: No, no, no! Don't let them come in to me! You stay with them, Anne.

NURSE: Very well, ma'am. (*Shuts the door.*)

NORA (*pale with terror*): Deprave my little children? Poison my home? (*A short pause. Then she tosses her head.*) It's not true. It can't possibly be true.

ACT TWO

The same room. The Christmas tree is in the corner by the piano, stripped of its ornaments and with burned-down candle ends on its disheveled branches. NORA's *cloak and hat are lying on the sofa. She is alone in the room, walking about uneasily. She stops by the sofa and takes up her cloak.*

NORA (*drops the cloak*): Someone is coming now. (*Goes to the door and listens.*) No—it is no one. Of course no one will come today, Christmas Day—nor tomorrow either. But perhaps— (*Opens the door and looks out.*) No, nothing in the letter box; it is quite empty. (*Comes forward.*) What rubbish! Of course he can't be in earnest about it. Such a thing couldn't happen; it is impossible—I have three little children.

Enter the NURSE *from the room on the left, carrying a big cardboard box.*

NURSE: At last I have found the box with the fancy dress.
NORA: Thanks; put it on the table.
NURSE (*in doing so*): But it is very much in want of mending.
NORA: I should like to tear it into a hundred thousand pieces.

NURSE: What an idea! It can easily be put in order—just a little patience.

NORA: Yes, I will go and get Mrs. Linde to come and help me with it.

NURSE: What, out again? In this horrible weather? You will catch cold, ma'am, and make yourself ill.

NORA: Well, worse than that might happen. How are the children?

NURSE: The poor little souls are playing with their Christmas presents, but—

NORA: Do they ask much for me?

NURSE: You see, they are so accustomed to having their mamma with them.

NORA: Yes—but, Nurse, I shall not be able to be so much with them now as I was before.

NURSE: Oh well, young children easily get accustomed to anything.

NORA: Do you think so? Do you think they would forget their mother if she went away altogether?

NURSE: Good heavens!—went away altogether?

NORA: Nurse, I want you to tell me something I have often wondered about—how could you have the heart to put your own child out among strangers?

NURSE: I was obliged to if I wanted to be little Nora's nurse.

NORA: Yes, but how could you be willing to do it?

NURSE: What, when I was going to get such a good place by it? A poor girl who has got into trouble should be glad to. Besides, that wicked man didn't do a single thing for me.

NORA: But I suppose your daughter has quite forgotten you.

NURSE: No, indeed she hasn't. She wrote to me when she was confirmed and when she was married.

NORA (*putting her arms round her neck*): Dear old Anne, you were a good mother to me when I was little.

NURSE: Little Nora, poor dear, had no other mother but me.

NORA: And if my little ones had no other mother, I am sure you would— What nonsense I am talking! (*Opens the box.*) Go in to them. Now I must— You will see tomorrow how charming I shall look.

NURSE: I am sure there will be no one at the ball so charming as you, ma'am. (*Goes into the room on the left.*)

NORA (*begins to unpack the box but soon pushes it away from her*): If only I dared go out. If only no one would come. If only I could be sure nothing would happen here in the meantime. Stuff and nonsense! No one will come. Only I mustn't think about it. I will brush my muff. What lovely, lovely gloves! Out of my thoughts, out of my thoughts! One, two, three, four, five, six— (*Screams.*) Ah! there is someone coming. (*Makes a movement toward the door but stands irresolute.*)

Enter MRS. LINDE *from the hall, where she has taken off her cloak and hat.*

NORA: Oh, it's you, Christine. There is no one else out there, is there? How good of you to come!

MRS. LINDE: I heard you were up asking for me.

NORA: Yes, I was passing by. As a matter of fact, it is something you could help me with. Let us sit down here on the sofa. Look here. Tomorrow evening there is to be a fancy-dress ball at the Stenborgs', who live above us, and Torvald wants me to go as a Neapolitan fishergirl and dance the tarantella[3] that I learned at Capri.

MRS. LINDE: I see; you are going to keep up the character.

NORA: Yes, Torvald wants me to. Look, here is the dress; Torvald had it made for me there, but now it is all so torn, and I haven't any idea—

MRS. LINDE: We will easily put that right. It is only some of the trimming come unsewn here and there. Needle and thread? Now then, that's all we want.

NORA: It *is* nice of you.

MRS. LINDE (*sewing*): So you are going to be dressed up tomorrow, Nora. I will tell you what—I shall come in for a moment and see you in your fine feathers. But I have completely forgotten to thank you for a delightful evening yesterday.

NORA (*gets up and crosses the stage*): Well, I don't think yesterday was as pleasant as usual. You ought to have come down to town a little earlier, Christine. Certainly Torvald does understand how to make a house dainty and attractive.

MRS. LINDE: And so do you, it seems to me; you are not your father's daughter for nothing. But tell me, is Dr. Rank always as depressed as he was yesterday?

NORA: No; yesterday it was very noticeable. I must tell you that he suffers from a very dangerous disease. He has consumption of the spine, poor creature. His father was a horrible man who committed all sorts of excesses, and that is why his son was sickly from childhood, do you understand?

MRS. LINDE (*dropping her sewing*): But, my dearest Nora, how do you know anything about such things?

NORA (*walking about*): Pooh! When you have three children you get visits now and then from—from married women who know something of medical matters, and they talk about one thing and another.

MRS. LINDE (*goes on sewing. A short silence*): Does Dr. Rank come here every day?

NORA: Every day regularly. He is Torvald's most intimate friend and a friend of mine too. He is just like one of the family.

MRS. LINDE: But tell me this—is he perfectly sincere? I mean, isn't he the kind of man that is very anxious to make himself agreeable?

NORA: Not in the least. What makes you think that?

MRS. LINDE: When you introduced him to me yesterday he declared he had often heard my name mentioned in this house, but afterward I noticed that your husband hadn't the slightest idea who I was. So how could Dr. Rank—

NORA: That is quite right, Christine. Torvald is so absurdly fond of me that he wants me absolutely to himself, as he says. At first he used to seem almost jealous if I mentioned any of the dear folks at home, so naturally I gave up doing so. But I often talk about such things with Dr. Rank because he likes hearing about them.

MRS. LINDE: Listen to me, Nora. You are still very like a child in many things, and I am older than you in many ways and have a little more experience. Let me tell you this—you ought to make an end of it with Dr. Rank.

NORA: What ought I to make an end of?

MRS. LINDE: Of two things, I think. Yesterday you talked some nonsense about a rich admirer who was to leave you money—

NORA: An admirer who doesn't exist, unfortunately! But what then?

MRS. LINDE: Is Dr. Rank a man of means?

NORA: Yes, he is.

MRS. LINDE: And has no one to provide for?

NORA: No, no one; but—

MRS. LINDE: And comes here every day?

NORA: Yes, I told you so.

MRS. LINDE: But how can this well-bred man be so tactless?

NORA: I don't understand you at all.

MRS. LINDE: Don't prevaricate, Nora. Do you suppose I don't guess who lent you the two hundred and fifty pounds?

NORA: Are you out of your senses? How can you think of such a thing! A friend of ours, who comes here every day! Do you realize what a horribly painful position that would be?

MRS. LINDE: Then it really isn't he?

NORA: No, certainly not. It would never have entered into my head for a moment. Besides, he had no money to lend then; he came into his money afterward.

MRS. LINDE: Well, I think that was lucky for you, my dear Nora.

NORA: No, it would never have come into my head to ask Dr. Rank. Although I am quite sure that if I had asked him—

MRS. LINDE: But of course you won't.

NORA: Of course not. I have no reason to think it could possibly be necessary. But I am quite sure that if I told Dr. Rank—

MRS. LINDE: Behind your husband's back?

NORA: I must make an end of it with the other one, and that will be behind his back too. I *must* make an end of it with him.

MRS. LINDE: Yes, that is what I told you yesterday, but—

NORA (*walking up and down*): A man can put a thing like that straight much easier than a woman.

MRS. LINDE: One's husband, yes.

NORA: Nonsense! (*Standing still.*) When you pay off a debt you get your bond back, don't you?

MRS. LINDE: Yes, as a matter of course.

NORA: And can tear it into a hundred thousand pieces and burn it up—the nasty dirty paper!

MRS. LINDE (*looks hard at her, lays down her sewing and gets up slowly*): Nora, you are concealing something from me.

NORA: Do I look as if I were?

MRS. LINDE: Something has happened to you since yesterday morning. Nora, what is it?

NORA (*going nearer to her*): Christine! (*Listens.*) Hush! There's Torvald come home. Do you mind going in to the children for the present? Torvald can't bear to see dressmaking going on. Let Anne help you.

MRS. LINDE (*gathering some of the things together*): Certainly—but I am not going away from here till we have had it out with one another. (*She goes into the room on the left as* HELMER *comes in from the hall.*)

NORA (*going up to* HELMER): I have wanted you so much, Torvald dear.

HELMER: Was that the dressmaker?

NORA: No, it was Christine; she is helping me to put my dress in order. You will see I shall look quite smart.

HELMER: Wasn't that a happy thought of mine, now?

NORA: Splendid! But don't you think it is nice of me, too, to do as you wish?

HELMER: Nice?—because you do as your husband wishes? Well, well, you little rogue, I am sure you did not mean it in that way. But I am not going to disturb you; you will want to be trying on your dress, I expect.

NORA: I suppose you are going to work.

HELMER: Yes. (*Shows her a bundle of papers.*) Look at that. I have just been in to the bank. (*Turns to go into his room.*)

NORA: Torvald.

HELMER: Yes.

NORA: If your little squirrel were to ask you for something very, very prettily—

HELMER: What then?

NORA: Would you do it?

HELMER: I should like to hear what it is first.

NORA: Your squirrel would run about and do all her tricks if you would be nice and do what she wants.

HELMER: Speak plainly.

NORA: Your skylark would chirp, chirp about in every room, with her song rising and falling—

HELMER: Well, my skylark does that anyhow.

NORA: I would play the fairy and dance for you in the moon-light, Torvald.

HELMER: Nora—you surely don't mean that request you made of me this morning?

NORA (*going near him*): Yes, Torvald, I beg you so earnestly—

HELMER: Have you really the courage to open up that question again?

NORA: Yes, dear, you *must* do as I ask; you *must* let Krogstad keep his post in the bank.

HELMER: My dear Nora, it is his post that I have arranged Mrs. Linde shall have.

NORA: Yes, you have been awfully kind about that, but you could just as well dismiss some other clerk instead of Krogstad.

HELMER: This is simply incredible obstinacy! Because you chose to give him a thoughtless promise that you would speak for him I am expected to—

NORA: That isn't the reason, Torvald. It is for your own sake. This fellow writes in the most scurrilous newspapers; you have told me so yourself. He can do you an unspeakable amount of harm. I am frightened to death of him.

HELMER: Ah, I understand; it is recollections of the past that scare you.

NORA: What do you mean?

HELMER: Naturally you are thinking of your father.

NORA: Yes—yes, of course. Just recall to your mind what these malicious creatures wrote in the papers about Papa and how horribly they slandered him. I believe they would have procured his dismissal if the Department had not sent you over to inquire into it and if you had not been so kindly disposed and helpful to him.

HELMER: My little Nora, there is an important difference between your father and me. Your father's reputation as a public official was not above suspicion. Mine is, and I hope it will continue to be so as long as I hold my office.

NORA: You never can tell what mischief these men may contrive. We ought to be so well off, so snug and happy here in our peaceful home, and have no cares—you and I and the children, Torvald! That is why I beg you so earnestly—

HELMER: And it is just by interceding for him that you make it impossible for me to keep him. It is already known at the bank that I mean to dismiss Krogstad. Is it to get about now that the new manager has changed his mind at his wife's bidding?

NORA: And what if it did?

HELMER: Of course!—if only this obstinate little person can get her way! Do you suppose I am going to make myself ridiculous before my whole staff, to let people think I am a man to be swayed by all sorts of outside influence? I should very soon feel the consequences of it, I can tell you! And besides, there is one thing that makes it quite impossible for me to have Krogstad in the bank as long as I am manager.

NORA: Whatever is that?

HELMER: His moral failings I might perhaps have overlooked if necessary—

NORA: Yes, you could—couldn't you?

HELMER: And I hear he is a good worker too. But I knew him when we were boys. It was one of those rash friendships that so often prove an incubus in afterlife. I may as well tell you plainly, we were once on very intimate terms with one another. But this tactless fellow lays no restraint on himself when other people are present. On the contrary, he thinks it gives him the right to adopt a familiar tone with me, and every minute it is "I say, Helmer, old fellow!" and that sort of thing. I assure you it is extremely painful for me. He would make my position in the bank intolerable.

NORA: Torvald, I don't believe you mean that.

HELMER: Don't you? Why not?

NORA: Because it is such a narrow-minded way of looking at things.

HELMER: What are you saying? Narrow-minded? Do you think I am narrow-minded?

NORA: No, just the opposite, dear—and it is exactly for that reason—

HELMER: It's the same thing. You say my point of view is narrow-minded, so I must be so too. Narrow-minded! Very well—I must put an end to this. (*Goes to the hall door and calls.*) Helen!

NORA: What are you going to do?

HELMER (*looking among his papers*): Settle it. (*Enter* MAID.) Look here; take this letter and go downstairs with it at once. Find a messenger and tell him to deliver it and be quick. The address is on it, and here is the money.

MAID: Very well, sir. (*Exit with the letter.*)

HELMER (*putting his papers together*): Now then, little Miss Obstinate.

NORA (*breathlessly*): Torvald—what was that letter?

HELMER: Krogstad's dismissal.

NORA: Call her back, Torvald! There is still time. Oh, Torvald, call her back! Do it for my sake—for your own sake—for the children's sake! Do you hear me, Torvald? Call her back! You don't know what that letter can bring upon us.

HELMER: It's too late.

NORA: Yes, it's too late.

HELMER: My dear Nora, I can forgive the anxiety you are in, although really it is an insult to me. It is, indeed. Isn't it an insult to think that I should be afraid of a starving quill driver's vengeance? But I forgive you nevertheless, because it is such eloquent witness to your great love for me. (*Takes her in his arms.*) And that is as it should be, my own darling Nora. Come what will, you may be sure I shall have both courage and strength if they be needed. You will see I am man enough to take everything upon myself.

NORA (*in a horror-stricken voice*): What do you mean by that?

HELMER: Everything, I say.

NORA (*recovering herself*): You will never have to do that.

HELMER: That's right. Well, we will share it, Nora, as man and wife should. That is how it shall be. (*Caressing her.*) Are you content now? There! there!—not these frightened dove's eyes! The whole thing is only the wildest fancy! Now you must go and play through the tarantella and practice with your tambourine. I shall go into the inner office and shut the door, and I shall hear nothing; you can make as much noise as you please. (*Turns back at the door.*) And when Rank comes tell him where he will find me. (*Nods to her, takes his papers and goes into his room and shuts the door after him.*)

NORA (*bewildered with anxiety, stands as if rooted to the spot and whispers*): He was capable of doing it. He will do it. He will do it in spite of everything. No, not that! Never, never! Anything rather than that! Oh, for some help, some way out of it! (*The doorbell rings.*) Dr. Rank! Anything rather than that—anything, whatever it is! (*She puts her hands over her face, pulls herself together, goes to the door and opens it. RANK is standing without, hanging up his coat. During the following dialogue it begins to grow dark.)*

NORA: Good day, Dr. Rank. I knew your ring. But you mustn't go in to Torvald now; I think he is busy with something.

RANK: And you?

NORA *(brings him in and shuts the door after him)*: Oh, you know very well I always have time for you.

RANK: Thank you. I shall make use of as much of it as I can.

NORA: What do you mean by that? As much of it as you can?

RANK: Well, does that alarm you?

NORA: It was such a strange way of putting it. Is anything likely to happen?

RANK: Nothing but what I have long been prepared for. But I certainly didn't expect it to happen so soon.

NORA *(gripping him by the arm)*: What have you found out? Dr. Rank, you must tell me.

RANK *(sitting down by the stove)*: It is all up with me. And it can't be helped.

NORA *(with a sigh of relief)*: Is it about yourself?

RANK: Who else? It is no use lying to one's self. I am the most wretched of all my patients, Mrs. Helmer. Lately I have been taking stock of my internal economy. Bankrupt! Probably within a month I shall lie rotting in the churchyard.

NORA: What an ugly thing to say!

RANK: The thing itself is cursedly ugly, and the worst of it is that I shall have to face so much more that is ugly before that. I shall only make one more examination of myself; when I have done that I shall know pretty certainly when it will be that the horrors of dissolution will begin. There is something I want to tell you. Helmer's refined nature gives him an unconquerable disgust at everything that is ugly; I won't have him in my sickroom.

NORA: Oh, but, Dr. Rank—

RANK: I won't have him there. Not on any account. I bar my door to him. As soon as I am quite certain that the worst has come I shall send you my card with a black cross on it, and then you will know that the loathsome end has begun.

NORA: You are quite absurd today. And I wanted you so much to be in a really good humor.

RANK: With death stalking beside me? To have to pay this penalty for another man's sin! Is there any justice in that? And in every single family, in one way or another, some such inexorable retribution is being exacted.

NORA (putting her hands over her ears): Rubbish! Do talk of something cheerful.

RANK: Oh, it's a mere laughing matter, the whole thing. My poor innocent spine has to suffer for my father's youthful amusements.[4]

NORA (sitting at the table on the left): I suppose you mean that he was too partial to asparagus and pâté de foie gras, don't you?

RANK: Yes, and to truffles.

NORA: Truffles, yes. And oysters too, I suppose?

RANK: Oysters, of course; that goes without saying.

NORA: And heaps of port and champagne. It is sad that all these nice things should take their revenge on our bones.

RANK: Especially that they should revenge themselves on the unlucky bones of those who have not had the satisfaction of enjoying them.

NORA: Yes, that's the saddest part of it all.

RANK (with a searching look at her): Hm!

NORA (after a short pause): Why did you smile?

RANK: No, it was you that laughed.

NORA: No, it was you that smiled, Dr. Rank!

RANK (rising): You are a greater rascal than I thought.

NORA: I am in a silly mood today.

RANK: So it seems.

NORA (putting her hands on his shoulders): Dear, dear Dr. Rank, death mustn't take you away from Torvald and me.

RANK: It is a loss you would easily recover from. Those who are gone are soon forgotten.

NORA (looking at him anxiously): Do you believe that?

RANK: People form new ties, and then—

NORA: Who will form new ties?

RANK: Both you and Helmer, when I am gone. You yourself are already on the highroad to it, I think. What did that Mrs. Linde want here last night?

NORA: Oho! You don't mean to say that you are jealous of poor Christine?

RANK: Yes, I am. She will be my successor in this house. When I am done for, this woman will—

NORA: Hush! Don't speak so loud. She is in that room.

RANK: Today again. There, you see.

NORA: She has only come to sew my dress for me. Bless my soul, how unreasonable you are! *(Sits down on the sofa.)* Be nice now, Dr. Rank, and tomorrow you will see how beautifully I shall dance, and you can imagine I am doing it all for you—and for Torvald too, of course. *(Takes various things out of the box.)* Dr. Rank, come and sit down here, and I will show you something.

RANK *(sitting down)*: What is it?

NORA: Just look at those!

RANK: Silk stockings.

NORA: Flesh colored. Aren't they lovely? It is so dark here now, but tomorrow— No, no, no! You must only look at the feet. Oh well, you may have leave to look at the legs too.

RANK: Hm!

NORA: Why are you looking so critical? Don't you think they will fit me?

RANK: I have no means of forming an opinion about that.

NORA *(looks at him for a moment)*: For shame! *(Hits him lightly on the ear with the stockings.)* That's to punish you. *(Folds them up again.)*

RANK: And what other nice things am I to be allowed to see?

NORA: Not a single thing more, for being so naughty. *(She looks among the things, humming to herself.)*

RANK *(after a short silence)*: When I am sitting here talking to you as intimately as this I cannot imagine for a moment what would have become of me if I had never come into this house.

NORA (*smiling*): I believe you do feel thoroughly at home with us.

RANK (*in a lower voice, looking straight in front of him*): And to be obliged to leave it all—

NORA: Nonsense, you are not going to leave it.

RANK (*as before*): And not be able to leave behind one the slightest token of one's gratitude, scarcely even a fleeting regret—nothing but an empty place which the firstcomer can fill as well as any other.

NORA: And if I asked you now for a— No!

RANK: For what?

NORA: For a big proof of your friendship—

RANK: Yes, yes!

NORA: I mean a tremendously big favor—

RANK: Would you really make me so happy for once?

NORA: Ah, but you don't know what it is yet.

RANK: No—but tell me.

NORA: I really can't, Dr. Rank. It is something out of all reason; it means advice and help and a favor—

RANK: The bigger a thing it is, the better. I can't conceive what it is you mean. Do tell me. Haven't I your confidence?

NORA: More than anyone else. I know you are my truest and best friend, and so I will tell you what it is. Well, Dr. Rank, it is something you must help me to prevent. You know how devotedly, how inexpressibly deeply Torvald loves me; he would never for a moment hesitate to give his life for me.

RANK (*leaning toward her*): Nora—do you think he is the only one—

NORA (*with a slight start*): The only one—?

RANK: The only one who would gladly give his life for your sake.

NORA (*sadly*): Is that it?

RANK: I was determined you should know it before I went away, and there will never be a better opportunity than this. Now you know it, Nora. And now you know, too, that you can trust me as you would trust no one else.

NORA (*rises deliberately and quietly*): Let me pass.

RANK (*makes room for her to pass him but sits still*): Nora!

NORA (*at the hall door*): Helen, bring in the lamp. (*Goes over to the stove.*) Dear Dr. Rank, that was really horrid of you.

RANK: To have loved you as much as anyone else does? Was that horrid?

NORA: No, but to go and tell me so. There was really no need—

RANK: What do you mean? Did you know? (MAID *enters with lamp, puts it down on the table and goes out.*) Nora—Mrs. Helmer—tell me, had you any idea of this?

NORA: Oh, how do I know whether I had or whether I hadn't? I really can't tell you. To think you could be so clumsy, Dr. Rank! We were getting on so nicely.

RANK: Well, at all events you know that you can command me body and soul. So won't you speak out?

NORA (*looking at him*): After what happened?

RANK: I beg you to let me know what it is.

NORA: I can't tell you anything now.

RANK: Yes, yes. You mustn't punish me in that way. Let me have permission to do for you whatever a man may do.

NORA: You can do nothing for me now. Besides, I really don't need any help at all. You will find that the whole thing is merely fancy on my part. It really is so—of course it is! (*Sits down in the rocking chair and looks at him with a smile.*) You are a nice sort of man, Dr. Rank! Don't you feel ashamed of yourself now the lamp has come?

RANK: Not a bit. But perhaps I had better go—forever?

NORA: No indeed, you shall not. Of course you must come here just as before. You know very well Torvald can't do without you.

RANK: Yes, but you?

NORA: Oh, I am always tremendously pleased when you come.

RANK: It is just that that put me on the wrong track. You are a riddle to me. I have often thought that you would almost as soon be in my company as in Helmer's.

NORA: Yes—you see, there are some people one loves best and others whom one would almost always rather have as companions.

RANK: Yes, there is something in that.

NORA: When I was at home of course I loved Papa best. But I always thought it tremendous fun if I could steal down into the maids' room, because they never moralized at all and talked to each other about such entertaining things.

RANK: I see—it is *their* place I have taken.

NORA (*jumping up and going to him*): Oh, dear, nice Dr. Rank, I never meant that at all. But surely you can understand that being with Torvald is a little like being with Papa—

Enter MAID *from the hall.*

MAID: If you please, ma'am. (*Whispers and hands her a card.*)

NORA (*glancing at the card*): Oh! (*Puts it in her pocket.*)

RANK: Is there anything wrong?

NORA: No, no, not in the least. It is only something—it is my new dress—

RANK: What? Your dress is lying there.

NORA: Oh yes, that one; but this is another. I ordered it. Torvald mustn't know about it.

RANK: Oho! Then that was the great secret.

NORA: Of course. Just go in to him; he is sitting in the inner room. Keep him as long as—

RANK: Make your mind easy; I won't let him escape. (*Goes into* HELMER's *room.*)

NORA (*to the* MAID): And he is standing waiting in the kitchen?

MAID: Yes; he came up the back stairs.

NORA: But didn't you tell him no one was in?

MAID: Yes, but it was no good.

NORA: He won't go away?

MAID: No; he says he won't until he has seen you, ma'am.

NORA: Well, let him come in—but quietly. Helen, you

mustn't say anything about it to anyone. It is a surprise for my husband.

MAID: Yes, ma'am, I quite understand. (*Exit.*)

NORA: This dreadful thing is going to happen! It will happen in spite of me! No, no, no, it can't happen—it shan't happen! (*She bolts the door of* HELMER's *room. The* MAID *opens the hall door for* KROGSTAD *and shuts it after him. He is wearing a fur coat, high boots and a fur cap.*)

NORA (*advancing toward him*): Speak low—my husband is at home.

KROGSTAD: No matter about that.

NORA: What do you want of me?

KROGSTAD: An explanation of something.

NORA: Make haste then. What is it?

KROGSTAD: You know, I suppose, that I have got my dismissal.

NORA: I couldn't prevent it, Mr. Krogstad. I fought as hard as I could on your side, but it was no good.

KROGSTAD: Does your husband love you so little then? He knows what I can expose you to, and yet he ventures—

NORA: How can you suppose that he has any knowledge of the sort?

KROGSTAD: I didn't suppose so at all. It would not be the least like our dear Torvald Helmer to show so much courage—

NORA: Mr. Krogstad, a little respect for my husband, please.

KROGSTAD: Certainly—all the respect he deserves. But since you have kept the matter so carefully to yourself, I make bold to suppose that you have a little clearer idea than you had yesterday of what it actually is that you have done?

NORA: More than you could ever teach me.

KROGSTAD: Yes, such a bad lawyer as I am.

NORA: What is it you want of me?

KROGSTAD: Only to see how you were, Mrs. Helmer. I have been thinking about you all day long. A mere cashier, a quill driver, a—well, a man like me—even he has a little of what is called feeling, you know.

NORA: Show it then; think of my little children.

KROGSTAD: Have you and your husband thought of mine?

But never mind about that. I only wanted to tell you that you need not take this matter too seriously. In the first place there will be no accusation made on my part.

NORA: No, of course not; I was sure of that.

KROGSTAD: The whole thing can be arranged amicably; there is no reason why anyone should know anything about it. It will remain a secret between us three.

NORA: My husband must never get to know anything about it.

KROGSTAD: How will you be able to prevent it? Am I to understand that you can pay the balance that is owing?

NORA: No, not just at present.

KROGSTAD: Or perhaps that you have some expedient for raising the money soon?

NORA: No expedient that I mean to make use of.

KROGSTAD: Well, in any case it would have been of no use to you now. If you stood there with ever so much money in your hand, I would never part with your bond.

NORA: Tell me what purpose you mean to put it to.

KROGSTAD: I shall only preserve it—keep it in my possession. No one who is not concerned in the matter shall have the slightest hint of it. So that if the thought of it has driven you to any desperate resolution—

NORA: It has.

KROGSTAD: If you had it in your mind to run away from your home—

NORA: I had.

KROGSTAD: Or even something worse—

NORA: How could you know that?

KROGSTAD: Give up the idea.

NORA: How did you know I had thought of *that*?

KROGSTAD: Most of us think of that at first. I did too—but I hadn't the courage.

NORA (*faintly*): No more than I.

KROGSTAD (*in a tone of relief*): No, that's it, isn't it—you hadn't the courage either?

NORA: No, I haven't—I haven't.

KROGSTAD: Besides, it would have been a great piece of folly.

Once the first storm at home is over— I have a letter for
your husband in my pocket.

NORA: Telling him everything?

KROGSTAD: In as lenient a manner as I possibly could.

NORA (*quickly*): He mustn't get the letter. Tear it up. I will
find some means of getting money.

KROGSTAD: Excuse me, Mrs. Helmer, but I think I told you
just now—

NORA: I am not speaking of what I owe you. Tell me what sum
you are asking my husband for, and I will get the money.

KROGSTAD: I am not asking your husband for a penny.

NORA: What do you want then?

KROGSTAD: I will tell you. I want to rehabilitate myself, Mrs.
Helmer; I want to get on, and in that your husband must
help me. For the last year and a half I have not had a hand
in anything dishonorable, and all that time I have been
struggling in most restricted circumstances. I was content
to work my way up step by step. Now I am turned out, and
I am not going to be satisfied with merely being taken into
favor again. I want to get on, I tell you. I want to get into
the bank again, in a higher position. Your husband must
make a place for me—

NORA: That he will never do!

KROGSTAD: He will; I know him; he dare not protest. And as
soon as I am in there again with him then you will see! Within
a year I shall be the manager's right hand. It will be Nils
Krogstad and not Torvald Helmer who manages the bank.

NORA: That's a thing you will never see!

KROGSTAD: Do you mean that you will—

NORA: I have courage enough for it now.

KROGSTAD: Oh, you can't frighten me. A fine, spoiled lady
like you—

NORA: You will see, you will see.

KROGSTAD: Under the ice, perhaps? Down into the cold,
coal-black water? And then, in the spring, to float up to
the surface, all horrible and unrecognizable, with your
hair fallen out—

NORA: You can't frighten me.

KROGSTAD: Nor you me. People don't do such things, Mrs. Helmer. Besides, what use would it be? I should have him completely in my power all the same.

NORA: Afterward? When I am no longer—

KROGSTAD: Have you forgotten that it is I who have the keeping of your reputation? (NORA *stands speechlessly looking at him.*) Well, now, I have warned you. Do not do anything foolish. When Helmer has had my letter I shall expect a message from him. And be sure you remember that it is your husband himself who has forced me into such ways as this again. I will never forgive him for that. Good-bye, Mrs. Helmer. (*Exit through the hall.*)

NORA (*goes to the hall door, opens it slightly and listens*): He is going. He is not putting the letter in the box. Oh no, no! that's impossible! (*Opens the door by degrees.*) What is that? He is standing outside. He is not going downstairs. Is he hesitating? Can he— (*A letter drops in the box; then* KROGSTAD's *footsteps are heard, till they die away as he goes downstairs.* NORA *utters a stifled cry and runs across the room to the table by the sofa. A short pause.*) In the letter box. (*Steals across to the hall door.*) There it lies— Torvald, Torvald, there is no hope for us now!

MRS. LINDE *comes in from the room on the left, carrying the dress.*

MRS. LINDE: There, I can't see anything more to mend now. Would you like to try it on?

NORA (*in a hoarse whisper*): Christine, come here.

MRS. LINDE (*throwing the dress down on the sofa*): What is the matter with you? You look so agitated!

NORA: Come here. Do you see that letter? There, look—you can see it through the glass in the letter box.

MRS. LINDE: Yes, I see it.

NORA: That letter is from Krogstad.

MRS. LINDE: Nora—it was Krogstad who lent you the money!

NORA: Yes, and now Torvald will know all about it.

MRS. LINDE: Believe me, Nora, that's the best thing for both of you.

NORA: You don't know all. I forged a name.

MRS. LINDE: Good heavens!

NORA: I only want to say this to you, Christine—you must be my witness.

MRS. LINDE: Your witness? What do you mean? What am I to—

NORA: If I should go out of my mind—and it might easily happen—

MRS. LINDE: Nora!

NORA: Or if anything else should happen to me—anything, for instance, that might prevent my being here—

MRS. LINDE: Nora! Nora! you are quite out of your mind.

NORA: And if it should happen that there were someone who wanted to take all the responsibility, all the blame, you understand—

MRS. LINDE: Yes, yes—but how can you suppose—

NORA: Then you must be my witness, that it is not true, Christine. I am not out of my mind at all; I am in my right senses now, and I tell you no one else has known anything about it; I, and I alone, did the whole thing. Remember that.

MRS. LINDE: I will, indeed. But I don't understand all this.

NORA: How should you understand it? A wonderful thing is going to happen.

MRS. LINDE: A wonderful thing?

NORA: Yes, a wonderful thing! But it is so terrible. Christine, it *mustn't* happen, not for all the world.

MRS. LINDE: I will go at once and see Krogstad.

NORA: Don't go to him; he will do you some harm.

MRS. LINDE: There was a time when he would gladly do anything for my sake.

NORA: He?

MRS. LINDE: Where does he live?

NORA: How should I know? Yes—(*feeling in her pocket*)—here is his card. But the letter, the letter!

HELMER (*calls from his room, knocking at the door*): Nora!

NORA (*cries out anxiously*): Oh, what's that? What do you want?

HELMER: Don't be so frightened. We are not coming in; you have locked the door. Are you trying on your dress?

NORA: Yes, that's it. I look so nice, Torvald.

MRS. LINDE (*who has read the card*): I see he lives at the corner here.

NORA: Yes, but it's no use. It is hopeless. The letter is lying there in the box.

MRS. LINDE: And your husband keeps the key?

NORA: Yes, always.

MRS. LINDE: Krogstad must ask for his letter back unread, he must find some pretense—

NORA: But it is just at this time that Torvald generally—

MRS. LINDE: You must delay him. Go in to him in the meantime. I will come back as soon as I can. (*She goes out hurriedly through the hall door.*)

NORA (*goes to* HELMER's *door, opens it and peeps in*): Torvald!

HELMER (*from the inner room*): Well? May I venture at last to come into my own room again? Come along, Rank, now you will see— (*Halting in the doorway.*) But what is this?

NORA: What is what, dear?

HELMER: Rank led me to expect a splendid transformation.

RANK (*in the doorway*): I understood so, but evidently I was mistaken.

NORA: Yes, nobody is to have the chance of admiring me in my dress until tomorrow.

HELMER: But, my dear Nora, you look so worn out. Have you been practicing too much?

NORA: No, I have not practiced at all.

HELMER: But you will need to—

NORA: Yes, indeed I shall, Torvald. But I can't get on a bit without you to help me; I have absolutely forgotten the whole thing.

HELMER: Oh, we will soon work it up again.

NORA: Yes, help me, Torvald. Promise that you will! I am so nervous about it—all the people— You must give yourself up to me entirely this evening. Not the tiniest bit of

business—you mustn't even take a pen in your hand. Will
you promise, Torvald dear?

HELMER: I promise. This evening I will be wholly and absolutely at your service, you helpless little mortal. Ah, by
the way, first of all I will just—(*Goes toward the hall door.*)

NORA: What are you going to do there?

HELMER: Only see if any letters have come.

NORA: No, no! Don't do that, Torvald!

HELMER: Why not?

NORA: Torvald, please don't. There is nothing there.

HELMER: Well, let me look. (*Turns to go to the letter box.
NORA, at the piano, plays the first bars of the tarantella.
HELMER stops in the doorway.*) Aha!

NORA: I can't dance tomorrow if I don't practice with you.

HELMER (*going up to her*): Are you really so afraid of it, dear?

NORA: Yes, so dreadfully afraid of it. Let me practice at once;
there is time now, before we go to dinner. Sit down and
play for me, Torvald dear; criticize me and correct me as
you play.

HELMER: With great pleasure, if you wish me to. (*Sits down
at the piano.*)

NORA (*takes out of the box a tambourine and a long varie-
gated shawl. She hastily drapes the shawl round her. Then
she springs to the front of the stage and calls out*): Now
play for me! I am going to dance!

HELMER *plays and* NORA *dances.* RANK *stands by the
piano behind* HELMER *and looks on.*

HELMER (*as he plays*): Slower, slower!

NORA: I can't do it any other way.

HELMER: Not so violently, Nora!

NORA: This is the way.

HELMER (*stops playing*): No, no—that is not a bit right.

NORA (*laughing and swinging the tambourine*): Didn't I tell
you so?

RANK: Let me play for her.

HELMER (*getting up*): Yes, do. I can correct her better then.

RANK *sits down at the piano and plays.* NORA *dances more and more wildly.* HELMER *has taken up a position by the stove and during her dance gives her frequent instructions. She does not seem to hear him; her hair comes down and falls over her shoulders; she pays no attention to it but goes on dancing. Enters* MRS. LINDE.

MRS. LINDE (*standing as if spellbound in the doorway*): Oh!

NORA (*as she dances*): Such fun, Christine!

HELMER: My dear darling Nora, you are dancing as if your life depended on it.

NORA: So it does.

HELMER: Stop, Rank; this is sheer madness. Stop, I tell you! (RANK *stops playing, and* NORA *suddenly stands still.* HELMER *goes up to her.*) I could never have believed it. You have forgotten everything I taught you.

NORA (*throwing away the tambourine*): There, you see.

HELMER: You will want a lot of coaching.

NORA: Yes, you see how much I need it. You must coach me up to the last minute. Promise me that, Torvald!

HELMER: You can depend on me.

NORA: You must not think of anything but me, either today or tomorrow; you mustn't open a single letter—not even open the letter box—

HELMER: Ah, you are still afraid of that fellow—

NORA: Yes, indeed I am.

HELMER: Nora, I can tell from your looks that there is a letter from him lying there.

NORA: I don't know; I think there is; but you must not read anything of that kind now. Nothing horrid must come between us till this is all over.

RANK (*whispers to* HELMER): You mustn't contradict her.

HELMER (*taking her in his arms*): The child shall have her way. But tomorrow night, after you have danced—

NORA: Then you will be free. (*The* MAID *appears in the doorway to the right.*)

MAID: Dinner is served, ma'am.

NORA: We will have champagne, Helen.

MAID: Very good, ma'am. (*Exit.*)

HELMER: Hullo!—are we going to have a banquet?

NORA: Yes, a champagne banquet till the small hours. (*Calls out.*) And a few macaroons, Helen—lots, just for once!

HELMER: Come, come, don't be so wild and nervous. Be my own little skylark, as you used to be.

NORA: Yes, dear, I will. But go in now, and you too, Dr. Rank. Christine, you must help me to do up my hair.

RANK (*whispers to* HELMER *as they go out*): I suppose there is nothing—she is not expecting anything?

HELMER: Far from it, my dear fellow; it is simply nothing more than this childish nervousness I was telling you of. (*They go into the right-hand room.*)

NORA: Well!

MRS. LINDE: Gone out of town.

NORA: I could tell from your face.

MRS. LINDE: He is coming home tomorrow evening. I wrote a note for him.

NORA: You should have let it alone; you must prevent nothing. After all, it is splendid to be waiting for a wonderful thing to happen.

MRS. LINDE: What is it that you are waiting for?

NORA: Oh, you wouldn't understand. Go in to them, I will come in a moment. (MRS. LINDE *goes into the dining room.* NORA *stands still for a little while, as if to compose herself. Then she looks at her watch.*) Five o'clock. Seven hours till midnight; and then four-and-twenty hours till the next midnight. Then the tarantella will be over. Twenty-four and seven? Thirty-one hours to live.

HELMER (*from the doorway on the right*): Where's my little skylark?

NORA (*going to him with her arms outstretched*): Here she is!

ACT THREE

The same room. The table has been placed in the middle of the stage with chairs round it. A lamp is burning on the table. The door into the hall stands open. Dance music is heard in the room above. MRS. LINDE *is sitting at the table idly turning over the leaves of a book; she tries to read but does not seem able to collect her thoughts. Every now and then she listens intently for a sound at the outer door.*

MRS. LINDE *(looking at her watch)*: Not yet—and the time is nearly up. If only he does not—*(Listens again.)* Ah, there he is. *(Goes into the hall and opens the outer door carefully. Light footsteps are heard on the stairs. She whispers.)* Come in. There is no one here.

KROGSTAD *(in the doorway)*: I found a note from you at home. What does this mean?

MRS. LINDE: It is absolutely necessary that I should have a talk with you.

KROGSTAD: Really? And it is absolutely necessary that it should be here?

MRS. LINDE: It is impossible where I live; there is no private entrance to my rooms. Come in; we are quite alone.

The maid is asleep, and the Helmers are at the dance upstairs.

KROGSTAD (*coming into the room*): Are the Helmers really at a dance tonight?

MRS. LINDE: Yes, why not?

KROGSTAD: Certainly—why not?

MRS. LINDE: Now, Nils, let us have a talk.

KROGSTAD: Can we two have anything to talk about?

MRS. LINDE: We have a great deal to talk about.

KROGSTAD: I shouldn't have thought so.

MRS. LINDE: No, you have never properly understood me.

KROGSTAD: Was there anything else to understand except what was obvious to all the world—a heartless woman jilts a man when a more lucrative chance turns up?

MRS. LINDE: Do you believe I am as absolutely heartless as all that? And do you believe it with a light heart?

KROGSTAD: Didn't you?

MRS. LINDE: Nils, did you really think that?

KROGSTAD: If it were as you say, why did you write to me as you did at the time?

MRS. LINDE: I could do nothing else. As I had to break with you, it was my duty also to put an end to all that you felt for me.

KROGSTAD (*wringing his hands*): So that was it. And all this— only for the sake of money!

MRS. LINDE: You mustn't forget that I had a helpless mother and two little brothers. We couldn't wait for you, Nils; your prospects seemed hopeless then.

KROGSTAD: That may be so, but you had no right to throw me over for anyone else's sake.

MRS. LINDE: Indeed, I don't know. Many a time did I ask myself if I had the right to do it.

KROGSTAD (*more gently*): When I lost you it was as if all the solid ground went from under my feet. Look at me now— I am a shipwrecked man clinging to a bit of wreckage.

MRS. LINDE: But help may be near.

KROGSTAD: It *was* near, but then you came and stood in my way.

MRS. LINDE: Unintentionally, Nils. It was only today that I learned it was your place I was going to take in the bank.

KROGSTAD: I believe you, if you say so. But now that you know it, are you not going to give it up to me?

MRS. LINDE: No, because that would not benefit you in the least.

KROGSTAD: Oh, benefit, benefit—I would have done it whether or no.

MRS. LINDE: I have learned to act prudently. Life and hard, bitter necessity have taught me that.

KROGSTAD: And life has taught me not to believe in fine speeches.

MRS. LINDE: Then life has taught you something very reasonable. But deeds you must believe in.

KROGSTAD: What do you mean by that?

MRS. LINDE: You said you were like a shipwrecked man clinging to some wreckage.

KROGSTAD: I had good reason to say so.

MRS. LINDE: Well, I am like a shipwrecked woman clinging to some wreckage—no one to mourn for, no one to care for.

KROGSTAD: It was your own choice.

MRS. LINDE: There was no other choice—then.

KROGSTAD: Well, what now?

MRS. LINDE: Nils, how would it be if we two shipwrecked people could join forces?

KROGSTAD: What are you saying?

MRS. LINDE: Two on the same piece of wreckage would stand a better chance than each on their own.

KROGSTAD: Christine!

MRS. LINDE: What do you suppose brought me to town?

KROGSTAD: Do you mean that you gave me a thought?

MRS. LINDE: I could not endure life without work. All my life, as long as I can remember, I have worked, and it has been my greatest and only pleasure. But now I am quite alone in the world—my life is so dreadfully empty and I feel so forsaken. There is not the least pleasure in working for one's self. Nils, give me someone and something to work for.

KROGSTAD: I don't trust that. It is nothing but a woman's overstrained sense of generosity that prompts you to make such an offer of yourself.

MRS. LINDE: Have you ever noticed anything of the sort in me?

KROGSTAD: Could you really do it? Tell me—do you know all about my past life?

MRS. LINDE: Yes.

KROGSTAD: And do you know what they think of me here?

MRS. LINDE: You seemed to me to imply that with me you might have been quite another man.

KROGSTAD: I am certain of it.

MRS. LINDE: Is it too late now?

KROGSTAD: Christine, are you saying this deliberately? Yes, I am sure you are. I see it in your face. Have you really the courage, then—

MRS. LINDE: I want to be a mother to someone, and your children need a mother. We two need each other. Nils, I have faith in your real character—I can dare anything with you.

KROGSTAD (grasps her hands): Thanks, thanks, Christine! Now I shall find a way to clear myself in the eyes of the world. Ah, but I forgot—

MRS. LINDE (listening): Hush! The tarantella! Go, go!

KROGSTAD: Why? What is it?

MRS. LINDE: Do you hear them up there? When that is over we may expect them back.

KROGSTAD: Yes, yes—I will go. But it is all no use. Of course you are not aware what steps I have taken in the matter of the Helmers.

MRS. LINDE: Yes, I know all about that.

KROGSTAD: And in spite of that have you the courage to—

MRS. LINDE: I understand very well to what lengths a man like you might be driven by despair.

KROGSTAD: If I could only undo what I have done!

MRS. LINDE: You cannot. Your letter is lying in the letter box now.

KROGSTAD: Are you sure of that?

MRS. LINDE: Quite sure, but—

KROGSTAD (*with a searching look at her*): Is that what it all means?—that you want to save your friend at any cost? Tell me frankly. Is that it?

MRS. LINDE: Nils, a woman who has once sold herself for another's sake doesn't do it a second time.

KROGSTAD: I will ask for my letter back.

MRS. LINDE: No, no.

KROGSTAD: Yes, of course I will. I will wait here till Helmer comes; I will tell him he must give me my letter back— that it only concerns my dismissal—that he is not to read it—

MRS. LINDE: No, Nils, you must not recall your letter.

KROGSTAD: But, tell me, wasn't it for that very purpose that you asked me to meet you here?

MRS. LINDE: In my first moment of fright it was. But twenty-four hours have elapsed since then, and in that time I have witnessed incredible things in this house. Helmer must know all about it. This unhappy secret must be disclosed; they must have a complete understanding between them, which is impossible with all this concealment and false-hood going on.

KROGSTAD: Very well, if you will take the responsibility. But there is one thing I can do in any case, and I shall do it at once.

MRS. LINDE (*listening*): You must be quick and go! The dance is over; we are not safe a moment longer.

KROGSTAD: I will wait for you below.

MRS. LINDE: Yes, do. You must see me back to my door.

KROGSTAD: I have never had such an amazing piece of good fortune in my life! (*Goes out through the outer door. The door between the room and the hall remains open.*)

MRS. LINDE (*tidying up the room and laying her hat and*

cloak ready): What a difference! What a difference! Someone to work for and live for—a home to bring comfort into. That I will do, indeed. I wish they would be quick and come. (*Listens.*) Ah, there they are now. I must put on my things. (*Takes up her hat and cloak.* HELMER's *and* NORA's *voices are heard outside; a key is turned, and* HELMER *brings* NORA *almost by force into the hall. She is in an Italian costume with a large black shawl round her; he is in evening dress and a black domino*[5] *which is flying open.*)

NORA (*hanging back in the doorway and struggling with him*): No, no, no!—don't take me in. I want to go upstairs again; I don't want to leave so early.

HELMER: But, my dearest Nora—

NORA: Please, Torvald dear—please, *please*—only an hour more.

HELMER: Not a single minute, my sweet Nora. You know that was our agreement. Come along into the room; you are catching cold standing there. (*He brings her gently into the room in spite of her resistance.*)

MRS. LINDE: Good evening.

NORA: Christine!

HELMER: You here so late, Mrs. Linde?

MRS. LINDE: Yes, you must excuse me; I was so anxious to see Nora in her dress.

NORA: Have you been sitting here waiting for me?

MRS. LINDE: Yes; unfortunately I came too late—you had already gone upstairs—and I thought I couldn't go away again without having seen you.

HELMER (*taking off* NORA's *shawl*): Yes, take a good look at her. I think she is worth looking at. Isn't she charming, Mrs. Linde?

MRS. LINDE: Yes, indeed she is.

HELMER: Doesn't she look remarkably pretty? Everyone thought so at the dance. But she is terribly self-willed, this sweet little person. What are we to do with her? You will hardly believe that I had almost to bring her away by force.

NORA: Torvald, you will repent not having let me stay, even if it were only for half an hour.

HELMER: Listen to her, Mrs. Linde! She had danced her tarantella, and it had been a tremendous success, as it deserved—although possibly the performance was a trifle too realistic—a little more so, I mean, than was strictly compatible with the limitations of art. But never mind about that! The chief thing is, she had made a success—she had made a tremendous success. Do you think I was going to let her remain there after that and spoil the effect? No indeed! I took my charming little Capri maiden [6]—my capricious little Capri maiden, I should say—on my arm, took one quick turn round the room, a curtsey on either side, and, as they say in novels, the beautiful apparition disappeared. An exit ought always to be effective, Mrs. Linde; but that is what I cannot make Nora understand. Pooh! this room is hot. (*Throws his domino on a chair and opens the door of his room.*) Hullo! it's all dark in here. Oh, of course—excuse me. (*He goes in and lights some candles.*)

NORA (*in a hurried and breathless whisper*): Well?

MRS. LINDE (*in a low voice*): I have had a talk with him.

NORA: Yes, and—

MRS. LINDE: Nora, you must tell your husband all about it.

NORA (*in an expressionless voice*): I knew it.

MRS. LINDE: You have nothing to be afraid of as far as Krogstad is concerned, but you must tell him.

NORA: I won't tell him.

MRS. LINDE: Then the letter will.

NORA: Thank you, Christine. Now I know what I must do. Hush!

HELMER (*coming in again*): Well, Mrs. Linde, have you admired her?

MRS. LINDE: Yes, and now I will say good night.

HELMER: What, already? Is this yours, this knitting?

MRS. LINDE *(taking it)*: Yes, thank you. I had very nearly forgotten it.

HELMER: So you knit?

MRS. LINDE: Of course.

HELMER: Do you know, you ought to embroider.

MRS. LINDE: Really? Why?

HELMER: Yes, it's far more becoming. Let me show you. You hold the embroidery thus in your left hand and use the needle with the right—like this—with a long easy sweep. Do you see?

MRS. LINDE: Yes, perhaps—

HELMER: Yes, but in the case of knitting—that can never be anything but ungraceful; look here—the arms close together, the knitting needles going up and down—it has a sort of Chinese effect. . . . That was really excellent champagne they gave us.

MRS. LINDE: Well—good night, Nora, and don't be self-willed anymore.

HELMER: That's right, Mrs. Linde.

MRS. LINDE: Good night, Mr. Helmer.

HELMER *(accompanying her to the door)*: Good night, good night. I hope you will get home all right. I should be very happy to— But you haven't any great distance to go. Good night, good night. *(She goes out; he shuts the door after her and comes in again.)* Ah!—at last we have got rid of her. She is a frightful bore, that woman.

NORA: Aren't you very tired, Torvald?

HELMER: No, not in the least.

NORA: Nor sleepy?

HELMER: Not a bit. On the contrary I feel extraordinarily lively. And you?—you really look both tired and sleepy.

NORA: Yes, I am very tired. I want to go to sleep at once.

HELMER: There, you see it was quite right of me not to let you stay there any longer.

NORA: Everything you do is quite right, Torvald.

HELMER *(kissing her on the forehead)*: Now my little skylark is speaking reasonably. Did you notice what good spirits Rank was in this evening?

NORA: Really? Was he? I didn't speak to him at all.

HELMER: And I very little, but I have not for a long time seen him in such good form. (*Looks for a while at her and then goes nearer to her.*) It is delightful to be at home by ourselves again, to be all alone with you—you fascinating, charming little darling!

NORA: Don't look at me like that, Torvald.

HELMER: Why shouldn't I look at my dearest treasure?—at all the beauty that is mine, all my very own?

NORA (*going to the other side of the table*): You mustn't say things like that to me tonight.

HELMER (*following her*): You have still got the tarantella in your blood, I see. And it makes you more captivating than ever. Listen—the guests are beginning to go now. (*In a lower voice.*) Nora—soon the whole house will be quiet.

NORA: Yes, I hope so.

HELMER: Yes, my own darling Nora. Do you know, when I am out at a party with you like this, why I speak so little to you, keep away from you and only send a stolen glance in your direction now and then?—do you know why I do that? It is because I make believe to myself that we are secretly in love and you are my secretly promised bride and that no one suspects there is anything between us.

NORA: Yes, yes—I know very well your thoughts are with me all the time.

HELMER: And when we are leaving and I am putting the shawl over your beautiful young shoulders—on your lovely neck—then I imagine that you are my young bride and that we have just come from our wedding and I am bringing you, for the first time, into our home—to be alone with you for the first time—quite alone with my shy little darling! All this evening I have longed for nothing but you. When I watched the seductive figures of the tarantella my blood was on fire; I could endure it no longer, and that was why I brought you down so early—

NORA: Go away, Torvald! You must let me go. I won't—

HELMER: What's that? You're joking, my little Nora! You won't—you won't? Am I not your husband? *(A knock is heard at the outer door.)*

NORA *(starting)*: Did you hear—

HELMER *(going into the hall)*: Who is it?

RANK *(outside)*: It is I. May I come in for a moment?

HELMER *(in a fretful whisper)*: Oh, what does he want now? *(Aloud.)* Wait a minute. *(Unlocks the door.)* Come, that's kind of you not to pass by our door.

RANK: I thought I heard your voice, and I felt as if I should like to look in. *(With a swift glance round.)* Ah yes!—these dear familiar rooms. You are very happy and cosy in here, you two.

HELMER: It seems to me that you looked after yourself pretty well upstairs too.

RANK: Excellently. Why shouldn't I? Why shouldn't one enjoy everything in this world?—at any rate as much as one can and as long as one can. The wine was capital—

HELMER: Especially the champagne.

RANK: So you noticed that too? It is almost incredible how much I managed to put away!

NORA: Torvald drank a great deal of champagne tonight too.

RANK: Did he?

NORA: Yes, and he is always in such good spirits afterward.

RANK: Well, why should one not enjoy a merry evening after a well-spent day?

HELMER: Well-spent? I am afraid I can't take credit for that.

RANK *(clapping him on the back)*: But I can, you know!

HELMER: Exactly.

NORA: Dr. Rank, you must have been occupied with some scientific investigation today.

HELMER: Just listen!—little Nora talking about scientific investigations!

NORA: And may I congratulate you on the result?

RANK: Indeed you may.

NORA: Was it favorable, then?

RANK: The best possible, for both doctor and patient—certainty.

NORA (*quickly and searchingly*): Certainty?

RANK: Absolute certainty. So wasn't I entitled to make a merry evening of it after that?

NORA: Yes, you certainly were, Dr. Rank.

HELMER: I think so too, so long as you don't have to pay for it in the morning.

RANK: Oh well, one can't have anything in this life without paying for it.

NORA: Dr. Rank—are you fond of fancy-dress balls?

RANK: Yes, if there is a fine lot of pretty costumes.

NORA: Tell me—what shall we two wear at the next?

HELMER: Little featherbrain!—are you thinking of the next already?

RANK: We two? Yes, I can tell you. You shall go as a good fairy—

HELMER: Yes, but what do you suggest as an appropriate costume for that?

RANK: Let your wife go dressed just as she is in everyday life.

HELMER: That was really very prettily turned. But can't you tell us what you will be?

RANK: Yes, my dear friend, I have quite made up my mind about that.

HELMER: Well?

RANK: At the next fancy-dress ball I shall be invisible.

HELMER: That's a good joke!

RANK: There is a big black hat—have you ever heard of hats that make you invisible? If you put one on, no one can see you.

HELMER (*suppressing a smile*): Yes, you are quite right.

RANK: But I am clean forgetting what I came for. Helmer, give me a cigar—one of the dark Havanas.

HELMER: With the greatest pleasure. (*Offers him his case.*)

RANK (*takes a cigar and cuts off the end*): Thanks.

NORA (*striking a match*): Let me give you a light.

RANK: Thank you. (*She holds the match for him to light his cigar.*) And now good-bye!

HELMER: Good-bye good-bye, dear old man!

NORA: Sleep well, Dr. Rank.

RANK: Thank you for that wish.

NORA: Wish me the same.

RANK: You? Well, if you want me to sleep well! And thanks for the light. (*He nods to them both and goes out.*)

HELMER (*in a subdued voice*): He has drunk more than he ought.

NORA (*absently*): Maybe. (HELMER *takes a bunch of keys out of his pocket and goes into the hall.*) Torvald! What are you going to do there?

HELMER: Empty the letter box; it is quite full; there will be no room to put the newspaper in tomorrow morning.

NORA: Are you going to work tonight?

HELMER: You know quite well I'm not. What is this? Someone has been at the lock.

NORA: At the lock?

HELMER: Yes, someone has. What can it mean? I should never have thought the maid— Here is a broken hairpin. Nora, it is one of yours.

NORA (*quickly*): Then it must have been the children.

HELMER: Then you must get them out of those ways. There, at last I have got it open. (*Takes out the contents of the letter box and calls to the kitchen.*) Helen! Helen, put out the light over the front door. (*Goes back into the room and shuts the door into the hall. He holds out his hand full of letters.*) Look at that—look what a heap of them there are. (*Turning them over.*) What on earth is that?

NORA (*at the window*): The letter— No! Torvald, no!

HELMER: Two cards—of Rank's.

NORA: Of Dr. Rank's?

HELMER (*looking at them*): Dr. Rank. They were on the top. He must have put them in when he went out.

NORA: Is there anything written on them?

HELMER: There is a black cross over the name. Look there— what an uncomfortable idea! It looks as if he were announcing his own death.

NORA: It is just what he is doing.

HELMER: What? Do you know anything about it? Has he said anything to you?

NORA: Yes. He told me that when the cards came it would be his leave-taking from us. He means to shut himself up and die.

HELMER: My poor old friend. Certainly I knew we should not have him very long with us. But so soon! And so he hides himself away like a wounded animal.

NORA: If it has to happen, it is best it should be without a word—don't you think so, Torvald?

HELMER (*walking up and down*): He had so grown into our lives. I can't think of him as having gone out of them. He, with his sufferings and his loneliness, was like a cloudy background to our sunlit happiness. Well, perhaps it is best so. For him, anyway. (*Standing still.*) And perhaps for us too, Nora. We two are thrown quite upon each other now. (*Puts his arms round her.*) My darling wife, I don't feel as if I could hold you tight enough. Do you know, Nora, I have often wished that you might be threatened by some great danger, so that I might risk my life's blood and everything for your sake.

NORA (*disengages herself and says firmly and decidedly*): Now you must read your letters, Torvald.

HELMER: No, no; not tonight. I want to be with you, my darling wife.

NORA: With the thought of your friend's death—

HELMER: You are right; it has affected us both. Something ugly has come between us—the thought of the horrors of death. We must try and rid our minds of that. Until then— we will each go to our own room.

NORA (*hanging on his neck*): Good night, Torvald—good night!

HELMER (*kissing her on the forehead*): Good night, my little singing bird. Sleep sound, Nora. Now I will read my letters through. (*He takes his letters and goes into his room, shutting the door after him.*)

NORA (*gropes distractedly about, seizes* HELMER's *domino, throws it about her while she says in quick, hoarse, spasmodic whispers*): Never to see him again. Never! Never! (*Puts her shawl over her head.*) Never to see my children again either—never again. Never! Never! Ah! the icy black water—the unfathomable depths—if only it were over! He has got it now—now he is reading it. Good-bye, Torvald and my children! (*She is about to rush out through the hall when* HELMER *opens his door hurriedly and stands with an open letter in his hand.*)

HELMER: Nora!

NORA: Ah!

HELMER: What is this? Do you know what is in this letter?

NORA: Yes, I know. Let me go! Let me get out!

HELMER (*holding her back*): Where are you going?

NORA (*trying to get free*): You shan't save me, Torvald!

HELMER (*reeling*): True? Is this true, that I read here? Horrible! No, no—it is impossible that it is true.

NORA: It is true. I have loved you above everything else in the world.

HELMER: Oh, don't let us have any silly excuses.

NORA (*taking a step toward him*): Torvald!

HELMER: Miserable creature—what have you done?

NORA: Let me go. You shall not suffer for my sake. You shall not take it upon yourself.

HELMER: No tragedy airs, please. (*Locks the hall door.*) Here you shall stay and give me an explanation. Do you understand what you have done? Answer me! Do you understand what you have done?

NORA (*looks steadily at him and says with a growing look of coldness in her face*): Yes, now I am beginning to understand thoroughly.

HELMER (*walking about the room*): What a horrible awakening! All these eight years—she who was my joy and pride—a hypocrite, a liar—worse, worse—a criminal! The unutterable ugliness of it all! For shame! For shame! (NORA *is silent and looks steadily at him. He stops in front of her.*) I ought to have suspected that something of the sort would happen. I ought to have foreseen it. All your father's want of principle—be silent!—all your father's want of principle has come out in you. No religion, no morality, no sense of duty— How I am punished for having winked at what he did! I did it for your sake, and this is how you repay me.

NORA: Yes, that's just it.

HELMER: Now you have destroyed all my happiness. You have ruined all my future. It is horrible to think of! I am in the power of an unscrupulous man; he can do what he likes with me, ask anything he likes of me, give me any orders he pleases—I dare not refuse. And I must sink to such miserable depths because of a thoughtless woman!

NORA: When I am out of the way you will be free.

HELMER: No fine speeches, please. Your father always had plenty of those ready too. What good would it be to me if you were out of the way, as you say? Not the slightest. He can make the affair known everywhere; and if he does, I may be falsely suspected of having been a party to your criminal action. Very likely people will think I was behind it all—that it was I who prompted you! And I have to thank you for all this—you whom I have cherished during the whole of our married life. Do you understand now what it is you have done for me?

NORA (*coldly and quietly*): Yes.

HELMER: It is so incredible that I can't take it in. But we must come to some understanding. Take off that shawl. Take it off, I tell you. I must try and appease him in some way or another. The matter must be hushed up at any cost. And as for you and me, it must appear as if everything between us were just as before—but naturally only in the eyes of the world. You will still remain in my house, that is a matter of course. But I shall not allow you to bring up the children; I dare not trust them to you. To think that I should be obliged to say so to one whom I have loved so dearly and whom I still— No, that is all over. From this moment happiness is not the question; all that concerns us is to save the remains, the fragments, the appearance—

A ring is heard at the front-door bell.

HELMER *(with a start)*: What is that? So late! Can the worst—can he— Hide yourself, Nora. Say you are ill.

NORA *stands motionless.* HELMER *goes and unlocks the hall door.*

MAID *(half dressed, comes to the door)*: A letter for the mistress.

HELMER: Give it to me. *(Takes the letter and shuts the door.)* Yes, it is from him. You shall not have it; I will read it myself.

NORA: Yes, read it.

HELMER *(standing by the lamp)*: I scarcely have the courage to do it. It may mean ruin for the both of us. No, I must know. *(Tears open the letter, runs his eye over a few lines, looks at a paper enclosed and gives a shout of joy.)* Nora! *(She looks at him questioningly.)* Nora! No, I must read it once again. Yes, it is true! I am saved! Nora, I am saved!

NORA: And I?

HELMER: You too, of course; we are both saved, both you and I. Look, he sends you your bond back. He says he regrets and repents—that a happy change in his life— Never mind what he says! We are saved, Nora! No one can do anything to you. Oh, Nora, Nora— No, first I must destroy these hateful things. Let me see. *(Takes a look at the bond.)* No, no, I won't look at it. The whole thing shall be nothing but a bad dream to me. *(Tears up the bond and both letters, throws them all into the stove and watches them burn.)* There—now it doesn't exist any longer. He says that since Christmas Eve you— These must have been three dreadful days for you, Nora.

NORA: I have fought a hard fight these three days.

HELMER: And suffered agonies and seen no way out, but— No, we won't call any of the horrors to mind. We will only shout with joy and keep saying, "It's all over! It's all over!" Listen to me, Nora. You don't seem to realize that it is all over. What is this?—such a cold, set face! My poor little Nora, I quite understand; you don't feel as if you could believe that I have forgiven you. But it is true, Nora, I swear it; I have forgiven you everything. I know that what you did you did out of love for me.

NORA: That is true.

HELMER: You have loved me as a wife ought to love her husband. Only you had not sufficient knowledge to judge of the means you used. But do you suppose you are any the less dear to me because you don't understand how to act on your own responsibility? No, no; only lean on me; I will advise and direct you. I should not be a man if this womanly helplessness did not just give you a double attractiveness in my eyes. You must not think any more about the hard things I said in my first moment of consternation, when I thought everything was going to overwhelm me. I have forgiven you, Nora; I swear to you I have forgiven you.

NORA: Thank you for your forgiveness. (*She goes out through the door to the right.*)

HELMER: No, don't go. (*Looks in.*) What are you doing in there?

NORA (*from within*): Taking off my fancy dress.

HELMER (*standing at the open door*): Yes, do. Try and calm yourself and make your mind easy again, my frightened little singing bird. Be at rest and feel secure; I have broad wings to shelter you under. (*Walks up and down by the door.*) How warm and cosy our home is, Nora. Here is shelter for you; here I will protect you like a hunted dove that I have saved from a hawk's claws; I will bring peace to your poor beating heart. It will come, little by little, Nora, believe me. Tomorrow morning you will look upon it all quite differently; soon everything will be just as it was before. Very soon you won't need me to assure you that I have forgiven you; you will yourself feel the certainty that

I have done so. Can you suppose I should ever think of such a thing as repudiating you or even reproaching you? You have no idea what a true man's heart is like, Nora. There is something so indescribably sweet and satisfying, to a man, in the knowledge that he has forgiven his wife— forgiven her freely and with all his heart. It seems as if that had made her, as it were, doubly his own; he has given her a new life, so to speak, and she has in a way become both wife and child to him. So you shall be for me after this, my little scared, helpless darling. Have no anxiety about anything, Nora; only be frank and open with me, and I will serve as will and conscience both to you— What is this? Not gone to bed? Have you changed your things?

NORA *(in everyday dress)*: Yes, Torvald, I have changed my things now.

HELMER: But what for?—so late as this.

NORA: I shall not sleep tonight.

HELMER: But, my dear Nora—

NORA *(looking at her watch)*: It is not so very late. Sit down here, Torvald. You and I have much to say to one another. *(She sits down at one side of the table.)*

HELMER: Nora—what is this?—this cold, set face?

NORA: Sit down. It will take some time; I have a lot to talk over with you.

HELMER *(sits down at the opposite side of the table)*: You alarm me, Nora!—and I don't understand you.

NORA: No, that is just it. You don't understand me, and I have never understood you either—before tonight. No, you mustn't interrupt me. You must simply listen to what I say. Torvald, this is a settling of accounts.

HELMER: What do you mean by that?

NORA *(after a short silence)*: Isn't there one thing that strikes you as strange in our sitting here like this?

HELMER: What is that?

NORA: We have been married now eight years. Does it not occur to you that this is the first time we two, you and I, husband and wife, have had a serious conversation?

HELMER: What do you mean, serious?

NORA: In all these eight years—longer than that—from the very beginning of our acquaintance we have never exchanged a word on any serious subject.

HELMER: Was it likely that I would be continually and forever telling you about worries that you could not help me to bear?

NORA: I am not speaking about business matters. I say that we have never sat down in earnest together to try and get at the bottom of anything.

HELMER: But, dearest Nora, would it have been any good to you?

NORA: That is just it; you have never understood me. I have been greatly wronged, Torvald—first by Papa and then by you.

HELMER: What! By us two—by us two who have loved you better than anyone else in the world?

NORA (shaking her head): You have never loved me. You have only thought it pleasant to be in love with me.

HELMER: Nora, what do I hear you saying?

NORA: It is perfectly true, Torvald. When I was at home with Papa he told me his opinion about everything, and so I had the same opinions; and if I differed from him I concealed the fact, because he would not have liked it. He called me his doll child, and he played with me just as I used to play with my dolls. And when I came to live with you—

HELMER: What sort of an expression is that to use about our marriage?

NORA (undisturbed): I mean that I was simply transferred from Papa's hands to yours. You arranged everything according to your own taste, and so I got the same tastes as you—or else I pretended to. I am really not quite sure which—I think sometimes the one and sometimes the other. When I look back on it it seems to me as if I have been living here like a poor woman—just from hand to mouth. I have existed merely to perform tricks for you,

Torvald. But you would have it so. You and Papa have committed a great sin against me. It is your fault that I have made nothing of my life.

HELMER: How unreasonable and how ungrateful you are, Nora! Have you not been happy here?

NORA: No, I have never been happy. I thought I was, but it has never really been so.

HELMER: Not—not happy!

NORA: No, only merry. And you have always been so kind to me. But our home has been nothing but a playroom. I have been your doll wife, just as at home I was Papa's doll child; and here the children have been my dolls. I thought it great fun when you played with me, just as they thought it great fun when I played with them. That is what our marriage has been, Torvald.

HELMER: There is some truth in what you say—exaggerated and strained as your view of it is. But for the future it shall be different. Playtime shall be over and lesson time shall begin.

NORA: Whose lessons? Mine or the children's?

HELMER: Both yours and the children's, my darling Nora.

NORA: Alas, Torvald, you are not the man to educate me into being a proper wife for you.

HELMER: And you can say that!

NORA: And I—how am I fitted to bring up the children?

HELMER: Nora!

NORA: Didn't you say so yourself a little while ago—that you dare not trust me to bring them up?

HELMER: In a moment of anger! Why do you pay any heed to that?

NORA: Indeed, you were perfectly right. I am not fit for the task. There is another task I must undertake first. I must try and educate myself—you are not the man to help me in that. I must do that for myself. And that is why I am going to leave you now.

HELMER (*springing up*): What do you say?

NORA: I must stand quite alone if I am to understand myself

and everything about me. It is for that reason that I cannot remain with you any longer.

HELMER: Nora, Nora!

NORA: I am going away from here now, at once. I am sure Christine will take me in for the night.

HELMER: You are out of your mind! I won't allow it! I forbid you!

NORA: It is no use forbidding me anything any longer. I will take with me what belongs to myself. I will take nothing from you, either now or later.

HELMER: What sort of madness is this?

NORA: Tomorrow I shall go home—I mean to my old home. It will be easiest for me to find something to do there.

HELMER: You blind, foolish woman!

NORA: I must try and get some sense, Torvald.

HELMER: To desert your home, your husband and your children! And you don't consider what people will say!

NORA: I cannot consider that at all. I only know that it is necessary for me.

HELMER: It's shocking. This is how you would neglect your most sacred duties.

NORA: What do you consider my most sacred duties?

HELMER: Do I need to tell you that? Are they not your duties to your husband and your children?

NORA: I have other duties just as sacred.

HELMER: That you have not. What duties could those be?

NORA: Duties to myself.

HELMER: Before all else you are a wife and a mother.

NORA: I don't believe that any longer. I believe that before all else I am a reasonable human being just as you are—or, at all events, that I must try and become one. I know quite well, Torvald, that most people would think you right and that views of that kind are to be found in books; but I can no longer content myself with what most people say or with what is found in books. I must think over things for myself and get to understand them.

HELMER: Can you understand your place in your own home?

Have you not a reliable guide in such matters as that?—
have you no religion?

NORA: I am afraid, Torvald, I do not exactly know what religion is.

HELMER: What are you saying?

NORA: I know nothing but what the clergyman said when I
went to be confirmed. He told us that religion was this and
that and the other. When I am away from all this and am
alone I will look into that matter too. I will see if what the
clergyman said is true, or at all events if it is true for me.

HELMER: This is unheard of in a girl of your age! But if religion
cannot lead you aright, let me try and awaken your
conscience. I suppose you have some moral sense? Or—
answer me—am I to think you have none?

NORA: I assure you, Torvald, that is not an easy question to
answer. I really don't know. The thing perplexes me altogether.
I only know that you and I look at it in quite a different
light. I am learning, too, that the law is quite
another thing from what I supposed; but I find it impossible
to convince myself that the law is right. According to it
a woman has no right to spare her old dying father or to
save her husband's life. I can't believe that.

HELMER: You talk like a child. You don't understand the conditions
of the world in which you live.

NORA: No, I don't. But now I am going to try. I am going to
see if I can make out who is right, the world or I.

HELMER: You are ill, Nora; you are delirious; I almost think
you are out of your mind.

NORA: I have never felt my mind so clear and certain as
tonight.

HELMER: And is it with a clear and certain mind that you forsake
your husband and your children?

NORA: Yes, it is.

HELMER: Then there is only one possible explanation.

NORA: What is that?

HELMER: You do not love me anymore.

NORA: No, that is just it.

HELMER: Nora!—and you can say that?

NORA: It gives me great pain, Torvald, for you have always been so kind to me, but I cannot help it. I do not love you anymore.

HELMER (*regaining his composure*): Is that a clear and certain conviction too?

NORA: Yes, absolutely clear and certain. That is the reason why I will not stay here any longer.

HELMER: And can you tell me what I have done to forfeit your love?

NORA: Yes, indeed I can. It was tonight, when the wonderful thing did not happen; then I saw you were not the man I had thought you.

HELMER: Explain yourself better—I don't understand you.

NORA: I have waited so patiently for eight years; for, goodness knows, I knew very well that wonderful things don't happen every day. Then this horrible misfortune came upon me, and then I felt quite certain that the wonderful thing was going to happen at last. When Krogstad's letter was lying out there never for a moment did I imagine that you would consent to accept this man's conditions. I was so absolutely certain that you would say to him: Publish the thing to the whole world. And when that was done—

HELMER: Yes, what then—when I had exposed my wife to shame and disgrace?

NORA: When that was done I was so absolutely certain you would come forward and take everything upon yourself and say: I am the guilty one.

HELMER: Nora!

NORA: You mean that I would never have accepted such a sacrifice on your part? No, of course not. But what would my assurances have been worth against yours? That was the wonderful thing which I hoped for and feared, and it was to prevent that that I wanted to kill myself.

HELMER: I would gladly work night and day for you, Nora— bear sorrow and want for your sake. But no man would sacrifice his honor for the one he loves.

NORA: It is a thing hundreds of thousands of women have done.

HELMER: Oh, you think and talk like a heedless child.

NORA: Maybe. But you neither think nor talk like the man I could bind myself to. As soon as your fear was over—and it was not fear for what threatened me but for what might happen to you—when the whole thing was past, as far as you were concerned it was exactly as if nothing at all had happened. Exactly as before, I was your little skylark, your doll, which you would in the future treat with doubly gentle care because it was so brittle and fragile. (*Getting up.*) Torvald—it was then it dawned upon me that for eight years I had been living here with a strange man and had borne him three children. Oh, I can't bear to think of it! I could tear myself into little bits!

HELMER (*sadly*): I see, I see. An abyss has opened between us—there is no denying it. But, Nora, would it not be possible to fill it up?

NORA: As I am now, I am no wife for you.

HELMER: I have it in me to become a different man.

NORA: Perhaps—if your doll is taken away from you.

HELMER: But to part—to part from you! No, no, Nora; I can't understand that idea.

NORA (*going out to the right*): That makes it all the more certain that it must be done. (*She comes back with her cloak and hat and a small bag which she puts on a chair by the table.*)

HELMER: Nora. Nora, not now! Wait till tomorrow.

NORA (*putting on her cloak*): I cannot spend the night in a strange man's room.

HELMER: But can't we live here like brother and sister?

NORA (*putting on her hat*): You know very well that would not last long. (*Puts the shawl round her.*) Good-bye, Torvald. I won't see the little ones. I know they are in better hands than mine. As I am now, I can be of no use to them.

HELMER: But someday, Nora—someday?

NORA: How can I tell? I have no idea what is going to become of me.

HELMER: But you are my wife, whatever becomes of you.

NORA: Listen, Torvald. I have heard that when a wife deserts her husband's house, as I am doing now, he is legally freed from all obligations toward her. In any case I set you free from all your obligations. You are not to feel yourself bound in the slightest way, any more than I shall. There must be perfect freedom on both sides. See, here is your ring back. Give me mine.

HELMER: That too?

NORA: That too.

HELMER: Here it is.

NORA: That's right. Now it is all over. I have put the keys here. The maids know all about everything in the house—better than I do. Tomorrow, after I have left her, Christine will come here and pack up my own things that I brought with me from home. I will have them sent after me.

HELMER: All over! All over! Nora, shall you never think of me again?

NORA: I know I shall often think of you and the children and this house.

HELMER: May I write to you, Nora?

NORA: No—never. You must not do that.

HELMER: But at least let me send you—

NORA: Nothing—nothing.

HELMER: Let me help you if you are in want.

NORA: No. I can receive nothing from a stranger.

HELMER: Nora—can I never be anything more than a stranger to you?

NORA (taking her bag): Ah, Torvald, the most wonderful thing of all would have to happen.

HELMER: Tell me what that would be!

NORA: Both you and I would have to be so changed that— Oh, Torvald, I don't believe any longer in wonderful things happening.

HELMER: But I will believe in it. Tell me. So changed that—

NORA: That our life together would be a real wedlock. Good-bye. (*She goes out through the hall.*)

HELMER (*sinks down on a chair at the door and buries his face in his hands*): Nora! Nora! (*Looks round and rises.*) Empty! She is gone. (*A hope flashes across his mind.*) The most wonderful thing of all—?

The sound of a door shutting is heard from below.

THE WILD DUCK

CHARACTERS

WERLE, a merchant, manufacturer, etc.

GREGERS WERLE, his son

OLD EKDAL

HIALMAR EKDAL, his son, a photographer

GINA EKDAL, Hialmar's wife

HEDVIG, their daughter, a girl of fourteen

MRS. SÖRBY, Werle's housekeeper

RELLING, a doctor

MOLVIK, student of theology

GRÅBERG, Werle's bookkeeper

PETTERSEN, Werle's servant

JENSEN, a hired waiter

A FLABBY GENTLEMAN

A THIN-HAIRED GENTLEMAN

A SHORTSIGHTED GENTLEMAN

SIX OTHER GENTLEMEN, guests at Werle's dinner party

SEVERAL HIRED WAITERS

The first act passes in WERLE's house, the remaining acts at
HIALMAR EKDAL's.

Pronunciation of Names: GREGERS WERLE = Grayghers
Verlë; HIALMAR EKDAL = Yalmar Aykdal; GINA =
Cheena; GRÅBERG = Groberg; JENSEN = Yensen.

ACT ONE

At WERLE's *house. A richly and comfortably furnished study;
bookcases and upholstered furniture; a writing table, with
papers and documents, in the center of the room; lighted
lamps with green shades, giving a subdued light. At the
back, open folding doors with curtains drawn back. Within
is seen a large and handsome room, brilliantly lighted with
lamps and branching candlesticks. In front, on the right
(in the study), a small baize door leads into* WERLE's *office. On the left, in front, a fireplace with a glowing coal
fire, and farther back a double door leading into the dining room.*

WERLE's *servant,* PETTERSEN, *in livery, and* JENSEN, *the
hired waiter, in black, are putting the study in order. In
the large room, two or three other hired waiters are moving about, arranging things and lighting more candles.
From the dining room, the hum of conversation and
laughter of many voices are heard; a glass is tapped with a
knife; silence follows, and a toast is proposed; shouts of
"Bravo!" and then again a buzz of conversation.*

PETTERSEN (*lights a lamp on the chimney place and places a shade over it*): Hark to them, Jensen! now the old man's on his legs holding a long palaver about Mrs. Sörby.

JENSEN (*pushing forward an armchair*): Is it true, what folks say, that they're—very good friends, eh?

PETTERSEN: Lord knows.

JENSEN: I've heard tell as he's been a lively customer in his day.[1]

PETTERSEN: Maybe.

JENSEN: And he's giving this spread in honor of his son, they say.

PETTERSEN: Yes. His son came home yesterday.

JENSEN: This is the first time I ever heard as Mr. Werle had a son.

PETTERSEN: Oh, yes, he has a son, right enough. But he's a fixture, as you might say, up at the Höidal works.[2] He's never once come to town all the years I've been in service here.

A WAITER (*in the doorway of the other room*): Pettersen, here's an old fellow wanting—

PETTERSEN (*mutters*): The devil—who's this now?

OLD EKDAL *appears from the right, in the inner room. He is dressed in a threadbare overcoat with a high collar; he wears woolen mittens and carries in his hand a stick and a fur cap. Under his arm, a brown paper parcel. Dirty red-brown wig and small gray mustache.*

PETTERSEN (*goes toward him*): Good Lord—what do you want here?

EKDAL (*in the doorway*): Must get into the office, Pettersen.

PETTERSEN: The office was closed an hour ago, and—

EKDAL: So they told me at the front door. But Gråberg's in there still. Let me slip in this way, Pettersen; there's a good fellow. (*Points toward the baize door.*) It's not the first time I've come this way.

PETTERSEN: Well, you may pass. (*Opens the door.*) But mind you go out again the proper way, for we've got company.

EKDAL: I know, I know—hm! Thanks, Pettersen, good old friend! Thanks! (*Mutters softly.*) Ass!

He goes into the office; PETTERSEN *shuts the door after him.*

JENSEN: Is he one of the office people?

PETTERSEN: No he's only an outside hand that does odd jobs of copying. But he's been a tip-topper in his day, has old Ekdal.

JENSEN: You can see he's been through a lot.

PETTERSEN: Yes; he was an army officer, you know.

JENSEN: You don't say so?

PETTERSEN: No mistake about it. But then he went into the timber trade or something of the sort. They say he once played Mr. Werle a very nasty trick. They were partners in the Höidal works at the time. Oh, I know old Ekdal well, I do. Many a nip of bitters and bottle of ale we two have drunk at Madam Eriksen's.

JENSEN: He don't look as if he'd much to stand treat with.

PETTERSEN: Why, bless you, Jensen, it's me that stands treat. I always think there's no harm in being a bit civil to folks that have seen better days.

JENSEN: Did he go bankrupt, then?

PETTERSEN: Worse than that. He went to prison.

JENSEN: To prison!

PETTERSEN: Or perhaps it was the penitentiary. (*Listens.*) Sh! They're leaving the table.

The dining room door is thrown open from within by a couple of waiters. MRS. SÖRBY *comes out conversing with two gentlemen. Gradually the whole company follows, among them* WERLE. *Last come* HIALMAR EKDAL *and* GREGERS WERLE.

MRS. SÖRBY (*in passing, to the servant*): Tell them to serve the coffee in the music room, Pettersen.

PETTERSEN: Very well, Madam.

*She goes with the two gentlemen into the inner room and
thence out to the right.* PETTERSEN *and* JENSEN *go out the
same way.*

A FLABBY GENTLEMAN (*to a* THIN-HAIRED GENTLEMAN):
Whew! What a dinner!—It was no joke to do it justice!

THE THIN-HAIRED GENTLEMAN: Oh, with a little goodwill
one can get through a lot in three hours.

THE FLABBY GENTLEMAN: Yes, but afterward, afterward, my
dear Chamberlain!

A THIRD GENTLEMAN: I hear the coffee and maraschino[3] are
to be served in the music room.

THE FLABBY GENTLEMAN: Bravo! Then perhaps Mrs. Sörby
will play us something.

THE THIN-HAIRED GENTLEMAN (*in a low voice*): I hope Mrs.
Sörby mayn't play us a tune we don't like, one of these
days!

THE FLABBY GENTLEMAN: Oh, no, not she! Bertha will
never turn against her old friends.

They laugh and pass into the inner room.

WERLE (*in a low voice, dejectedly*): I don't think anybody noticed it, Gregers.

GREGERS (*looks at him*): Noticed what?

WERLE: Did you not notice it either?

GREGERS: What do you mean?

WERLE: We were thirteen at table.

GREGERS: Indeed? Were there thirteen of us?

WERLE (*glances toward* HIALMAR EKDAL): Our usual party
is twelve. (*To the others.*) This way, gentlemen!

WERLE *and the others, all except* HIALMAR *and* GREGERS,
go out by the back, to the right.

HIALMAR (*who has overheard the conversation*): You ought
not to have invited me, Gregers.

GREGERS: What! Not ask my best and only friend to a party
supposed to be in my honor—?

HIALMAR: But I don't think your father likes it. You see I am quite outside his circle.

GREGERS: So I hear. But I wanted to see you and have a talk with you, and I certainly shan't be staying long.—Ah, we two old schoolfellows have drifted far apart from each other. It must be sixteen or seventeen years since we met.

HIALMAR: Is it so long?

GREGERS: It is indeed. Well, how goes it with you? You look well. You have put on flesh and grown almost stout.

HIALMAR: Well, "stout" is scarcely the word; but I daresay I look a little more of a man than I used to.

GREGERS: Yes, you do; your outer man is in first-rate condition.

HIALMAR (in a tone of gloom): Ah, but the inner man! That is a very different matter, I can tell you! Of course you know of the terrible catastrophe that has befallen me and mine since last we met.

GREGERS (more softly): How are things going with your father now?

HIALMAR: Don't let us talk of it, old fellow. Of course my poor unhappy father lives with me. He hasn't another soul in the world to care for him. But you can understand that this is a miserable subject for me.—Tell me, rather, how you have been getting on up at the works.

GREGERS: I have had a delightfully lonely time of it—plenty of leisure to think and think about things. Come over here; we may as well make ourselves comfortable.

He seats himself in an armchair by the fire and draws HIALMAR *down into another alongside of it.*

HIALMAR (sentimentally): After all, Gregers, I thank you for inviting me to your father's table; for I take it as a sign that you have got over your feeling against me.

GREGERS (surprised): How could you imagine I had any feeling against you?

HIALMAR: You had at first, you know.

GREGERS: How at first?

HIALMAR: After the great misfortune. It was natural enough
that you should. Your father was within an ace of being
drawn into that—well, that terrible business.

GREGERS: Why should that give me any feeling against you?
Who can have put that into your head?

HIALMAR: I know it did, Gregers; your father told me so himself.

GREGERS (starts): My father! Oh, indeed. Hm.—Was that
why you never let me hear from you?—not a single word.

HIALMAR: Yes.

GREGERS: Not even when you made up your mind to become
a photographer?

HIALMAR: Your father said I had better not write to you at all,
about anything.

GREGERS (looking straight before him): Well, well, perhaps
he was right.—But tell me now, Hialmar: are you pretty
well satisfied with your present position?

HIALMAR (with a little sigh): Oh, yes, I am; I have really no
cause to complain. At first, as you may guess, I felt it a little strange. It was such a totally new state of things for me.
But of course my whole circumstances were totally
changed. Father's utter, irretrievable ruin,—the shame
and disgrace of it, Gregers—

GREGERS (affected): Yes, yes; I understand.

HIALMAR: I couldn't think of remaining at college; there
wasn't a shilling to spare; on the contrary, there were
debts—mainly to your father, I believe—

GREGERS: Hm—

HIALMAR: In short, I thought it best to break, once for all,
with my old surroundings and associations. It was your father that specially urged me to it; and since he interested
himself so much in me—

GREGERS: My father did?

HIALMAR: Yes, you surely knew that, didn't you? Where do
you suppose I found the money to learn photography, and
to furnish a studio and make a start? All that cost a pretty
penny, I can tell you.

GREGERS: And my father provided the money?

HIALMAR: Yes, my dear fellow, didn't you know? I understood him to say he had written to you about it.

GREGERS: Not a word about his part in the business. He must have forgotten it. Our correspondence has always been purely a business one. So it was my father that—!

HIALMAR: Yes, certainly. He didn't wish it to be generally known; but he it was. And of course it was he, too, that put me in a position to marry. Don't you—don't you know about that either?

GREGERS: No, I haven't heard a word of it. (*Shakes him by the arm.*) But, my dear Hialmar, I can't tell you what pleasure all this gives me—pleasure, and self-reproach. I have perhaps done my father injustice after all—in some things. This proves that he has a heart. It shows a sort of compunction—

HIALMAR: Compunction—?

GREGERS: Yes, yes—whatever you like to call it. Oh, I can't tell you how glad I am to hear this of Father.—So you are a married man, Hialmar! That is further than I shall ever get. Well, I hope you are happy in your married life?

HIALMAR: Yes, thoroughly happy. She is as good and capable a wife as any man could wish for. And she is by no means without culture.

GREGERS (*rather surprised*): No, of course not.

HIALMAR: You see, life is itself an education. Her daily intercourse with me— And then we know one or two rather remarkable men, who come a good deal about us. I assure you, you would hardly know Gina again.

GREGERS: Gina?

HIALMAR: Yes; had you forgotten that her name was Gina?

GREGERS: Whose name? I haven't the slightest idea—

HIALMAR: Don't you remember that she used to be in service here?

GREGERS (*looks at him*): Is it Gina Hansen—?

HIALMAR: Yes, of course it is Gina Hansen.

GREGERS: —who kept house for us during the last year of my mother's illness?

HIALMAR: Yes, exactly. But, my dear friend, I'm quite sure your father told you that I was married.

GREGERS *(who has risen)*: Oh, yes, he mentioned it; but not that— *(Walking about the room.)* Stay—perhaps he did—now that I think of it. My father always writes such short letters. *(Half seats himself on the arm of the chair.)* Now tell me, Hialmar—this is interesting—how did you come to know Gina—your wife?

HIALMAR: The simplest thing in the world. You know Gina did not stay here long, everything was so much upset at that time, owing to your mother's illness and so forth, that Gina was not equal to it all; so she gave notice and left. That was the year before your mother died—or it may have been the same year.

GREGERS: It was the same year. I was up at the works then. But afterward—?

HIALMAR: Well, Gina lived at home with her mother, Madam Hansen, an excellent hardworking woman, who kept a little eating house. She had a room to let, too; a very nice comfortable room.

GREGERS: And I suppose you were lucky enough to secure it?

HIALMAR: Yes; in fact, it was your father that recommended it to me. So it was there, you see, that I really came to know Gina.

GREGERS: And then you got engaged?

HIALMAR: Yes. It doesn't take young people long to fall in love—; hm—

GREGERS *(rises and moves about a little)*: Tell me: was it after your engagement—was it then that my father—I mean was it then that you began to take up photography?

HIALMAR: Yes, precisely. I wanted to make a start and to set up house as soon as possible; and your father and I agreed that this photography business was the readiest way. Gina thought so, too. Oh, and there was another thing in its favor, by-the-bye: it happened, luckily, that Gina had learned to retouch.[4]

GREGERS: That chimed in marvelously.

HIALMAR *(pleased, rises)*: Yes, didn't it? Don't you think it was a marvelous piece of luck?

GREGERS: Oh, unquestionably. My father seems to have been almost a kind of providence for you.

HIALMAR *(with emotion)*: He did not forsake his old friend's son in the hour of his need. For he has a heart, you see.

MRS. SÖRBY *(enters, arm in arm with* WERLE): Nonsense, my dear Mr. Werle; you mustn't stop there any longer staring at all the lights. It's very bad for you.

WERLE *(lets go her arm and passes his hand over his eyes)*: I daresay you are right.

PETTERSEN *and* JENSEN *carry round refreshment trays.*

MRS. SÖRBY *(to the guests in the other room)*: This way, if you please, gentlemen. Whoever wants a glass of punch must be so good as to come in here.

THE FLABBY GENTLEMAN *(comes up to* MRS. SÖRBY): Surely, it isn't possible that you have suspended our cherished right to smoke?

MRS. SÖRBY: Yes. No smoking here, in Mr. Werle's sanctum, Chamberlain.

THE THIN-HAIRED GENTLEMAN: When did you enact these stringent amendments on the cigar law, Mrs. Sörby?

MRS. SÖRBY: After the last dinner, Chamberlain, when certain persons permitted themselves to overstep the mark.

THE THIN-HAIRED GENTLEMAN: And may one never overstep the mark a little bit, Madame Bertha? Not the least little bit?

MRS. SÖRBY: Not in any respect whatsoever, Mr. Balle.

Most of the guests have assembled in the study; servants hand round glasses of punch.

WERLE *(to* HIALMAR, *who is standing beside a table)*: What are you studying so intently, Ekdal?

HIALMAR: Only an album, Mr. Werle.

THE THIN-HAIRED GENTLEMAN (*who is wandering about*): Ah, photographs! They are quite in your line, of course.

THE FLABBY GENTLEMAN (*in an armchair*): Haven't you brought any of your own with you?

HIALMAR: No, I haven't.

THE FLABBY GENTLEMAN: You ought to have; it's very good for the digestion to sit and look at pictures.

THE THIN-HAIRED GENTLEMAN: And it contributes to the entertainment, you know.

THE SHORTSIGHTED GENTLEMAN: And all contributions are thankfully received.

MRS. SÖRBY: The Chamberlains think that when one is invited out to dinner, one ought to exert oneself a little in return, Mr. Ekdal.

THE FLABBY GENTLEMAN: Where one dines so well, that duty becomes a pleasure.

THE THIN-HAIRED GENTLEMAN: And when it's a case of the struggle for existence, you know—

MRS. SÖRBY: I quite agree with you!

They continue the conversation, with laughter and joking.

GREGERS (*softly*): You must join in, Hialmar.

HIALMAR (*writhing*): What am I to talk about?

THE FLABBY GENTLEMAN: Don't you think, Mr. Werle, that Tokay may be considered one of the more wholesome sorts of wine?

WERLE (*by the fire*): I can answer for the Tokay you had today, at any rate; it's one of the very finest seasons. Of course you would notice that.

THE FLABBY GENTLEMAN: Yes, it had a remarkably delicate flavor.

HIALMAR (*shyly*): Is there any difference between the seasons?

THE FLABBY GENTLEMAN (*laughs*): Come! That's good!

WERLE (*smiles*): It really doesn't pay to set fine wine before you.

THE THIN-HAIRED GENTLEMAN: Tokay is like photographs, Mr. Ekdal: they both need sunshine.[5] Am I not right?

HIALMAR: Yes, light is important no doubt.

MRS. SÖRBY: And it's exactly the same with Chamberlains—they, too, depend very much on sunshine, as the saying is.

THE THIN-HAIRED GENTLEMAN: Oh, fie! That's a very threadbare sarcasm!

THE SHORTSIGHTED GENTLEMAN: Mrs. Sörby is coming out—

THE FLABBY GENTLEMAN: —and at our expense, too. (*Holds up his finger reprovingly.*) Oh, Madame Bertha, Madame Bertha!

MRS. SÖRBY: Yes, and there's not the least doubt that the seasons differ greatly. The old vintages are the finest.

THE SHORTSIGHTED GENTLEMAN: Do you reckon me among the old vintages?

MRS. SÖRBY: Oh, far from it.

THE THIN-HAIRED GENTLEMAN: There now! But me, dear Mrs. Sörby—?

THE FLABBY GENTLEMAN: Yes, and me? What vintage should you say that we belong to?

MRS. SÖRBY: Why, to the sweet vintages, gentlemen.

She sips a glass of punch. The gentlemen laugh and flirt with her.

WERLE: Mrs. Sörby can always find a loophole—when she wants to. Fill your glasses, gentlemen! Pettersen, will you see to it—! Gregers, suppose we have a glass together. (GREGERS *does not move.*) Won't you join us, Ekdal? I found no opportunity of drinking with you at table.

GRÅBERG, *the bookkeeper, looks in at the baize door.*

GRÅBERG: Excuse me, sir, but I can't get out.

WERLE: Have you been locked in again?

GRÅBERG: Yes, and Flakstad has carried off the keys.

WERLE: Well, you can pass out this way.

GRÅBERG: But there's someone else—

WERLE: All right; come through, both of you. Don't be afraid.

GRÅBERG and OLD EKDAL come out of the office.

WERLE (*involuntarily*): Ugh!

The laughter and talk among the guests cease. HIALMAR *starts at the sight of his father, puts down his glass and turns toward the fireplace.*

EKDAL (*does not look up, but makes little bows to both sides as he passes, murmuring*): Beg pardon, come the wrong way. Door locked—door locked. Beg pardon.

He and GRÅBERG go out by the back, to the right.

WERLE (*between his teeth*): That idiot Gråberg.

GREGERS (*openmouthed and staring, to* HIALMAR): Why surely that wasn't—!

THE FLABBY GENTLEMAN: What's the matter? Who was it?

GREGERS: Oh, nobody, only the bookkeeper and someone with him.

THE SHORTSIGHTED GENTLEMAN (*to* HIALMAR): Did you know that man?

HIALMAR: I don't know—I didn't notice—

THE FLABBY GENTLEMAN: What the deuce has come over everyone?

He joins another group who are talking softly.

MRS. SÖRBY (*whispers to the servant*): Give him something to take with him;—something good, mind.

PETTERSEN (*nods*): I'll see to it. (*Goes out.*)

GREGERS (*softly and with emotion, to* HIALMAR): So that was really he!

HIALMAR: Yes.

GREGERS: And you could stand there and deny that you knew him!

HIALMAR (*whispers vehemently*): But how could I—!

GREGERS: —acknowledge your own father?

HIALMAR *(with pain)*: Oh, if you were in my place—

The conversation among the guests, which has been carried on in a low tone, now swells into constrained joviality.

THE THIN-HAIRED GENTLEMAN *(approaching HIALMAR and GREGERS in a friendly manner)*: Aha! Reviving old college memories, eh? Don't you smoke, Mr. Ekdal? May I give you a light? Oh, by-the-bye, we mustn't—

HIALMAR: No, thank you, I won't—

THE FLABBY GENTLEMAN: Haven't you a nice little poem you could recite to us, Mr. Ekdal? You used to recite so charmingly.

HIALMAR: I am sorry I can't remember anything.

THE FLABBY GENTLEMAN: Oh, that's a pity. Well, what shall we do, Balle?

Both gentlemen move away and pass into the other room.

HIALMAR *(gloomily)*: Gregers—I am going! When a man has felt the crushing hand of Fate, you see— Say good-bye to your father for me.

GREGERS: Yes, yes. Are you going straight home?

HIALMAR: Yes. Why?

GREGERS: Oh, because I may perhaps look in on you later.

HIALMAR: No, you mustn't do that. You must not come to my home. Mine is a melancholy abode, Gregers; especially after a splendid banquet like this. We can always arrange to meet somewhere in the town.

MRS. SÖRBY *(who has quietly approached)*: Are you going, Ekdal?

HIALMAR: Yes.

MRS. SÖRBY: Remember me to Gina.

HIALMAR: Thanks.

MRS. SÖRBY: And say I am coming up to see her one of these days.

HIALMAR: Yes, thank you. *(To GREGERS.)* Stay here; I will slip out unobserved.

*He saunters away, then into the other room, and so out to
the right.*

MRS. SÖRBY *(softly to the servant, who has come back)*: Well,
did you give the old man something?

PETTERSEN: Yes; I sent him off with a bottle of cognac.

MRS. SÖRBY: Oh, you might have thought of something better than that.

PETTERSEN: Oh, no, Mrs. Sörby; cognac is what he likes best
in the world.

THE FLABBY GENTLEMAN *(in the doorway with a sheet of
music in his hand)*: Shall we play a duet, Mrs. Sörby?

MRS. SÖRBY: Yes, suppose we do.

THE GUESTS: Bravo, bravo!

*She goes with all the guests through the back room, out to
the right.* GREGERS *remains standing by the fire.* WERLE *is
looking for something on the writing table and appears to
wish that* GREGERS *would go; as* GREGERS *does not move,*
WERLE *goes toward the door.*

GREGERS: Father, won't you stay a moment?

WERLE *(stops)*: What is it?

GREGERS: I must have a word with you.

WERLE: Can it not wait till we are alone?

GREGERS: No, it cannot; for perhaps we shall never be alone
together.

WERLE *(drawing nearer)*: What do you mean by that?

*During what follows, the pianoforte is faintly heard from
the distant music room.*

GREGERS: How has that family been allowed to go so miser-
ably to the wall?

WERLE: You mean the Ekdals, I suppose.

GREGERS: Yes, I mean the Ekdals. Lieutenant Ekdal was
once so closely associated with you.

WERLE: Much too closely; I have felt that to my cost for many a year. It is thanks to him that I—yes *I*—have had a kind of slur cast upon my reputation.

GREGERS (*softly*): Are you sure that he alone was to blame?

WERLE: Who else do you suppose—?

GREGERS: You and he acted together in that affair of the forests—

WERLE: But was it not Ekdal that drew the map of the tracts we had bought—that fraudulent map! It was he who felled all that timber illegally on Government ground. In fact, the whole management was in his hands. I was quite in the dark as to what Lieutenant Ekdal was doing.

GREGERS: Lieutenant Ekdal himself seems to have been very much in the dark as to what he was doing.

WERLE: That may be. But the fact remains that he was found guilty and I acquitted.

GREGERS: Yes, I know that nothing was proved against you.

WERLE: Acquittal is acquittal. Why do you rake up these old miseries that turned my hair gray before its time? Is that the sort of thing you have been brooding over up there, all these years? I can assure you, Gregers, here in the town the whole story has been forgotten long ago—so far as *I* am concerned.

GREGERS: But that unhappy Ekdal family—

WERLE: What would you have had me do for the people? When Ekdal came out of prison he was a broken-down being, past all help. There are people in the world who dive to the bottom the moment they get a couple of slugs in their body and never come to the surface again. You may take my word for it, Gregers, I have done all I could without positively laying myself open to all sorts of suspicion and gossip—

GREGERS: Suspicion—? Oh, I see.

WERLE: I have given Ekdal copying to do for the office, and I pay him far, far more for it than his work is worth—

GREGERS (*without looking at him*): Hm; that I don't doubt.

WERLE: You laugh? Do you think I am not telling you the

truth? Well, I certainly can't refer you to my books, for I never enter payments of that sort.

GREGERS (*smiles coldly*): No, there are certain payments it is best to keep no account of.

WERLE (*taken aback*): What do you mean by that?

GREGERS (*mustering up courage*): Have you entered what it cost you to have Hialmar Ekdal taught photography?

WERLE: I? How "entered" it?

GREGERS: I have learned that it was you who paid for his training. And I have learned, too, that it was you who enabled him to set up house so comfortably.

WERLE: Well, and yet you talk as though I had done nothing for the Ekdals! I can assure you these people have cost me enough in all conscience.

GREGERS: Have you entered any of these expenses in your books?

WERLE: Why do you ask?

GREGERS: Oh, I have my reasons. Now tell me: when you interested yourself so warmly in your old friend's son—it was just before his marriage, was it not?

WERLE: Why, deuce take it—after all these years, how can I—?

GREGERS: You wrote me a letter about that time—a business letter, of course; and in a postscript you mentioned—quite briefly—that Hialmar Ekdal had married a Miss Hansen.

WERLE: Yes, that was quite right. That was her name.

GREGERS: But you did not mention that this Miss Hansen was Gina Hansen—our former housekeeper.

WERLE (*with a forced laugh of derision*): No; to tell the truth, it didn't occur to me that you were so particularly interested in our former housekeeper.

GREGERS: No more I was. But (*lowers his voice*) there were others in this house who were particularly interested in her.

WERLE: What do you mean by that? (*Flaring up.*) You are not alluding to me, I hope?

GREGERS (*softly but firmly*): Yes, I am alluding to you.

WERLE: And you dare—! You presume to—! How can that

ungrateful hound—that photographer fellow—how dare he go making such insinuations!

GREGERS: Hialmar has never breathed a word about this. I don't believe he has the faintest suspicion of such a thing.

WERLE: Then where have you got it from? Who can have put such notions in your head?

GREGERS: My poor unhappy mother told me; and that the very last time I saw her.

WERLE: Your mother! I might have known as much! You and she—you always held together. It was she who turned you against me, from the first.

GREGERS: No, it was all that she had to suffer and submit to, until she broke down and came to such a pitiful end.

WERLE: Oh, she had nothing to suffer or submit to; not more than most people, at all events. But there's no getting on with morbid, overstrained creatures—that I have learned to my cost.—And you could go on nursing such a suspicion—burrowing into all sorts of old rumors and slanders against your own father! I must say, Gregers, I really think that at your age you might find something more useful to do.

GREGERS: Yes, it is high time.

WERLE: Then perhaps your mind would be easier than it seems to be now. What can be your object in remaining up at the works, year out and year in, drudging away like a common clerk, and not drawing a farthing more than the ordinary monthly wage? It is downright folly.

GREGERS: Ah, if I were only sure of that.

WERLE: I understand you well enough. You want to be independent; you won't be beholden to me for anything. Well, now there happens to be an opportunity for you to become independent, your own master in everything.

GREGERS: Indeed? In what way—?

WERLE: When I wrote you insisting on your coming to town at once—hm—

GREGERS: Yes, what is it you really want of me? I have been waiting all day to know.

WERLE: I want to propose that you should enter the firm, as partner.

GREGERS: I! Join your firm? As partner?

WERLE: Yes. It would not involve our being constantly together. You could take over the business here in town, and I should move up to the works.

GREGERS: You would?

WERLE: The fact is, I am not so fit for work as I once was. I am obliged to spare my eyes, Gregers; they have begun to trouble me.

GREGERS: They have always been weak.

WERLE: Not as they are now. And, besides, circumstances might possibly make it desirable for me to live up there—for a time, at any rate.

GREGERS: That is certainly quite a new idea to me.

WERLE: Listen, Gregers: there are many things that stand between us; but we are father and son after all. We ought surely to be able to come to some sort of understanding with each other.

GREGERS: Outwardly, you mean, of course?

WERLE: Well, even that would be something. Think it over, Gregers. Don't you think it ought to be possible? Eh?

GREGERS (looking at him coldly): There is something behind all this.

WERLE: How so?

GREGERS: You want to make use of me in some way.

WERLE: In such a close relationship as ours, the one can always be useful to the other.

GREGERS: Yes, so people say.

WERLE: I want very much to have you at home with me for a time. I am a lonely man, Gregers; I have always felt lonely, all my life through; but most of all now that I am getting up in years. I feel the need of someone about me—

GREGERS: You have Mrs. Sörby.

WERLE: Yes, I have her; and she has become, I may say, almost indispensable to me. She is lively and even-tempered; she brightens up the house; and that is a very great thing for me.

GREGERS: Well, then, you have everything just as you wish it.

WERLE: Yes, but I am afraid it can't last. A woman so situated may easily find herself in a false position, in the eyes of the world. For that matter it does a man no good, either.

GREGERS: Oh, when a man gives such dinners as you give, he can risk a great deal.

WERLE: Yes, but how about the woman, Gregers? I fear she won't accept the situation much longer; and even if she did—even if, out of attachment to me, she were to take her chance of gossip and scandal and all that—? Do you think, Gregers—you with your strong sense of justice—

GREGERS (interrupts him): Tell me in one word: are you thinking of marrying her?

WERLE: Suppose I were thinking of it? What then?

GREGERS: That's what I say: what then?

WERLE: Should you be inflexibly opposed to it!

GREGERS: —Not at all. Not by any means.

WERLE: I was not sure whether your devotion to your mother's memory—

GREGERS: I am not overstrained.

WERLE: Well, whatever you may or may not be, at all events you have lifted a great weight from my mind. I am extremely pleased that I can reckon on your concurrence in this matter.

GREGERS (looking intently at him): Now I see the use you want to put me to.

WERLE: Use to put you to? What an expression!

GREGERS: Oh, don't let us be nice in our choice of words—not when we are alone together, at any rate. (With a short laugh.) Well, well. So this is what made it absolutely essential that I should come to town in person. For the sake of Mrs. Sörby, we are to get up a pretense at family life in the house—a tableau of filial affection! That will be something new indeed.

WERLE: How dare you speak in that tone!

GREGERS: Was there ever any family life here? Never since I can remember. But now, forsooth, your plans demand something of the sort. No doubt it will have an excellent effect when it is reported that the son has hastened home, on the wings of filial piety, to the gray-haired father's wedding feast. What will then remain of all the rumors as to the wrongs the poor dead mother had to submit to? Not a vestige. Her son annihilates them at one stroke.

WERLE: Gregers—I believe there is no one in the world you detest as you do me.

GREGERS (*softly*): I have seen you at too close quarters.

WERLE: You have seen me with your mother's eyes. (*Lowers his voice a little.*) But you should remember that her eyes were—clouded now and then.

GREGERS (*quivering*): I see what you are hinting at. But who was to blame for Mother's unfortunate weakness? Why you, and all those—! The last of them was this woman that you palmed off upon Hialmar Ekdal, when you were— Ugh!

WERLE (*shrugs his shoulders*): Word for word as if it were your mother speaking!

GREGERS (*without heeding*): And there he is now, with his great, confiding, childlike mind, compassed about with all this treachery—living under the same roof with such a creature and never dreaming that what he calls his home is built upon a lie! (*Comes a step nearer.*) When I look back upon your past, I seem to see a battlefield with shattered lives on every hand.

WERLE: I begin to think the chasm that divides us is too wide.

GREGERS (*bowing, with self-command*): So I have observed; and therefore I take my hat and go.

WERLE: You are going! Out of the house?

GREGERS: Yes. For at last I see my mission in life.

WERLE: What mission?

GREGERS: You would only laugh if I told you.

WERLE: A lonely man doesn't laugh so easily, Gregers.

GREGERS *(pointing toward the background)*: Look, Father,— the Chamberlains are playing blindman's-buff[6] with Mrs. Sörby.—Good night and good-bye.

He goes out by the back to the right. Sounds of laughter and merriment from the company, who are now visible in the outer room.

WERLE (muttering contemptuously after GREGERS): Ha—! Poor wretch—and he says he is not overstrained!

Act Two

HIALMAR EKDAL's *studio, a good-sized room, evidently in the top story of the building. On the right, a sloping roof of large panes of glass, half-covered by a blue curtain. In the right-hand corner, at the back, the entrance door; farther forward, on the same side, a door leading to the sitting room. Two doors on the opposite side, and between them an iron stove. At the back, a wide double sliding door. The studio is plainly but comfortably fitted up and furnished. Between the doors on the right, standing out a little from the wall, a sofa with a table and some chairs; on the table a lighted lamp with a shade; beside the stove an old armchair. Photographic instruments and apparatus of different kinds lying about the room. Against the back wall, to the left of the double door, stands a bookcase containing a few books, boxes, and bottles of chemicals, instruments, tools, and other objects. Photographs and small articles, such as camel's-hair pencils, paper, and so forth, lie on the table.*

GINA EKDAL *sits on a chair by the table, sewing.* HEDVIG *is sitting on the sofa, with her hands shading her eyes and her thumbs in her ears, reading a book.*

GINA (*glances once or twice at* HEDVIG, *as if with secret anxiety; then says*): Hedvig!

HEDVIG *does not hear.*

GINA (*repeats more loudly*): Hedvig!

HEDVIG (*takes away her hands and looks up*): Yes, Mother?

GINA: Hedvig dear, you mustn't sit reading any longer now.

HEDVIG: Oh, Mother, mayn't I read a little more? Just a little bit?

GINA: No, no, you must put away your book now. Father doesn't like it; he never reads hisself in the evening.

HEDVIG (*shuts the book*): No, Father doesn't care much about reading.

GINA (*puts aside her sewing and takes up a lead pencil and a little account book from the table*): Can you remember how much we paid for the butter today?

HEDVIG: It was one crown sixty-five.

GINA: That's right. (*Puts it down.*) It's terrible what a lot of butter we get through in this house. Then there was the smoked sausage, and the cheese—let me see—(*Writes*)—and the ham—(*Adds up.*) Yes, that makes just—

HEDVIG: And then the beer.

GINA: Yes, to be sure. (*Writes.*) How it do mount up! But we can't manage with no less.

HEDVIG: And then you and I didn't need anything hot for dinner, as Father was out.

GINA: No; that was so much to the good. And then I took eight crowns fifty for the photographs.

HEDVIG: Really! So much as that?

GINA: Exactly eight crowns fifty.

Silence. GINA *takes up her sewing again,* HEDVIG *takes paper and pencil and begins to draw, shading her eyes with her left hand.*

HEDVIG: Isn't it jolly to think that Father is at Mr. Werle's big dinner party?

GINA: You know he's not really Mr. Werle's guest. It was the son invited him. *(After a pause.)* We have nothing to do with that Mr. Werle.

HEDVIG: I'm longing for Father to come home. He promised to ask Mrs. Sörby for something nice for me.

GINA: Yes, there's plenty of good things going in that house, I can tell you.

HEDVIG *(goes on drawing)*: And I believe I'm a little hungry, too.

OLD EKDAL, *with the paper parcel under his arm and another parcel in his coat pocket, comes in by the entrance door.*

GINA: How late you are today, Grandfather!

EKDAL: They had locked the office door. Had to wait in Gråberg's room. And then they let me through—hm.

HEDVIG: Did you get some more copying to do, Grandfather?

EKDAL: This whole packet. Just look.

GINA: That's capital.

HEDVIG: And you have another parcel in your pocket.

EKDAL: Eh? Oh, never mind, that's nothing. *(Puts his stick away in a corner.)* This work will keep me going a long time, Gina. *(Opens one of the sliding doors in the back wall a little.)* Hush! *(Peeps into the room for a moment, then pushes the door carefully to again.)* Hee-hee! They're fast asleep, all the lot of them. And she's gone into the basket herself. Hee-hee!

HEDVIG: Are you sure she isn't cold in that basket, Grandfather?

EKDAL: Not a bit of it! Cold? With all that straw? *(Goes toward the farther door on the left.)* There are matches in here, I suppose.

GINA: The matches is on the drawers.

EKDAL *goes into his room.*

HEDVIG: It's nice that Grandfather has got all that copying.

GINA: Yes, poor old Father; it means a bit of pocket money for him.

HEDVIG: And he won't be able to sit the whole forenoon down at that horrid Madam Eriksen's.

GINA: No more he won't.

Short silence.

HEDVIG: Do you suppose they are still at the dinner table?

GINA: Goodness knows; as like as not.

HEDVIG: Think of all the delicious things Father is having to eat! I'm certain he'll be in splendid spirits when he comes. Don't you think so, Mother?

GINA: Yes; and if only we could tell him that we'd got the room let—

HEDVIG: But we don't need that this evening.

GINA: Oh, we'd be none the worst of it, I can tell you. It's no use to us as it is.

HEDVIG: I mean we don't need it this evening, for Father will be in a good humor at any rate. It is best to keep the letting of the room for another time.

GINA *(looks across at her)*: You like having some good news to tell Father when he comes home in the evening?

HEDVIG: Yes; for then things are pleasanter somehow.

GINA *(thinking to herself)*: Yes, yes, there's something in that.

OLD EKDAL *comes in again and is going out by the foremost door to the left.*

GINA *(half turning in her chair)*: Do you want something out of the kitchen, Grandfather?

EKDAL: Yes, yes, I do. Don't you trouble. *(Goes out.)*

GINA: He's not poking away at the fire, is he? *(Waits a moment.)* Hedvig, go and see what he's about.

EKDAL *comes in again with a small jug of steaming hot water.*

HEDVIG: Have you been getting some hot water, Grandfather?

EKDAL: Yes, hot water. Want it for something. Want to write, and the ink has got as thick as porridge—hm.

GINA: But you'd best have your supper, first, Grandfather. It's laid in there.

EKDAL: Can't be bothered with supper, Gina. Very busy, I tell you. No one's to come to my room. No one—hm.

He goes into his room; GINA and HEDVIG look at each other.

GINA *(softly)*: Can you imagine where he's got money from?

HEDVIG: From Gråberg, perhaps.

GINA: Not a bit of it. Gråberg always sends the money to me.

HEDVIG: Then he must have got a bottle on credit somewhere.

GINA: Poor Grandfather, who'd give him credit?

HIALMAR EKDAL, in an overcoat and gray felt hat, comes in from the right.

GINA *(throws down her sewing and rises)*: Why, Ekdal, is that you already?

HEDVIG *(at the same time jumping up)*: Fancy your coming so soon, Father!

HIALMAR *(taking off his hat)*: Yes, most of the people were coming away.

HEDVIG: So early?

HIALMAR: Yes, it was a dinner party, you know. *(Taking off his overcoat.)*

GINA: Let me help you.

HEDVIG: Me, too.

They draw off his coat; GINA hangs it up on the back wall.

HEDVIG: Were there many people there, Father?

HIALMAR: Oh, no, not many. We were about twelve or fourteen at table.

GINA: And you had some talk with them all?

HIALMAR: Oh, yes, a little; but Gregers took me up most of the time.

GINA: Is Gregers as ugly as ever?

HIALMAR: Well, he's not very much to look at. Hasn't the old man come home?

HEDVIG: Yes, Grandfather is in his room, writing.

HIALMAR: Did he say anything?

GINA: No, what should he say?

HIALMAR: Didn't he say anything about—? I heard something about his having been with Gråberg. I'll go in and see him for a moment.

GINA: No, no, better not.

HIALMAR: Why not? Did he say he didn't want me to go in?

GINA: I don't think he wants to see nobody this evening—

HEDVIG *(making signs)*: Hm—hm!

GINA *(not noticing)*: —he has been in to fetch hot water—

HIALMAR: Aha! Then he's—

GINA: Yes, I suppose so.

HIALMAR: Oh, God! my poor old white-haired father!— Well, well; there let him sit and get all the enjoyment he can.

OLD EKDAL, *in an indoor coat and with a lighted pipe, comes from his room.*

EKDAL: Got home? Thought it was you I heard talking.

HIALMAR: Yes, I have just come.

EKDAL: You didn't see me, did you?

HIALMAR: No, but they told me you had passed through—so I thought I would follow you.

EKDAL: Hm, good of you, Hialmar.—Who were they, all those fellows?

HIALMAR: —Oh, all sorts of people. There was Chamberlain Flor, and Chamberlain Balle, and Chamberlain Kaspersen and Chamberlain—this, that, and the other—I don't know who all—

EKDAL *(nodding)*: Hear that, Gina! Chamberlains every one of them!

GINA: Yes, I hear as they're terrible genteel in that house nowadays.

HEDVIG: Did the Chamberlains sing, Father? Or did they read aloud?

HIALMAR: No, they only talked nonsense. They wanted me to recite something for them; but I knew better than that.

EKDAL: You weren't to be persuaded, eh?

GINA: Oh, you might have done it.

HIALMAR: No; one mustn't be at everybody's beck and call. *(Walks about the room.)* That's not my way, at any rate.

EKDAL: No, no; Hialmar's not to be had for the asking, he isn't.

HIALMAR: I don't see why *I* should bother myself to entertain people on the rare occasions when I go into society. Let the others exert themselves. These fellows go from one great dinner table to the next and gorge and guzzle day out and day in. It's for them to bestir themselves and do something in return for all the good feeding they get.

GINA: But you didn't say that?

HIALMAR *(humming)*: Ho-ho-ho—; faith, I gave them a bit of my mind.

EKDAL: Not the Chamberlains?

HIALMAR: Oh, why not? *(Lightly.)* After that, we had a little discussion about Tokay.

EKDAL: Tokay! There's a fine wine for you!

HIALMAR *(comes to a standstill)*: It may be a fine wine. But of course you know the vintages differ; it all depends on how much sunshine the grapes have had.

GINA: Why, you know everything, Ekdal.

EKDAL: And did they dispute that?

HIALMAR: They tried to; but they were requested to observe that it was just the same with Chamberlains—that with them, too, different batches were of different qualities.

GINA: What things you do think of!

EKDAL: Hee-hee! So they got that in their pipes, too?

HIALMAR: Right in their teeth.

EKDAL: Do you hear that, Gina? He said it right in the very teeth of all the Chamberlains.

GINA: Fancy—! Right in their teeth!

HIALMAR: Yes, but I don't want it talked about. One doesn't speak of such things. The whole affair passed off quite amicably of course. They were nice, genial fellows; I didn't want to wound them—not I!

EKDAL: Right in their teeth, though—!

HEDVIG (*caressingly*): How nice it is to see you in a dress coat! It suits you so well, Father.

HIALMAR: Yes, don't you think so? And this one really sits to perfection. It fits almost as if it had been made for me;—a little tight in the armholes perhaps;—help me, Hedvig (*takes off the coat*). I think I'll put on my jacket. Where is my jacket, Gina?

GINA: Here it is. (*Brings the jacket and helps him.*)

HIALMAR: That's it! Don't forget to send the coat back to Molvik first thing tomorrow morning.

GINA (*laying it away*): I'll be sure and see to it.

HIALMAR (*stretching himself*): After all, there's a more homely feeling about this. A free-and-easy indoor costume suits my whole personality better. Don't you think so, Hedvig?

HEDVIG: Yes, Father.

HIALMAR: When I loosen my necktie into a pair of flowing ends—like this—eh?

HEDVIG: Yes, that goes so well with your mustache and the sweep of your curls.

HIALMAR: I should not call them curls exactly; I should rather say locks.

HEDVIG: Yes, they are too big for curls.

HIALMAR: Locks describes them better.

HEDVIG (*after a pause, twitching his jacket*): Father!

HIALMAR: Well, what is it?

HEDVIG: Oh, you know very well.

HIALMAR: No, really I don't—

HEDVIG (*half laughing, half whispering*): Oh, yes, Father; now don't tease me any longer!

HIALMAR: Why, what do you mean?

HEDVIG (*shaking him*): Oh, what nonsense; come, where are

they, Father? All the good things you promised me, you know?

HIALMAR: Oh—if I haven't forgotten all about them!

HEDVIG: Now you're only teasing me, Father! Oh, it's too bad of you! Where have you put them?

HIALMAR: No, I positively forgot to get anything. But wait a little! I have something else for you, Hedvig.

Goes and searches in the pockets of the coat.

HEDVIG *(skipping and clapping her hands)*: Oh, Mother, Mother!

GINA: There, you see; if you only give him time—

HIALMAR *(with a paper)*: Look, here it is.

HEDVIG: That? Why, that's only a paper.

HIALMAR: That is the bill of fare, my dear; the whole bill of fare. Here you see: "Menu"—that means bill of fare.

HEDVIG: Haven't you anything else?

HIALMAR: I forgot the other things, I tell you. But you may take my word for it, these dainties are very unsatisfying. Sit down at the table and read the bill of fare, and then I'll describe to you how the dishes taste. Here you are, Hedvig.

HEDVIG *(gulping down her tears)*: Thank you. *(She seats herself, but does not read; GINA makes signs to her; HIALMAR notices it.)*

HIALMAR *(pacing up and down the room)*: It's monstrous what absurd things the father of a family is expected to think of; and if he forgets the smallest trifle, he is treated to sour faces at once. Well, well, one gets used to that, too. *(Stops near the stove, by the old man's chair.)* Have you peeped in there this evening, Father?

EKDAL: Yes, to be sure I have. She's gone into the basket.

HIALMAR: Ah, she has gone into the basket. Then she's beginning to get used to it.

EKDAL: Yes; just as I prophesied. But you know there are still a few little things—

HIALMAR: A few improvements, yes.

EKDAL: They've got to be made, you know.

HIALMAR: Yes, let us have a talk about the improvements, Father. Come, let us sit on the sofa.

EKDAL: All right. Hm—think I'll just fill my pipe first. Must clean it out, too. Hm. (*He goes into his room.*)

GINA (*smiling to* HIALMAR): His pipe!

HIALMAR: Oh, yes, yes, Gina; let him alone—the poor shipwrecked old man.—Yes, these improvements—we had better get them out of hand tomorrow.

GINA: You'll hardly have time tomorrow, Ekdal.

HEDVIG (*interposing*): Oh, yes he will, Mother!

GINA: —for remember them prints that has to be retouched; they've sent for them time after time.

HIALMAR: There now! those prints again! I shall get them finished all right! Have any new orders come in?

GINA: No, worse luck; tomorrow I have nothing but those two sittings, you know.

HIALMAR: Nothing else? Oh, no, if people won't set about things with a will—

GINA: But what more can I do? Don't I advertise in the papers as much as we can afford?

HIALMAR: Yes, the papers, the papers; you see how much good they do. And I suppose no one has been to look at the room either?

GINA: No, not yet.

HIALMAR: That was only to be expected. If people won't keep their eyes open—. Nothing can be done without a real effort, Gina!

HEDVIG (*going toward him*): Shall I fetch you the flute, Father?

HIALMAR: No; no flute for me; *I* want no pleasures in this world. (*Pacing about.*) Yes, indeed I will work tomorrow; you shall see if I don't. You may be sure I shall work as long as my strength holds out.

GINA: But my dear, good Ekdal, I didn't mean it in that way.

HEDVIG: Father, mayn't I bring in a bottle of beer?

HIALMAR: No, certainly not. I require nothing, nothing—

(Comes to a standstill.) Beer? Was it beer you were talking about?

HEDVIG *(cheerfully)*: Yes, Father; beautiful, fresh beer.

HIALMAR: Well—since you insist upon it, you may bring in a bottle.

GINA: Yes, do; and we'll be nice and cosy.

HEDVIG *runs toward the kitchen door.*

HIALMAR *(by the stove, stops her, looks at her, puts his arm round her neck and presses her to him)*: Hedvig, Hedvig!

HEDVIG *(with tears of joy)*: My dear, kind father!

HIALMAR: No, don't call me that. Here have I been feasting at the rich man's table,—battening at the groaning board—! And I couldn't even—!

GINA *(sitting at the table)*: Oh, nonsense, nonsense, Ekdal.

HIALMAR: It's not nonsense! And yet you mustn't be too hard upon me. You know that I love you for all that.

HEDVIG *(throwing her arms round him)*: And we love you, oh, so dearly, Father!

HIALMAR: And if I am unreasonable once in a while,—why then—you must remember that I am a man beset by a host of cares. There, there! *(Dries his eyes.)* No beer at such a moment as this. Give me the flute.

HEDVIG *runs to the bookcase and fetches it.*

HIALMAR: Thanks! That's right. With my flute in my hand and you two at my side—ah—!

HEDVIG *seats herself at the table near* GINA; HIALMAR *paces backward and forward, pipes up vigorously and plays a Bohemian peasant dance, but in a slow plaintive tempo, and with sentimental expression.*

HIALMAR *(breaking off the melody, holds out his left hand to* GINA *and says with emotion)*: Our roof may be poor and humble, Gina; but it is home. And with all my heart I say: here dwells my happiness.

He begins to play again; almost immediately after, a knocking is heard at the entrance door.

GINA *(rising)*: Hush, Ekdal,—I think there's someone at the door.

HIALMAR *(laying the flute on the bookcase)*: There! Again!

GINA *goes and opens the door.*

GREGERS WERLE *(in the passage)*: Excuse me—

GINA *(starting back slightly)*: Oh!

GREGERS: —does not Mr. Ekdal, the photographer, live here?

GINA: Yes, he does.

HIALMAR *(going toward the door)*: Gregers! You here after all? Well, come in then.

GREGERS *(coming in)*: I told you I would come and look you up.

HIALMAR: But this evening—? Have you left the party?

GREGERS: I have left both the party and my father's house.— Good evening, Mrs. Ekdal. I don't know whether you recognize me?

GINA: Oh, yes; it's not difficult to know young Mr. Werle again.

GREGERS: No, I am like my mother; and no doubt you remember her.

HIALMAR: Left your father's house, did you say?

GREGERS: Yes, I have gone to a hotel.

HIALMAR: Indeed. Well, since you're here, take off your coat and sit down.

GREGERS: Thanks.

He takes off his overcoat. He is now dressed in a plain gray suit of a countrified cut.

HIALMAR: Here, on the sofa. Make yourself comfortable.

GREGERS *seats himself on the sofa;* HIALMAR *takes a chair at the table.*

GREGERS (*looking around him*): So these are your quarters, Hialmar—this is your home.

HIALMAR: This is the studio, as you see—

GINA: But it's the largest of our rooms, so we generally sit here.

HIALMAR: We used to live in a better place; but this flat has one great advantage: there are such capital outer rooms—

GINA: And we have a room on the other side of the passage that we can let.

GREGERS (*to* HIALMAR): Ah—so you have lodgers, too?

HIALMAR: No, not yet. They're not so easy to find, you see; you have to keep your eyes open. (*To* HEDVIG.) What about the beer, eh?

HEDVIG *nods and goes out into the kitchen.*

GREGERS: So that is your daughter?

HIALMAR: Yes, that is Hedvig.

GREGERS: And she is your only child?

HIALMAR: Yes, the only one. She is the joy of our lives, and— (*lowering his voice*)—at the same time our deepest sorrow, Gregers.

GREGERS: What do you mean?

HIALMAR: She is in serious danger of losing her eyesight.

GREGERS: Becoming blind?

HIALMAR: Yes. Only the first symptoms have appeared as yet, and she may not feel it much for some time. But the doctor has warned us. It is coming, inexorably.

GREGERS: What a terrible misfortune! How do you account for it?

HIALMAR (*sighs*): Hereditary, no doubt.

GREGERS (*starting*): Hereditary?

GINA: Ekdal's mother had weak eyes.

HIALMAR: Yes, so my father says; I can't remember her.

GREGERS: Poor child! And how does she take it?

HIALMAR: Oh, you can imagine we haven't the heart to tell her of it. She dreams of no danger. Gay and careless and chirping like a little bird, she flutters onward into a life of endless night. *(Overcome.)* Oh, it is cruelly hard on me, Gregers.

HEDVIG *brings a tray with beer and glasses, which she sets upon the table.*

HIALMAR *(stroking her hair)*: Thanks, thanks, Hedvig.

HEDVIG *puts her arm around his neck and whispers in his ear.*

HIALMAR: No, no bread and butter just now. *(Looks up.)* But perhaps you would like some, Gregers.

GREGERS *(with a gesture of refusal)*: No, no, thank you.

HIALMAR *(still melancholy)*: Well, you can bring in a little all the same. If you have a crust, that is all I want. And plenty of butter on it, mind.

HEDVIG *nods gaily and goes out into the kitchen again.*

GREGERS *(who has been following her with his eyes)*: She seems quite strong and healthy otherwise.

GINA: Yes. In other ways there's nothing amiss with her, thank goodness.

GREGERS: She promises to be very like you, Mrs. Ekdal. How old is she now?

GINA: Hedvig is close on fourteen; her birthday is the day after tomorrow.

GREGERS: She is pretty tall for her age, then.

GINA: Yes, she's shot up wonderful this last year.

GREGERS: It makes one realize one's own age to see these young people growing up.—How long is it now since you were married?

GINA: We've been married—let me see—just on fifteen years.

GREGERS: Is it so long as that?

GINA *(becomes attentive; looks at him)*: Yes, it is indeed.

HIALMAR: Yes, so it is. Fifteen years all but a few months. *(Changing his tone.)* They must have been long years for you, up at the works, Gregers.

GREGERS: They seemed long while I was living them; now they are over, I hardly know how the time has gone.

OLD EKDAL *comes from his room without his pipe, but with his old-fashioned uniform cap on his head; his gait is somewhat unsteady.*

EKDAL: Come now, Hialmar, let's sit down and have a good talk about this—hm—what was it again?

HIALMAR *(going toward him)*: Father, we have a visitor here—Gregers Werle.—I don't know if you remember him.

EKDAL *(looking at* GREGERS, *who has risen)*: Werle? Is that the son? What does he want with me?

HIALMAR: Nothing; it's me he has come to see.

EKDAL: Oh! Then there's nothing wrong?

HIALMAR: No, no, of course not.

EKDAL *(with a large gesture)*: Not that I'm afraid, you know; but—

GREGERS *(goes over to him)*: I bring you a greeting from your old hunting grounds, Lieutenant Ekdal.

EKDAL: Hunting grounds?

GREGERS: Yes, up in Höidal, about the works, you know.

EKDAL: Oh, up there. Yes, I knew all those places well in the old days.

GREGERS: You were a great sportsman then.

EKDAL: So I was, I don't deny it. You're looking at my uniform cap. I don't ask anybody's leave to wear it in the house. So long as I don't go out in the streets with it—

HEDVIG *brings a plate of bread and butter, which she puts upon the table.*

HIALMAR: Sit down, Father, and have a glass of beer. Help yourself, Gregers.

EKDAL *mutters and stumbles over to the sofa.* GREGERS *seats himself on the chair nearest to him,* HIALMAR *on the other side of* GREGERS. GINA *sits a little way from the table, sewing;* HEDVIG *stands beside her father.*

GREGERS: Can you remember, Lieutenant Ekdal, how Hialmar and I used to come up and visit you in the summer and at Christmas?

EKDAL: Did you? No, no, no; I don't remember it. But sure enough I've been a tidy bit of a sportsman in my day. I've shot bears, too. I've shot nine of 'em, no less.

GREGERS (*looking sympathetically at him*): And now you never get any shooting?

EKDAL: Can't just say that, sir. Get a shot now and then perhaps. Of course not in the old way. For the woods you see—the woods, the woods—! (*Drinks.*) Are the woods fine up there now?

GREGERS: Not so fine as in your time. They have been thinned a good deal.

EKDAL: Thinned? (*More softly, and as if afraid.*) It's dangerous work that. Bad things come of it. The woods revenge themselves.

HIALMAR (*filling up his glass*): Come—a little more, Father.

GREGERS: How can a man like you—such a man for the open air—live in the midst of a stuffy town, boxed within four walls?

EKDAL (*laughs quietly and glances at* HIALMAR): Oh, it's not so bad here. Not at all so bad.

GREGERS: But don't you miss all the things that used to be a part of your very being—the cool sweeping breezes, the free life in the woods and on the uplands, among beasts and birds—?

EKDAL (*smiling*): Hialmar, shall we let him see it?

HIALMAR (*hastily and a little embarrassed*): Oh, no, no, Father; not this evening.

GREGERS: What does he want to show me?

HIALMAR: Oh, it's only something—you can see it another time.

GREGERS (*continues, to the old man*): You see I have been thinking, Lieutenant Ekdal, that you should come up with me to the works; I am sure to be going back soon. No doubt you could get some copying there, too. And here, you have nothing on earth to interest you—nothing to liven you up.

EKDAL (*stares in astonishment at him*): Have *I* nothing on earth to—!

GREGERS: Of course you have Hialmar; but then he has his own family. And a man like you, who has always had such a passion for what is free and wild—

EKDAL (*thumps the table*): Hialmar, he shall see it!

HIALMAR: Oh, do you think it's worthwhile, Father? It's all dark.

EKDAL: Nonsense; it's moonlight. (*Rises*). He shall see it, I tell you. Let me pass! Come and help me, Hialmar.

HEDVIG: Oh, yes, do, Father!

HIALMAR (*rising*): Very well then.

GREGERS (*to* GINA): What is it?

GINA: Oh, nothing so very wonderful, after all.

EKDAL *and* HIALMAR *have gone to the back wall and are each pushing back a side of the sliding door;* HEDVIG *helps the old man;* GREGERS *remains standing by the sofa;* GINA *sits still and sews. Through the open doorway a large, deep irregular garret*[7] *is seen with odd nooks and corners; a couple of stovepipes running through it, from rooms below. There are skylights through which clear moonbeams shine in on some parts of the great room; others lie in deep shadow.*

EKDAL (*to* GREGERS): You may come close up if you like.

GREGERS (*going over to them*): Why, what is it?

EKDAL: Look for yourself. Hm.

HIALMAR (*somewhat embarrassed*): This belongs to Father, you understand.

GREGERS (*at the door, looks into the garret*): Why, you keep poultry, Lieutenant Ekdal.

EKDAL: Should think we did keep poultry. They've gone to roost now. But you should just see our fowls by daylight, sir!

HEDVIG: And there's a—

EKDAL: Sh—sh! don't say anything about it yet.

GREGERS: And you have pigeons, too, I see.

EKDAL: Oh, yes, haven't we just got pigeons! They have their nest-boxes up there under the roof-tree;[8] for pigeons like to roost high, you see.

HIALMAR: They aren't all common pigeons.

EKDAL: Common! Should think not indeed! We have tumblers and a pair of pouters,[9] too. But come here! Can you see that hutch[10] down there by the wall?

GREGERS: Yes; what do you use it for?

EKDAL: That's where the rabbits sleep, sir.

GREGERS: Dear me; so you have rabbits, too?

EKDAL: Yes, you may take my word for it, we have rabbits! He wants to know if we have rabbits, Hialmar! Hm! But now comes the thing, let me tell you! Here we have it! Move away, Hedvig. Stand here; that's right,—and now look down there.—Don't you see a basket with straw in it?

GREGERS: Yes. And I can see a fowl lying in the basket.

EKDAL: Hm—"a fowl"—

GREGERS: Isn't it a duck?

EKDAL (hurt): Why, of course it's a duck.

HIALMAR: But what kind of duck, do you think?

HEDVIG: It's not just a common duck—

EKDAL: Sh!

GREGERS: And it's not a Muscovy[11] duck either.

EKDAL: No, Mr.—Werle; it's not a Muscovy duck; for it's a wild duck!

GREGERS: Is it really? A wild duck?

EKDAL: Yes, that's what it is. That "fowl" as you call it—is the wild duck. It's our wild duck, sir.

HEDVIG: My wild duck. It belongs to me.

GREGERS: And can it live up here in the garret? Does it thrive?

EKDAL: Of course it has a trough of water to splash about in, you know.

HIALMAR: Fresh water every other day.

GINA (*turning toward* HIALMAR): But my dear Ekdal, it's getting icy cold here.

EKDAL: Hm, we had better shut up then. It's as well not to disturb their night's rest, too. Close up, Hedvig.

HIALMAR *and* HEDVIG *push the garret doors together.*

EKDAL: Another time you shall see her properly. (*Seats himself in the armchair by the stove.*) Oh, they're curious things, these wild ducks, I can tell you.

GREGERS: How did you manage to catch it, Lieutenant Ekdal?

EKDAL: *I* didn't catch it. There's a certain man in this town whom we have to thank for it.

GREGERS (*starts slightly*): That man was not my father, was he?

EKDAL: You've hit it. Your father and no one else. Hm.

HIALMAR: Strange that you should guess that, Gregers.

GREGERS: You were telling me that you owed so many things to my father; and so I thought perhaps—

GINA: But we didn't get the duck from Mr. Werle himself—

EKDAL: It's Håkon Werle we have to thank for her, all the same, Gina. (*To* GREGERS.) He was shooting from a boat, you see, and he brought her down. But your father's sight is not very good now. Hm; she was only wounded.

GREGERS: Ah! She got a couple of slugs in her body, I suppose.

HIALMAR: Yes, two or three.

HEDVIG: She was hit under the wing, so that she couldn't fly.

GREGERS: And I suppose she dived to the bottom, eh?

EKDAL (*sleepily, in a thick voice*): Of course. Always do that, wild ducks do. They shoot to the bottom as deep as they can get, sir—and bite themselves fast in the tangle and seaweed—and all the devil's own mess that grows down there. And they never come up again.

GREGERS: But your wild duck came up again, Lieutenant Ekdal.

EKDAL: He had such an amazingly clever dog, your father had. And that dog—he dived in after the duck and fetched her up again.

GREGERS *(who has turned to* HIALMAR*)*: And then she was sent to you here?

HIALMAR: Not at once; at first your father took her home. But she wouldn't thrive there; so Pettersen was told to put an end to her—

EKDAL *(half asleep)*: Hm—yes—Pettersen—that ass—

HIALMAR *(speaking more softly)*: That was how we got her, you see; for Father knows Pettersen a little; and when he heard about the wild duck he got him to hand her over to us.

GREGERS: And now she thrives as well as possible in the garret there?

HIALMAR: Yes, wonderfully well. She has got fat. You see, she has lived in there so long now that she has forgotten her natural wild life; and it all depends on that.

GREGERS: You are right there, Hialmar. Be sure you never let her get a glimpse of the sky and the sea—. But I mustn't stay any longer; I think your father is asleep.

HIALMAR: Oh, as for that—

GREGERS: But, by-the-bye—you said you had a room to let—a spare room?

HIALMAR: Yes; what then? Do you know of anybody—?

GREGERS: Can *I* have that room?

HIALMAR: You?

GINA: Oh, no, Mr. Werle, you—

GREGERS: May I have the room? If so, I'll take possession first thing tomorrow morning.

HIALMAR: Yes, with the greatest pleasure—

GINA: But, Mr. Werle, I'm sure it's not at all the sort of room for you.

HIALMAR: Why, Gina! how can you say that?

GINA: Why, because the room's neither large enough nor light enough, and—

GREGERS: That really doesn't matter, Mrs. Ekdal.

HIALMAR: I call it quite a nice room, and not at all badly furnished either.

GINA: But remember the pair of them underneath.

GREGERS: What pair?

GINA: Well, there's one as has been a tutor—

HIALMAR: That's Molvik—Mr. Molvik, B.A.

GINA: And then there's a doctor, by the name of Relling.

GREGERS: Relling? I know him a little; he practiced for a time up in Höidal.

GINA: They're a regular rackety pair, they are. As often as not, they're out on the loose in the evenings; and then they come home at all hours, and they're not always just—

GREGERS: One soon gets used to that sort of thing. I daresay I shall be like the wild duck—

GINA: Hm; I think you ought to sleep upon it first, anyway.

GREGERS: You seem very unwilling to have me in the house, Mrs. Ekdal.

GINA: Oh, no! What makes you think that?

HIALMAR: Well, you really behave strangely about it, Gina. (*To* GREGERS.) Then I suppose you intend to remain in the town for the present?

GREGERS (*putting on his overcoat*): Yes, now I intend to remain here.

HIALMAR: And yet not at your father's? What do you propose to do, then?

GREGERS: Ah, if I only knew that, Hialmar, I shouldn't be so badly off! But when one has the misfortune to be called Gregers—! "Gregers"—and then "Werle" after it; did you ever hear anything so hideous?

HIALMAR: Oh, I don't think so at all.

GREGERS: Ugh! Bah! I feel I should like to spit upon the fellow that answers to such a name. But when a man is once for all doomed to be Gregers—Werle in this world, as I am—

HIALMAR (*laughs*): Ha, ha! If you weren't Gregers Werle, what would you like to be?

GREGERS: If I should choose, I should like best to be a clever dog.

GINA: A dog!

HEDVIG (*involuntarily*): Oh, no!

GREGERS: Yes, an amazingly clever dog; one that goes to the bottom after wild ducks when they dive and bite themselves fast in tangle and seaweed, down among the ooze.

HIALMAR: Upon my word now, Gregers—I don't in the least know what you're driving at.

GREGERS: Oh, well, you might not be much the wiser if you did. It's understood, then, that I move in early tomorrow morning. (*To* GINA.) I won't give you any trouble; I do everything for myself. (*To* HIALMAR.) We can talk about the rest tomorrow.—Good night, Mrs. Ekdal. (*Nods to* HEDVIG.) Good night.

GINA: Good night, Mr. Werle.

HEDVIG: Good night.

HIALMAR (*who has lighted a candle*): Wait a moment; I must show you a light; the stairs are sure to be dark.

GREGERS *and* HIALMAR *go out by the passage door.*

GINA (*looking straight before her, with her sewing in her lap*): Wasn't that queer-like talk about wanting to be a dog?

HEDVIG: Do you know, Mother—I believe he meant something quite different by that.

GINA: Why, what should he mean?

HEDVIG: Oh, I don't know; but it seemed to me he meant something different from what he said—all the time.

GINA: Do you think so? Yes, it was sort of queer.

HIALMAR (*comes back*): The lamp was still burning. (*Puts out the candle and sets it down.*) Ah, now one can get a mouthful of food at last. (*Begins to eat the bread and butter.*) Well, you see, Gina—if only you keep your eyes open—

GINA: How, keep your eyes open—?

HIALMAR: Why, haven't we at last had the luck to get the room let? And just think—to a person like Gregers—a good old friend.

GINA: Well, I don't know what to say about it.

HEDVIG: Oh, Mother, you'll see; it'll be such fun!

HIALMAR: You're very strange. You were so bent upon getting the room let before; and now you don't like it.

GINA: Yes, I do, Ekdal; if it had only been to someone else— But what do you suppose Mr. Werle will say?

HIALMAR: Old Werle? It doesn't concern him.

GINA: But surely you can see that there's something amiss between them again, or the young man wouldn't be leaving home. You know very well those two can't get on with each other.

HIALMAR: Very likely not, but—

GINA: And now Mr. Werle may fancy it's you that has egged him on—

HIALMAR: Let him fancy so, then! Mr. Werle has done a great deal for me; far be it from me to deny it. But that doesn't make me everlastingly dependent upon him.

GINA: But, my dear Ekdal, maybe Grandfather'll suffer for it. He may lose the little bit of work he gets from Gråberg.

HIALMAR: I could almost say: so much the better! Is it not humiliating for a man like me to see his gray-haired father treated as a pariah? But now I believe the fullness of time is at hand. (*Takes a fresh piece of bread and butter.*) As sure as I have a mission in life, I mean to fulfill it now!

HEDVIG: Oh, yes, Father, do!

GINA: Hush! Don't wake him!

HIALMAR (*more softly*): I will fulfill it, I say. The day shall come when— And that is why I say it's a good thing we have let the room; for that makes me more independent. The man who has a mission in life must be independent. (*By the armchair, with emotion.*) Poor old white-haired

Father! Rely on your Hialmar. He has broad shoulders—strong shoulders, at any rate. You shall yet wake up some fine day and—(*To* GINA.) Do you not believe it?

GINA *(rising)*: Yes, of course I do; but in the meantime suppose we see about getting him to bed.

HIALMAR: Yes, come.

They take hold of the old man carefully.

ACT THREE

HIALMAR EKDAL's *studio. It is morning: the daylight shines through the large window in the slanting roof; the curtain is drawn back.*

> HIALMAR *is sitting at the table, busy retouching a photograph; several others lie before him. Presently* GINA, *wearing her hat and cloak, enters by the passage door; she has a covered basket on her arm.*

HIALMAR: Back already, Gina?

GINA: Oh, yes, one can't let the grass grow under one's feet.

Sets her basket on a chair and takes off her things.

HIALMAR: Did you look in at Gregers' room?

GINA: Yes, that I did. It's a rare sight, I can tell you; he's made a pretty mess to start off with.

HIALMAR: How so?

GINA: He was determined to do everything for himself, he said; so he sets to work to light the stove, and what must he do but screw down the damper till the whole room is full of smoke. Ugh! There was a smell fit to—

HIALMAR: Well, really!

138

GINA: But that's not the worst of it; for then he thinks he'll put out the fire, and goes and empties his water jug into the stove and so makes the whole floor one filthy puddle.

HIALMAR: How annoying!

GINA: I've got the porter's wife to clear up after him, pig that he is! But the room won't be fit to live in till the afternoon.

HIALMAR: What's he doing with himself in the meantime?

GINA: He said he was going out for a little while.

HIALMAR: I looked in upon him, too, for a moment—after you had gone.

GINA: So I heard. You've asked him to lunch.

HIALMAR: Just to a little bit of early lunch, you know. It's his first day—we can hardly do less. You've got something in the house, I suppose?

GINA: I shall have to find something or other.

HIALMAR: And don't cut it too fine, for I fancy Relling and Molvik are coming up, too. I just happened to meet Relling on the stairs, you see; so I had to—

GINA: Oh, are we to have those two as well?

HIALMAR: Good Lord—couple more or less can't make any difference.

OLD EKDAL (opens his door and looks in): I say, Hialmar— (Sees GINA.) Oh!

GINA: Do you want anything, Grandfather?

EKDAL: Oh, no, it doesn't matter. Hm! (Retires again.)

GINA (takes up the basket): Be sure you see that he doesn't go out.

HIALMAR: All right, all right. And, Gina, a little herring salad wouldn't be a bad idea; Relling and Molvik were out on the loose again last night.

GINA: If only they don't come before I'm ready for them—

HIALMAR: No, of course they won't; take your own time.

GINA: Very well; and meanwhile you can be working a bit.

HIALMAR: Well, I am working! I am working as hard as I can!

GINA: Then you'll have that job off your hands, you see.

She goes out to the kitchen with her basket. HIALMAR *sits for a time penciling away at the photograph, in an indolent and listless manner.*

EKDAL (*peeps in, looks round the studio and says softly*): Are you busy?

HIALMAR: Yes, I'm toiling at these wretched pictures—

EKDAL: Well, well, never mind,—since you're so busy—hm! (*He goes out again; the door stands open.*)

HIALMAR (*continues for some time in silence; then he lays down his brush and goes over to the door*): Are you busy, Father?

EKDAL (*in a grumbling tone, within*): If you're busy, I'm busy, too. Hm!

HIALMAR: Oh, very well, then. (*Goes to his work again.*)

EKDAL (*presently, coming to the door again*): Hm; I say, Hialmar, I'm not so very busy, you know.

HIALMAR: I thought you were writing.

EKDAL: Oh, the devil take it! Can't Gråberg wait a day or two? After all, it's not a matter of life and death.

HIALMAR: No; and you're not his slave either.

EKDAL: And about that other business in there—

HIALMAR: Just what I was thinking of. Do you want to go in? Shall I open the door for you?

EKDAL: Well, it wouldn't be a bad notion.

HIALMAR (*rises*): Then we'd have that off our hands.

EKDAL: Yes, exactly. It's got to be ready first thing tomorrow. It is tomorrow, isn't it? Hm?

HIALMAR: Yes, of course it's tomorrow.

HIALMAR *and* EKDAL *push aside each his half of the sliding door. The morning sun is shining in through the skylights; some doves are flying about; others sit cooing, upon the perches; the hens are heard clucking now and then, further back in the garret.*

HIALMAR: There; now you can get to work, Father.

EKDAL (*goes in*): Aren't you coming, too?

HIALMAR: Well, really, do you know—; I almost think— (*Sees* GINA *at the kitchen door.*) I? No; I haven't time; I must work.—But now for our new contrivance—

He pulls a cord, a curtain slips down inside, the lower part consisting of a piece of old sailcloth, the upper part of a stretched fishing net. The floor of the garret is thus no longer visible.

HIALMAR (*goes to the table*): So! Now, perhaps I can sit in peace for a little while.

GINA: Is he rampaging in there again?

HIALMAR: Would you rather have had him slip down to Madam Eriksen's? (*Seats himself.*) Do you want anything? You know you said—

GINA: I only wanted to ask if you think we can lay the table for lunch here?

HIALMAR: Yes; we have no early appointment, I suppose?

GINA: No, I expect no one today except those two sweethearts that are to be taken together.

HIALMAR: Why the deuce couldn't they be taken together another day!

GINA: Don't you know, I told them to come in the afternoon, when you are having your nap.

HIALMAR: Oh, that's capital. Very well, let us have lunch here then.

GINA: All right; but there's no hurry about laying the cloth; you can have the table for a good while yet.

HIALMAR: Do you think I am not sticking at my work? I'm at it as hard as I can!

GINA: Then you'll be free later on, you know.

Goes out into the kitchen again. Short pause.

EKDAL (*in the garret doorway, behind the net*): Hialmar!

HIALMAR: Well?

EKDAL: Afraid we shall have to move the water trough, after all.

HIALMAR: What else have I been saying all along?

EKDAL: Hm—hm—hm.

Goes away from the door again. HIALMAR *goes on working a little; glances toward the garret and half rises.* HEDVIG *comes in from the kitchen.*

HIALMAR *(sits down again hurriedly)*: What do you want?

HEDVIG: I only wanted to come in beside you, Father.

HIALMAR *(after a pause)*: What makes you go prying around like that? Perhaps you are told off to watch me?

HEDVIG: No, no.

HIALMAR: What is your mother doing out there?

HEDVIG: Oh, Mother's in the middle of making the herring salad. *(Goes to the table.)* Isn't there any little thing I could help you with, Father?

HIALMAR: Oh, no. It is right that I should bear the whole burden—so long as my strength holds out. Set your mind at rest, Hedvig; if only your father keeps his health—

HEDVIG: Oh, no, Father! You mustn't talk in that horrid way.

She wanders about a little, stops by the doorway and looks into the garret.

HIALMAR: Tell me, what is he doing?

HEDVIG: I think he's making a new path to the water trough.

HIALMAR: He can never manage that by himself! And here am I doomed to sit—!

HEDVIG *(goes to him)*: Let me take the brush, Father; I can do it, quite well.

HIALMAR: Oh, nonsense; you will only hurt your eyes.

HEDVIG: Not a bit. Give me the brush.

HIALMAR *(rising)*: Well, it won't take more than a minute or two.

HEDVIG: Pooh, what harm can it do then? *(Takes the brush.)* There! *(Seats herself.)* I can begin upon this one.

HIALMAR: But mind you don't hurt your eyes! Do you hear? *I* won't be answerable; you do it on your own responsibility—understand that.

HEDVIG *(retouching)*: Yes, yes, I understand.

HIALMAR: You are quite clever at it, Hedvig. Only a minute or two, you know.

He slips through by the edge of the curtain into the garret. HEDVIG *sits at her work.* HIALMAR *and* EKDAL *are heard disputing inside.*

HIALMAR (*appears behind the net*): I say, Hedvig—give me those pincers that are lying on the shelf. And the chisel. (*Turns away inside.*) Now you shall see, Father. Just let me show you first what I mean!

HEDVIG *has fetched the required tools from the shelf and hands them to him through the net.*

HIALMAR: Ah, thanks. I didn't come a moment too soon.

Goes back from the curtain again; they are heard carpentering and talking inside. HEDVIG *stands looking in at them. A moment later there is a knock at the passage door; she does not notice it.*

GREGERS WERLE (*bareheaded, in indoor dress, enters and stops near the door*): Hm—!
HEDVIG (*turns and goes toward him*): Good morning. Please come in.
GREGERS: Thank you. (*Looking toward the garret.*) You seem to have workpeople in the house.
HEDVIG: No, it is only Father and Grandfather. I'll tell them you are here.
GREGERS: No, no, don't do that; I would rather wait a little. (*Seats himself on the sofa.*)
HEDVIG: It looks so untidy here— (*Begins to clear away the photographs.*)
GREGERS: Oh, don't take them away. Are those prints that have to be finished off?
HEDVIG: Yes, they are a few I was helping Father with.
GREGERS: Please don't let me disturb you.
HEDVIG: Oh, no.

She gathers the things to her and sits down to work;
GREGERS *looks at her, meanwhile, in silence.*

GREGERS: Did the wild duck sleep well last night?

HEDVIG: Yes, I think so, thanks.

GREGERS *(turning toward the garret)*: It looks quite different by day from what it did last night in the moonlight.

HEDVIG: Yes, it changes ever so much. It looks different in the morning and in the afternoon; and it's different on rainy days from what it is in fine weather.

GREGERS: Have you noticed that?

HEDVIG: Yes, how could I help it?

GREGERS: Are you, too, fond of being in there with the wild duck?

HEDVIG: Yes, when I can manage it—

GREGERS: But I suppose you haven't much spare time; you go to school, no doubt.

HEDVIG: No, not now; Father is afraid of my hurting my eyes.

GREGERS: Oh; then he reads with you himself?

HEDVIG: Father has promised to read with me; but he has never had time yet.

GREGERS: Then is there nobody else to give you a little help?

HEDVIG: Yes, there is Mr. Molvik; but he is not always exactly—quite—

GREGERS: Sober?

HEDVIG: Yes, I suppose that's it!

GREGERS: Why, then you must have any amount of time on your hands. And in there I suppose it is a sort of world by itself?

HEDVIG: Oh, yes, quite. And there are such lots of wonderful things.

GREGERS: Indeed?

HEDVIG: Yes, there are big cupboards full of books; and a great many of the books have pictures in them.

GREGERS: Aha!

HEDVIG: And there's an old bureau with drawers and flaps,

and a big clock with figures that go out and in. But the
clock isn't going now.

GREGERS: So time has come to a standstill in there—in the
wild duck's domain.

HEDVIG: Yes. And then there's an old paint box and things of
that sort; and all the books.

GREGERS: And you read the books, I suppose?

HEDVIG: Oh, yes, when I get the chance. Most of them are
English, though, and I don't understand English. But then
I look at the pictures.—There is one great big book called
"Harrison's History of London."[12] It must be a hundred
years old; and there are such heaps of pictures in it. At the
beginning there is Death with an hourglass and a woman.[13]
I think that is horrid. But then there are all the other pictures of churches, and castles, and streets and great ships
sailing on the sea.

GREGERS: But tell me, where did all those wonderful things
come from?

HEDVIG: Oh, an old sea captain once lived here, and he
brought them home with him. They used to call him "The
Flying Dutchman."[14] That was curious, because he wasn't
a Dutchman at all.

GREGERS: Was he not?

HEDVIG: No. But at last he was drowned at sea; and so he left
all those things behind him.

GREGERS: Tell me now—when you are sitting in there looking at the pictures, don't you wish you could travel and see
the real world for yourself?

HEDVIG: Oh, no! I mean always to stay at home and help
Father and Mother.

GREGERS: To retouch photographs?

HEDVIG: No, not only that. I should love above everything to
learn to engrave[15] pictures like those in the English books.

GREGERS: Hm. What does your father say to that?

HEDVIG: I don't think Father likes it; Father is strange about
such things. Only think, he talks of my learning basket

making and straw plaiting! But I don't think that would be much good.

GREGERS: Oh, no, I don't think so either.

HEDVIG: But Father was right in saying that if I had learned basket making I could have made the new basket, for the wild duck.

GREGERS: So you could; and it was you that ought to have done it, wasn't it?

HEDVIG: Yes, for it's my wild duck.

GREGERS: Of course it is.

HEDVIG: Yes, it belongs to me. But I lend it to Father and Grandfather as often as they please.

GREGERS: Indeed? What do they do with it?

HEDVIG: Oh, they look after it, and build places for it, and so on.

GREGERS: I see; for no doubt the wild duck is by far the most distinguished inhabitant of the garret?

HEDVIG: Yes, indeed she is; for she is a real wild fowl, you know. And then she is so much to be pitied; she has no one to care for, poor thing.

GREGERS: She has no family, as the rabbits have—

HEDVIG: No. The hens, too, many of them, were chickens together; but she has been taken right away from all her friends. And then there is so much that is strange about the wild duck. Nobody knows her, and nobody knows where she came from either.

GREGERS: And she has been down in the depths of the sea.

HEDVIG (*with a quick glance at him, represses a smile and asks*): Why do you say "depths of the sea"?

GREGERS: What else should I say?

HEDVIG: You could say "the bottom of the sea."

GREGERS: Oh, mayn't I just as well say the depths of the sea?

HEDVIG: Yes; but it sounds so strange to me when other people speak of the depths of the sea.

GREGERS: Why so? Tell me why?

HEDVIG: No, I won't; it's so stupid.

GREGERS: Oh, no, I am sure it's not. Do tell me why you smiled.

HEDVIG: Well, this is the reason: whenever I come to realize suddenly—in a flash—what is in there, it always seems to me that the whole room and everything in it should be called "the depths of the sea."—But that is so stupid.

GREGERS: You mustn't say that.

HEDVIG: Oh, yes, for you know it is only a garret.

GREGERS (*looks fixedly at her*): Are you so sure of that?

HEDVIG (*astonished*): That it's a garret?

GREGERS: Are you quite certain of it?

HEDVIG *is silent, and looks at him openmouthed.* GINA *comes in from the kitchen with the table things.*

GREGERS (*rising*): I have come in upon you too early.

GINA: Oh, you must be somewhere; and we're nearly ready now, anyway. Clear the table, Hedvig.

HEDVIG *clears away her things; she and* GINA *lay the cloth during what follows.* GREGERS *seats himself in the armchair and turns over an album.*

GREGERS: I hear you can retouch, Mrs. Ekdal.

GINA (*with a side glance*): Yes, I can.

GREGERS: That was exceedingly lucky.

GINA: How—lucky?

GREGERS: Since Ekdal took to photography, I mean.

HEDVIG: Mother can take photographs, too.

GINA: Oh, yes; I was bound to learn that.

GREGERS: So it is really you that carry on the business, I suppose?

GINA: Yes, when Ekdal hasn't time himself—

GREGERS: He is a great deal taken up with his old father, I daresay.

GINA: Yes; and then you can't expect a man like Ekdal to do nothing but take car-de-visits of Dick, Tom and Harry.

GREGERS: I quite agree with you; but having once gone in for the thing—

GINA: You can surely understand, Mr. Werle, that Ekdal's not like one of your common photographers.

GREGERS: Of course not; but still—

A shot is fired within the garret.

GREGERS *(starting up)*: What's that?

GINA: Ugh! now they're firing again!

GREGERS: Have they firearms in there?

HEDVIG: They are out shooting.

GREGERS: What! *(At the door of the garret.)* Are you shooting, Hialmar?

HIALMAR *(inside the net)*: Are you there? I didn't know; I was so taken up— *(To HEDVIG.)* Why did you not let us know? *(Comes into the studio.)*

GREGERS: Do you go shooting in the garret?

HIALMAR *(showing a double-barreled pistol)*: Oh, only with this thing.

GINA: Yes, you and Grandfather will do yourselves a mischief some day with that there pigstol.

HIALMAR *(with irritation)*: I believe I have told you that this kind of firearm is called a pistol.

GINA: Oh, that doesn't make it much better, that I can see.

GREGERS: So you have become a sportsman, too, Hialmar?

HIALMAR: Only a little rabbit shooting now and then. Mostly to please Father, you understand.

GINA: Men are strange beings; they must always have something to pervert theirselves with.

HIALMAR *(snappishly)*: Just so; we must always have something to divert ourselves with.

GINA: Yes, that's just what I say.

HIALMAR: Hm. *(To GREGERS)*. You see the garret is fortunately so situated that no one can hear us shooting. *(Lays the pistol on the top shelf of the bookcase.)* Don't touch the pistol, Hedvig! One of the barrels is loaded; remember that.

GREGERS (*looking through the net*): You have a fowling piece, too, I see.

HIALMAR: That is Father's old gun. It's of no use now; something has gone wrong with the lock. But it's fun to have it all the same; for we can take it to pieces now and then, and clean and grease it, and screw it together again.—Of course, it's mostly Father that fiddle-faddles with all that sort of thing.

HEDVIG (*beside* GREGERS): Now you can see the wild duck properly.

GREGERS: I was just looking at her. One of her wings seems to me to droop a bit.

HEDVIG: Well, no wonder; her wing was broken, you know.

GREGERS: And she trails one foot a little. Isn't that so?

HIALMAR: Perhaps a very little bit.

HEDVIG: Yes, it was by that foot the dog took hold of her.

HIALMAR: But otherwise she hasn't the least thing the matter with her; and that is simply marvelous for a creature that has a charge of shot in her body and has been between a dog's teeth—

GREGERS (*with a glance at* HEDVIG): —and that has lain in the depths of the sea—so long.

HEDVIG (*smiling*): Yes.

GINA (*laying the table*): That blessed wild duck! What a lot of fuss you do make over her.

HIALMAR: Hm;—will lunch soon be ready?

GINA: Yes, directly. Hedvig, you must come and help me now.

GINA *and* HEDVIG *go out into the kitchen.*

HIALMAR (*in a low voice*): I think you had better not stand there looking in at Father; he doesn't like it. (GREGERS *moves away from the garret door.*) Besides, I may as well shut up before the others come. (*Claps his hands to drive the fowls back.*) Shh—shh, in with you! (*Draws up the curtain and pulls the doors together.*) All the contrivances are my own invention. It's really quite amusing to have things of this sort to potter with and to put to rights when they get out of order. And it's absolutely necessary, too; for Gina objects to having rabbits and fowls in the studio.

GREGERS: To be sure; and I suppose the studio is your wife's special department?

HIALMAR: As a rule, I leave the everyday details of business to her; for then I can take refuge in the parlor and give my mind to more important things.

GREGERS: What things may they be, Hialmar?

HIALMAR: I wonder you have not asked that question sooner. But perhaps you haven't heard of the invention?

GREGERS: The invention? No.

HIALMAR: Really? Have you not? Oh, no, out there in the wilds—

GREGERS: So you have invented something, have you?

HIALMAR: It is not quite completed yet; but I am working at it. You can easily imagine that when I resolved to devote myself to photography, it wasn't simply with the idea of taking likenesses of all sorts of commonplace people.

GREGERS: No; your wife was saying the same thing just now.

HIALMAR: I swore that if I consecrated my powers to this handicraft, I would so exalt it that it should become both an art and a science. And to that end I determined to make this great invention.

GREGERS: And what is the nature of the invention? What purpose does it serve?

HIALMAR: Oh, my dear fellow, you mustn't ask for details yet. It takes time, you see. And you must not think that my motive is vanity. It is not for my own sake that I am working. Oh, no; it is my life's mission that stands before me night and day.

GREGERS: What is your life's mission?

HIALMAR: Do you forget the old man with the silver hair?

GREGERS: Your poor father? Well, but what can you do for him?

HIALMAR: I can raise up his self-respect from the dead, by restoring the name of Ekdal to honor and dignity.

GREGERS: Then that is your life's mission?

HIALMAR: Yes. I will rescue the shipwrecked man. For shipwrecked he was, by the very first blast of the storm. Even while those terrible investigations were going on, he was no longer himself. That pistol there—the one we use to shoot rabbits with—has played its part in the tragedy of the house of Ekdal.

GREGERS: The pistol? Indeed?

HIALMAR: When the sentence of imprisonment was passed—he had the pistol in his hand—

GREGERS: Had he—?

HIALMAR: Yes; but he dared not use it. His courage failed him! So broken, so demoralized was he even then! Oh, can you understand it? He, a soldier; he, who had shot nine bears, and who was descended from two lieutenant-colonels—one after the other, of course. Can you understand it, Gregers?

GREGERS: Yes, I understand it well enough.

HIALMAR: I cannot. And once more the pistol played a part in the history of our house. When he had put on the gray clothes [16] and was under lock and key—oh, that was a terrible time for me, I can tell you. I kept the blinds drawn down over both my windows. When I peeped out, I saw the sun shining as if nothing had happened. I could not understand it. I saw people going along the street, laughing and talking about indifferent things. I could not understand it. It seemed to me that the whole of existence must be at a standstill—as if under an eclipse.

GREGERS: I felt that, too, when my mother died.

HIALMAR: It was in such an hour that Hialmar Ekdal pointed the pistol at his own breast.

GREGERS: You, too, thought of—!

HIALMAR: Yes.

GREGERS: But you did not fire?

HIALMAR: No. At the decisive moment I won the victory over myself. I remained in life. But I can assure you it takes some courage to choose life under circumstances like those.

GREGERS: Well, that depends on how you look at it.

HIALMAR: Yes, indeed, it takes courage. But I am glad I was firm: for now I shall soon perfect my invention; and Dr. Relling thinks, as I do myself, that Father may be allowed to wear his uniform again.[17] I will demand that as my sole reward.

GREGERS: So that is what he meant about his uniform—?

HIALMAR: Yes, that is what he most yearns for. You can't think how my heart bleeds for him. Every time we celebrate any little family festival—Gina's and my wedding day, or whatever it may be—in comes the old man in the lieutenant's uniform of happier days. But if he only hears a knock at the door—for he daren't show himself to strangers, you know—he hurries back to his room again as fast as his old legs can carry him. Oh, it's heartrending for a son to see such things!

GREGERS: How long do you think it will take you to finish your invention?

HIALMAR: Come now, you mustn't expect me to enter into particulars like that. An invention is not a thing completely under one's own control. It depends largely on inspiration—on intuition—and it is almost impossible to predict when the inspiration may come.

GREGERS: But it's advancing?

HIALMAR: Yes, certainly, it is advancing. I turn it over in my mind every day; I am full of it. Every afternoon, when I have had my dinner, I shut myself up in the parlor, where I can ponder undisturbed. But I can't be goaded to it; it's not a bit of good; Relling says so, too.

GREGERS: And you don't think that all that business in the garret draws you off and distracts you too much?

HIALMAR: No, no, no; quite the contrary. You mustn't say that. I cannot be everlastingly absorbed in the same laborious train of thought. I must have something alongside of it to fill up the time of waiting. The inspiration, the intuition, you see—when it comes, it comes, and there's an end of it.

GREGERS: My dear Hialmar, I almost think you have something of the wild duck in you.

HIALMAR: Something of the wild duck? How do you mean?

GREGERS: You have dived down and bitten yourself fast in the undergrowth.

HIALMAR: Are you alluding to the well-nigh fatal shot that has broken my father's wing—and mine, too?

GREGERS: Not exactly to that. I don't say that your wing has been broken; but you have strayed into a poisonous marsh, Hialmar; an insidious disease has taken hold of you, and you have sunk down to die in the dark.

HIALMAR: I? To die in the dark? Look here, Gregers, you must really leave off talking such nonsense.

GREGERS: Don't be afraid; I shall find a way to help you up again. I, too, have a mission in life now; I found it yesterday.

HIALMAR: That's all very well; but you will please leave me out of it. I can assure you that—apart from my very natural melancholy, of course—I am as contented as anyone can wish to be.

GREGERS: Your contentment is an effect of the marsh poison.

HIALMAR: Now, my dear Gregers, pray do not go on about disease and poison; I am not used to that sort of talk. In my house nobody ever speaks to me about unpleasant things.

GREGERS: Ah, that I can easily believe.

HIALMAR: It's not good for me, you see. And there are no marsh poisons here, as you express it. The poor photographer's roof is lowly, I know—and my circumstances are narrow. But I am an inventor, and I am the breadwinner of a family. That exalts me above my mean surroundings.—Ah, here comes lunch!

GINA and HEDVIG *bring bottles of ale, a decanter of brandy, glasses, etc. At the same time,* RELLING *and*

MOLVIK *enter from the passage; they are both without hat or overcoat.* MOLVIK *is dressed in black.*

GINA *(placing the things upon the table)*: Ah, you two have come in the nick of time.

RELLING: Molvik got it into his head that he could smell herring salad, and then there was no holding him.—Good morning again, Ekdal.

HIALMAR: Gregers, let me introduce you to Mr. Molvik. Doctor—. Oh, you know Relling, don't you?

GREGERS: Yes, slightly.

RELLING: Oh, Mr. Werle, junior! Yes, we two have had one or two little skirmishes up at the Höidal works. You've just moved in?

GREGERS: I moved in this morning.

RELLING: Molvik and I live right under you; so you haven't far to go for the doctor and the clergyman, if you should need anything in that line.

GREGERS: Thanks, it's not quite unlikely; for yesterday we were thirteen at table.

HIALMAR: Oh, come now, don't let us get upon unpleasant subjects again!

RELLING: You may make your mind easy, Ekdal; I'll be hanged if the finger of fate points to you.

HIALMAR: I should hope not, for the sake of my family. But let us sit down now, and eat and drink and be merry.

The men seat themselves at the table, and eat and drink. GINA and HEDVIG go in and out and wait upon them.

RELLING: Molvik was frightfully screwed yesterday, Mrs. Ekdal.

GINA: Really? Yesterday again?

RELLING: Didn't you hear him when I brought him home last night?

GINA: No, I can't say I did.

RELLING: That was a good thing, for Molvik was disgusting last night.

GINA: Is that true, Molvik?

MOLVIK: Let us draw a veil over last night's proceedings. That sort of thing is totally foreign to my better self.

RELLING (*to* GREGERS): It comes over him like a sort of possession, and then I have to go out on the loose with him. Mr. Molvik is demonic, you see.

GREGERS: Demonic?

RELLING: Molvik is demonic, yes.

GREGERS: Hm.

RELLING: And demonic natures are not made to walk straight through the world; they must meander a little now and then.—Well, so you still stick up there at those horrible grimy works?

GREGERS: I have stuck there until now.

RELLING: And did you ever manage to collect that claim[18] you went about presenting?

GREGERS: Claim? (*Understands him.*) Ah, I see.

HIALMAR: Have you been presenting claims, Gregers?

GREGERS: Oh, nonsense.

RELLING: Faith, but he has, though! He went around to all the cottars' cabins presenting something he called "the claim of the ideal."

GREGERS: I was young then.

RELLING: You're right; you were very young. And as for the claim of the ideal—you never got it honored while *I* was up there.

GREGERS: Nor since either.

RELLING: Ah, then you've learned to knock a little discount off, I expect.

GREGERS: Never, when I have a true man to deal with.

HIALMAR: No, I should think not, indeed. A little butter, Gina.

RELLING: And a slice of bacon for Molvik.

MOLVIK: Ugh; not bacon!

A knock at the garret door.

HIALMAR: Open the door, Hedvig; Father wants to come out.

HEDVIG *goes over and opens the door a little way;* EKDAL *enters with a fresh rabbit skin; she closes the door after him.*

EKDAL: Good morning, gentlemen! Good sport today. Shot a big one.

HIALMAR: And you've gone and skinned it without waiting for me—!

EKDAL: Salted it, too. It's good tender meat, is rabbit; it's sweet; it tastes like sugar. Good appetite to you, gentlemen! *(Goes into his room.)*

MOLVIK *(rising):* Excuse me—; I can't—; I must get downstairs immediately—

RELLING: Drink some soda water, man!

MOLVIK *(hurrying away):* Ugh—ugh! *(Goes out by the passage door.)*

RELLING *(to* HIALMAR*):* Let us drain a glass to the old hunter.

HIALMAR *(clinks glasses with him):* To the undaunted sportsman who has looked death in the face!

RELLING: To the gray-haired— *(Drinks.)* By-the-bye, is his hair gray or white?

HIALMAR: Something between the two, I fancy; for that matter, he has very few hairs left of any color.

RELLING: Well, well, one can get through the world with a wig. After all, you are a happy man, Ekdal; you have your noble mission to labor for—

HIALMAR: And I do labor, I can tell you.

RELLING: And then you have your excellent wife, shuffling quietly in and out in her felt slippers, and that seesaw walk of hers, and making everything cosy and comfortable about you.

HIALMAR: Yes, Gina—*(nods to her)*—you were a good helpmate on the path of life.

GINA: Oh, don't sit there cricketizing me.

RELLING: And your Hedvig, too, Ekdal!

HIALMAR (*affected*): The child, yes! The child before everything! Hedvig, come here to me. (*Strokes her hair.*) What day is it tomorrow, eh?

HEDVIG (*shaking him*): Oh, no, you're not to say anything, Father.

HIALMAR: It cuts me to the heart when I think what a poor affair it will be; only a little festivity in the garret—

HEDVIG: Oh, but that's just what I like!

RELLING: Just you wait till the wonderful invention sees the light, Hedvig!

HIALMAR: Yes, indeed—then you shall see—! Hedvig, I have resolved to make your future secure. You shall live in comfort all your days. I will demand—something or other—on your behalf. That shall be the poor inventor's sole reward.

HEDVIG (*whispering, with her arms round his neck*): Oh, you dear, kind father!

RELLING (*to* GREGERS): Come now, don't you find it pleasant, for once in a way, to sit at a well-spread table in a happy family circle?

HIALMAR: Ah, yes, I really prize these social hours.

GREGERS: For my part, I don't thrive in marsh vapors.

RELLING: Marsh vapors?

HIALMAR: Oh, don't begin with that stuff again!

GINA: Goodness knows there's no vapors in this house, Mr. Werle; I give the place a good airing every blessed day.

GREGERS (*leaves the table*): No airing you can give will drive out the taint I mean.

HIALMAR: Taint!

GINA: Yes, what do you say to that, Ekdal!

RELLING: Excuse me—may it not be you yourself that have brought the taint from those mines up there?

GREGERS: It is like you to call what I bring into this house a taint.

RELLING (*goes up to him*): Look here, Mr. Werle, junior: I have a strong suspicion that you are still carrying about that "claim of the ideal" large as life, in your coattail pocket.

GREGERS: I carry it in my breast.

RELLING: Well, wherever you carry it, I advise you not to come dunning us with it here, so long as *I* am on the premises.

GREGERS: And if I do so nonetheless?

RELLING: Then you'll go head-foremost down the stairs; now I've warned you.

HIALMAR *(rising)*: Oh, but Relling—!

GREGERS: Yes, you may turn me out—

GINA *(interposing between them)*: We can't have that, Relling. But I must say, Mr. Werle, it ill becomes you to talk about vapors and taints, after all the mess you made with your stove.

A knock at the passage door.

HEDVIG: Mother, there's somebody knocking.

HIALMAR: There now, we're going to have a whole lot of people!

GINA: I'll go— *(Goes over and opens the door, starts, and draws back.)* Oh—oh, dear!

WERLE, *in a fur coat, advances one step into the room.*

WERLE: Excuse me; but I think my son is staying here.

GINA *(with a gulp)*: Yes.

HIALMAR *(approaching him)*: Won't you do us the honor to—?

WERLE: Thank you, I merely wish to speak to my son.

GREGERS: What is it? Here I am.

WERLE: I want a few words with you, in your room.

GREGERS: In my room? Very well— *(About to go.)*

GINA: No, no, your room's not in a fit state—

WERLE: Well then, out in the passage here; I want to have a few words with you alone.

HIALMAR: You can have them here, sir. Come into the parlor, Relling.

HIALMAR *and* RELLING *go off to the right.* GINA *takes* HEDVIG *with her into the kitchen.*

GREGERS *(after a short pause)*: Well, now we are alone.

WERLE: From something you let fall last evening, and from your coming to lodge with the Ekdals, I can't help inferring that you intend to make yourself unpleasant to me, in one way or another.

GREGERS: I intend to open Hialmar Ekdal's eyes. He shall see his position as it really is—that is all.

WERLE: Is that the mission in life you spoke of yesterday?

GREGERS: Yes. You have left me no other.

WERLE: Is it I, then, that have crippled your mind, Gregers?

GREGERS: You have crippled my whole life. I am not thinking of all that about Mother— But it's thanks to you that I am continually haunted and harassed by a guilty conscience.

WERLE: Indeed! It is your conscience that troubles you, is it?

GREGERS: I ought to have taken a stand against you when the trap was set for Lieutenant Ekdal. I ought to have cautioned him; for I had a misgiving as to what was in the wind.

WERLE: Yes, that was the time to have spoken.

GREGERS: I did not dare to, I was so cowed and spiritless. I was mortally afraid of you—not only then, but long afterward.

WERLE: You have got over that fear now, it appears.

GREGERS: Yes, fortunately. The wrong done to old Ekdal, both by me and by—others, can never be undone; but Hialmar I can rescue from all the falsehood and deception that are bringing him to ruin.

WERLE: Do you think that will be doing him a kindness?

GREGERS: I have not the least doubt of it.

WERLE: You think our worthy photographer is the sort of man to appreciate such friendly offices?

GREGERS: Yes, I do.

WERLE: Hm—we shall see.

GREGERS: Besides, if I am to go on living, I must try to find some cure for my sick conscience.

WERLE: It will never be sound. Your conscience has been sickly from childhood. That is a legacy from your mother, Gregers—the only one she left you.

GREGERS (*with a scornful half smile*): Have you not yet forgiven her for the mistake you made in supposing she would bring you a fortune?

WERLE: Don't let us wander from the point.—Then you hold to your purpose of setting young Ekdal upon what you imagine to be the right scent?

GREGERS: Yes, that is my fixed resolve.

WERLE: Well, in that case I might have spared myself this visit; for, of course, it is useless to ask whether you will return home with me?

GREGERS: Quite useless.

WERLE: And I suppose you won't enter the firm either?

GREGERS: No.

WERLE: Very good. But as I am thinking of marrying again, your share in the property [19] will fall to you at once.

GREGERS (*quickly*): No, I do not want that.

WERLE: You don't want it?

GREGERS: No, I dare not take it, for conscience' sake.

WERLE (*after a pause*): Are you going up to the works again?

GREGERS: No; I consider myself released from your service.

WERLE: But what are you going to do?

GREGERS: Only to fulfill my mission; nothing more.

WERLE: Well, but afterward? What are you going to live upon?

GREGERS: I have laid by a little out of my salary.

WERLE: How long will that last?

GREGERS: I think it will last my time.

WERLE: What do you mean?

GREGERS: I shall answer no more questions.

WERLE: Good-bye then, Gregers.

GREGERS: Good-bye.

WERLE *goes.*

HIALMAR *(peeping in)*: He's gone, isn't he?
GREGERS: Yes.

> HIALMAR *and* RELLING *enter; also* GINA *and* HEDVIG *from the kitchen.*

RELLING: That luncheon party was a failure.
GREGERS: Put on your coat, Hialmar; I want you to come for a long walk with me.
HIALMAR: With pleasure. What was it your father wanted? Had it anything to do with me?
GREGERS: Come along. We must have a talk. I'll go and put on my overcoat. *(Goes out by the passage door.)*
GINA: You shouldn't go out with him, Ekdal.
RELLING: No, don't you do it. Stay where you are.
HIALMAR *(gets his hat and overcoat)*: Oh, nonsense! When a friend of my youth feels impelled to open his mind to me in private—
RELLING: But devil take it—don't you see that the fellow's mad, cracked, demented!
GINA: There, what did I tell you! His mother before him had crazy fits like that sometimes.
HIALMAR: The more need for a friend's watchful eye. *(To* GINA.*)* Be sure you have dinner ready in good time. Good-bye for the present. *(Goes out by the passage door.)*
RELLING: It's a thousand pities the fellow didn't go to hell through one of the Höidal mines.
GINA: Good Lord! what makes you say that?
RELLING *(muttering)*: Oh, I have my own reasons.
GINA: Do you think young Werle is really mad?
RELLING: No, worse luck; he's no madder than most other people. But one disease he has certainly got in his system.
GINA: What is it that's the matter with him?
RELLING: Well, I'll tell you, Mrs. Ekdal. He is suffering from an acute attack of integrity.

GINA: Integrity?

HEDVIG: Is that a kind of disease?

RELLING: Yes, it's a national disease; but it only appears sporadically. (*Nods to* GINA.) Thanks for your hospitality. (*He goes out by the passage door.*)

GINA (*moving restlessly to and fro*): Ugh, that Gregers Werle—he was always a wretched creature.

HEDVIG (*standing by the table and looking searchingly at her*): I think all this is very strange.

ACT FOUR

HIALMAR EKDAL'S *studio. A photograph has just been taken; a camera with the cloth over it, a pedestal, two chairs, a folding table, etc., are standing out in the room. Afternoon light; the sun is going down; a little later it begins to grow dusk.*

GINA *stands in the passage doorway, with a little box and a wet glass plate in her hand, and is speaking to somebody outside.*

GINA: Yes, certainly. When I make a promise I keep it. The first dozen shall be ready on Monday. Good afternoon.

Someone is heard going downstairs. GINA *shuts the door, slips the plate into the box and puts it into the covered camera.*

HEDVIG (*comes in from the kitchen*): Are they gone?

GINA (*tidying up*): Yes, thank goodness, I've got rid of them at last.

HEDVIG: But can you imagine why Father hasn't come home yet?

GINA: Are you sure he's not down in Relling's room?

HEDVIG: No, he's not; I ran down the kitchen stair just now and asked.

GINA: And his dinner standing and getting cold, too.

HEDVIG: Yes, I can't understand it. Father's always so careful to be home to dinner!

GINA: Oh, he'll be here directly, you'll see.

HEDVIG: I wish he would come; everything seems so queer today.

GINA (*calls out*): There he is!

HIALMAR EKDAL *comes in at the passage door.*

HEDVIG (*going to him*): Father! Oh, what a time we've been waiting for you!

GINA (*glancing sidelong at him*): You've been out a long time, Ekdal.

HIALMAR (*without looking at her*): Rather long, yes.

He takes off his overcoat; GINA *and* HEDVIG *go to help him; he motions them away.*

GINA: Perhaps you've had dinner with Werle?

HIALMAR (*hanging up his coat*): No.

GINA (*going toward the kitchen door*): Then I'll bring some in for you.

HIALMAR: No; let the dinner alone. I want nothing to eat.

HEDVIG (*going nearer to him*): Are you not well, Father?

HIALMAR: Well? Oh, yes, well enough. We have had a tiring walk, Gregers and I.

GINA: You didn't ought to have gone so far, Ekdal; you're not used to it.

HIALMAR: Hm; there's many a thing a man must get used to in this world. (*Wanders about the room.*) Has anyone been here while I was out?

GINA: Nobody but the two sweethearts.

HIALMAR: No new orders?

GINA: No, not today.

HEDVIG: There will be some tomorrow, Father, you'll see.

HIALMAR: I hope there will; for tomorrow I am going to set to work in real earnest.

HEDVIG: Tomorrow! Don't you remember what day it is tomorrow?

HIALMAR: Oh, yes, by-the-bye—. Well, the day after, then. Henceforth I mean to do everything myself; I shall take all the work into my own hands.

GINA: Why, what can be the good of that, Ekdal? It'll only make your life a burden to you. I can manage the photography all right; and you can go on working at your invention.

HEDVIG: And think of the wild duck, Father,—and all the hens and rabbits and—!

HIALMAR: Don't talk to me of all that trash! From tomorrow I will never set foot in the garret again.

HEDVIG: Oh, but Father, you promised that we should have a little party—

HIALMAR: Hm, true. Well, then, from the day after tomorrow. I should almost like to wring that cursed wild duck's neck!

HEDVIG (shrieks): The wild duck!

GINA: Well, I never!

HEDVIG (shaking him): Oh, no, Father; you know it's my wild duck!

HIALMAR: That is why I don't do it. I haven't the heart to— for your sake, Hedvig. But in my inmost soul I feel that I ought to do it. I ought not to tolerate under my roof a creature that has been through those hands.

GINA: Why, good gracious, even if Grandfather did get it from that poor creature, Pettersen—

HIALMAR (wandering about): There are certain claims— what shall I call them?—let me say claims of the ideal— certain obligations, which a man cannot disregard without injury to his soul.

HEDVIG (going after him): But think of the wild duck,—the poor wild duck!

HIALMAR *(stops)*: I tell you I will spare it—for your sake. Not a hair of its head shall be—I mean, it shall be spared. There are greater problems than that to be dealt with. But you should go out a little now, Hedvig, as usual; it is getting dusk enough for you now.

HEDVIG: No, I don't care about going out now.

HIALMAR: Yes, do; it seems to me your eyes are blinking a great deal; all these vapors in here are bad for you. The air is heavy under this roof.

HEDVIG: Very well, then, I'll run down the kitchen stair and go for a little walk. My cloak and hat?—oh, they're in my own room. Father—be sure you don't do the wild duck any harm while I'm out.

HIALMAR: Not a feather of its head shall be touched. *(Draws her to him.)* You and I, Hedvig—we two—! Well, go along.

HEDVIG *nods to her parents and goes out through the kitchen.*

HIALMAR *(walks about without looking up)*: Gina.

GINA: Yes?

HIALMAR: From tomorrow—or, say, from the day after tomorrow—I should like to keep the household account book myself.

GINA: Do you want to keep the accounts, too, now?

HIALMAR: Yes; or to check the receipts at any rate.

GINA: Lord help us! that's soon done.

HIALMAR: One would hardly think so; at any rate, you seem to make the money go a very long way. *(Stops and looks at her.)* How do you manage it?

GINA: It's because me and Hedvig, we need so little.

HIALMAR: Is it the case that Father is very liberally paid for the copying he does for Mr. Werle?

GINA: I don't know as he gets anything out of the way. I don't know the rates for that sort of work.

HIALMAR: Well, what does he get, about? Let me hear!

GINA: Oh, it varies; I daresay it'll come to about as much as he costs us, with a little pocket money over.

HIALMAR: As much as he costs us! And you have never told me this before!

GINA: No, how could I tell you? It pleased you so much to think he got everything from you.

HIALMAR: And he gets it from Mr. Werle.

GINA: Oh, well, he has plenty and to spare, he has.

HIALMAR: Light the lamp for me, please!

GINA *(lighting the lamp)*: And, of course, we don't know as it's Mr. Werle himself; it may be Gråberg—

HIALMAR: Why attempt such an evasion?

GINA: I don't know; I only thought—

HIALMAR: Hm.

GINA: It wasn't me that got Grandfather that copying. It was Bertha, when she used to come about us.

HIALMAR: It seems to me your voice is trembling.

GINA *(putting the lamp shade on)*: Is it?

HIALMAR: And your hands are shaking, are they not?

GINA *(firmly)*: Come right out with it, Ekdal. What has he been saying about me?

HIALMAR: Is it true—can it be true that—that there was an—an understanding between you and Mr. Werle, while you were in service there?

GINA: That's not true. Not at that time. Mr. Werle did come after me, that's a fact. And his wife thought there was something in it, and then she made such a hocus-pocus and hurly-burly, and she hustled me and bustled me about so that I left her service.

HIALMAR: But afterward, then?

GINA: Well, then I went home. And Mother—well, she wasn't the woman you took her for, Ekdal; she kept on worrying and worrying at me about one thing and another—for Mr. Werle was a widower by that time.

HIALMAR: Well, and then?

GINA: I suppose you've got to know it. He gave me no peace until he'd had his way.

HIALMAR *(striking his hands together)*: And this is the mother of my child! How could you hide this from me?

GINA: Yes, it was wrong of me; I ought certainly to have told you long ago.

HIALMAR: You should have told me at the very first;—then I should have known the sort of woman you were.

GINA: But would you have married me all the same?

HIALMAR: How can you dream that I would?

GINA: That's just why I didn't dare tell you anything, then. For I'd come to care for you so much, you see; and I couldn't go and make myself utterly miserable—

HIALMAR *(walks about)*: And this is my Hedvig's mother. And to know that all I see before me—*(kicks a chair)*—all that I call my home—I owe to a favored predecessor! Oh, that scoundrel Werle!

GINA: Do you repent of the fourteen—the fifteen years we've lived together?

HIALMAR *(placing himself in front of her)*: Have you not every day, every hour, repented of the spider's web of deceit you have spun around me? Answer me that! How could you help writhing with penitence and remorse?

GINA: Oh, my dear Ekdal, I've had all I could do to look after the house and get through the day's work—

HIALMAR: Then you never think of reviewing your past?

GINA: No; Heaven knows I'd almost forgotten those old stories.

HIALMAR: Oh, this dull, callous contentment! To me there is something revolting about it. Think of it—never so much as a twinge of remorse!

GINA: But tell me, Ekdal—what would have become of you if you hadn't had a wife like me?

HIALMAR: Like you—!

GINA: Yes; for you know I've always been a bit more practical and wide awake than you. Of course I'm a year or two older.

HIALMAR: What would have become of me!

GINA: You'd got into all sorts of bad ways when first you met me; that you can't deny.

HIALMAR: "Bad ways" do you call them? Little do you know

what a man goes through when he is in grief and despair—especially a man of my fiery temperament.

GINA: Well, well, that may be so. And I've no reason to crow over you, neither; for you turned a moral of a husband, that you did, as soon as ever you had a house and home of your own.—And now we'd got everything so nice and cosy about us; and me and Hedvig was just thinking we'd soon be able to let ourselves go a bit, in the way of both food and clothes.

HIALMAR: In the swamp of deceit, yes.

GINA: I wish to goodness that detestable thing had never set his foot inside our doors!

HIALMAR: And I, too, thought my home such a pleasant one. That was a delusion. Where shall I now find the elasticity of spirit to bring my invention into the world of reality? Perhaps it will die with me; and then it will be your past, Gina, that will have killed it.

GINA (*nearly crying*): You mustn't say such things, Ekdal. Me, that has only wanted to do the best I could for you, all my days!

HIALMAR: I ask you, what becomes of the breadwinner's dream? When I used to lie in there on the sofa and brood over my invention, I had a clear enough presentiment that it would sap my vitality to the last drop. I felt even then that the day when I held the patent in my hand—that day—would bring my—release. And then it was my dream that you should live on after me, the dead inventor's well-to-do widow.

GINA (*drying her tears*): No, you mustn't talk like that, Ekdal. May the Lord never let me see the day I am left a widow!

HIALMAR: Oh, the whole dream has vanished. It is all over now. All over!

GREGERS WERLE *opens the passage door cautiously and looks in.*

GREGERS: May I come in?

HIALMAR: Yes, come in.

GREGERS (*comes forward, his face beaming with satisfaction, and holds out both his hands to them*): Well, dear friends—! (*Looks from one to the other and whispers to* HIALMAR.) Have you not done it yet?

HIALMAR (*aloud*): It is done.

GREGERS: It is?

HIALMAR: I have passed through the bitterest moments of my life.

GREGERS: But also, I trust, the most ennobling.

HIALMAR: Well, at any rate, we have got through it for the present.

GINA: God forgive you, Mr. Werle.

GREGERS (*in great surprise*): But I don't understand this.

HIALMAR: What don't you understand?

GREGERS: After so great a crisis—a crisis that is to be the starting point of an entirely new life—of a communion founded on truth, and free from all taint of deception—

HIALMAR: Yes, yes, I know; I know that quite well.

GREGERS: I confidently expected, when I entered the room, to find the light of transfiguration shining upon me from both husband and wife. And now I see nothing but dullness, oppression, gloom—

GINA: Oh, is that it? (*Takes off the lamp shade.*)

GREGERS: You will not understand me, Mrs. Ekdal. Ah, well, you, I suppose, need time to—. But you, Hialmar? Surely you feel a new consecration after the great crisis.

HIALMAR: Yes, of course I do. That is—in a sort of way.

GREGERS: For surely nothing in the world can compare with the joy of forgiving one who has erred and raising her up to oneself in love.

HIALMAR: Do you think a man can so easily throw off the bitter cup I have drained?

GREGERS: No, not a common man, perhaps. But a man like you—!

HIALMAR: Good God! I know that well enough. But you must keep me up to it, Gregers. It takes time, you know.

GREGERS: You have much of the wild duck in you, Hialmar.

RELLING *has come in at the passage door.*

RELLING: Oho! is the wild duck to the fore again?

HIALMAR: Yes; Mr. Werle's wing-broken victim.

RELLING: Mr. Werle's—? So it's him you are talking about?

HIALMAR: Him and—ourselves.

RELLING (*in an undertone to* GREGERS): May the devil fly away with you!

HIALMAR: What is that you are saying?

RELLING: Only uttering a heartfelt wish that this quack-salver would take himself off. If he stays here, he is quite equal to making an utter mess of life, for both of you.

GREGERS: These two will not make a mess of life, Mr. Relling. Of course I won't speak of Hialmar—him we know. But she, too, in her innermost heart, has certainly something loyal and sincere—

GINA (*almost crying*): You might have let me alone for what I was, then.

RELLING (*to* GREGERS): Is it rude to ask what you really want in this house?

GREGERS: To lay the foundations of a true marriage.

RELLING: So you don't think Ekdal's marriage is good enough as it is?

GREGERS: No doubt it is as good a marriage as most others, worse luck. But a true marriage it has yet to become.

HIALMAR: You have never had eyes for the claims of the ideal, Relling.

RELLING: Rubbish, my boy!—but excuse me, Mr. Werle: how many—in round numbers—how many true marriages have you seen in the course of your life?

GREGERS: Scarcely a single one.

RELLING: Nor I either.

GREGERS: But I have seen innumerable marriages of the opposite kind. And it has been my fate to see at close quarters what ruin such a marriage can work in two human souls.

HIALMAR: A man's whole moral basis may give away beneath his feet; that is the terrible part of it.

RELLING: Well, I can't say I've ever been exactly married, so I don't pretend to speak with authority. But this I know, that the child enters into the marriage problem. And you must leave the child in peace.

HIALMAR: Oh—Hedvig! my poor Hedvig!

RELLING: Yes, you must be good enough to keep Hedvig outside of all this. You two are grown-up people; you are free, in God's name, to make what mess and muddle you please of your life. But you must deal cautiously with Hedvig, I tell you; else you may do her a great injury.

HIALMAR: An injury!

RELLING: Yes, or she may do herself an injury—and perhaps others, too.

GINA: How can you know that, Relling?

HIALMAR: Her sight is in no immediate danger, is it?

RELLING: I am not talking about her sight. Hedvig is at a critical age. She may be getting all sorts of mischief into her head.

GINA: That's true—I've noticed it already! She's taken to carrying on with the fire, out in the kitchen. She calls it playing at house-on-fire. I'm often scared for fear she really sets fire to the house.

RELLING: You see; I thought as much.

GREGERS (to RELLING): But how do you account for that?

RELLING (sullenly): Her constitution's changing, sir.

HIALMAR: So long as the child has me—! So long as I am above ground—!

A knock at the door.

GINA: Hush, Ekdal; there's someone in the passage. (*Calls out.*) Come in!

MRS. SÖRBY, *in walking dress, comes in.*

MRS. SÖRBY: Good evening.

GINA (*going toward her*): Is it really you, Bertha?

MRS. SÖRBY: Yes, of course it is. But I'm disturbing you, I'm afraid?

HIALMAR: No, not at all; an emissary from that house—

MRS. SÖRBY (*to* GINA): To tell the truth, I hoped your menfolk would be out at this time. I just ran up to have a little chat with you, and to say good-bye.

GINA: Good-bye? Are you going away, then?

MRS. SÖRBY: Yes, tomorrow morning,—up to Höidal. Mr. Werle started this afternoon. (*Lightly to* GREGERS.) He asked me to say good-bye for him.

GINA: Only fancy—!

HIALMAR: So Mr. Werle has gone? And now you are going after him?

MRS. SÖRBY: Yes, what do you say to that, Ekdal?

HIALMAR: I say: beware!

GREGERS: I must explain the situation. My father and Mrs. Sörby are going to be married.

HIALMAR: Going to be married!

GINA: Oh, Bertha! So it's come to that at last!

RELLING (*his voice quivering a little*): This is surely not true?

MRS. SÖRBY: Yes, my dear Relling, it's true enough.

RELLING: You are going to marry again?

MRS. SÖRBY: Yes, it looks like it. Werle has got a special license, and we are going to be married quite quietly, up at the works.

GREGERS: Then I must wish you all happiness, like a dutiful stepson.

MRS. SÖRBY: Thank you very much—if you mean what you say. I certainly hope it will lead to happiness, both for Werle and for me.

RELLING: You have every reason to hope that. Mr. Werle never gets drunk—so far as I know; and I don't suppose he's in the habit of thrashing his wives, like the late lamented horse doctor.

MRS. SÖRBY: Come now, let Sörby rest in peace. He had his good points, too.

RELLING: Mr. Werle has better ones, I have no doubt.

MRS. SÖRBY: He hasn't frittered away all that was good in him, at any rate. The man who does that must take the consequences.

RELLING: I shall go out with Molvik this evening.

MRS. SÖRBY: You mustn't do that, Relling. Don't do it—for my sake.

RELLING: There's nothing else for it. (*To* HIALMAR.) If you're going with us, come along.

GINA: No, thank you. Ekdal doesn't go in for that sort of dissertation.

HIALMAR (*half aloud, in vexation*): Oh, do hold your tongue!

RELLING: Good-bye, Mrs.—Werle. (*Goes out through the passage door.*)

GREGERS (*to* MRS. SÖRBY): You seem to know Dr. Relling pretty intimately.

MRS. SÖRBY: Yes, we have known each other for many years. At one time it seemed as if things might have gone further between us.

GREGERS: It was surely lucky for you that they did not.

MRS. SÖRBY: You may well say that. But I have always been wary of acting on impulse. A woman can't afford absolutely to throw herself away.

GREGERS: Are you not in the least afraid that I may let my father know about this old friendship?

MRS. SÖRBY: Why, of course, I have told him all about it myself.

GREGERS: Indeed?

MRS. SÖRBY: Your father knows every single thing that can, with any truth, be said about me. I have told him all; it was the first thing I did when I saw what was in his mind.

GREGERS: Then you have been franker than most people, I think.

MRS. SÖRBY: I have always been frank. We women find that the best policy.

HIALMAR: What do you say to that, Gina?

GINA: Oh, we're not all alike, us women aren't. Some are made one way, some another.

MRS. SÖRBY: Well, for my part, Gina, I believe it's wisest to do as I've done. And Werle has no secrets either, on his side. That's really the great bond between us, you see. Now he can talk to me as openly as a child. He has never had the chance to do that before. Fancy a man like him, full of health and vigor, passing his whole youth and the best years of his life in listening to nothing but penitential sermons! And very often the sermons had for their text the most imaginary offenses—at least so I understand.

GINA: That's true enough.

GREGERS: If you ladies are going to follow up this topic, I had better withdraw.

MRS. SÖRBY: You can stay as far as that's concerned. I shan't say a word more. But I wanted you to know that I had done nothing secretly or in an underhand way. I may seem to have come in for a great piece of luck; and so I have, in a sense. But after all, I don't think I am getting any more than I am giving. I shall stand by him always, and I can tend and care for him as no one else can, now that he is getting helpless.

HIALMAR: Getting helpless?

GREGERS (to MRS. SÖRBY): Hush, don't speak of that here.

MRS. SÖRBY: There is no disguising it any longer, however much he would like to. He is going blind.

HIALMAR (starts): Going blind? That's strange. He, too, going blind!

GINA: Lots of people do.

MRS. SÖRBY: And you can imagine what that means to a business man. Well, I shall try as well as I can to make my eyes take the place of his. But I mustn't stay any longer; I have heaps of things to do.—Oh, by-the-bye, Ekdal, I was to tell you that if there is anything Werle can do for you, you must just apply to Gråberg.

GREGERS: That offer I am sure Hialmar Ekdal will decline with thanks.

MRS. SÖRBY: Indeed? I don't think he used to be so—

GINA: No, Bertha, Ekdal doesn't need anything from Mr. Werle now.

HIALMAR (*slowly, and with emphasis*): Will you present my compliments to your future husband and say that I intend very shortly to call upon Mr. Gråberg—

GREGERS: What! You don't really mean that?

HIALMAR: To call upon Mr. Gråberg, I say, and obtain an account of the sum I owe his principal. I will pay that debt of honor—ha ha ha! a debt of honor, let us call it! In any case, I will pay the whole with five percent interest.

GINA: But, my dear Ekdal, God knows we haven't got the money to do it.

HIALMAR: Be good enough to tell your future husband that I am working assiduously at my invention. Please tell him that what sustains me in this laborious task is the wish to free myself from a torturing burden of debt. That is my reason for proceeding with the invention. The entire profits shall be devoted to releasing me from my pecuniary obligations to your future husband.

MRS. SÖRBY: Something has happened here.

HIALMAR: Yes, you are right.

MRS. SÖRBY: Well, good-bye. I had something else to speak to you about, Gina; but it must keep till another time. Good-bye.

HIALMAR *and* GREGERS *bow silently.* GINA *follows* MRS. SÖRBY *to the door.*

HIALMAR: Not beyond the threshold, Gina!

MRS. SÖRBY *goes;* GINA *shuts the door after her.*

HIALMAR: There now, Gregers; I have got that burden of debt off my mind.

GREGERS: You soon will, at all events.

HIALMAR: I think my attitude may be called correct.

GREGERS: You are the man I have always taken you for.

HIALMAR: In certain cases, it is impossible to disregard the claim of the ideal. Yet, as the breadwinner of a family, I cannot but writhe and groan under it. I can tell you it is no joke for a man without capital to attempt the repayment of a long-standing obligation, over which, so to speak, the dust of oblivion had gathered. But it cannot be helped: the Man in me demands his rights.

GREGERS (*laying his hand on* HIALMAR's *shoulder*): My dear Hialmar—was it not a good thing I came?

HIALMAR: Yes.

GREGERS: Are you not glad to have had your true position made clear to you?

HIALMAR (*somewhat impatiently*): Yes, of course I am. But there is one thing that is revolting to my sense of justice.

GREGERS: And what is that?

HIALMAR: It is that—but I don't know whether I ought to express myself so unreservedly about your father.

GREGERS: Say what you please, so far as I am concerned.

HIALMAR: Well, then, is it not exasperating to think that it is not I, but he, who will realize the true marriage?

GREGERS: How can you say such a thing?

HIALMAR: Because it is clearly the case. Isn't the marriage between your father and Mrs. Sörby founded upon complete confidence, upon entire and unreserved candor on both sides? They hide nothing from each other, they keep no secrets in the background; their relation is based, if I may put it so, on mutual confession and absolution.

GREGERS: Well, what then?

HIALMAR: Well, is not that the whole thing? Did you not yourself say that this was precisely the difficulty that had to be overcome in order to found a true marriage?

GREGERS: But this is a totally different matter, Hialmar. You surely don't compare either yourself or your wife with those two—? Oh, you understand me well enough.

HIALMAR: Say what you like, there is something in all this that hurts and offends my sense of justice. It really looks as if there were no just providence to rule the world.

GINA: Oh, no, Ekdal; for God's sake don't say such things.

GREGERS: Hm; don't let us get upon those questions.

HIALMAR: And yet, after all, I cannot but recognize the guiding finger of fate. He is going blind.

GINA: Oh, you can't be sure of that.

HIALMAR: There is no doubt about it. At all events there ought not to be; for in that very fact lies the righteous retribution. He has hoodwinked a confiding fellow creature in days gone by—

GREGERS: I fear he has hoodwinked many.

HIALMAR: And now comes inexorable, mysterious Fate and demands Werle's own eyes.

GINA: Oh, how dare you say such dreadful things! You make me quite scared.

HIALMAR: It is profitable, now and then, to plunge deep into the night side of existence.

HEDVIG, *in her hat and cloak, comes in by the passage door. She is pleasurably excited and out of breath.*

GINA: Are you back already?

HEDVIG: Yes, I didn't care to go any farther. It was a good thing, too; for I've just met someone at the door.

HIALMAR: It must have been that Mrs. Sörby.

HEDVIG: Yes.

HIALMAR (*walks up and down*): I hope you have seen her for the last time.

Silence. HEDVIG, *discouraged, looks first at one and then at the other, trying to divine their frame of mind.*

HEDVIG (*approaching, coaxingly*): Father.

HIALMAR: Well—what is it, Hedvig?

HEDVIG: Mrs. Sörby had something with her for me.

HIALMAR (*stops*): For you?

HEDVIG: Yes. Something for tomorrow.

GINA: Bertha has always given you some little thing on your birthday.

HIALMAR: What is it?

HEDVIG: Oh, you mustn't see it now. Mother is to give it to me tomorrow morning before I'm up.

HIALMAR: What is all this hocus-pocus that I am to be in the dark about!

HEDVIG (quickly): Oh, no, you may see it if you like. It's a big letter.

Takes the letter out of her cloak pocket.

HIALMAR: A letter, too?

HEDVIG: Yes, it is only a letter. The rest will come afterward, I suppose. But fancy—a letter! I've never had a letter before. And there's "Miss" written upon it. (Reads.) "Miss Hedvig Ekdal." Only fancy—that's me!

HIALMAR: Let me see that letter.

HEDVIG (hands it to him): There it is.

HIALMAR: That is Mr. Werle's hand.

GINA: Are you sure of that, Ekdal?

HIALMAR: Look for yourself.

GINA: Oh, what do I know about such-like things?

HIALMAR: Hedvig, may I open the letter—and read it?

HEDVIG: Yes, of course you may, if you want to.

GINA: No, not tonight, Ekdal; it's to be kept till tomorrow.

HEDVIG (softly): Oh, can't you let him read it! It's sure to be something good; and then Father will be glad, and everything will be nice again.

HIALMAR: I may open it, then?

HEDVIG: Yes, do, Father. I'm so anxious to know what it is.

HIALMAR: Well and good. (Opens the letter, takes out a paper, reads it through and appears bewildered.) What is this—!

GINA: What does it say?

HEDVIG: Oh, yes, Father—tell us!

HIALMAR: Be quiet. (Reads it through again; he has turned pale, but says with self-control): It is a deed of gift, Hedvig.

HEDVIG: Is it? What sort of gift am I to have?

HIALMAR: Read for yourself.

HEDVIG goes over and reads for a time by the lamp.

HIALMAR *(half aloud, clenching his hands)*: The eyes! The eyes—and then that letter!

HEDVIG *(leaves off reading)*: Yes, but it seems to me that it's Grandfather that's to have it.

HIALMAR *(takes letter from her)*: Gina—can you understand this?

GINA: I know nothing whatever about it; tell me what's the matter.

HIALMAR: Mr. Werle writes to Hedvig that her old grandfather need not trouble himself any longer with the copying, but that he can henceforth draw on the office for a hundred crowns a month—

GREGERS: Aha!

HEDVIG: A hundred crowns, Mother! I read that.

GINA: What a good thing for Grandfather!

HIALMAR: —a hundred crowns a month so long as he needs it—that means, of course, so long as he lives.

GINA: Well, so he's provided for, poor dear.

HIALMAR: But there is more to come. You didn't read that, Hedvig. Afterward this gift is to pass on to you.

HEDVIG: To me! The whole of it?

HIALMAR: He says that the same amount is assured to you for the whole of your life. Do you hear that, Gina?

GINA: Yes, I hear.

HEDVIG: Fancy—all that money for me! *(Shakes him.)* Father, Father, aren't you glad—?

HIALMAR *(eluding her)*: Glad? *(Walks about.)* Oh what vistas—what perspectives open up before me! It is Hedvig, Hedvig that he showers these benefactions upon!

GINA: Yes, because it's Hedvig's birthday—

HEDVIG: And you'll get it all the same, Father! You know quite well I shall give all the money to you and Mother.

HIALMAR: To Mother, yes! There we have it.

GREGERS: Hialmar, this is a trap he is setting for you.

HIALMAR: Do you think it's another trap?

GREGERS: When he was here this morning he said: Hialmar Ekdal is not the man you imagine him to be.

HIALMAR: Not the man—!

GREGERS: That you shall see, he said.

HIALMAR: He meant you should see that I would let myself be bought off—!

HEDVIG: Oh, Mother, what does all this mean?

GINA: Go and take off your things.

HEDVIG *goes out by the kitchen door, half crying.*

GREGERS: Yes, Hialmar—now is the time to show who was right, he or I.

HIALMAR (*slowly tears the paper across, lays both pieces on the table and says*): Here is my answer.

GREGERS: Just what I expected.

HIALMAR (*goes over to* GINA, *who stands by the stove, and says in a low voice*): Now please make a clean breast of it. If the connection between you and him was quite over when you—came to care for me, as you call it—why did he place us in a position to marry?

GINA: I suppose he thought as he could come and go in our house.

HIALMAR: Only that? Was not he afraid of a possible contingency?

GINA: I don't know what you mean.

HIALMAR: I want to know whether—your child has the right to live under my roof.

GINA (*draws herself up; her eyes flash*): You ask that!

HIALMAR: You shall answer me this one question: Does Hedvig belong to me—or—? Well!

GINA (*looking at him with cold defiance*): I don't know.

HIALMAR (*quivering a little*): You don't know!

GINA: How should *I* know. A creature like me—

HIALMAR (*quietly turning away from her*): Then I have nothing more to do in this house.

GREGERS: Take care, Hialmar! Think what you are doing!

HIALMAR (*puts on his overcoat*): In this case, there is nothing for a man like me to think twice about.

GREGERS: Yes, indeed, there are endless things to be considered. You three must be together if you are to attain the true frame of mind for self-sacrifice and forgiveness.

HIALMAR: I don't want to attain it. Never, never! My hat! *(Takes his hat.)* My home has fallen in ruins about me. *(Bursts into tears.)* Gregers, I have no child!

HEDVIG *(who has opened the kitchen door)*: What is that you're saying? *(Coming to him.)* Father, Father!

GINA: There, you see!

HIALMAR: Don't come near me, Hedvig! Keep far away. I cannot bear to see you. Oh! those eyes—! Good-bye. *(Makes for the door.)*

HEDVIG *(clinging close to him and screaming loudly)*: No! no! Don't leave me!

GINA *(cries out)*: Look at the child, Ekdal! Look at the child!

HIALMAR: I will not! I cannot! I must get out—away from all this!

He tears himself away from HEDVIG *and goes out by the passage door.*

HEDVIG *(with despairing eyes)*: He is going away from us, Mother! He is going away from us! He will never come back again!

GINA: Don't cry, Hedvig. Father's sure to come back again.

HEDVIG *(throws herself sobbing on the sofa)*: No, no, he'll never come home to us anymore.

GREGERS: Do you believe I meant all for the best, Mrs. Ekdal?

GINA: Yes, I daresay you did; but God forgive you, all the same.

HEDVIG *(lying on the sofa)*: Oh, this will kill me! What have I done to him? Mother, you must fetch him home again!

GINA: Yes, yes yes; only be quiet, and I'll go out and look for him. *(Puts on her outdoor things.)* Perhaps he's gone in to Relling's. But you mustn't lie there and cry. Promise me!

HEDVIG *(weeping convulsively)*: Yes, I'll stop, I'll stop; if only Father comes back!

GREGERS (to GINA, who is going): After all, had you not better leave him to fight out his bitter fight to the end?

GINA: Oh, he can do that afterward. First of all, we must get the child quieted. (Goes out by the passage door.)

HEDVIG (sits up and dries her tears): Now you must tell me what all this means. Why doesn't Father want me anymore?

GREGERS: You mustn't ask that till you are a big girl—quite grown-up.

HEDVIG (sobs): But I can't go on being as miserable as this till I'm grown-up.—I think I know what it is.—Perhaps I'm not really Father's child.

GREGERS (uneasily): How could that be?

HEDVIG: Mother might have found me. And perhaps Father has just got to know it; I've read of such things.

GREGERS: Well, but if it were so—

HEDVIG: I think he might be just as fond of me for all that. Yes, fonder almost. We got the wild duck in a present, you know, and I love it so dearly all the same.

GREGERS (turning the conversation): Ah, the wild duck, by-the-bye! Let us talk about the wild duck a little, Hedvig.

HEDVIG: The poor wild duck! He doesn't want to see it anymore either. Only think, he wanted to wring its neck!

GREGERS: Oh, he won't do that.

HEDVIG: No; but he said he would like to. And I think it was horrid of Father to say it; for I pray for the wild duck every night and ask that it may be preserved from death and all that is evil.

GREGERS (looking at her): Do you say your prayers every night?

HEDVIG: Yes.

GREGERS: Who taught you to do that?

HEDVIG: I myself; one time when Father was very ill, and had leeches on his neck and said that death was staring him in the face.

GREGERS: Well?

HEDVIG: Then I prayed for him as I lay in bed; and since then I have always kept it up.

GREGERS: And now you pray for the wild duck, too?

HEDVIG: I thought it was best to bring in the wild duck; for she was so weakly at first.

GREGERS: Do you pray in the morning, too?

HEDVIG: No, of course not.

GREGERS: Why not in the morning as well?

HEDVIG: In the morning it's light, you know, and there's nothing in particular to be afraid of.

GREGERS: And your father was going to wring the neck of the wild duck that you love so dearly?

HEDVIG: No; he said he ought to wring its neck, but he would spare it for my sake; and that was kind of Father.

GREGERS (*coming a little nearer*): But suppose you were to sacrifice the wild duck of your own free will for his sake.

HEDVIG (*rising*): The wild duck!

GREGERS: Suppose you were to make a free-will offering, for his sake, of the dearest treasure you have in the world!

HEDVIG: Do you think that would do any good?

GREGERS: Try it, Hedvig.

HEDVIG (*softly, with flashing eyes*): Yes, I will try it.

GREGERS: Have you really the courage for it, do you think?

HEDVIG: I'll ask Grandfather to shoot the wild duck for me.

GREGERS: Yes, do. But not a word to your mother about it.

HEDVIG: Why not?

GREGERS: She doesn't understand us.

HEDVIG: The wild duck! I'll try it tomorrow morning.

GINA *comes in by the passage door.*

HEDVIG (*going toward her*): Did you find him, Mother?

GINA: No, but I heard as he had called and taken Relling with him.

GREGERS: Are you sure of that?

GINA: Yes, the porter's wife said so. Molvik went with them, too, she said.

GREGERS: This evening, when his mind so sorely needs to wrestle in solitude—!

GINA (*takes off her things*): Yes, men are strange creatures, so they are. The Lord only knows where Relling has dragged him to! I ran over to Madam Eriksen's, but they weren't there.

HEDVIG (*struggling to keep back her tears*): Oh, if he should never come home anymore!

GREGERS: He will come home again. I shall have news to give him tomorrow; and then you shall see how he comes home. You may rely upon that, Hedvig, and sleep in peace. Good night. (*He goes out by the passage door.*)

HEDVIG (*throws herself sobbing on* GINA's *neck*): Mother, Mother!

GINA (*pats her shoulder and sighs*): Ah, yes; Relling was right, he was. That's what comes of it when crazy creatures go about presenting the claims of the—what-you-may-call-it.

Act Five

━━━━━━◆━━━━━━

HIALMAR EKDAL's *studio. Cold, gray morning light. Wet snow lies upon the large panes of the sloping roof-window.*

GINA comes from the kitchen with an apron and bib on, and carrying a dusting brush and a duster; she goes toward the sitting room door. At the same moment HEDVIG *comes hurriedly in from the passage.*

GINA (*stops*): Well?

HEDVIG: Oh, Mother, I almost think he's down at Relling's—

GINA: There, you see!

HEDVIG: —because the porter's wife says she could hear that Relling had two people with him when he came home last night.

GINA: That's just what I thought.

HEDVIG: But it's no use his being there, if he won't come up to us.

GINA: I'll go down and speak to him at all events.

OLD EKDAL, in dressing gown and slippers, and with a lighted pipe, appears at the door of his room.

186

EKDAL: Hialmar— Isn't Hialmar at home?

GINA: No, he's gone out.

EKDAL: So early? And in such a tearing snowstorm? Well, well; just as he pleases; I can take my morning walk alone.

He slides the garret door aside; HEDVIG *helps him; he goes in; she closes it after him.*

HEDVIG *(in an undertone)*: Only think, Mother, when poor Grandfather hears that Father is going to leave us.

GINA: Oh, nonsense; Grandfather mustn't hear anything about it. It was a heaven's mercy he wasn't at home yesterday in all that hurly-burly.

HEDVIG: Yes, but—

GREGERS *comes in by the passage door.*

GREGERS: Well, have you any news of him?

GINA: They say he's down at Relling's.

GREGERS: At Relling's! Has he really been out with those creatures?

GINA: Yes, like enough.

GREGERS: When he ought to have been yearning for solitude, to collect and clear his thoughts—

GINA: Yes, you may well say so.

RELLING *enters from the passage.*

HEDVIG *(going to him)*: Is Father in your room?

GINA *(at the same time)*: Is he there?

RELLING: Yes, to be sure he is.

HEDVIG: And you never let us know!

RELLING: Yes; I'm a brute. But in the first place I had to look after the other brute; I mean our demonic friend, of course; and then I fell so dead asleep that—

GINA: What does Ekdal say today?

RELLING: He says nothing whatever.

HEDVIG: Doesn't he speak?

RELLING: Not a blessed word.

GREGERS: No, no; I can understand that very well.

GINA: But what's he doing then?

RELLING: He's lying on the sofa, snoring.

GINA: Oh, is he? Yes, Ekdal's a rare one to snore.

HEDVIG: Asleep? Can he sleep?

RELLING: Well, it certainly looks like it.

GREGERS: No wonder, after the spiritual conflict that has rent him—

GINA: And then he's never been used to gadding about out of doors at night.

HEDVIG: Perhaps it's a good thing that he's getting sleep, Mother.

GINA: Of course it is; and we must take care we don't wake him up too early. Thank you, Relling. I must get the house cleaned up a bit now, and then— Come and help me, Hedvig.

GINA *and* HEDVIG *go into the sitting room.*

GREGERS (*turning to* RELLING): What is your explanation of the spiritual tumult that is now going on in Hialmar Ekdal?

RELLING: Devil a bit of a spiritual tumult have *I* noticed in him.

GREGERS: What! Not at such a crisis, when his whole life has been placed on a new foundation—? How can you think that such an individuality as Hialmar's—?

RELLING: Oh, individuality—he! If he ever had any tendency to the abnormal developments you call individuality, I can assure you it was rooted out of him while he was still in his teens.

GREGERS: That would be strange indeed,—considering the loving care with which he was brought up.

RELLING: By those two high-flown, hysterical maiden aunts, you mean?

GREGERS: Let me tell you that they were women who never forgot the claim of the ideal—but of course you will only jeer at me again.

RELLING: No, I'm in no humor for that. I know all about those ladies; for he has ladled out no end of rhetoric on the subject of his "two soul-mothers." But I don't think he has much to thank them for. Ekdal's misfortune is that in his own circle he has always been looked upon as a shining light—

GREGERS: Not without reason, surely. Look at the depth of his mind!

RELLING: *I* have never discovered it. That his father believed in it I don't so much wonder; the old lieutenant has been an ass all his days.

GREGERS: He has had a childlike mind all his days; that is what you cannot understand.

RELLING: Well, so be it. But then, when our dear, sweet Hialmar went to college, he at once passed for the great light of the future among his comrades, too! He was handsome, the rascal—red and white—a shopgirl's dream of manly beauty; and with his superficially emotional temperament, and his sympathetic voice and his talent for declaiming other people's verses and other people's thoughts—

GREGERS *(indignantly)*: Is it Hialmar Ekdal you are talking about in this strain?

RELLING: Yes, with your permission; I am simply giving you an inside view of the idol you are groveling before.

GREGERS: I should hardly have thought I was quite stone blind.

RELLING: Yes, you are—or not far from it. You are a sick man, too, you see.

GREGERS: You are right there.

RELLING: Yes. Yours is a complicated case. First of all there is that plague integrity-fever; and then—what's worse—you are always in a delirium of hero worship; you must always have something to adore, outside yourself.

GREGERS: Yes, I must certainly seek it outside myself.

RELLING: But you make such shocking mistakes about every new phoenix you think you have discovered. Here again you have come to a cottar's cabin with your claim of the ideal; and the people of the house are insolvent.

GREGERS: If you don't think better than that of Hialmar Ekdal, what pleasure can you find in being everlastingly with him?

RELLING: Well, you see, I'm supposed to be a sort of a doctor—save the mark! I can't but give a hand to the poor sick folk who live under the same roof with me.

GREGERS: Oh, indeed! Hialmar Ekdal is sick, too, is he!

RELLING: Most people are, worse luck.

GREGERS: And what remedy are you applying in Hialmar's case?

RELLING: My usual one. I am cultivating the life-illusion in him.

GREGERS: Life—illusion? I didn't catch what you said.

RELLING: Yes, I said illusion. For illusion, you know, is the stimulating principle.

GREGERS: May I ask with what illusion Hialmar is inoculated?

RELLING: No, thank you; I don't betray professional secrets to quack-salvers. You would probably go and muddle his case still more than you have already. But my method is infallible. I have applied it to Molvik as well. I have made him "demonic." That's the blister I have to put on his neck.

GREGERS: Is he not really demonic, then?

RELLING: What the devil do you mean by demonic? It's only a piece of gibberish I've invented to keep up a spark of life in him. But for that, the poor harmless creature would have succumbed to self-contempt and despair many a long year ago. And then the old lieutenant! But he has hit upon his own cure, you see.

GREGERS: Lieutenant Ekdal? What of him?

RELLING: Just think of the old bear-hunter shutting himself up in that dark garret to shoot rabbits! I tell you there is not a happier sportsman in the world than that old man pottering about in there among all that rubbish. The four or five withered Christmas trees he has saved up are the same to him as the whole great fresh Höidal forest; the cock and the hens are big game birds in the fir tops; and the rabbits that flop about the garret floor are the bears he has to battle with—the mighty hunter of the mountains!

GREGERS: Poor unfortunate old man! Yes; he has indeed had to narrow the ideals of his youth.

RELLING: While I think of it, Mr. Werle, junior—don't use that foreign word: ideals. We have the excellent native word: lies.

GREGERS: Do you think the two things are related?

RELLING: Yes, just about as closely as typhus and putrid fever.

GREGERS: Dr. Relling, I shall not give up the struggle until I have rescued Hialmar from your clutches!

RELLING: So much the worse for him. Rob the average man of his life-illusion, and you rob him of his happiness at the same stroke. (*To* HEDVIG, *who comes in from the sitting room.*) Well, little wild-duck-mother, I'm just going down to see whether papa is still lying meditating upon that wonderful invention of his. (*Goes out by passage door.*)

GREGERS (*approaches* HEDVIG): I can see by your face that you have not yet done it.

HEDVIG: What? Oh, that about the wild duck! No.

GREGERS: I suppose your courage failed when the time came.

HEDVIG: No, that wasn't it. But when I awoke this morning and remembered what we had been talking about, it seemed so strange.

GREGERS: Strange?

HEDVIG: Yes, I don't know— Yesterday evening, at the moment, I thought there was something so delightful about it; but since I have slept and thought of it again, it somehow doesn't seem worthwhile.

GREGERS: Ah, I thought you could not have grown up quite unharmed in this house.

HEDVIG: I don't care about that, if only Father would come up—

GREGERS: Oh, if only your eyes had been opened to that which gives life its value—if you possessed the true, joyous, fearless, spirit of sacrifice, you would soon see how he would come up to you.—But I believe in you still, Hedvig.

He goes out by the passage door. HEDVIG *wanders about the room for a time; she is on the point of going into the kitchen when a knock is heard at the garret door.* HEDVIG *goes over and opens it a little; old* EKDAL *comes out; she pushes the door to again.*

EKDAL: Hm, it's not much fun to take one's morning walk alone.

HEDVIG: Wouldn't you like to go shooting, Grandfather?

EKDAL: It's not the weather for it today. It's so dark there, you can scarcely see where you're going.

HEDVIG: Do you never want to shoot anything besides the rabbits?

EKDAL: Do you think the rabbits aren't good enough?

HEDVIG: Yes, but what about the wild duck?

EKDAL: Ho-ho! are you afraid I shall shoot your wild duck? Never in the world. Never.

HEDVIG: No, I suppose you couldn't; they say it's very difficult to shoot wild ducks.

EKDAL: Couldn't! Should rather think I could.

HEDVIG: How would you set about it, Grandfather?—I don't mean with my wild duck, but with others?

EKDAL: I should take care to shoot them in the breast, you know; that's the surest place. And then you must shoot against the feathers, you see—not the way of the feathers.

HEDVIG: Do they die then, Grandfather?

EKDAL: Yes, they die right enough—when you shoot properly. Well, I must go and brush up a bit. Hm—understand—hm. (*Goes into his room.*)

HEDVIG *waits a little, glances toward the sitting room door, goes over to the bookcase, stands on tiptoe, takes the double-barreled pistol down from the shelf and looks at it.*

GINA, *with brush and duster, comes from the sitting room.*
HEDVIG *hastily lays down the pistol, unobserved.*

GINA: Don't stand raking among Father's things, Hedvig.

HEDVIG (*goes away from the bookcase*): I was only going to
tidy up a little.

GINA: You'd better go into the kitchen and see if the coffee's
keeping hot; I'll take his breakfast on a tray, when I go
down to him.

HEDVIG *goes out.* GINA *begins to sweep and clean up the
studio. Presently the passage door is opened with hesitation, and* HIALMAR EKDAL *looks in. He has on his overcoat, but not his hat; he is unwashed, and his hair is
disheveled and unkempt. His eyes are dull and heavy.*

GINA (*standing with the brush in her hand and looking at
him*): Oh, there now, Ekdal—so you've come after all!

HIALMAR (*comes in and answers in a toneless voice*): I
come—only to depart again immediately.

GINA: Yes, yes, I suppose so. But, Lord help us! what a sight
you are!

HIALMAR: A sight?

GINA: And your nice winter coat, too! Well, that's done for.

HEDVIG (*at the kitchen door*): Mother, hadn't I better—?
(*Sees* HIALMAR, *gives a loud scream of joy and runs to
him.*) Oh, Father, Father!

HIALMAR (*turns away and makes a gesture of repulsion*):
Away, away, away! (*To* GINA). Keep her away from me,
I say!

GINA (*in a low tone*): Go into the sitting room, Hedvig.

HEDVIG *does so without a word.*

HIALMAR (*fussily pulls out the table drawer*): I must have my
books with me. Where are my books?

GINA: Which books?

HIALMAR: My scientific books, of course; the technical magazines I require for my invention.

GINA (*searches in the bookcase*): Is it these here paper-covered ones?

HIALMAR: Yes, of course.

GINA (*lays a heap of magazines on the table*): Shan't I get Hedvig to cut them for you?

HIALMAR: I don't require to have them cut for me.

Short silence.

GINA: Then you're still set on leaving us, Ekdal?

HIALMAR (*rummaging among the books*): Yes, that is a matter of course, I should think.

GINA: Well, well.

HIALMAR (*vehemently*): How can I live here, to be stabbed to the heart every hour of the day?

GINA: God forgive you for thinking such vile things of me.

HIALMAR: Prove—!

GINA: I think it's you as has got to prove.

HIALMAR: After a past like yours? There are certain claims—I may almost call them claims of the ideal—

GINA: But what about Grandfather? What's to become of him, poor dear!

HIALMAR: I know my duty; my helpless father will come with me. I am going out into the town to make arrangements—Hm—(*hesitatingly*)—has anyone found my hat on the stairs?

GINA: No. Have you lost your hat?

HIALMAR: Of course I had it on when I came in last night; there's no doubt about that; but I couldn't find it this morning.

GINA: Lord help us! where have you been to with those two ne'er-do-wells?

HIALMAR: Oh, don't bother me about trifles. Do you suppose I am in the mood to remember details?

GINA: If only you haven't caught cold, Ekdal—(*Goes out into the kitchen.*)

HIALMAR (*talks to himself in a low tone of irritation, while he empties the table drawer*): You're a scoundrel, Relling!—

You're a low fellow!—Ah, you shameless tempter!—I wish I could get someone to stick a knife into you!

He lays some old letters on one side, finds the torn document of yesterday, takes it up and looks at the pieces; puts it down hurriedly as GINA *enters.*

GINA *(sets a tray with coffee, etc., on the table)*: Here's a drop of something hot, if you'd fancy it. And there's some bread and butter and a snack of salt meat.

HIALMAR *(glancing at the tray)*: Salt meat? Never under this roof! It's true I have not had a mouthful of solid food for nearly twenty-four hours; but no matter.—My memoranda! The commencement of my autobiography! What has become of my diary, and all my important papers? *(Opens the sitting room door but draws back.)* She is there, too?

GINA: Good Lord! the child must be somewhere!

HIALMAR: Come out.

He makes room, HEDVIG *comes, scared, into the studio.*

HIALMAR *(with his hand upon the door handle, says to* GINA*)*: In these, the last moments I spend in my former home, I wish to be spared from interlopers— *(Goes into the room.)*

HEDVIG *(with a bound toward her mother, asks softly, trembling)*: Does that mean me?

GINA: Stay out in the kitchen, Hedvig; or no—you'd best go into your own room. *(Speaks to* HIALMAR *as she goes in to him.)* Wait a bit, Ekdal; don't rummage so in the drawers; *I* know where everything is.

HEDVIG *(stands a moment immovable, in terror and perplexity, biting her lips to keep back the tears; then she clenches her hands convulsively and says softly)*: The wild duck.

She steals over and takes the pistol from the shelf, opens the garret door a little way, creeps in and draws the door to after her. HIALMAR *and* GINA *can be heard disputing in the sitting room.*

HIALMAR (*comes in with some manuscript books and old loose papers, which he lays upon the table*): That portmanteau is of no use! There are a thousand and one things I must drag with me.

GINA (*following with the portmanteau*): Why not leave all the rest for the present and only take a shirt and a pair of woolen drawers with you?

HIALMAR: Whew!—all these exhausting preparations—!

Pulls off his overcoat and throws it upon the sofa.

GINA: And there's the coffee getting cold.

HIALMAR: Hm.

Drinks a mouthful without thinking of it and then another.

GINA (*dusting the backs of the chairs*): A nice job you'll have to find such another big garret for the rabbits.

HIALMAR: What! Am I to drag all those rabbits with me, too?

GINA: You don't suppose Grandfather can get on without his rabbits.

HIALMAR: He must just get used to doing without them. Have not *I* to sacrifice very much greater things than rabbits!

GINA (*dusting the bookcase*): Shall I put the flute in the portmanteau for you?

HIALMAR: No. No flute for me. But give me the pistol!

GINA: Do you want to take the pistol with you?

HIALMAR: Yes. My loaded pistol.

GINA (*searching for it*): It's gone. He must have taken it in with him.

HIALMAR: Is he in the garret?

GINA: Yes, of course he's in the garret.

HIALMAR: Hm—poor lonely old man.

He takes a piece of bread and butter, eats it and finishes his cup of coffee.

GINA: If we hadn't have let that room, you could have moved in there.

HIALMAR: And continued to live under the same roof with—! Never,—never!

GINA: But couldn't you put up with the sitting room for a day or two? You could have it all to yourself.

HIALMAR: Never within these walls!

GINA: Well, then, down with Relling and Molvik.

HIALMAR: Don't mention those wretches' names to me! The very thought of them almost takes away my appetite.— Oh, no, I must go out into the storm and the snowdrift,— go from house to house and seek shelter for my father and myself.

GINA: But you've got no hat, Ekdal! You've been and lost your hat, you know.

HIALMAR: Oh, those two brutes, those slaves of all the vices! A hat must be procured. *(Takes another piece of bread and butter.)* Some arrangements must be made. For I have no mind to throw away my life, either. *(Looks for something on the tray.)*

GINA: What are you looking for?

HIALMAR: Butter.

GINA: I'll get some at once. *(Goes out into the kitchen.)*

HIALMAR *(calls after her)*: Oh, it doesn't matter; dry bread is good enough for me.

GINA *(brings a dish of butter)*: Look here; this is fresh churned.

She pours out another cup of coffee for him; he seats himself on the sofa, spreads more butter on the already buttered bread and eats and drinks awhile in silence.

HIALMAR: Could I, without being subject to intrusion— intrusion of any sort—could I live in the sitting room there for a day or two?

GINA: Yes, to be sure you could, if you only would.

HIALMAR: For I see no possibility of getting all Father's things out in such a hurry.

GINA: And, besides, you've surely got to tell him first as you don't mean to live with us others no more.

HIALMAR (*pushes away his coffee cup*): Yes, there is that, too; I shall have to lay bare the whole tangled story to him— I must turn matters over; I must have breathing time; I cannot take all these burdens on my shoulders in a single day.

GINA: No, especially in such horrible weather as it is outside.

HIALMAR (*touching* WERLE's *letter*): I see that paper is still lying about here.

GINA: Yes, *I* haven't touched it.

HIALMAR: So far as I am concerned it is mere waste paper—

GINA: Well, *I* have certainly no notion of making any use of it.

HIALMAR: —but we had better not let it get lost all the same;—in all the upset when I move, it might easily—

GINA: I'll take good care of it, Ekdal.

HIALMAR: The donation is in the first instance made to Father, and it rests with him to accept or decline it.

GINA (*sighs*): Yes, poor old Father—

HIALMAR: To make quite safe—Where shall I find some gum?

GINA (*goes to the bookcase*): Here's the gum-pot.

HIALMAR: And a brush?

GINA: The brush is here, too. (*Brings him the things.*)

HIALMAR (*takes a pair of scissors*): Just a strip of paper at the back— (*Clips and gums.*) Far be it from me to lay hands upon what is not my own—and least of all upon what belongs to a destitute old man—and to—the other as well.— There now. Let it lie there for a time; and when it is dry, take it away. I wish never to see that document again. Never!

GREGERS WERLE *enters from the passage.*

GREGERS (*somewhat surprised*): What,—are you sitting here, Hialmar?

HIALMAR (*rises hurriedly*): I had sunk down from fatigue.

GREGERS: You have been having breakfast, I see.

HIALMAR: The body sometimes makes its claims felt, too.

GREGERS: What have you decided to do?

HIALMAR: For a man like me, there is only one course possible. I am just putting my most important things together. But it takes time, you know.

GINA (*with a touch of impatience*): Am I to get the room ready for you, or am I to pack your portmanteau?

HIALMAR (*after a glance of annoyance at* GREGERS): Pack—and get the room ready!

GINA (*takes the portmanteau*): Very well; then I'll put in the shirt and the other things.

Goes into the sitting room and draws the door to after her.

GREGERS (*after a short silence*): I never dreamed that this would be the end of it. Do you really feel it a necessity to leave house and home?

HIALMAR (*wanders about restlessly*): What would you have me do?—I am not fitted to bear unhappiness, Gregers. I must feel secure and at peace in my surroundings.

GREGERS: But can you not feel that here? Just try it. I should have thought you had firm ground to build upon now—if only you start afresh. And, remember, you have your invention to live for.

HIALMAR: Oh, don't talk about my invention. It's perhaps still in the dim distance.

GREGERS: Indeed!

HIALMAR: Why, great heavens, what would you have me invent? Other people have invented almost everything already. It becomes more and more difficult every day—

GREGERS: And you have devoted so much labor to it.

HIALMAR: It was that blackguard Relling that urged me to it.

GREGERS: Relling?

HIALMAR: Yes, it was he that first made me realize my aptitude for making some notable discovery in photography.

GREGERS: Aha—it was Relling!

HIALMAR: Oh, I have been so truly happy over it! Not so much for the sake of the invention itself, as because Hedvig believed in it—believed in it with a child's whole eagerness of faith.—At least, I have been fool enough to go and imagine that she believed in it.

GREGERS: Can you really think Hedvig has been false toward you?

HIALMAR: I can think anything now. It is Hedvig that stands in my way. She will blot out the sunlight from my whole life.

GREGERS: Hedvig! Is it Hedvig you are talking of? How should she blot out your sunlight?

HIALMAR (*without answering*): How unutterably I have loved that child! How unutterably happy I have felt every time I came home to my humble room, and she flew to meet me, with her sweet little blinking eyes. Oh, confiding fool that I have been! I loved her unutterably;—and I yielded myself up to the dream, the delusion, that she loved me unutterably in return.

GREGERS: Do you call that a delusion?

HIALMAR: How should I know? I can get nothing out of Gina; and besides, she is totally blind to the ideal side of these complications. But to you I feel impelled to open my mind, Gregers. I cannot shake off this frightful doubt—perhaps Hedvig has never really and honestly loved me.

GREGERS: What would you say if she were to give you a proof of her love? (*Listens.*) What's that? I thought I heard the wild duck—?

HIALMAR: It's the wild duck quacking. Father's in the garret.

GREGERS: Is he? (*His face lights up with joy.*) I say, you may yet have proof that your poor misunderstood Hedvig loves you!

HIALMAR: Oh, what proof can she give me? I dare not believe in any assurance from that quarter.

GREGERS: Hedvig does not know what deceit means.

HIALMAR: Oh, Gregers, that is just what I cannot be sure of. Who knows what Gina and that Mrs. Sörby may many a time have sat here whispering and tattling about? And Hedvig usually has her ears open, I can tell you. Perhaps

the deed of gift was not such a surprise to her, after all. In
fact, I'm not sure but that I noticed something of the sort.

GREGERS: What spirit is this that has taken possession of you?

HIALMAR: I have had my eyes opened. Just you notice;—
you'll see, the deed of gift is only a beginning. Mrs. Sörby
has always been a good deal taken up with Hedvig; and
now she has the power to do whatever she likes for the
child. They can take her from me whenever they please.

GREGERS: Hedvig will never, never leave you.

HIALMAR: Don't be so sure of that. If only they beckon to her
and throw out a golden bait—! And, oh! I have loved her
so unspeakably! I would have counted it my highest happiness to take her tenderly by the hand and lead her, as
one leads a timid child through a great dark empty
room!—I am cruelly certain now that the poor photographer in his humble attic has never really and truly been
anything to her. She has only cunningly contrived to keep
on a good footing with him until the time came.

GREGERS: You don't believe that yourself, Hialmar.

HIALMAR: That is just the terrible part of it—I don't know
what to believe,—I never can know it. But can you really
doubt that it must be as I say? Ho-ho, you have far too
much faith in the claim of the ideal, my good Gregers! If
those others came, with the glamour of wealth about
them, and called to the child:—"Leave him: come to us:
here life awaits you—!"

GREGERS (quickly): Well, what then?

HIALMAR: If I then asked her: Hedvig, are you willing to re-
nounce that life for me? (Laughs scornfully.) No thank
you! You would soon hear what answer I should get.

A pistol shot is heard from within the garret.

GREGERS (loudly and joyfully): Hialmar!

HIALMAR: There now; he must needs go shooting, too.

GINA (comes in): Oh, Ekdal, I can hear Grandfather blazing
away in the garret by hisself.

HIALMAR: I'll look in—

GREGERS (*eagerly, with emotion*): Wait a moment! Do you know what that was?

HIALMAR: Yes, of course I know.

GREGERS: No, you don't know. But *I* do. That was the proof!

HIALMAR: What proof?

GREGERS: It was a child's free-will offering. She has got your father to shoot the wild duck.

HIALMAR: To shoot the wild duck!

GINA: Oh, think of that—!

HIALMAR: What was that for?

GREGERS: She wanted to sacrifice to you her most cherished possession; for then she thought you would surely come to love her again.

HIALMAR (*tenderly, with emotion*): Oh, poor child!

GINA: What things she does think of!

GREGERS: She only wanted your love again, Hialmar. She could not live without it.

GINA (*struggling with her tears*): There, you can see for yourself, Ekdal.

HIALMAR: Gina, where is she?

GINA (*sniffs*): Poor dear, she's sitting out in the kitchen, I daresay.

HIALMAR (*goes over, tears open the kitchen door and says*): Hedvig, come, come in to me! (*Looks around.*) No, she's not here.

GINA: Then she must be in her own little room.

HIALMAR (*without*): No, she's not here either. (*Comes in.*) She must have gone out.

GINA: Yes, you wouldn't have her anywheres in the house.

HIALMAR: Oh, if she would only come home quickly, so that I can tell her— Everything will come right now, Gregers; now I believe we can begin life afresh.

GREGERS (*quietly*): I knew it; I knew the child would make amends.

OLD EKDAL *appears at the door of his room; he is in full uniform and is busy buckling on his sword.*

HIALMAR (*astonished*): Father! Are you there?

GINA: Have you been firing in your room?

EKDAL (*resentfully, approaching*): So you go shooting alone, do you, Hialmar?

HIALMAR (*excited and confused*): Then it wasn't you that fired that shot in the garret?

EKDAL: Me that fired? Hm.

GREGERS (*calls out to* HIALMAR): She has shot the wild duck herself!

HIALMAR: What can it mean? (*Hastens to the garret door, tears it aside, looks in and calls loudly*): Hedvig!

GINA (*runs to the door*): Good God, what's that!

HIALMAR (*goes in*): She's lying on the floor!

GREGERS: Hedvig! lying on the floor! (*Goes in to* HIALMAR.)

GINA (*at the same time*): Hedvig! (*Inside the garret.*) No, no, no!

EKDAL: Ho-ho! does she go shooting, too, now?

HIALMAR, GINA *and* GREGERS *carry* HEDVIG *into the studio; in her dangling right hand she holds the pistol fast clasped in her fingers.*

HIALMAR (*distracted*): The pistol has gone off. She has wounded herself. Call for help! Help!

GINA (*runs into the passage and calls down*): Relling! Relling! Dr. Relling; come up as quick as you can!

HIALMAR *and* GREGERS *lay* HEDVIG *down on the sofa.*

EKDAL (*quietly*): The woods avenge themselves.

HIALMAR (*on his knees beside* HEDVIG): She'll soon come to now. She's coming to—; yes, yes, yes.

GINA (*who has come in again*): Where has she hurt herself? I can't see anything—

RELLING *comes hurriedly, and immediately after him* MOLVIK; *the latter without his waistcoat and necktie, and with his coat open.*

RELLING: What's the matter here?

GINA: They say Hedvig has shot herself.

HIALMAR: Come and help us!

RELLING: Shot herself!

He pushes the table aside and begins to examine her.

HIALMAR (*kneeling and looking anxiously up at him*): It can't be dangerous? Speak, Relling! She is scarcely bleeding at all. It can't be dangerous?

RELLING: How did it happen?

HIALMAR: Oh, we don't know—

GINA: She wanted to shoot the wild duck.

RELLING: The wild duck?

HIALMAR: The pistol must have gone off.

RELLING: Hm. Indeed.

EKDAL: The woods avenge themselves. But I'm not afraid, all the same. (*Goes into the garret and closes the door after him.*)

HIALMAR: Well, Relling,—why don't you say something?

RELLING: The ball has entered the breast.

HIALMAR: Yes, but she's coming to!

RELLING: Surely you can see that Hedvig is dead.

GINA (*bursts into tears*): Oh, my child, my child—

GREGERS (*huskily*): In the depths of the sea—

HIALMAR (*jumps up*): No, no, she must live! Oh, for God's sake, Relling—only a moment—only just till I can tell her how unspeakably I loved her all the time!

RELLING: The bullet has gone through her heart. Internal hemorrhage. Death must have been instantaneous.

HIALMAR: And I! I hunted her from me like an animal! And she crept terrified into the garret and died for love of me! (*Sobbing.*) I can never atone to her! I can never tell her—! (*Clenches his hands and cries, upward.*) O thou above—! If thou be indeed! Why hast thou done this thing to me?

GINA: Hush, hush, you mustn't go on that awful way. We had no right to keep her, I suppose.

MOLVIK: The child is not dead, but sleepeth.

RELLING: Bosh.

HIALMAR *(becomes calm, goes over to the sofa, folds his arms and looks at* HEDVIG*)*: There she lies so stiff and still.

RELLING *(tries to loosen the pistol)*: She's holding it so tight, so tight.

GINA: No, no, Relling, don't break her fingers; let the pistol be.

HIALMAR: She shall take it with her.

GINA: Yes, let her. But the child mustn't lie here for a show. She shall go to her own room, so she shall. Help me, Ekdal.

HIALMAR *and* GINA *take* HEDVIG *between them.*

HIALMAR *(as they are carrying her)*: Oh, Gina, Gina, can you survive this!

GINA: We must help each other to bear it. For now at least she belongs to both of us.

MOLVIK *(stretches out his arms and mumbles)*: Blessed be the Lord; to earth thou shalt return; to earth thou shalt return—

RELLING *(whispers)*: Hold your tongue, you fool; you're drunk.

HIALMAR *and* GINA *carry the body out through the kitchen door.* RELLING *shuts it after them.* MOLVIK *slinks out into the passage.*

RELLING *(goes over to* GREGERS *and says)*: No one shall ever convince me that the pistol went off by accident.

GREGERS *(who has stood terrified, with convulsive twitchings)*: Who can say how the dreadful thing happened?

RELLING: The powder has burned the body of her dress. She must have pressed the pistol right against her breast and fired.

GREGERS: Hedvig has not died in vain. Did you not see how sorrow set free what is noble in him?

RELLING: Most people are ennobled by the actual presence of death. But how long do you suppose this nobility will last in him?

GREGERS: Why should it not endure and increase throughout his life?

RELLING: Before a year is over, little Hedvig will be nothing to him but a pretty theme for declamation.

GREGERS: How dare you say that of Hialmar Ekdal?

RELLING: We will talk of this again, when the grass has first withered on her grave. Then you'll hear him spouting about "the child too early torn from her father's heart"; then you'll see him steep himself in a syrup of sentiment and self-admiration and self-pity. Just you wait!

GREGERS: If you are right and I am wrong, then life is not worth living.

RELLING: Oh, life would be quite tolerable, after all, if only we could be rid of the confounded duns that keep on pestering us, in our poverty, with the claim of the ideal.

GREGERS (*looking straight before him*): In that case, I am glad that my destiny is what is.

RELLING: May I inquire,—what is your destiny?

GREGERS (*going*): To be the thirteenth at table.

RELLING: The devil it is.

HEDDA GABLER

CHARACTERS

GEORGE TESMAN
HEDDA TESMAN, his wife
MISS JULIANA TESMAN, his aunt
MRS. ELVSTED
JUDGE BRACK
EILERT LÖVBORG
BERTA, servant at the Tesmans'

The scene of the action is TESMAN's villa, in the west end of
    Christiania.[1]

ACT ONE

A spacious, handsome, and tastefully furnished drawing room, decorated in dark colors. In the back, a wide doorway with curtains drawn back, leading into a smaller room decorated in the same style as the drawing room. In the right-hand wall of the front room, a folding door leading out to the hall. In the opposite wall, on the left, a glass door, also with curtains drawn back. Through the panes can be seen part of a verandah outside, and trees covered with autumn foliage. An oval table, with a cover on it, and surrounded by chairs, stands well forward. In front, by the wall on the right, a wide stove of dark porcelain, a high-backed armchair, a cushioned footrest, and two footstools. A settee, with a small round table in front of it, fills the upper right-hand corner. In front, on the left, a little way from the wall, a sofa. Further back than the glass door, a piano. On either side of the doorway at the back a whatnot with terra-cotta and majolica ornaments.— Against the back wall of the inner room a sofa, with a table, and one or two chairs. Over the sofa hangs the portrait of a handsome elderly man in a General's uniform. Over the table a hanging lamp, with an opal glass shade.—A number of bouquets are arranged about the drawing room, in vases and

*glasses. Others lie upon the tables. The floors in both rooms
are covered with thick carpets.—Morning light. The sun
shines in through the glass door.*

MISS JULIANA TESMAN, *with her bonnet on and carrying a
parasol, comes in from the hall, followed by* BERTA, *who
carries a bouquet wrapped in paper.* MISS TESMAN *is a
comely and pleasant-looking lady of about sixty-five. She
is nicely but simply dressed in a gray walking costume.*
BERTA *is a middle-aged woman of plain and rather countrified appearance.*

MISS TESMAN (*stops close to the door, listens, and says softly*):
Upon my word, I don't believe they are stirring yet!

BERTA (*also softly*): I told you so, Miss. Remember how late
the steamboat got in last night. And then, when they got
home!—good Lord, what a lot the young mistress had to
unpack before she could get to bed.

MISS TESMAN: Well, well—let them have their sleep out. But
let us see that they get a good breath of the fresh morning
air when they do appear. (*She goes to the glass door and
throws it open.*)

BERTA (*beside the table, at a loss what to do with the bouquet
in her hand*): I declare there isn't a bit of room left. I think
I'll put it down here, Miss. (*She places it on the piano.*)

MISS TESMAN: So you've got a new mistress now, my dear
Berta. Heaven knows it was a wrench to me to part
with you.

BERTA (*on the point of weeping*): And do you think it wasn't
hard for me too, Miss? After all the blessed years I've been
with you and Miss Rina.

MISS TESMAN: We must make the best of it, Berta. There was
nothing else to be done. George can't do without you, you
see—he absolutely can't. He has had you to look after him
ever since he was a little boy.

BERTA: Ah but, Miss Julia, I can't help thinking of Miss Rina
lying helpless at home there, poor thing. And with only

that new girl too! She'll never learn to take proper care of an invalid.

MISS TESMAN: Oh, I shall manage to train her. And of course, you know, I shall take most of it upon myself. You needn't be uneasy about my poor sister, my dear Berta.

BERTA: Well, but there's another thing, Miss. I'm so mortally afraid I shan't be able to suit the young mistress.

MISS TESMAN: Oh well—just at first there may be one or two things—

BERTA: Most like she'll be terrible grand in her ways.

MISS TESMAN: Well, you can't wonder at that—General Gabler's daughter! Think of the sort of life she was accustomed to in her father's time. Don't you remember how we used to see her riding down the road along with the General? In that long black habit²—and with feathers in her hat?

BERTA: Yes, indeed—I remember well enough—! But good Lord, I should never have dreamt in those days that she and Master George would make a match of it.

MISS TESMAN: Nor I.—But, by-the-bye, Berta—while I think of it: in future you mustn't say Master George. You must say Dr. Tesman.

BERTA: Yes, the young mistress spoke of that too—last night—the moment they set foot in the house. Is it true then, Miss?

MISS TESMAN: Yes, indeed it is. Only think, Berta—some foreign university has made him a doctor—while he has been abroad, you understand. I hadn't heard a word about it, until he told me himself upon the pier.

BERTA: Well, well, he's clever enough for anything, he is. But I didn't think he'd have gone in for doctoring people too.

MISS TESMAN: No, no, it's not that sort of doctor he is. (Nods significantly.) But let me tell you, we may have to call him something still grander before long.

BERTA: You don't say so! What can that be, Miss?

MISS TESMAN (smiling): Hm—wouldn't you like to know! (With emotion.) Ah, dear, dear—if my poor brother could only look up from his grave now, and see what his little boy has grown into! (*Looks around.*) But bless me, Berta— why have you done this? Taken the chintz covers off all the furniture?

BERTA: The mistress told me to. She can't abide covers on the chairs, she says.

MISS TESMAN: Are they going to make this their everyday sitting room then?

BERTA: Yes, that's what I understood—from the mistress. Master George—the doctor—he said nothing.

GEORGE TESMAN *comes from the right into the inner room, humming to himself, and carrying an unstrapped empty portmanteau. He is a middle-sized, young-looking man of thirty-three, rather stout, with a round, open, cheerful face, fair hair and beard. He wears spectacles, and is somewhat carelessly dressed in comfortable indoor clothes.*

MISS TESMAN: Good morning, good morning, George.

TESMAN (*in the doorway between the rooms*): Aunt Julia! Dear Aunt Julia! (*Goes up to her and shakes hands warmly.*) Come all this way—so early! Eh?

MISS TESMAN: Why, of course I had to come and see how you were getting on.

TESMAN: In spite of your having had no proper night's rest?

MISS TESMAN: Oh, that makes no difference to me.

TESMAN: Well, I suppose you got home all right from the pier? Eh?

MISS TESMAN: Yes, quite safely, thank goodness. Judge Brack was good enough to see me right to my door.

TESMAN: We were so sorry we couldn't give you a seat in the carriage. But you saw what a pile of boxes Hedda had to bring with her.

MISS TESMAN: Yes, she had certainly plenty of boxes.

BERTA (*to* TESMAN): Shall I go in and see if there's anything I can do for the mistress?

TESMAN: No, thank you, Berta—you needn't. She said she would ring if she wanted anything.

BERTA (*going toward the right*): Very well.

TESMAN: But look here—take this portmanteau with you.

BERTA (*taking it*): I'll put it in the attic. (*She goes out by the hall door.*)

TESMAN: Fancy, Auntie—I had the whole of that portmanteau chock full of copies of documents. You wouldn't believe how much I have picked up from all the archives I have been examining—curious old details that no one has had any idea of—

MISS TESMAN: Yes, you don't seem to have wasted your time on your wedding trip, George.

TESMAN: No, that I haven't. But do take off your bonnet, Auntie. Look here! Let me untie the strings—eh?

MISS TESMAN (*while he does so*): Well, well—this is just as if you were still at home with us.

TESMAN (*with the bonnet in his hand, looks at it from all sides*): Why, what a gorgeous bonnet you've been investing in!

MISS TESMAN: I bought it on Hedda's account.

TESMAN: On Hedda's account? Eh?

MISS TESMAN: Yes, so that Hedda needn't be ashamed of me if we happened to go out together.

TESMAN (*patting her cheek*): You always think of everything, Aunt Julia. (*Lays the bonnet on a chair beside the table.*) And now, look here—suppose we sit comfortably on the sofa and have a little chat, till Hedda comes. (*They seat themselves. She places her parasol in the corner of the sofa.*)

MISS TESMAN (*takes both his hands and looks at him*): What a delight it is to have you again, as large as life, before my very eyes, George! My George—my poor brother's own boy!

TESMAN: And it's a delight for me, too, to see you again, Aunt Julia! You, who have been father and mother in one to me.

MISS TESMAN: Oh, yes, I know you will always keep a place in your heart for your old aunts.

TESMAN: And what about Aunt Rina? No improvement—eh?

MISS TESMAN: Oh, no—we can scarcely look for any improvement in her case, poor thing. There she lies, helpless, as she has lain for all these years. But heaven grant I
may not lose her yet awhile! For if I did, I don't know what
I should make of my life, George—especially now that I
haven't you to look after anymore.

TESMAN (*patting her back*): There, there, there—!

MISS TESMAN (*suddenly changing her tone*): And to think
that here are you a married man, George!—And that you
should be the one to carry off Hedda Gabler—the beautiful Hedda Gabler! Only think of it—she, that was so beset
with admirers!

TESMAN (*hums a little and smiles complacently*): Yes, I fancy
I have several good friends about town who would like to
stand in my shoes—eh?

MISS TESMAN: And then this fine long wedding tour you have
had! More than five—nearly six months—

TESMAN: Well, for me it has been a sort of tour of research
as well. I have had to do so much grubbing among old
records—and to read no end of books too, Auntie.

MISS TESMAN: Oh, yes, I suppose so. (*More confidentially,
and lowering her voice a little.*) But listen now, George—
have you nothing—nothing special to tell me?

TESMAN: As to our journey?

MISS TESMAN: Yes.

TESMAN: No, I don't know of anything except what I have
told you in my letters. I had a doctor's degree conferred on
me—but that I told you yesterday.

MISS TESMAN: Yes, yes, you did. But what I mean is—haven't
you any—any—expectations—?

TESMAN: Expectations?

MISS TESMAN: Why, you know, George—I'm your old auntie!

TESMAN: Why, of course I have expectations.

MISS TESMAN: Ah!

TESMAN: I have every expectation of being a professor one of
these days.

MISS TESMAN: Oh, yes, a professor—

TESMAN: Indeed, I may say I am certain of it. But my dear Auntie—you know all about that already!

MISS TESMAN (*laughing to herself*): Yes, of course I do. You are quite right there. (*Changing the subject.*) But we were talking about your journey. It must have cost a great deal of money, George?

TESMAN: Well, you see—my handsome traveling scholarship went a good way.

MISS TESMAN: But I can't understand how you can have made it go far enough for two.

TESMAN: No, that's not so easy to understand—eh?

MISS TESMAN: And especially traveling with a lady—they tell me that makes it ever so much more expensive.

TESMAN: Yes, of course—it makes it a little more expensive. But Hedda had to have this trip, Auntie! She really had to. Nothing else would have done.

MISS TESMAN: No, no, I suppose not. A wedding tour seems to be quite indispensable nowadays.—But tell me now—have you gone thoroughly over the house yet?

TESMAN: Yes, you may be sure I have. I have been afoot ever since daylight.

MISS TESMAN: And what do you think of it all?

TESMAN: I'm delighted! Quite delighted! Only I can't think what we are to do with the two empty rooms between this inner parlor and Hedda's bedroom.

MISS TESMAN (*laughing*): Oh, my dear George, I daresay you may find some use for them—in the course of time.

TESMAN: Why of course you are quite right, Aunt Julia! You mean as my library increases—eh?

MISS TESMAN: Yes, quite so, my dear boy. It was your library I was thinking of.

TESMAN: I am specially pleased on Hedda's account. Often and often, before we were engaged, she said that she would never care to live anywhere but in Secretary Falk's villa.

MISS TESMAN: Yes, it was lucky that this very house should come into the market, just after you had started.

TESMAN: Yes, Aunt Julia, the luck was on our side, wasn't it—eh?

MISS TESMAN: But the expense, my dear George! You will find it very expensive, all this.

TESMAN (*looks at her, a little cast down*): Yes, I suppose I shall, Aunt!

MISS TESMAN: Oh, frightfully!

TESMAN: How much do you think? In round numbers?— Eh?

MISS TESMAN: Oh, I can't even guess until all the accounts come in.

TESMAN: Well, fortunately, Judge Brack has secured the most favorable terms for me,—so he said in a letter to Hedda.

MISS TESMAN: Yes, don't be uneasy, my dear boy.—Besides, I have given security for the furniture and all the carpets.

TESMAN: Security? You? My dear Aunt Julia—what sort of security could you give?

MISS TESMAN: I have given a mortgage on our annuity.[3]

TESMAN (*jumps up*): What! On your—and Aunt Rina's annuity!

MISS TESMAN: Yes, I knew of no other plan, you see.

TESMAN (*placing himself before her*): Have you gone out of your senses, Auntie! Your annuity—it's all that you and Aunt Rina have to live upon.

MISS TESMAN: Well, well, don't get so excited about it. It's only a matter of form you know—Judge Brack assured me of that. It was he that was kind enough to arrange the whole affair for me. A mere matter of form, he said.

TESMAN: Yes, that may be all very well. But nevertheless—

MISS TESMAN: You will have your own salary to depend upon now. And, good heavens, even if we did have to pay up a little—! To eke things out a bit at the start—! Why, it would be nothing but a pleasure to us.

TESMAN: Oh, Auntie—will you never be tired of making sacrifices for me!

MISS TESMAN (*rises and lays her hands on his shoulders*):

Have I any other happiness in this world except to smooth your way for you, my dear boy? You, who have had neither father nor mother to depend on. And now we have reached the goal, George! Things have looked black enough for us, sometimes; but, thank heaven, now you have nothing to fear.

TESMAN: Yes, it is really marvelous how everything has turned out for the best.

MISS TESMAN: And the people who opposed you—who wanted to bar the way for you—now you have them at your feet. They have fallen, George. Your most dangerous rival—his fall was the worst.—And now he has to lie on the bed he has made for himself—poor misguided creature.

TESMAN: Have you heard anything of Eilert? Since I went away, I mean.

MISS TESMAN: Only that he is said to have published a new book.

TESMAN: What! Eilert Lövborg! Recently—eh?

MISS TESMAN: Yes, so they say. Heaven knows whether it can be worth anything! Ah, when your new book appears— that will be another story, George! What is it to be about?

TESMAN: It will deal with the domestic industries of Brabant during the Middle Ages.

MISS TESMAN: Fancy—to be able to write on such a subject as that!

TESMAN: However, it may be some time before the book is ready. I have all these collections to arrange first, you see.

MISS TESMAN: Yes, collecting and arranging—no one can beat you at that. There you are my poor brother's own son.

TESMAN: I am looking forward eagerly to setting to work at it; especially now that I have my own delightful home to work in.

MISS TESMAN: And, most of all, now that you have got the wife of your heart, my dear George.

TESMAN (*embracing her*): Oh, yes, yes, Aunt Julia. Hedda— she is the best part of it all! (*Looks toward the doorway.*) I believe I hear her coming—eh?

HEDDA *enters from the left through the inner room. She is a woman of nine-and-twenty. Her face and figure show refinement and distinction. Her complexion is pale and opaque. Her steel-gray eyes express a cold, unruffled repose. Her hair is of an agreeable medium brown, but not particularly abundant. She is dressed in a tasteful, somewhat loose-fitting morning gown.*

MISS TESMAN (*going to meet* HEDDA): Good morning, my dear Hedda! Good morning, and a hearty welcome.

HEDDA (*holds out her hand*): Good morning, dear Miss Tesman! So early a call! That is kind of you.

MISS TESMAN (*with some embarrassment*): Well—has the bride slept well in her new home?

HEDDA: Oh yes, thanks. Passably.

TESMAN (*laughing*): Passably! Come, that's good, Hedda! You were sleeping like a stone when I got up.

HEDDA: Fortunately. Of course one has always to accustom one's self to new surroundings, Miss Tesman—little by little. (*Looking toward the left.*) Oh—there the servant has gone and opened the verandah door, and let in a whole flood of sunshine.

MISS TESMAN (*going toward the door*): Well, then, we will shut it.

HEDDA: No, no, not that! Tesman, please draw the curtains. That will give a softer light.

TESMAN (*at the door*): All right—all right. There now, Hedda, now you have both shade and fresh air.

HEDDA: Yes, fresh air we certainly must have, with all these stacks of flowers—But—won't you sit down, Miss Tesman?

MISS TESMAN: No, thank you. Now that I have seen that everything is all right here—thank heaven!—I must be getting home again. My sister is lying longing for me, poor thing.

TESMAN: Give her my very best love, Auntie; and say I shall look in and see her later in the day.

MISS TESMAN: Yes, yes, I'll be sure to tell her. But by-the-bye, George—(*feeling in her dress pocket*)—I had almost forgotten—I have something for you here.

TESMAN: What is it, Auntie? Eh?

MISS TESMAN (*produces a flat parcel wrapped in newspaper and hands it to him*): Look here, my dear boy.

TESMAN (*opening the parcel*): Well, I declare!—Have you really saved them for me, Aunt Julia! Hedda! isn't this touching—eh?

HEDDA (*beside the whatnot on the right*): Well, what is it?

TESMAN: My old morning shoes! My slippers.

HEDDA: Indeed. I remember you often spoke of them while we were abroad.

TESMAN: Yes, I missed them terribly. (*Goes up to her.*) Now you shall see them, Hedda!

HEDDA (*going toward the stove*): Thanks, I really don't care about it.

TESMAN (*following her*): Only think—ill as she was, Aunt Rina embroidered these for me. Oh you can't think how many associations cling to them.

HEDDA (*at the table*): Scarcely for me.

MISS TESMAN: Of course not for Hedda, George.

TESMAN: Well, but now that she belongs to the family, I thought—

HEDDA (*interrupting*): We shall never get on with this servant, Tesman.

MISS TESMAN: Not get on with Berta?

TESMAN: Why, dear, what puts that in your head? Eh?

HEDDA (*pointing*): Look there! She has left her old bonnet lying about on a chair.

TESMAN (*in consternation, drops the slippers on the floor*): Why, Hedda—

HEDDA: Just fancy, if anyone should come in and see it!

TESMAN: But Hedda—that's Aunt Julia's bonnet.

HEDDA: Is it!

MISS TESMAN (*taking up the bonnet*): Yes, indeed it's mine. And, what's more, it's not old, Madam Hedda.

HEDDA: I really did not look closely at it, Miss Tesman.

MISS TESMAN (*trying on the bonnet*): Let me tell you it's the first time I have worn it—the very first time.

TESMAN: And a very nice bonnet it is too—quite a beauty!

MISS TESMAN: Oh, it's no such great things, George. (*Looks around her.*) My parasol—? Ah, here. (*Takes it.*) For this is mine too—(*mutters*)—not Berta's.

TESMAN: A new bonnet and a new parasol! Only think, Hedda!

HEDDA: Very handsome indeed.

TESMAN: Yes, isn't it? Eh? But Auntie, take a good look at Hedda before you go! See how handsome she is!

MISS TESMAN: Oh, my dear boy, there's nothing new in that. Hedda was always lovely. (*She nods and goes toward the right.*)

TESMAN (*following*): Yes, but have you noticed what splendid condition she is in? How she has filled out on the journey?

HEDDA (*crossing the room*): Oh, do be quiet—!

MISS TESMAN (*who has stopped and turned*): Filled out?

TESMAN: Of course you don't notice it so much now that she has that dress on. But I, who can see—

HEDDA (*at the glass door, impatiently*): Oh, you can't see anything.

TESMAN: It must be the mountain air in the Tyrol—

HEDDA (*curtly, interrupting*): I am exactly as I was when I started.

TESMAN: So you insist; but I'm quite certain you are not. Don't you agree with me, Auntie?

MISS TESMAN (*who has been gazing at her with folded hands*): Hedda is lovely—lovely—lovely. (*Goes up to her, takes her head between both hands, draws it downward, and kisses her hair.*) God bless and preserve Hedda Tesman—for George's sake.

HEDDA (*gently freeing herself*): Oh—! Let me go.

MISS TESMAN (*in quiet emotion*): I shall not let a day pass without coming to see you.

TESMAN: No you won't, will you, Auntie? Eh?

MISS TESMAN: Good-bye—good-bye!

She goes out by the hall door. TESMAN *accompanies her. The door remains half open.* TESMAN *can be heard repeating his message to Aunt Rina and his thanks for the slippers.*

In the meantime, HEDDA *walks about the room, raising her arms and clenching her hands as if in desperation. Then she flings back the curtains from the glass door, and stands there looking out.*

Presently TESMAN *returns and closes the door behind him.*

TESMAN (*picks up the slippers from the floor*): What are you looking at, Hedda?

HEDDA (*once more calm and mistress of herself*): I am only looking at the leaves. They are so yellow—so withered.

TESMAN (*wraps up the slippers and lays them on the table*): Well you see, we are well into September now.

HEDDA (*again restless*): Yes, to think of it!—Already in—in September.

TESMAN: Don't you think Aunt Julia's manner was strange, dear? Almost solemn? Can you imagine what was the matter with her? Eh?

HEDDA: I scarcely know her, you see. Is she not often like that?

TESMAN: No, not as she was today.

HEDDA (*leaving the glass door*): Do you think she was annoyed about the bonnet?

TESMAN: Oh, scarcely at all. Perhaps a little, just at the moment—

HEDDA: But what an idea, to pitch her bonnet about in the drawing room! No one does that sort of thing.

TESMAN: Well you may be sure Aunt Julia won't do it again.

HEDDA: In any case, I shall manage to make my peace with her.

TESMAN: Yes, my dear, good Hedda, if you only would.

HEDDA: When you call this afternoon, you might invite her to spend the evening here.

TESMAN: Yes, that I will. And there's one thing more you could do that would delight her heart.

HEDDA: What is it?

TESMAN: If you could only prevail on yourself to say *du*⁴ to her. For my sake, Hedda? Eh?

HEDDA: No no, Tesman—you really mustn't ask that of me. I have told you so already. I shall try to call her "Aunt"; and you must be satisfied with that.

TESMAN: Well, well. Only I think now that you belong to the family, you—

HEDDA: Hm—I can't in the least see why— (*She goes up toward the middle doorway.*)

TESMAN (*after a pause*): Is there anything the matter with you, Hedda? Eh?

HEDDA: I'm only looking at my old piano. It doesn't go at all well with all the other things.

TESMAN: The first time I draw my salary, we'll see about exchanging it.

HEDDA: No, no—no exchanging. I don't want to part with it. Suppose we put it there in the inner room, and then get another here in its place. When it's convenient, I mean.

TESMAN (*a little taken aback*): Yes—of course we could do that.

HEDDA (*takes up the bouquet from the piano*): These flowers were not here last night when we arrived.

TESMAN: Aunt Julia must have brought them for you.

HEDDA (*examining the bouquet*): A visiting card. (*Takes it out and reads:*) "Shall return later in the day." Can you guess whose card it is?

TESMAN: No. Whose? Eh?

HEDDA: The name is "Mrs. Elvsted."

TESMAN: Is it really? Sheriff Elvsted's wife? Miss Rysing that was.

HEDDA: Exactly. The girl with the irritating hair, that she was always showing off. An old flame of yours I've been told.

TESMAN (*laughing*): Oh, that didn't last long; and it was before I knew you, Hedda. But fancy her being in town!

HEDDA: It's odd that she should call upon us. I have scarcely seen her since we left school.

TESMAN: I haven't seen her either for—heaven knows how long. I wonder how she can endure to live in such an out-of-the-way hole—eh?

HEDDA (*after a moment's thought says suddenly*): Tell me, Tesman—isn't it somewhere near there that he—that—Eilert Lövborg is living?

TESMAN: Yes, he is somewhere in that part of the country.

BERTA *enters by the hall door.*

BERTA: That lady, ma'am, that brought some flowers a little while ago, is here again. (*Pointing.*) The flowers you have in your hand, ma'am.

HEDDA: Ah, is she? Well, please show her in.

BERTA *opens the door for* MRS. ELVSTED, *and goes out herself.*—MRS. ELVSTED *is a woman of fragile figure, with pretty, soft features. Her eyes are light blue, large, round, and somewhat prominent, with a startled, inquiring expression. Her hair is remarkably light, almost flaxen, and unusually abundant and wavy. She is a couple of years younger than* HEDDA. *She wears a dark visiting dress, tasteful, but not quite in the latest fashion.*

HEDDA (*receives her warmly*): How do you do, my dear Mrs. Elvsted? It's delightful to see you again.

MRS. ELVSTED (*nervously, struggling for self-control*): Yes, it's a very long time since we met.

TESMAN (*gives her his hand*): And we too—eh?

HEDDA: Thanks for your lovely flowers—

MRS. ELVSTED: Oh, not at all—I would have come straight here yesterday afternoon; but I heard that you were away—

TESMAN: Have you just come to town? Eh?

MRS. ELVSTED: I arrived yesterday, about midday. Oh, I was quite in despair when I heard that you were not at home.

HEDDA: In despair! How so?

TESMAN: Why, my dear Mrs. Rysing—I mean Mrs. Elvsted—

HEDDA: I hope that you are not in any trouble?

MRS. ELVSTED: Yes, I am. And I don't know another living creature here that I can turn to.

HEDDA (*laying the bouquet on the table*): Come—let us sit here on the sofa—

MRS. ELVSTED: Oh, I am too restless to sit down.

HEDDA: Oh no, you're not. Come here. (*She draws* MRS. ELVSTED *down upon the sofa and sits at her side.*)

TESMAN: Well? What is it, Mrs. Elvsted?

HEDDA: Has anything particular happened to you at home?

MRS. ELVSTED: Yes—and no. Oh—I am so anxious you should not misunderstand me—

HEDDA: Then your best plan is to tell us the whole story, Mrs. Elvsted.

TESMAN: I suppose that's what you have come for—eh?

MRS. ELVSTED: Yes, yes—of course it is. Well then, I must tell you—if you don't already know—that Eilert Lövborg is in town, too.

HEDDA: Lövborg—!

TESMAN: What! Has Eilert Lövborg come back? Fancy that, Hedda!

HEDDA: Well, well—I hear it.

MRS. ELVSTED: He has been here a week already. Just fancy—a whole week! In this terrible town, alone! With so many temptations on all sides.

HEDDA: But my dear Mrs. Elvsted—how does he concern you so much?

MRS. ELVSTED (*looks at her with a startled air, and says rapidly*): He was the children's tutor.

HEDDA: Your children's?

MRS. ELVSTED: My husband's. I have none.

HEDDA: Your stepchildren's, then?

MRS. ELVSTED: Yes.

TESMAN (*somewhat hesitatingly*): Then was he—I don't know how to express it—was he—regular enough in his habits to be fit for the post? Eh?

MRS. ELVSTED: For the last two years his conduct has been irreproachable.

TESMAN: Has it indeed? Fancy that, Hedda!

HEDDA: I hear it.

MRS. ELVSTED: Perfectly irreproachable, I assure you! In every respect. But all the same—now that I know he is here—in this great town—and with a large sum of money in his hands—I can't help being in mortal fear for him.

TESMAN: Why did he not remain where he was? With you and your husband? Eh?

MRS. ELVSTED: After his book was published he was too restless and unsettled to remain with us.

TESMAN: Yes, by-the-bye, Aunt Julia told me he had published a new book.

MRS. ELVSTED: Yes, a big book, dealing with the march of civilization—in broad outline, as it were. It came out about a fortnight ago. And since it has sold so well, and been so much read—and made such a sensation—

TESMAN: Has it indeed? It must be something he has had lying by since his better days.

MRS. ELVSTED: Long ago, you mean?

TESMAN: Yes.

MRS. ELVSTED: No, he has written it all since he has been with us—within the last year.

TESMAN: Isn't that good news, Hedda? Think of that.

MRS. ELVSTED: Ah, yes, if only it would last!

HEDDA: Have you seen him here in town?

MRS. ELVSTED: No, not yet. I have had the greatest difficulty in finding out his address. But this morning I discovered it at last.

HEDDA (looks searchingly at her): Do you know, it seems to me a little odd of your husband—hm—

MRS. ELVSTED (starting nervously): Of my husband! What?

HEDDA: That he should send you to town on such an errand—that he does not come himself and look after his friend.

MRS. ELVSTED: Oh no, no—my husband has no time. And besides, I—I had some shopping to do.

HEDDA (with a slight smile): Ah, that is a different matter.

MRS. ELVSTED (rising quickly and uneasily): And now I beg and implore you, Mr. Tesman—receive Eilert Lövborg kindly if he comes to you! And that he is sure to do. You see you were such great friends in the old days. And then you are interested in the same studies—the same branch of science—so far as I can understand.

TESMAN: We used to be, at any rate.

MRS. ELVSTED: That is why I beg so earnestly that you—you too—will keep a sharp eye upon him. Oh, you will promise me that, Mr. Tesman—won't you?

TESMAN: With the greatest of pleasure, Mrs. Rysing—

HEDDA: Elvsted.

TESMAN: I assure you I shall do all I possibly can for Eilert. You may rely upon me.

MRS. ELVSTED: Oh, how very, very kind of you! (Presses his hands.) Thanks, thanks, thanks! (Frightened.) You see, my husband is so very fond of him!

HEDDA (rising): You ought to write to him, Tesman. Perhaps he may not care to come to you of his own accord.

TESMAN: Well, perhaps it would be the right thing to do, Hedda? Eh?

HEDDA: And the sooner the better. Why not at once?

MRS. ELVSTED (imploringly): Oh, if you only would!

TESMAN: I'll write this moment. Have you his address, Mrs.—Mrs. Elvsted.

MRS. ELVSTED: Yes. (Takes a slip of paper from her pocket, and hands it to him.) Here it is.

TESMAN: Good, good. Then I'll go in— (Looks about him.) By-the-bye,—my slippers? Oh, here. (Takes the packet, and is about to go.)

HEDDA: Be sure you write him a cordial, friendly letter. And a good long one too.

TESMAN: Yes, I will.

MRS. ELVSTED: But please, please don't say a word to show that I have suggested it.

TESMAN: No, how could you think I would? Eh? *(He goes out to the right, through the inner room.)*

HEDDA *(goes up to* MRS. ELVSTED, *smiles, and says in a low voice)*: There! We have killed two birds with one stone.

MRS. ELVSTED: What do you mean?

HEDDA: Could you not see that I wanted him to go?

MRS. ELVSTED: Yes, to write the letter—

HEDDA: And that I might speak to you alone.

MRS. ELVSTED *(confused)*: About the same thing?

HEDDA: Precisely.

MRS. ELVSTED *(apprehensively)*: But there is nothing more, Mrs. Tesman! Absolutely nothing!

HEDDA: Oh, yes, but there is. There is a great deal more—I can see that. Sit here—and we'll have a cosy, confidential chat. *(She forces* MRS. ELVSTED *to sit in the easy chair beside the stove, and seats herself on one of the footstools.)*

MRS. ELVSTED *(anxiously, looking at her watch)*: But, my dear Mrs. Tesman—I was really on the point of going.

HEDDA: Oh, you can't be in such a hurry.—Well? Now tell me something about your life at home.

MRS. ELVSTED: Oh, that is just what I care least to speak about.

HEDDA: But to me, dear—? Why, weren't we schoolfellows?

MRS. ELVSTED: Yes, but you were in the class above me. Oh, how dreadfully afraid of you I was then!

HEDDA: Afraid of me?

MRS. ELVSTED: Yes, dreadfully. For when we met on the stairs you used always to pull my hair.

HEDDA: Did I, really?

MRS. ELVSTED: Yes, and once you said you would burn it off my head.

HEDDA: Oh, that was all nonsense, of course.

MRS. ELVSTED: Yes, but I was so silly in those days.—And since then, too—we have drifted so far—far apart from each other. Our circles have been so entirely different.

HEDDA: Well then, we must try to drift together again. Now listen! At school we said *du* to each other; and we called each other by our Christian names—

MRS. ELVSTED: No, I am sure you must be mistaken.

HEDDA: No, not at all! I can remember quite distinctly. So now we are going to renew our old friendship. (*Draws the footstool closer to* MRS. ELVSTED.) There now! (*Kisses her cheek.*) You must say *du* to me and call me Hedda.

MRS. ELVSTED (*presses and pats her hands*): Oh, how good and kind you are! I am not used to such kindness.

HEDDA: There, there, there! And I shall say *du* to you, as in the old days, and call you my dear Thora.

MRS. ELVSTED: My name is Thea.

HEDDA: Why, of course! I meant Thea. (*Looks at her compassionately.*) So you are not accustomed to goodness and kindness, Thea? Not in your own home?

MRS. ELVSTED: Oh, if I only had a home! But I haven't any; I have never had a home.

HEDDA (*looks at her for a moment*): I almost suspected as much.

MRS. ELVSTED (*gazing helplessly before her*): Yes—yes—yes.

HEDDA: I don't quite remember—was it not as housekeeper that you first went to Mr. Elvsted's?

MRS. ELVSTED: I really went as governess. But his wife—his late wife—was an invalid,—and rarely left her room. So I had to look after the housekeeping as well.

HEDDA: And then—at last—you became mistress of the house.

MRS. ELVSTED (*sadly*): Yes, I did.

HEDDA: Let me see—about how long ago was that?

MRS. ELVSTED: My marriage?

HEDDA: Yes.

MRS. ELVSTED: Five years ago.

HEDDA: To be sure; it must be that.

MRS. ELVSTED: Oh, those five years—! Or at all events the last two or three of them! Oh, if you could only imagine—

HEDDA (*giving her a little slap on the hand*): De?[5] Fie, Thea!

MRS. ELVSTED: Yes, yes, I will try— Well, if—you could only imagine and understand—

HEDDA (*lightly*): Eilert Lövborg has been in your neighborhood about three years, hasn't he?

MRS. ELVSTED (*looks at her doubtfully*): Eilert Lövborg? Yes—he has.

HEDDA: Had you known him before, in town here?

MRS. ELVSTED: Scarcely at all. I mean—I knew him by name of course.

HEDDA: But you saw a good deal of him in the country?

MRS. ELVSTED: Yes, he came to us every day. You see, he gave the children lessons; for in the long run I couldn't manage it all myself.

HEDDA: No, that's clear.—And your husband—? I suppose he is often away from home?

MRS. ELVSTED: Yes. Being sheriff, you know, he has to travel about a good deal in his district.

HEDDA (*leaning against the arm of the chair*): Thea—my poor, sweet Thea—now you must tell me everything—exactly as it stands.

MRS. ELVSTED: Well then, you must question me.

HEDDA: What sort of man is your husband, Thea? I mean—you know—in everyday life. Is he kind to you?

MRS. ELVSTED (*evasively*): I am sure he means well in everything.

HEDDA: I should think he must be altogether too old for you. There is at least twenty years' difference between you, is there not?

MRS. ELVSTED (*irritably*): Yes, that is true, too. Everything about him is repellent to me! We have not a thought in common. We have no single point of sympathy—he and I.

HEDDA: But is he not fond of you all the same? In his own way?

MRS. ELVSTED: Oh, I really don't know. I think he regards me simply as a useful property. And then it doesn't cost much to keep me. I am not expensive.

HEDDA: That is stupid of you.

MRS. ELVSTED (*shakes her head*): It cannot be otherwise—not with him. I don't think he really cares for anyone but himself—and perhaps a little for the children.

HEDDA: And for Eilert Lövborg, Thea.

MRS. ELVSTED (*looking at her*): For Eilert Lövborg? What puts that into your head?

HEDDA: Well, my dear—I should say, when he sends you after him all the way to town— (*Smiling almost imperceptibly.*) And besides, you said so yourself, to Tesman.

MRS. ELVSTED (*with a little nervous twitch*): Did I? Yes, I suppose I did. (*Vehemently, but not loudly.*) No—I may just as well make a clean breast of it at once! For it must all come out in any case.

HEDDA: Why, my dear Thea—?

MRS. ELVSTED: Well, to make a long story short: My husband did not know that I was coming.

HEDDA: What! Your husband didn't know it!

MRS. ELVSTED: No, of course not. For that matter, he was away from home himself—he was traveling. Oh, I could bear it no longer, Hedda! I couldn't indeed—so utterly alone as I should have been in the future.

HEDDA: Well? And then?

MRS. ELVSTED: So I put together some of my things—what I needed most—as quietly as possible. And then I left the house.

HEDDA: Without a word?

MRS. ELVSTED: Yes—and took the train straight to town.

HEDDA: Why, my dear, good Thea—to think of you daring to do it!

MRS. ELVSTED (*rises and moves about the room*): What else could I possibly do?

HEDDA: But what do you think your husband will say when you go home again?

MRS. ELVSTED (*at the table, looks at her*): Back to him?

HEDDA: Of course.

MRS. ELVSTED: I shall never go back to him again.

HEDDA (*rising and going toward her*): Then you have left your home—for good and all?

MRS. ELVSTED: Yes. There was nothing else to be done.

HEDDA: But then—to take flight so openly.

MRS. ELVSTED: Oh, it's impossible to keep things of that sort secret.

HEDDA: But what do you think people will say of you, Thea?

MRS. ELVSTED: They may say what they like, for aught *I* care. (*Seats herself wearily and sadly on the sofa.*) I have done nothing but what I had to do.

HEDDA (*after a short silence*): And what are your plans now? What do you think of doing?

MRS. ELVSTED: I don't know yet. I only know this, that I must live here, where Eilert Lövborg is—if I am to live at all.

HEDDA (*takes a chair from the table, seats herself beside her, and strokes her hands*): My dear Thea—how did this—this friendship—between you and Eilert Lövborg come about?

MRS. ELVSTED: Oh, it grew up gradually. I gained a sort of influence over him.

HEDDA: Indeed?

MRS. ELVSTED: He gave up his old habits. Not because I asked him to, for I never dared do that. But of course he saw how repulsive they were to me; and so he dropped them.

HEDDA (*concealing an involuntary smile of scorn*): Then you have reclaimed him—as the saying goes—my little Thea.

MRS. ELVSTED: So he says himself, at any rate. And he, on his side, has made a real human being of me—taught me to think, and to understand so many things.

HEDDA: Did he give you lessons too, then?

MRS. ELVSTED: No, not exactly lessons. But he talked to me—talked about such an infinity of things. And then came the lovely, happy time when I began to share in his work—when he allowed me to help him!

HEDDA: Oh, he did, did he?

MRS. ELVSTED: Yes! He never wrote anything without my assistance.

HEDDA: You were two good comrades, in fact?

MRS. ELVSTED (*eagerly*): Comrades! Yes, fancy, Hedda—that is the very word he used!—Oh, I ought to feel perfectly happy; and yet I cannot; for I don't know how long it will last.

HEDDA: Are you no surer of him than that?

MRS. ELVSTED (*gloomily*): A woman's shadow stands between Eilert Lövborg and me.

HEDDA (*looks at her anxiously*): Who can that be?

MRS. ELVSTED: I don't know. Someone he knew in his—in his past. Someone he has never been able wholly to forget.

HEDDA: What has he told you—about this?

MRS. ELVSTED: He has only once—quite vaguely—alluded to it.

HEDDA: Well! And what did he say?

MRS. ELVSTED: He said that when they parted, she threatened to shoot him with a pistol.

HEDDA (*with cold composure*): Oh, nonsense! No one does that sort of thing here.

MRS. ELVSTED: No. And that is why I think it must have been that red-haired singing-woman whom he once—

HEDDA: Yes, very likely.

MRS. ELVSTED: For I remember they used to say of her that she carried loaded firearms.

HEDDA: Oh—then of course it must have been she.

MRS. ELVSTED (*wringing her hands*): And now just fancy, Hedda—I hear that this singing-woman—that she is in town again! Oh, I don't know what to do—

HEDDA (*glancing toward the inner room*): Hush! Here comes Tesman. (*Rises and whispers.*) Thea—all this must remain between you and me.

MRS. ELVSTED (*springing up*): Oh, yes, yes! for heaven's sake—!

GEORGE TESMAN, *with a letter in his hand, comes from the right through the inner room.*

TESMAN: There now—the epistle is finished.

HEDDA: That's right. And now Mrs. Elvsted is just going. Wait a moment—I'll go with you to the garden gate.

TESMAN: Do you think Berta could post the letter, Hedda dear?

HEDDA *(takes it)*: I will tell her to.

BERTA *enters from the hall.*

BERTA: Judge Brack wishes to know if Mrs. Tesman will receive him.

HEDDA: Yes, ask Judge Brack to come in. And look here—put this letter in the post.

BERTA *(taking the letter)*: Yes, ma'am.

She opens the door for JUDGE BRACK *and goes out herself. BRACK is a man of forty-five; thick-set, but well-built and elastic in his movements. His face is roundish with an aristocratic profile. His hair is short, still almost black, and carefully dressed. His eyes are lively and sparkling. His eyebrows thick. His mustache is also thick, with short-cut ends. He wears a well-cut walking suit, a little too youthful for his age. He uses an eyeglass, which he now and then lets drop.*

JUDGE BRACK *(with his hat in his hand, bowing)*: May one venture to call so early in the day?

HEDDA: Of course one may.

TESMAN *(presses his hand)*: You are welcome at any time. *(Introducing him.)* Judge Brack—Miss Rysing—

HEDDA: Oh—!

BRACK *(bowing)*: Ah—delighted—

HEDDA *(looks at him and laughs)*: It's nice to have a look at you by daylight, Judge!

BRACK: Do you find me—altered?

HEDDA: A little younger, I think.

BRACK: Thank you so much.

TESMAN: But what do you think of Hedda—eh? Doesn't she look flourishing? She has actually—

HEDDA: Oh, do leave me alone. You haven't thanked Judge Brack for all the trouble he has taken—

BRACK: Oh, nonsense—it was a pleasure to me—

HEDDA: Yes, you are a friend indeed. But here stands Thea all impatience to be off—so *au revoir* Judge. I shall be back again presently. (*Mutual salutations.* MRS. ELVSTED *and* HEDDA *go out by the hall door.*)

BRACK: Well,—is your wife tolerably satisfied—

TESMAN: Yes, we can't thank you sufficiently. Of course she talks of a little rearrangement here and there; and one or two things are still wanting. We shall have to buy some additional trifles.

BRACK: Indeed!

TESMAN: But we won't trouble you about these things. Hedda says she herself will look after what is wanting.— Shan't we sit down? Eh?

BRACK: Thanks, for a moment. (*Seats himself beside the table.*) There is something I wanted to speak to you about, my dear Tesman.

TESMAN: Indeed? Ah, I understand! (*Seating himself.*) I suppose it's the serious part of the frolic that is coming now. Eh?

BRACK: Oh, the money question is not so very pressing; though, for that matter, I wish we had gone a little more economically to work.

TESMAN: But that would never have done, you know! Think of Hedda, my dear fellow! You, who know her so well—. I couldn't possibly ask her to put up with a shabby style of living!

BRACK: No, no—that is just the difficulty.

TESMAN: And then—fortunately—it can't be long before I receive my appointment.

BRACK: Well, you see—such things are often apt to hang fire for a time.

TESMAN: Have you heard anything definite? Eh?

BRACK: Nothing exactly definite—(*Interrupting himself.*) But, by-the-bye—I have one piece of news for you.

TESMAN: Well?

BRACK: Your old friend, Eilert Lövborg, has returned to town.

TESMAN: I know that already.

BRACK: Indeed! How did you learn it?

TESMAN: From that lady who went out with Hedda.

BRACK: Really? What was her name? I didn't quite catch it.

TESMAN: Mrs. Elvsted.

BRACK: Aha—Sheriff Elvsted's wife? Of course—he has been living up in their regions.

TESMAN: And fancy—I'm delighted to hear that he is quite a reformed character!

BRACK: So they say.

TESMAN: And then he has published a new book—eh?

BRACK: Yes, indeed he has.

TESMAN: And I hear it has made some sensation!

BRACK: Quite an unusual sensation.

TESMAN: Fancy—isn't that good news! A man of such extraordinary talents—I felt so grieved to think that he had gone irretrievably to ruin.

BRACK: That was what everybody thought.

TESMAN: But I cannot imagine what he will take to now! How in the world will he be able to make his living? Eh?

During the last words, HEDDA *has entered by the hall door.*

HEDDA (*to* BRACK, *laughing with a touch of scorn*): Tesman is forever worrying about how people are to make their living.

TESMAN: Well, you see, dear—we were talking about poor Eilert Lövborg.

HEDDA (*glancing at him rapidly*): Oh, indeed? (*Seats herself in the armchair beside the stove and asks indifferently.*) What is the matter with him?

TESMAN: Well—no doubt he has run through all his property long ago; and he can scarcely write a new book every year—eh? So I really can't see what is to become of him.

BRACK: Perhaps I can give you some information on that point.

TESMAN: Indeed!

BRACK: You must remember that his relations have a good deal of influence.

TESMAN: Oh, his relations, unfortunately, have entirely washed their hands of him.

BRACK: At one time they called him the hope of the family.

TESMAN: At one time, yes! But he has put an end to all that.

HEDDA: Who knows? *(With a slight smile.)* I hear they have reclaimed him up at Sheriff Elvsted's—

BRACK: And then this book that he has published—

TESMAN: Well, well, I hope to goodness they may find something for him to do. I have just written to him. I asked him to come and see us this evening, Hedda dear.

BRACK: But, my dear fellow, you are booked for my bachelor's party this evening. You promised on the pier last night.

HEDDA: Had you forgotten, Tesman?

TESMAN: Yes, I had utterly forgotten.

BRACK: But it doesn't matter, for you may be sure he won't come.

TESMAN: What makes you think that? Eh?

BRACK *(with a little hesitation, rising and resting his hands on the back of his chair)*: My dear Tesman—and you too, Mrs. Tesman—I think I ought not to keep you in the dark about something that—that—

TESMAN: That concerns Eilert—?

BRACK: Both you and him.

TESMAN: Well, my dear Judge, out with it.

BRACK: You must be prepared to find your appointment deferred longer than you desired or expected.

TESMAN *(jumping up uneasily)*: Is there some hitch about it? Eh?

BRACK: The nomination may perhaps be made conditional on the result of a competition—

TESMAN: Competition! Think of that, Hedda!

HEDDA (*leans farther back in the chair*): Aha—aah!

TESMAN: But who can my competitor be? Surely not—?

BRACK: Yes, precisely—Eilert Lövborg.

TESMAN (*clasping his hands*): No, no—it's quite inconceivable! Quite impossible! Eh?

BRACK: Hm—that is what it may come to, all the same.

TESMAN: Well but, Judge Brack—it would show the most incredible lack of consideration for me. (*Gesticulates with his arms.*) For—just think—I'm a married man! We have married on the strength of these prospects, Hedda and I; and run deep into debt; and borrowed money from Aunt Julia too. Good heavens, they had as good as promised me the appointment. Eh?

BRACK: Well, well, well—no doubt you will get it in the end; only after a contest.

HEDDA (*immovable in her armchair*): Fancy, Tesman, there will be a sort of sporting interest in that.

TESMAN: Why, my dearest Hedda, how can you be so indifferent about it?

HEDDA (*as before*): I am not at all indifferent. I am most eager to see who wins.

BRACK: In any case, Mrs. Tesman, it is best that you should know how matters stand. I mean—before you set about the little purchases I hear you are threatening.

HEDDA: This can make no difference.

BRACK: Indeed! Then I have no more to say. Good-bye! (*To* TESMAN.) I shall look in on my way back from my afternoon walk, and take you home with me.

TESMAN: Oh yes, yes—your news has quite upset me.

HEDDA (*reclining, holds out her hand*): Good-bye, Judge; and be sure you call in the afternoon.

BRACK: Many thanks. Good-bye, good-bye!

TESMAN (*accompanying him to the door*): Good-bye, my dear Judge! You must really excuse me— (JUDGE BRACK *goes out by the hall door.*)

TESMAN (*crosses the room*): Oh, Hedda—one should never rush into adventures. Eh?

HEDDA (*looks at him, smiling*): Do you do that?

TESMAN: Yes, dear—there is no denying—it was adventurous to go and marry and set up house upon mere expectations.

HEDDA: Perhaps you are right there.

TESMAN: Well—at all events, we have our delightful home, Hedda! Fancy, the home we both dreamed of—the home we were in love with, I may almost say. Eh?

HEDDA (*rising slowly and wearily*): It was part of our compact that we were to go into society—to keep open house.

TESMAN: Yes, if you only knew how I had been looking forward to it! Fancy—to see you as hostess—in a select circle! Eh? Well, well, well—for the present we shall have to get on without society, Hedda—only to invite Aunt Julia now and then.—Oh, I intended you to lead such an utterly different life, dear—!

HEDDA: Of course I cannot have my man in livery just yet.

TESMAN: Oh no, unfortunately. It would be out of the question for us to keep a footman, you know.

HEDDA: And the saddle horse I was to have had—

TESMAN (*aghast*): The saddle horse!

HEDDA: —I suppose I must not think of that now.

TESMAN: Good heavens, no!—that's as clear as daylight.

HEDDA (*goes up the room*): Well, I shall have one thing at least to kill time with in the meanwhile.

TESMAN (*beaming*): Oh, thank heaven for that! What is it, Hedda? Eh?

HEDDA (*in the middle doorway, looks at him with covert scorn*): My pistols, George.

TESMAN (*in alarm*): Your pistols!

HEDDA (*with cold eyes*): General Gabler's pistols. (*She goes out through the inner room, to the left.*)

TESMAN (*rushes up to the middle doorway and calls after her*): No, for heaven's sake, Hedda darling—don't touch those dangerous things! For my sake, Hedda! Eh?

ACT TWO

The room at the TESMANS' *as in the first act, except that the piano has been removed, and an elegant little writing table with bookshelves put in its place. A smaller table stands near the sofa on the left. Most of the bouquets have been taken away.* MRS. ELVSTED'S *bouquet is upon the large table in front.—It is afternoon.*

> HEDDA, *dressed to receive callers, is alone in the room. She stands by the open glass door, loading a revolver. The fellow to it lies in an open pistol case on the writing table.*

HEDDA (*looks down the garden, and calls*): So you are here again, Judge!

BRACK (*is heard calling from a distance*): As you see, Mrs. Tesman!

HEDDA (*raises the pistol and points*): Now I'll shoot you, Judge Brack!

BRACK (*calling unseen*): No, no, no! Don't stand aiming at me!

HEDDA: This is what comes of sneaking in by the back way. (*She fires.*)

BRACK (*nearer*): Are you out of your senses—!

HEDDA: Dear me—did I happen to hit you?

BRACK *(still outside)*: I wish you would let these pranks alone!

HEDDA: Come in then, Judge.

JUDGE BRACK, *dressed as though for a men's party, enters by the glass door. He carries a light overcoat over his arm.*

BRACK: What the deuce—haven't you tired of that sport, yet? What are you shooting at?

HEDDA: Oh, I am only firing in the air.

BRACK *(gently takes the pistol out of her hand)*: Allow me, madam! *(Looks at it.)* Ah—I know this pistol well! *(Looks around.)* Where is the case? Ah, here it is. *(Lays the pistol in it, and shuts it.)* Now we won't play at that game anymore today.

HEDDA: Then what in heaven's name would you have me do with myself?

BRACK: Have you had no visitors?

HEDDA *(closing the glass door)*: Not one. I suppose all our set are still out of town.

BRACK: And is Tesman not at home either?

HEDDA *(at the writing table, putting the pistol case in a drawer which she shuts)*: No. He rushed off to his aunt's directly after lunch; he didn't expect you so early.

BRACK: Hm—how stupid of me not to have thought of that!

HEDDA *(turning her head to look at him)*: Why stupid?

BRACK: Because if I had thought of it I should have come a little—earlier.

HEDDA *(crossing the room)*: Then you would have found no one to receive you; for I have been in my room changing my dress ever since lunch.

BRACK: And is there no sort of little chink that we could hold a parley through?[6]

HEDDA: You have forgotten to arrange one.

BRACK: That was another piece of stupidity.

HEDDA: Well, we must just settle down here—and wait. Tesman is not likely to be back for some time yet.

BRACK: Never mind; I shall not be impatient.

HEDDA *seats herself in the corner of the sofa.* BRACK *lays his overcoat over the back of the nearest chair, and sits down, but keeps his hat in his hand. A short silence. They look at each other.*

HEDDA: Well?

BRACK *(in the same tone)*: Well?

HEDDA: I spoke first.

BRACK *(bending a little forward)*: Come, let us have a cosy little chat, Mrs. Hedda.

HEDDA *(leaning further back in the sofa)*: Does it not seem like a whole eternity since our last talk? Of course I don't count those few words yesterday evening and this morning.

BRACK: You mean since our last confidential talk? Our last *tête-à-tête?*

HEDDA: Well, yes—since you put it so.

BRACK: Not a day has passed but I have wished that you were home again.

HEDDA: And I have done nothing but wish the same thing.

BRACK: You? Really, Mrs. Hedda? And I thought you had been enjoying your tour so much!

HEDDA: Oh, yes, you may be sure of that!

BRACK: But Tesman's letters spoke of nothing but happiness.

HEDDA: Oh, Tesman! You see, he thinks nothing so delightful as grubbing in libraries and making copies of old parchments, or whatever you call them.

BRACK *(with a spice of malice)*: Well, that is his vocation in life—or part of it at any rate.

HEDDA: Yes, of course; and no doubt when it's your vocation—But *I!* Oh, my dear Mr. Brack, how mortally bored I have been.

BRACK *(sympathetically)*: Do you really say so? In downright earnest?

HEDDA: Yes, you can surely understand it—! To go for six whole months without meeting a soul that knew anything of our circle, or could talk about the things we are interested in.

BRACK: Yes, yes—I too should feel that a deprivation.

HEDDA: And then, what I found most intolerable of all—

BRACK: Well?

HEDDA: —was being everlastingly in the company of—one and the same person—

BRACK *(with a nod of assent)*: Morning, noon, and night, yes—at all possible times and seasons.

HEDDA: I said "everlastingly."

BRACK: Just so. But I should have thought, with our excellent Tesman, one could—

HEDDA: Tesman is—a specialist, my dear Judge.

BRACK: Undeniably.

HEDDA: And specialists are not at all amusing to travel with. Not in the long run at any rate.

BRACK: Not even—the specialist one happens to love?

HEDDA: Faugh—don't use that sickening word!

BRACK *(taken aback)*: What do you say, Mrs. Hedda?

HEDDA *(half laughing, half irritated)*: You should just try it! To hear of nothing but the history of civilization, morning, noon, and night—

BRACK: Everlastingly.

HEDDA: Yes, yes, yes! And then all this about the domestic industry of the middle ages—! That's the most disgusting part of it!

BRACK *(looks searchingly at her)*: But tell me—in that case, how am I to understand your—? Hm—

HEDDA: My accepting George Tesman, you mean?

BRACK: Well, let us put it so.

HEDDA: Good heavens, do you see anything so wonderful in that?

BRACK: Yes and no—Mrs. Hedda.

HEDDA: I had positively danced myself tired, my dear Judge. My day was done— *(With a slight shudder.)* Oh no—I won't say that; nor think it either.

BRACK: You have assuredly no reason to.

HEDDA: Oh, reasons— *(Watching him closely.)* And George

Tesman—after all, you must admit that he is correctness itself.

BRACK: His correctness and respectability are beyond all question.

HEDDA: And I don't see anything absolutely ridiculous about him.—Do you?

BRACK: Ridiculous? N—no—I shouldn't exactly say so—

HEDDA: Well—and his powers of research, at all events, are untiring.—I see no reason why he should not one day come to the front, after all.

BRACK (looks at her hesitatingly): I thought that you, like everyone else, expected him to attain the highest distinction.

HEDDA (with an expression of fatigue): Yes, so I did.—And then, since he was bent, at all hazards, on being allowed to provide for me—I really don't know why I should not have accepted his offer?

BRACK: No—if you look at it in that light—

HEDDA: It was more than my other adorers were prepared to do for me, my dear Judge.

BRACK (laughing): Well, I can't answer for all the rest; but as for myself, you know quite well that I have always entertained a—a certain respect for the marriage tie—for marriage as an institution, Mrs. Hedda.

HEDDA (jestingly): Oh, I assure you I have never cherished any hopes with respect to you.

BRACK: All I require is a pleasant and intimate interior where I can make myself useful in every way, and am free to come and go as—as a trusted friend—

HEDDA: Of the master of the house, do you mean?

BRACK (bowing): Frankly—of the mistress first of all; but of course of the master, too, in the second place. Such a triangular friendship—if I may call it so—is really a great convenience for all parties, let me tell you.

HEDDA: Yes, I have many a time longed for someone to make a third on our travels. Oh—those railway-carriage tête-à-têtes—!

BRACK: Fortunately your wedding journey is over now.

HEDDA (*shaking her head*): Not by a long—long way. I have only arrived at a station on the line.

BRACK: Well, then the passengers jump out and move about a little, Mrs. Hedda.

HEDDA: I never jump out.

BRACK: Really?

HEDDA: No—because there is always someone standing by to—

BRACK (*laughing*): To look at your ankles, do you mean?

HEDDA: Precisely.

BRACK: Well but, dear me—

HEDDA (*with a gesture of repulsion*): I won't have it. I would rather keep my seat where I happen to be—and continue the *tête-à-tête*.

BRACK: But suppose a third person were to jump in and join the couple.

HEDDA: Ah—that is quite another matter!

BRACK: A trusted, sympathetic friend—

HEDDA: —with a fund of conversation on all sorts of lively topics—

BRACK: —and not the least bit of a specialist!

HEDDA (*with an audible sigh*): Yes, that would be a relief indeed.

BRACK (*hears the front door open, and glances in that direction*): The triangle is completed.

HEDDA (*half aloud*): And on goes the train.

GEORGE TESMAN, *in a gray walking suit, with a soft felt hat, enters from the hall. He has a number of unbound books under his arm and in his pockets.*

TESMAN (*goes up to the table beside the corner settee*): Ouf—what a load for a warm day—all these books. (*Lays them on the table.*) I'm positively perspiring, Hedda. Hallo—are you there already, my dear Judge? Eh? Berta didn't tell me.

BRACK (*rising*): I came in through the garden.

HEDDA: What books have you got there?

TESMAN (*stands looking them through*): Some new books on my special subjects—quite indispensable to me.

HEDDA: Your special subjects?

BRACK: Yes, books on his special subjects, Mrs. Tesman. (BRACK *and* HEDDA *exchange a confidential smile.*)

HEDDA: Do you need still more books on your special subjects?

TESMAN: Yes, my dear Hedda, one can never have too many of them. Of course one must keep up with all that is written and published.

HEDDA: Yes, I suppose one must.

TESMAN (*searching among his books*): And look here—I have got hold of Eilert Lövborg's new book too. (*Offering it to her.*) Perhaps you would like to glance through it, Hedda? Eh?

HEDDA: No, thank you. Or rather—afterward perhaps.

TESMAN: I looked into it a little on the way home.

BRACK: Well, what do you think of it—as a specialist?

TESMAN: I think it shows quite remarkable soundness of judgment. He never wrote like that before. (*Putting the books together.*) Now I shall take all these into my study. I'm longing to cut the leaves—! And then I must change my clothes. (*To* BRACK.) I suppose we needn't start just yet? Eh?

BRACK: Oh, dear no—there is not the slightest hurry.

TESMAN: Well then, I will take my time. (*Is going with his books, but stops in the doorway and turns.*) By-the-bye, Hedda—Aunt Julia is not coming this evening.

HEDDA: Not coming? Is it that affair of the bonnet that keeps her away?

TESMAN: Oh, not at all. How could you think such a thing of Aunt Julia? Just fancy—! The fact is, Aunt Rina is very ill.

HEDDA: She always is.

TESMAN: Yes, but today she is much worse than usual, poor dear.

HEDDA: Oh, then it's only natural that her sister should remain with her. I must bear my disappointment.

TESMAN: And you can't imagine, dear, how delighted Aunt
Julia seemed to be—because you had come home looking
so flourishing!

HEDDA (half aloud, rising): Oh, those everlasting aunts!

TESMAN: What?

HEDDA (going to the glass door): Nothing.

TESMAN: Oh, all right. (He goes through the inner room, out
to the right.)

BRACK: What bonnet were you talking about?

HEDDA: Oh, it was a little episode with Miss Tesman this
morning. She had laid down her bonnet on the chair
there—(looks at him and smiles)—And I pretended to
think it was the servant's.

BRACK (shaking his head): Now my dear Mrs. Hedda, how
could you do such a thing? To that excellent old lady, too!

HEDDA (nervously crossing the room): Well, you see—these
impulses come over me all of a sudden; and I cannot resist
them. (Throws herself down in the easy chair by the
stove.) Oh, I don't know how to explain it.

BRACK (behind the easy chair): You are not really happy—
that is at the bottom of it.

HEDDA (looking straight before her): I know of no reason why
I should be—happy. Perhaps you can give me one?

BRACK: Well—among other things, because you have got exactly the home you had set your heart on.

HEDDA (looks up at him and laughs): Do you too believe in
that legend?

BRACK: Is there nothing in it, then?

HEDDA: Oh, yes, there is something in it.

BRACK: Well?

HEDDA: There is this in it, that I made use of Tesman to see
me home from evening parties last summer—

BRACK: I, unfortunately, had to go quite a different way.

HEDDA: That's true. I know you were going a different way
last summer.

BRACK (*laughing*): Oh fie, Mrs. Hedda! Well, then—you and Tesman—?

HEDDA: Well, we happened to pass here one evening; Tesman, poor fellow, was writhing in the agony of having to find conversations; so I took pity on the learned man—

BRACK (*smiles doubtfully*): You took pity? Hm—

HEDDA: Yes, I really did. And so—to help him out of his torment—I happened to say, in pure thoughtlessness, that I should like to live in this villa.

BRACK: No more than that?

HEDDA: Not that evening.

BRACK: But afterward?

HEDDA: Yes, my thoughtlessness had consequences, my dear Judge.

BRACK: Unfortunately that too often happens, Mrs. Hedda.

HEDDA: Thanks! So you see it was this enthusiasm for Secretary Falk's villa that first constituted a bond of sympathy between George Tesman and me. From that came our engagement and our marriage, and our wedding journey, and all the rest of it. Well, well, my dear Judge—as you make your bed so you must lie, I could almost say.

BRACK: This is exquisite! And you really cared not a rap about it all the time?

HEDDA: No, heaven knows I didn't.

BRACK: But now? Now that we have made it so homelike for you?

HEDDA: Uh—the rooms all seem to smell of lavender and dried rose leaves.—But perhaps it's Aunt Julia that has brought that scent with her.

BRACK (*laughing*): No, I think it must be a legacy from the late Mrs. Secretary Falk.

HEDDA: Yes, there is an odor of mortality about it. It reminds me of a bouquet—the day after the ball. (*Clasps her hands behind her head, leans back in her chair and looks at him.*) Oh, my dear Judge—you cannot imagine how horribly I shall bore myself here.

BRACK: Why should not you, too, find some sort of vocation in life, Mrs. Hedda?

HEDDA: A vocation—that should attract me?

BRACK: If possible, of course.

HEDDA: Heaven knows what sort of vocation that could be. I often wonder whether— *(Breaking off.)* But that would never do either.

BRACK: Who can tell? Let me hear what it is.

HEDDA: Whether I might not get Tesman to go into politics, I mean.

BRACK *(laughing)*: Tesman? No, really now, political life is not the thing for him—not at all in his line.

HEDDA: No, I daresay not.—But if I could get him into it all the same?

BRACK: Why—what satisfaction could you find in that? If he is not fitted for that sort of thing, why should you want to drive him into it?

HEDDA: Because I am bored, I tell you! *(After a pause.)* So you think it quite out of the question that Tesman should ever get into the ministry?

BRACK: Hm—you see, my dear Mrs. Hedda—to get into the ministry, he would have to be a tolerably rich man.

HEDDA *(rising impatiently)*: Yes, there we have it! It is this genteel poverty I have managed to drop into—! *(Crosses the room.)* That is what makes life so pitiable! So utterly ludicrous!—For that's what it is.

BRACK: Now *I* should say the fault lay elsewhere.

HEDDA: Where, then?

BRACK: You have never gone through any really stimulating experience.

HEDDA: Anything serious, you mean?

BRACK: Yes, you may call it so. But now you may perhaps have one in store.

HEDDA *(tossing her head)*: Oh, you're thinking of the annoyances about this wretched professorship! But that must be Tesman's own affair. I assure you I shall not waste a thought upon it.

BRACK: No, no, I daresay not. But suppose now that what people call—in elegant language—a solemn responsibility were to come upon you? (*Smiling.*) A new responsibility, Mrs. Hedda?

HEDDA (*angrily*): Be quiet! Nothing of that sort will ever happen!

BRACK (*warily*): We will speak of this again a year hence—at the very outside.

HEDDA (*curtly*): I have no turn for anything of the sort, Judge Brack. No responsibilities for me!

BRACK: Are you so unlike the generality of women as to have no turn for duties which—?

HEDDA (*beside the glass door*): Oh, be quiet, I tell you!—I often think there is only one thing in the world I have any turn for.

BRACK (*drawing near to her*): And what is that, if I may ask?

HEDDA (*stands looking out*): Boring myself to death. Now you know it. (*Turns, looks toward the inner room, and laughs.*) Yes, as I thought! Here comes the Professor.

BRACK (*softly, in a tone of warning*): Come, come, come, Mrs. Hedda!

GEORGE TESMAN, *dressed for the party, with his gloves and hat in his hand, enters from the right through the inner room.*

TESMAN: Hedda, has no message come from Eilert Lövborg? Eh?

HEDDA: No.

TESMAN: Then you'll see he'll be here presently.

BRACK: Do you really think he will come?

TESMAN: Yes, I am almost sure of it. For what you were telling us this morning must have been a mere floating rumor.

BRACK: You think so?

TESMAN: At any rate, Aunt Julia said she did not believe for a moment that he would ever stand in my way again. Fancy that!

BRACK: Well then, that's all right.

TESMAN (*placing his hat and gloves on a chair on the right*): Yes, but you must really let me wait for him as long as possible.

BRACK: We have plenty of time yet. None of my guests will arrive before seven or half-past.

TESMAN: Then meanwhile we can keep Hedda company, and see what happens. Eh?

HEDDA (*placing* BRACK's *hat and overcoat upon the corner settee*): And at the worst Mr. Lövborg can remain here with me.

BRACK (*offering to take his things*): Oh, allow me, Mrs. Tesman!—What do you mean by "At the worst"?

HEDDA: If he won't go with you and Tesman.

TESMAN (*looks dubiously at her*): But, Hedda dear—do you think it would quite do for him to remain with you? Eh? Remember, Aunt Julia can't come.

HEDDA: No, but Mrs. Elvsted is coming. We three can have a cup of tea together.

TESMAN: Oh, yes, that will be all right.

BRACK (*smiling*): And that would perhaps be the safest plan for him.

HEDDA: Why so?

BRACK: Well, you know, Mrs. Tesman, how you used to gird at my little bachelor parties. You declared they were adapted only for men of the strictest principles.

HEDDA: But no doubt Mr. Lövborg's principles are strict enough now. A converted sinner— (BERTA *appears at the hall door.*)

BERTA: There's a gentleman asking if you are at home, ma'am—

HEDDA: Well, show him in.

TESMAN (*softly*): I'm sure it is he! Fancy that!

EILERT LÖVBORG *enters from the hall. He is slim and lean; of the same age as* TESMAN, *but looks older and somewhat worn-out. His hair and beard are of a blackish brown, his face long and pale, but with patches of color on the cheekbones. He is dressed in a well-cut black visiting suit, quite new. He has dark gloves and a silk hat. He stops near the door, and makes a rapid bow, seeming somewhat embarrassed.*

TESMAN *(goes up to him and shakes him warmly by the hand)*: Well, my dear Eilert—so at last we meet again!

EILERT LÖVBORG *(speaks in a subdued voice)*: Thanks for your letter, Tesman. *(Approaching* HEDDA.*)* Will you too shake hands with me, Mrs. Tesman?

HEDDA *(taking his hand)*: I am glad to see you, Mr. Lövborg. *(With a motion of her hand.)* I don't know whether you two gentlemen—?

LÖVBORG *(bowing slightly)*: Judge Brack, I think.

BRACK *(doing likewise)*: Oh yes,—in the old days—

TESMAN *(to* LÖVBORG, *with his hands on his shoulders)*: And now you must make yourself entirely at home, Eilert! Mustn't he, Hedda?—For I hear you are going to settle in town again? Eh?

LÖVBORG: Yes, I am.

TESMAN: Quite right, quite right. Let me tell you, I have got hold of your new book; but I haven't had time to read it yet.

LÖVBORG: You may spare yourself the trouble.

TESMAN: Why so?

LÖVBORG: Because there is very little in it.

TESMAN: Just fancy—how can you say so?

BRACK: But it has been very much praised, I hear.

LÖVBORG: That was what I wanted; so I put nothing into the book but what everyone would agree with.

BRACK: Very wise of you.

TESMAN: Well but, my dear Eilert—!

LÖVBORG: For now I mean to win myself a position again—to make a fresh start.

TESMAN *(a little embarrassed)*: Ah, that is what you wish to do? Eh?

LÖVBORG (*smiling, lays down his hat, and draws a packet, wrapped in paper, from his coat pocket*): But when this one appears, George Tesman, you will have to read it. For this is the real book—the book I have put my true self into.

TESMAN: Indeed? And what is it?

LÖVBORG: It is the continuation.

TESMAN: The continuation? Of what?

LÖVBORG: Of the book.

TESMAN: Of the new book?

LÖVBORG: Of course.

TESMAN: Why, my dear Eilert—does it not come down to our own days?

LÖVBORG: Yes, it does; and this one deals with the future.

TESMAN: With the future! But, good heavens, we know nothing of the future!

LÖVBORG: No; but there is a thing or two to be said about it all the same. (*Opens the packet.*) Look here—

TESMAN: Why, that's not your handwriting.

LÖVBORG: I dictated it. (*Turning over the pages.*) It falls into two sections. The first deals with the civilizing forces of the future. And here is the second—(*running through the pages toward the end*)—forecasting the probable line of development.

TESMAN: How odd now! I should never have thought of writing anything of that sort.

HEDDA (*at the glass door, drumming on the pane*): Hm— I daresay not.

LÖVBORG (*replacing the manuscript in its paper and laying the packet on the table*): I brought it, thinking I might read you a little of it this evening.

TESMAN: That was very good of you, Eilert. But this evening—? (*Looking at* BRACK.) I don't quite see how we can manage it—

LÖVBORG: Well then, some other time. There is no hurry.

BRACK: I must tell you, Mr. Lövborg—there is a little gathering at my house this evening—mainly in honor of Tesman, you know—

LÖVBORG (*looking for his hat*): Oh—then I won't detain you—

BRACK: No, but listen—will you not do me the favor of joining us?

LÖVBORG (*curtly and decidedly*): No, I can't—thank you very much.

BRACK: Oh, nonsense—do! We shall be quite a select little circle. And I assure you we shall have a "lively time," as Mrs. Hed—as Mrs. Tesman says.

LÖVBORG: I have no doubt of it. But nevertheless—

BRACK: And then you might bring your manuscript with you, and read it to Tesman at my house. I could give you a room to yourselves.

TESMAN: Yes, think of that, Eilert,—why shouldn't you? Eh?

HEDDA (*interposing*): But, Tesman, if Mr. Lövborg would really rather not! I am sure Mr. Lövborg is much more inclined to remain here and have supper with me.

LÖVBORG (*looking at her*): With you, Mrs. Tesman?

HEDDA: And with Mrs. Elvsted.

LÖVBORG: Ah— (*Lightly.*) I saw her for a moment this morning.

HEDDA: Did you? Well, she is coming this evening. So you see you are almost bound to remain, Mr. Lövborg, or she will have no one to see her home.

LÖVBORG: That's true. Many thanks, Mrs. Tesman—in that case I will remain.

HEDDA: Then I have one or two orders to give the servant— (*She goes to the hall door and rings.* BERTA *enters.* HEDDA *talks to her in a whisper, and points toward the inner room.* BERTA *nods and goes out again.*)

TESMAN (*at the same time, to* LÖVBORG): Tell me, Eilert—is it this new subject—the future—that you are going to lecture about?

LÖVBORG: Yes.

TESMAN: They told me at the bookseller's that you are going to deliver a course of lectures this autumn.

LÖVBORG: That is my intention. I hope you won't take it ill, Tesman.

TESMAN: Oh no, not in the least! But—?

LÖVBORG: I can quite understand that it must be disagreeable to you.

TESMAN (*cast down*): Oh, I can't expect you, out of consideration for me, to—

LÖVBORG: But I shall wait till you have received your appointment.

TESMAN: Will you wait? Yes, but—yes, but—are you not going to compete with me? Eh?

LÖVBORG: No; it is only the moral victory I care for.

TESMAN: Why, bless me—then Aunt Julia was right after all! Oh yes—I knew it! Hedda! Just fancy—Eilert Lövborg is not going to stand in our way!

HEDDA (*curtly*): Our way? Pray leave me out of the question. (*She goes up toward the inner room, where* BERTA *is placing a tray with decanters and glasses on the table.* HEDDA *nods approval, and comes forward again.* BERTA *goes out.*)

TESMAN (*at the same time*): And you, Judge Brack—what do you say to this? Eh?

BRACK: Well, I say that a moral victory—hm—may be all very fine—

TESMAN: Yes, certainly. But all the same—

HEDDA (*looking at* TESMAN *with a cold smile*): You stand there looking as if you were thunderstruck—

TESMAN: Yes—so I am—I almost think—

BRACK: Don't you see, Mrs. Tesman, a thunderstorm has just passed over?

HEDDA (*pointing toward the inner room*): Will you not take a glass of cold punch, gentlemen?

BRACK (*looking at his watch*): A stirrup cup[7]? Yes, it wouldn't come amiss.

TESMAN: A capital idea, Hedda! Just the thing! Now that the weight has been taken off my mind—

HEDDA: Will you not join them, Mr. Lövborg?

LÖVBORG (*with a gesture of refusal*): No, thank you. Nothing for me.

BRACK: Why, bless me—cold punch is surely not poison.

LÖVBORG: Perhaps not for everyone.

HEDDA: I will keep Mr. Lövborg company in the meantime.

TESMAN: Yes, yes, Hedda dear, do.

He and BRACK *go into the inner room, seat themselves, drink punch, smoke cigarettes, and carry on a lively conversation during what follows.* EILERT LÖVBORG *remains standing beside the stove.* HEDDA *goes to the writing table.*

HEDDA (*raising her voice a little*): Do you care to look at some photographs, Mr. Lövborg? You know Tesman and I made a tour in the Tyrol[8] on our way home? (*She takes up an album, and places it on the table beside the sofa, in the further corner of which she seats herself.* EILERT LÖVBORG *approaches, stops, and looks at her. Then he takes a chair and seats himself to her left, with his back toward the inner room.*

HEDDA (*opening the album*): Do you see this range of mountains, Mr. Lövborg? It's the Ortler group. Tesman has written the name underneath. Here it is: "The Ortler group near Meran."

LÖVBORG (*who has never taken his eyes off her, says softly and slowly*): Hedda—Gabler!

HEDDA (*glancing hastily at him*): Ah! Hush!

LÖVBORG (*repeats softly*): Hedda Gabler!

HEDDA (*looking at the album*): That was my name in the old days—when we two knew each other.

LÖVBORG: And I must teach myself never to say Hedda Gabler again—never, as long as I live.

HEDDA (*still turning over the pages*): Yes, you must. And I think you ought to practice in time. The sooner the better, I should say.

LÖVBORG (*in a tone of indignation*): Hedda Gabler married? And married to—George Tesman!

HEDDA: Yes—so the world goes.

LÖVBORG: Oh, Hedda, Hedda—how could you throw your-self away!

HEDDA (*looks sharply at him*): What? I can't allow this!

LÖVBORG: What do you mean? (TESMAN *comes into the room and goes toward the sofa.*)

HEDDA (*hears him coming and says in an indifferent tone*): And this is a view from the Val d'Ampezzo, Mr. Lövborg. Just look at these peaks! (*Looks affectionately up at* TESMAN.) What's the name of these curious peaks, dear?

TESMAN: Let me see. Oh, those are the Dolomites.

HEDDA: Yes, that's it!—Those are the Dolomites, Mr. Löv-borg.

TESMAN: Hedda dear,—I only wanted to ask whether I shouldn't bring you a little punch after all? For yourself at any rate—eh?

HEDDA: Yes, do, please; and perhaps a few biscuits.

TESMAN: No cigarettes?

HEDDA: No.

TESMAN: Very well. (*He goes into the inner room and out to the right.* BRACK *sits in the inner room, and keeps an eye from time to time on* HEDDA *and* LÖVBORG.)

LÖVBORG (*softly, as before*): Answer me, Hedda—how could you go and do this?

HEDDA (*apparently absorbed in the album*): If you continue to say *du* to me I won't talk to you.

LÖVBORG: May I not say *du* when we are alone?

HEDDA: No. You may think it; but you mustn't say it.

LÖVBORG: Ah, I understand. It is an offense against George Tesman, whom you—love.

HEDDA (*glances at him and smiles*): Love? What an idea!

LÖVBORG: You don't love him then!

HEDDA: But I won't hear of any sort of unfaithfulness! Re-member that.

LÖVBORG: Hedda—answer me one thing—

HEDDA: Hush! (TESMAN *enters with a small tray from the inner room.*)

TESMAN: Here you are! Isn't this tempting? (*He puts the tray on the table.*)

HEDDA: Why do you bring it yourself?

TESMAN (*filling the glasses*): Because I think it's such fun to wait upon you, Hedda.

HEDDA: But you have poured out two glasses. Mr. Lövborg said he wouldn't have any—

TESMAN: No, but Mrs. Elvsted will soon be here, won't she?

HEDDA: Yes, by-the-bye—Mrs. Elvsted—

TESMAN: Had you forgotten her? Eh?

HEDDA: We were so absorbed in these photographs. (*Shows him a picture.*) Do you remember this little village?

TESMAN: Oh, it's that one just below the Brenner Pass. It was there we passed the night—

HEDDA: —and met that lively party of tourists.

TESMAN: Yes, that was the place. Fancy—if we could only have had you with us, Eilert! Eh? (*He returns to the inner room and sits beside* BRACK.)

LÖVBORG: Answer me this one thing, Hedda—

HEDDA: Well?

LÖVBORG: Was there no love in your friendship for me either? Not a spark—not a tinge of love in it?

HEDDA: I wonder if there was? To me it seems as though we were two good comrades—two thoroughly intimate friends. (*Smilingly.*) You especially were frankness itself.

LÖVBORG: It was you that made me so.

HEDDA: As I look back upon it all, I think there was really something beautiful, something fascinating—something daring—in—in that secret intimacy—that comradeship which no living creature so much as dreamed of.

LÖVBORG: Yes, yes, Hedda! Was there not?—When I used to come to your father's in the afternoon—and the General sat over at the window reading his papers—with his back toward us—

HEDDA: And we two on the corner sofa—

LÖVBORG: Always with the same illustrated paper before us—

HEDDA: For want of an album, yes.

LÖVBORG: Yes, Hedda, and when I made my confessions to you—told you about myself, things that at that time no one else knew! There I would sit and tell you of my escapades—my days and nights of devilment. Oh, Hedda—what was the power in you that forced me to confess these things?

HEDDA: Do you think it was any power in me?

LÖVBORG: How else can I explain it? And all those—those roundabout questions you used to put to me—

HEDDA: Which you understood so particularly well—

LÖVBORG: How could you sit and question me like that? Question me quite frankly—

HEDDA: In roundabout terms, please observe.

LÖVBORG: Yes, but frankly nevertheless. Cross-question me about—all that sort of thing?

HEDDA: And how could you answer, Mr. Lövborg?

LÖVBORG: Yes, that is just what I can't understand—in looking back upon it. But tell me now, Hedda—was there not love at the bottom of our friendship? On your side, did you not feel as though you might purge my stains away—if I made you my confessor? Was it not so?

HEDDA: No, not quite.

LÖVBORG: What was your motive, then?

HEDDA: Do you think it quite incomprehensible that a young girl—when it can be done—without anyone knowing—

LÖVBORG: Well?

HEDDA: —should be glad to have a peep, now and then, into a world which—

LÖVBORG: Which—?

HEDDA: —which she is forbidden to know anything about?

LÖVBORG: So that was it?

HEDDA: Partly. Partly—I almost think.

LÖVBORG: Comradeship in the thirst for life. But why should not that, at any rate, have continued?

HEDDA: The fault was yours.

LÖVBORG: It was you that broke with me.

HEDDA: Yes, when our friendship threatened to develop into something more serious. Shame upon you, Eilert Lövborg! How could you think of wronging your—your frank comrade?

LÖVBORG *(clenching his hands)*: Oh, why did you not carry out your threat? Why did you not shoot me down?

HEDDA: Because I have such a dread of scandal.

LÖVBORG: Yes, Hedda, you are a coward at heart.

HEDDA: A terrible coward. *(Changing her tone.)* But it was a lucky thing for you. And now you have found ample consolation at the Elvsteds'.

LÖVBORG: I know what Thea has confided to you.

HEDDA: And perhaps you have confided to her something about us?

LÖVBORG: Not a word. She is too stupid to understand anything of that sort.

HEDDA: Stupid?

LÖVBORG: She is stupid about matters of that sort.

HEDDA: And I am cowardly. *(Bends over toward him, without looking him in the face, and says more softly:)* But now I will confide something to you.

LÖVBORG *(eagerly)*: Well?

HEDDA: The fact that I dared not shoot you down—

LÖVBORG: Yes!

HEDDA: —that was not my most arrant cowardice—that evening.

LÖVBORG *(looks at her a moment, understands, and whispers passionately)*: Oh, Hedda! Hedda Gabler! Now I begin to see a hidden reason beneath our comradeship! You and I—! After all, then, it was your craving for life—

HEDDA *(softly, with a sharp glance)*: Take care! Believe nothing of the sort!

Twilight has begun to fall. The hall door is opened from without by BERTA.

HEDDA: *(Closes the album with a bang and calls smilingly)*: Ah, at last! My darling Thea,—come along!

MRS. ELVSTED *enters from the hall. She is in evening dress. The door is closed behind her.*

HEDDA (*on the sofa, stretches out her arms toward her*): My sweet Thea—you can't think how I have been longing for you!

MRS. ELVSTED, *in passing, exchanges slight salutations with the gentlemen in the inner room, then goes up to the table and gives* HEDDA *her hand.* EILERT LÖVBORG *has risen. He and* MRS. ELVSTED *greet each other with a silent nod.*

MRS. ELVSTED: Ought I to go in and talk to your husband for a moment?

HEDDA: Oh, not at all. Leave those two alone. They will soon be going.

MRS. ELVSTED: Are they going out?

HEDDA: Yes, to a supper party.

MRS. ELVSTED (*quickly, to* LÖVBORG): Not you?

LÖVBORG: No.

HEDDA: Mr. Lövborg remains with us.

MRS. ELVSTED (*takes a chair and is about to seat herself at his side*): Oh, how nice it is here!

HEDDA: No, thank you, my little Thea! Not there! You'll be good enough to come over here to me. I will sit between you.

MRS. ELVSTED: Yes, just as you please.

She goes round the table and seats herself on the sofa on HEDDA's *right.* LÖVBORG *reseats himself on his chair.*

LÖVBORG (*after a short pause, to* HEDDA): Is not she lovely to look at?

HEDDA (*lightly stroking her hair*): Only to look at?

LÖVBORG: Yes. For we two—she and I—we are two real comrades. We have absolute faith in each other; so we can sit and talk with perfect frankness—

HEDDA: Not roundabout, Mr. Lövborg?

LÖVBORG: Well—

MRS. ELVSTED (*softly clinging close to* HEDDA): Oh, how happy I am, Hedda; for, only think, he says I have inspired him too.

HEDDA (*looks at her with a smile*): Ah! Does he say that, dear?

LÖVBORG: And then she is so brave, Mrs. Tesman!

MRS. ELVSTED: Good heavens—am I brave?

LÖVBORG: Exceedingly—where your comrade is concerned.

HEDDA: Ah yes—courage! If one only had that!

LÖVBORG: What then? What do you mean?

HEDDA: Then life would perhaps be liveable, after all. (*With a sudden change of tone.*) But now, my dearest Thea, you really must have a glass of cold punch.

MRS. ELVSTED: No, thanks—I never take anything of that kind.

HEDDA: Well then, you, Mr. Lövborg.

LÖVBORG: Nor I, thank you.

MRS. ELVSTED: No, he doesn't either.

HEDDA (*looks fixedly at him*): But if I say you shall?

LÖVBORG: It would be no use.

HEDDA (*laughing*): Then I, poor creature, have no sort of power over you?

LÖVBORG: Not in that respect.

HEDDA: But seriously, I think you ought to—for your own sake.

MRS. ELVSTED: Why, Hedda—!

LÖVBORG: How so?

HEDDA: Or rather on account of other people.

LÖVBORG: Indeed?

HEDDA: Otherwise people might be apt to suspect that—in your heart of hearts—you did not feel quite secure—quite confident in yourself.

MRS. ELVSTED (*softly*): Oh please, Hedda—.

LÖVBORG: People may suspect what they like—for the present.

MRS. ELVSTED (*joyfully*): Yes, let them!

HEDDA: I saw it plainly in Judge Brack's face a moment ago.

LÖVBORG: What did you see?

HEDDA: His contemptuous smile, when you dared not go with them into the inner room.

LÖVBORG: Dared not? Of course I preferred to stop here and talk to you.

MRS. ELVSTED: What could be more natural, Hedda?

HEDDA: But the Judge could not guess that. And I saw, too, the way he smiled and glanced at Tesman when you dared not accept his invitation to this wretched little supper party of his.

LÖVBORG: Dared not! Do you say I dared not?

HEDDA: *I* don't say so. But that was how Judge Brack understood it.

LÖVBORG: Well, let him.

HEDDA: Then you are not going with them?

LÖVBORG: I will stay here with you and Thea.

MRS. ELVSTED: Yes, Hedda—how can you doubt that?

HEDDA (*smiles and nods approvingly to* LÖVBORG): Firm as a rock! Faithful to your principles, now and forever! Ah, that is how a man should be! (*Turns to* MRS. ELVSTED *and caresses her.*) Well now, what did I tell you, when you came to us this morning in such a state of distraction—

LÖVBORG (*surprised*): Distraction!

MRS. ELVSTED (*terrified*): Hedda—oh Hedda—!

HEDDA: You can see for yourself; you haven't the slightest reason to be in such mortal terror— (*Interrupting herself.*) There! Now we can all three enjoy ourselves!

LÖVBORG (*who has given a start*): Ah—what is all this, Mrs. Tesman?

MRS. ELVSTED: Oh my God, Hedda! What are you saying? What are you doing?

HEDDA: Don't get excited! That horrid Judge Brack is sitting watching you.

LÖVBORG: So she was in mortal terror! On my account!

MRS. ELVSTED (*softly and piteously*): Oh, Hedda—now you have ruined everything!

LÖVBORG: (*Looks fixedly at her for a moment. His face is distorted.*) So that was my comrade's frank confidence in me?

MRS. ELVSTED (*imploringly*): Oh, my dearest friend—only let me tell you—

LÖVBORG (*takes one of the glasses of punch, raises it to his lips, and says in a low, husky voice*): Your health, Thea!

He empties the glass, puts it down, and takes the second.

MRS. ELVSTED (*softly*): Oh, Hedda, Hedda—how could you do this?

HEDDA: *I* do it? *I*? Are you crazy?

LÖVBORG: Here's to your health too, Mrs. Tesman. Thanks for the truth. Hurrah for the truth!

He empties the glass and is about to refill it.

HEDDA (*lays her hand on his arm*): Come, come—no more for the present. Remember you are going out to supper.

MRS. ELVSTED: No, no, no!

HEDDA: Hush! They are sitting watching you.

LÖVBORG (*putting down the glass*): Now, Thea—tell me the truth—

MRS. ELVSTED: Yes.

LÖVBORG: Did your husband know that you had come after me?

MRS. ELVSTED (*wringing her hands*): Oh, Hedda—do you hear what he is asking?

LÖVBORG: Was it arranged between you and him that you were to come to town and look after me? Perhaps it was the Sheriff himself that urged you to come? Aha, my dear—no doubt he wanted my help in his office! Or was it at the card table that he missed me?

MRS. ELVSTED (*softly, in agony*): Oh, Lövborg, Lövborg—!

LÖVBORG (*seizes a glass and is on the point of filling it*): Here's a glass for the old Sheriff too!

HEDDA (*preventing him*): No more just now. Remember you have to read your manuscript to Tesman.

LÖVBORG (*calmly, putting down the glass*): It was stupid of

me all this, Thea—to take it in this way, I mean. Don't be
angry with me, my dear, dear comrade. You shall see—
both you and the others—that if I was fallen once—now I
have risen again! Thanks to you, Thea.

MRS. ELVSTED (*radiant with joy*): Oh, heaven be praised—!

BRACK *has in the meantime looked at his watch. He and*
TESMAN *rise and come into the drawing room.*

BRACK (*takes his hat and overcoat*): Well, Mrs. Tesman, our
time has come.

HEDDA: I suppose it has.

LÖVBORG (*rising*): Mine too, Judge Brack.

MRS. ELVSTED (*softly and imploringly*): Oh, Lövborg, don't
do it!

HEDDA (*pinching her arm*): They can hear you!

MRS. ELVSTED (*with a suppressed shriek*): Ow!

LÖVBORG (*to* BRACK): You were good enough to invite me.

BRACK: Well, are you coming after all?

LÖVBORG: Yes, many thanks.

BRACK: I'm delighted—

LÖVBORG (*to* TESMAN, *putting the parcel of manuscript in
his pocket*): I should like to show you one or two things before I send it to the printers.

TESMAN: Fancy—that will be delightful. But, Hedda dear,
how is Mrs. Elvsted to get home? Eh?

HEDDA: Oh, that can be managed somehow.

LÖVBORG (*looking toward the ladies*): Mrs. Elvsted? Of
course, I'll come again and fetch her. (*Approaching.*) At
ten or thereabouts, Mrs. Tesman? Will that do?

HEDDA: Certainly. That will do capitally.

TESMAN: Well, then, that's all right. But you must not expect
me so early, Hedda.

HEDDA: —Oh, you may stop as long—as long as ever you
please.

MRS. ELVSTED (*trying to conceal her anxiety*): Well then,
Mr. Lövborg—I shall remain here until you come.

LÖVBORG (*with his hat in his hand*): Pray do, Mrs. Elvsted.

BRACK: And now off goes the excursion train, gentlemen! I hope we shall have a lively time, as a certain fair lady puts it.

HEDDA: Ah, if only the fair lady could be present unseen—!

BRACK: Why unseen?

HEDDA: In order to hear a little of your liveliness at first hand, Judge Brack.

BRACK (*laughing*): I should not advise the fair lady to try it.

TESMAN (*also laughing*): Come, you're a nice one, Hedda! Fancy that!

BRACK: Well, good-bye, good-bye, ladies.

LÖVBORG (*bowing*): About ten o'clock, then.

BRACK, LÖVBORG, *and* TESMAN *go out by the hall door. At the same time,* BERTA *enters from the inner room with a lighted lamp, which she places on the dining room table; she goes out by the way she came.*

MRS. ELVSTED (*who has risen and is wandering restlessly about the room*): Hedda—Hedda—what will come of all this?

HEDDA: At ten o'clock—he will be here. I can see him already—with vine leaves in his hair—flushed and fearless—

MRS. ELVSTED: Oh, I hope he may.

HEDDA: And then, you see—then he will have regained control over himself. Then he will be a free man for all his days.

MRS. ELVSTED: Oh God!—if he would only come as you see him now!

HEDDA: He will come as I see him—so, and not otherwise! (*Rises and approaches* THEA.) You may doubt him as long as you please; *I* believe in him. And now we will try—

MRS. ELVSTED: You have some hidden motive in this, Hedda!

HEDDA: Yes, I have. I want for once in my life to have power to mold a human destiny.

MRS. ELVSTED: Have you not the power?

HEDDA: I have not—and have never had it.

MRS. ELVSTED: Not your husband's?

HEDDA: Do you think that is worth the trouble? Oh, if you could only understand how poor I am. And fate has made you so rich! (*Clasps her passionately in her arms.*) I think I must burn your hair off, after all.

MRS. ELVSTED: Let me go! Let me go! I am afraid of you, Hedda!

BERTA (*in the middle doorway*): Tea is laid in the dining room, ma'am.

HEDDA: Very well. We are coming.

MRS. ELVSTED: No, no, no! I would rather go home alone! At once!

HEDDA: Nonsense! First you shall have a cup of tea, you little stupid. And then—at ten o'clock—Eilert Lövborg will be here—with vine leaves in his hair.

She drags MRS. ELVSTED *almost by force toward the middle doorway.*

ACT THREE

The room at the TESMANS'. *The curtains are drawn over the middle doorway, and also over the glass door. The lamp, half turned down, and with a shade over it, is burning on the table. In the stove, the door of which stands open, there has been a fire, which is now nearly burned out.*

MRS. ELVSTED, *wrapped in a large shawl, and with her feet upon a footrest, sits close to the stove, sunk back in the armchair.* HEDDA, *fully dressed, lies sleeping upon the sofa, with a sofa blanket over her.*

MRS. ELVSTED (*after a pause, suddenly sits up in her chair, and listens eagerly. Then she sinks back again wearily, moaning to herself*): Not yet!—Oh God—oh God—not yet!

BERTA *slips cautiously in by the hall door. She has a letter in her hand.*

MRS. ELVSTED (*turns and whispers eagerly*): Well—has anyone come?

BERTA (*softly*): Yes, a girl has brought this letter.

MRS. ELVSTED (*quickly, holding out her hand*): A letter! Give it to me!

BERTA: No, it's for Dr. Tesman, ma'am.

MRS. ELVSTED: Oh, indeed.

BERTA: It was Miss Tesman's servant that brought it. I'll lay it here on the table.

MRS. ELVSTED: Yes, do.

BERTA (*laying down the letter*): I think I had better put out the lamp. It's smoking.

MRS. ELVSTED: Yes, put it out. It must soon be daylight now.

BERTA (*putting out the lamp*): It is daylight already, ma'am.

MRS. ELVSTED: Yes, broad day! And no one come back yet—!

BERTA: Lord bless you, ma'am—I guessed how it would be.

MRS. ELVSTED: You guessed?

BERTA: Yes, when I saw that a certain person had come back to town—and that he went off with them. For we've heard enough about that gentleman before now.

MRS. ELVSTED: Don't speak so loud. You will waken Mrs. Tesman.

BERTA (*looks toward the sofa and sighs*): No, no—let her sleep, poor thing. Shan't I put some wood on the fire?

MRS. ELVSTED: Thanks, not for me.

BERTA: Oh, very well. (*She goes softly out by the hall door.*)

HEDDA (*is awakened by the shutting of the door, and looks up*): What's that—?

MRS. ELVSTED: It was only the servant—

HEDDA (*looking about her*): Oh, we're here—! Yes, now I remember. (*Sits erect upon the sofa, stretches herself, and rubs her eyes.*) What o'clock is it, Thea?

MRS. ELVSTED (*looks at her watch*): It's past seven.

HEDDA: When did Tesman come home?

MRS. ELVSTED: He has not come.

HEDDA: Not come home yet?

MRS. ELVSTED (*rising*): No one has come.

HEDDA: Think of our watching and waiting here till four in the morning—

MRS. ELVSTED (*wringing her hands*): And how I watched and waited for him!

HEDDA (*yawns, and says with her hand before her mouth*): Well well—we might have spared ourselves the trouble.

MRS. ELVSTED: Did you get a little sleep?

HEDDA: Oh yes; I believe I have slept pretty well. Have you not?

MRS. ELVSTED: Not for a moment. I couldn't, Hedda!—not to save my life.

HEDDA (*rises and goes toward her*): There there there! There's nothing to be so alarmed about. I understand quite well what has happened.

MRS. ELVSTED: Well, what do you think? Won't you tell me?

HEDDA: Why, of course it has been a very late affair at Judge Brack's—

MRS. ELVSTED: Yes, yes, that is clear enough. But all the same—

HEDDA: And then, you see, Tesman hasn't cared to come home and ring us up in the middle of the night. (*Laughing.*) Perhaps he wasn't inclined to show himself either— immediately after a jollification.

MRS. ELVSTED: But in that case—where can he have gone?

HEDDA: Of course he has gone to his aunts' and slept there. They have his old room ready for him.

MRS. ELVSTED: No, he can't be with them; for a letter has just come for him from Miss Tesman. There it lies.

HEDDA: Indeed? (*Looks at the address.*) Why yes, it's addressed in Aunt Julia's own hand. Well then, he has remained at Judge Brack's. And as for Eilert Lövborg—he is sitting, with vine leaves in his hair, reading his manuscript.

MRS. ELVSTED: Oh Hedda, you are just saying things you don't believe a bit.

HEDDA: You really are a little blockhead, Thea.

MRS. ELVSTED: Oh yes, I suppose I am.

HEDDA: And how mortally tired you look.

MRS. ELVSTED: Yes, I am mortally tired.

HEDDA: Well then, you must do as I tell you. You must go into my room and lie down for a little while.

MRS. ELVSTED: Oh no, no—I shouldn't be able to sleep.

HEDDA: I am sure you would.

MRS. ELVSTED: Well, but your husband is certain to come soon now; and then I want to know at once—

HEDDA: I shall take care to let you know when he comes.

MRS. ELVSTED: Do you promise me, Hedda?

HEDDA: Yes, rely upon me. Just you go in and have a sleep in the meantime.

MRS. ELVSTED: Thanks; then I'll try to. (*She goes off through the inner room.*)

HEDDA goes up to the glass door and draws back the curtains. The broad daylight streams into the room. Then she takes a little hand glass from the writing table, looks at herself in it, and arranges her hair. Next she goes to the hall door and presses the bell button.

BERTA presently appears at the hall door.

BERTA: Did you want anything, ma'am?

HEDDA: Yes; you must put some more wood in the stove. I am shivering.

BERTA: Bless me—I'll make up the fire at once. (*She rakes the embers together and lays a piece of wood upon them; then stops and listens.*) That was a ring at the front door, ma'am.

HEDDA: Then go to the door. I will look after the fire.

BERTA: It'll soon burn up. (*She goes out by the hall door.*)

HEDDA kneels on the footrest and lays some more pieces of wood in the stove.

After a short pause, GEORGE TESMAN enters from the hall. He looks tired and rather serious. He steals on tiptoe toward the middle doorway and is about to slip through the curtains.

HEDDA (*at the stove, without looking up*): Good morning.

TESMAN (*turns*): Hedda! (*Approaching her.*) Good heavens— are you up so early? Eh?

HEDDA: Yes, I am up very early this morning.

TESMAN: And I never doubted you were still sound asleep! Fancy that, Hedda!

HEDDA: Don't speak so loud. Mrs. Elvsted is resting in my room.

TESMAN: Has Mrs. Elvsted been here all night?

HEDDA: Yes, since no one came to fetch her.

TESMAN: Ah, to be sure.

HEDDA (closes the door of the stove and rises): Well, did you enjoy yourselves at Judge Brack's?

TESMAN: Have you been anxious about me? Eh?

HEDDA: No, I should never think of being anxious. But I asked if you had enjoyed yourself.

TESMAN: Oh yes,—for once in a way. Especially the beginning of the evening; for then Eilert read me part of his book. We arrived more than an hour too early—fancy that! And Brack had all sorts of arrangements to make—so Eilert read to me.

HEDDA (seating herself by the table on the right): Well? Tell me, then—

TESMAN (sitting on a footstool near the stove): Oh, Hedda, you can't conceive what a book that is going to be! I believe it is one of the most remarkable things that have ever been written. Fancy that!

HEDDA: Yes, yes; I don't care about that—

TESMAN: I must make a confession to you, Hedda. When he had finished reading—a horrid feeling came over me.

HEDDA: A horrid feeling?

TESMAN: I felt jealous of Eilert for having had it in him to write such a book. Only think, Hedda!

HEDDA: Yes, yes, I am thinking!

TESMAN: And then how pitiful to think that he—with all his gifts—should be irreclaimable, after all.

HEDDA: I suppose you mean that he has more courage than the rest?

TESMAN: No, not at all—I mean that he is incapable of taking his pleasures in moderation.

HEDDA: And what came of it all—in the end?

TESMAN: Well, to tell the truth, I think it might best be described as an orgie, Hedda.

HEDDA: Had he vine leaves in his hair?

TESMAN: Vine leaves? No, I saw nothing of the sort. But he made a long, rambling speech in honor of the woman who had inspired him in his work—that was the phrase he used.

HEDDA: Did he name her?

TESMAN: No, he didn't; but I can't help thinking he meant Mrs. Elvsted. You may be sure he did.

HEDDA: Well—where did you part from him?

TESMAN: On the way to town. We broke up—the last of us at any rate—all together; and Brack came with us to get a breath of fresh air. And then, you see, we agreed to take Eilert home; for he had had far more than was good for him.

HEDDA: I daresay.

TESMAN: But now comes the strange part of it, Hedda; or, I should rather say, the melancholy part of it. I declare I am almost ashamed—on Eilert's account—to tell you—

HEDDA: Oh, go on—

TESMAN: Well, as we were getting near town, you see, I happened to drop a little behind the others. Only for a minute or two—fancy that!

HEDDA: Yes, yes, yes, but—?

TESMAN: And then, as I hurried after them—what do you think I found by the wayside? Eh?

HEDDA: Oh, how should I know!

TESMAN: You mustn't speak of it to a soul, Hedda! Do you hear! Promise me, for Eilert's sake. (*Draws a parcel, wrapped in paper, from his coat pocket.*) Fancy, dear—I found this.

HEDDA: Is not that the parcel he had with him yesterday?

TESMAN: Yes, it is the whole of his precious, irreplaceable manuscript! And he had gone and lost it, and knew nothing about it. Only fancy, Hedda! So deplorably—

HEDDA: But why did you not give him back the parcel at once?

TESMAN: I didn't dare to—in the state he was then in—

HEDDA: Did you not tell any of the others that you had found it?

TESMAN: Oh, far from it! You can surely understand that, for Eilert's sake, I wouldn't do that.

HEDDA: So no one knows that Eilert Lövborg's manuscript is in your possession?

TESMAN: No. And no one must know it.

HEDDA: Then what did you say to him afterward?

TESMAN: I didn't talk to him again at all; for when we got in among the streets, he and two or three of the others gave us the slip and disappeared. Fancy that!

HEDDA: Indeed! They must have taken him home then.

TESMAN: Yes, so it would appear. And Brack, too, left us.

HEDDA: And what have you been doing with yourself since?

TESMAN: Well, I and some of the others went home with one of the party, a jolly fellow, and took our morning coffee with him; or perhaps I should rather call it our night coffee—eh? But now, when I have rested a little, and given Eilert, poor fellow, time to have his sleep out, I must take this back to him.

HEDDA (holds out her hand for the packet): No—don't give it to him! Not in such a hurry, I mean. Let me read it first.

TESMAN: No, my dearest Hedda, I mustn't, I really mustn't.

HEDDA: You must not?

TESMAN: No—for you can imagine what a state of despair he will be in when he awakens and misses the manuscript. He has no copy of it, you must know! He told me so.

HEDDA (looking searchingly at him): Can such a thing not be reproduced? Written over again?

TESMAN: No, I don't think that would be possible. For the inspiration, you see—

HEDDA: Yes, yes—I suppose it depends on that. (Lightly.) But, by-the-bye—here is a letter for you.

TESMAN: Fancy—!

HEDDA (handing it to him): It came early this morning.

TESMAN: It's from Aunt Julia! What can it be? (*He lays the packet on the other footstool, opens the letter, runs his eye through it, and jumps up.*) Oh, Hedda—she says that poor Aunt Rina is dying!

HEDDA: Well, we were prepared for that.

TESMAN: And that if I want to see her again, I must make haste. I'll run in to them at once.

HEDDA (*suppressing a smile*): Will you run?

TESMAN: Oh, dearest Hedda—if you could only make up your mind to come with me! Just think!

HEDDA (*rises and says wearily, repelling the idea*): No, no, don't ask me. I will not look upon sickness and death. I loathe all sorts of ugliness.

TESMAN: Well, well, then—! (*Bustling around.*) My hat— My overcoat—? Oh, in the hall— I do hope I mayn't come too late, Hedda! Eh?

HEDDA: Oh, if you run—

BERTA *appears at the hall door.*

BERTA: Judge Brack is at the door, and wishes to know if he may come in.

TESMAN: At this time! No, I can't possibly see him.

HEDDA: But I can. (*To* BERTA.) Ask Judge Brack to come in. (BERTA *goes out.*)

HEDDA (*quickly, whispering*): The parcel, Tesman! (*She snatches it up from the stool.*)

TESMAN: Yes, give it to me!

HEDDA: No, no, I will keep it till you come back.

She goes to the writing table and places it in the bookcase. TESMAN *stands in a flurry of haste, and cannot get his gloves on.*

    JUDGE BRACK *enters from the hall.*

HEDDA (*nodding to him*): You are an early bird, I must say.

BRACK: Yes, don't you think so? (*To* TESMAN.) Are you on the move, too?

TESMAN: Yes, I must rush off to my aunts'. Fancy—the invalid one is lying at death's door, poor creature.

BRACK: Dear me, is she indeed? Then on no account let me detain you. At such a critical moment—

TESMAN: Yes, I must really rush— Good-bye! Good-bye! *(He hastens out by the hall door.)*

HEDDA *(approaching)*: You seem to have made a particularly lively night of it at your rooms, Judge Brack.

BRACK: I assure you I have not had my clothes off, Mrs. Hedda.

HEDDA: Not you, either?

BRACK: No, as you may see. But what has Tesman been telling you of the night's adventures?

HEDDA: Oh, some tiresome story. Only that they went and had coffee somewhere or other.

BRACK: I have heard about that coffee party already. Eilert Lövborg was not with them, I fancy?

HEDDA: No, they had taken him home before that.

BRACK: Tesman too?

HEDDA: No, but some of the others, he said.

BRACK *(smiling)*: George Tesman is really an ingenuous creature, Mrs. Hedda.

HEDDA: Yes, heaven knows he is. Then is there something behind all this?

BRACK: Yes, perhaps there may be.

HEDDA: Well then, sit down, my dear Judge, and tell your story in comfort.

She seats herself to the left of the table. BRACK *sits near her, at the long side of the table.*

HEDDA: Now then?

BRACK: I had special reasons for keeping track of my guests— or rather of some of my guests—last night.

HEDDA: Of Eilert Lövborg among the rest, perhaps?

BRACK: Frankly, yes.

HEDDA: Now you make me really curious—

BRACK: Do you know where he and one or two of the others finished the night, Mrs. Hedda?

HEDDA: If it is not quite unmentionable, tell me.

BRACK: Oh no, it's not at all unmentionable. Well, they put in an appearance at a particularly animated soirée.

HEDDA: Of the lively kind?

BRACK: Of the very liveliest—

HEDDA: Tell me more of this, Judge Brack—

BRACK: Lövborg, as well as the others, had been invited in advance. I knew all about it. But he had declined the invitation; for now, as you know, he has become a new man.

HEDDA: Up at the Elvsteds', yes. But he went after all, then?

BRACK: Well, you see, Mrs. Hedda—unhappily the spirit moved him at my rooms last evening—

HEDDA: Yes, I hear he found inspiration.

BRACK: Pretty violent inspiration. Well, I fancy that altered his purpose; for we menfolk are unfortunately not always so firm in our principles as we ought to be.

HEDDA: Oh, I am sure you are an exception, Judge Brack. But as to Lövborg—?

BRACK: To make a long story short—he landed at last in Mademoiselle Diana's rooms.

HEDDA: Mademoiselle Diana's?

BRACK: It was Mademoiselle Diana that was giving the soirée, to a select circle of her admirers and her lady friends.

HEDDA: Is she a red-haired woman?

BRACK: Precisely.

HEDDA: A sort of a—singer?

BRACK: Oh yes—in her leisure moments. And moreover a mighty huntress—of men—Mrs. Hedda. You have no doubt heard of her. Eilert Lövborg was one of her most enthusiastic protectors—in the days of his glory.

HEDDA: And how did all this end?

BRACK: Far from amicably, it appears. After a most tender meeting, they seem to have come to blows—

HEDDA: Lövborg and she?

BRACK: Yes. He accused her or her friends of having robbed him. He declared that his pocketbook had disappeared—and other things as well. In short, he seems to have made a furious disturbance.

HEDDA: And what came of it all?

BRACK: It came to a general scrimmage, in which the ladies as well as the gentlemen took part. Fortunately the police at last appeared on the scene.

HEDDA: The police too?

BRACK: Yes. I fancy it will prove a costly frolic for Eilert Lövborg, crazy being that he is.

HEDDA: How so?

BRACK: He seems to have made a violent resistance—to have hit one of the constables on the head and torn the coat off his back. So they had to march him off to the police station with the rest.

HEDDA: How have you learned all this?

BRACK: From the police themselves.

HEDDA (gazing straight before her): So that is what happened. Then he had no vine leaves in his hair.

BRACK: Vine leaves, Mrs. Hedda?

HEDDA (changing her tone): But tell me now, Judge—what is your real reason for tracking out Eilert Lövborg's movements so carefully?

BRACK: In the first place, it could not be entirely indifferent to me if it should appear in the police court that he came straight from my house.

HEDDA: Will the matter come into court then?

BRACK: Of course. However, I should scarcely have troubled so much about that. But I thought that, as a friend of the family, it was my duty to supply you and Tesman with a full account of his nocturnal exploits.

HEDDA: Why so, Judge Brack?

BRACK: Why, because I have a shrewd suspicion that he intends to use you as a sort of blind.

HEDDA: Oh, how can you think such a thing!

BRACK: Good heavens, Mrs. Hedda—we have eyes in our

head. Mark my words! This Mrs. Elvsted will be in no hurry to leave town again.

HEDDA: Well, even if there should be anything between them, I suppose there are plenty of other places where they could meet.

BRACK: Not a single home. Henceforth, as before, every respectable house will be closed against Eilert Lövborg.

HEDDA: And so ought mine to be, you mean?

BRACK: Yes. I confess it would be more than painful to me if this personage were to be made free of your house. How superfluous, how intrusive, he would be, if he were to force his way into—

HEDDA: —into the triangle?

BRACK: Precisely. It would simply mean that I should find myself homeless.

HEDDA (*looks at him with a smile*): So you want to be the one cock in the basket—that is your aim.

BRACK (*nods slowly and lowers his voice*): Yes, that is my aim. And for that I will fight—with every weapon I can command.

HEDDA (*her smile vanishing*): I see you are a dangerous person—when it comes to the point.

BRACK: Do you think so?

HEDDA: I am beginning to think so. And I am exceedingly glad to think—that you have no sort of hold over me.

BRACK (*laughing equivocally*): Well, well, Mrs. Hedda— perhaps you are right there. If I had, who knows what I might be capable of?

HEDDA: Come, come now, Judge Brack! That sounds almost like a threat.

BRACK (*rising*): Oh, not at all! The triangle, you know, ought, if possible, to be spontaneously constructed.

HEDDA: There I agree with you.

BRACK: Well, now I have said all I had to say; and I had better be getting back to town. Good-bye, Mrs. Hedda. (*He goes toward the glass door.*)

HEDDA (*rising*): Are you going through the garden?

BRACK: Yes, it's a short cut for me.

HEDDA: And then it is a back way, too.

BRACK: Quite so. I have no objection to back ways. They may be piquant enough at times.

HEDDA: When there is ball practice going on, you mean?

BRACK (*in the doorway, laughing to her*): Oh, people don't shoot their tame poultry, I fancy.

HEDDA (*also laughing*): Oh no, when there is only one cock in the basket—

They exchange laughing nods of farewell. He goes. She closes the door behind him.

HEDDA, who has become quite serious, stands for a moment looking out. Presently she goes and peeps through the curtain over the middle doorway. Then she goes to the writing table, takes LÖVBORG's packet out of the bookcase, and is on the point of looking through its contents. BERTA is heard speaking loudly in the hall.

HEDDA turns and listens. Then she hastily locks up the packet in the drawer, and lays the key on the inkstand.

EILERT LÖVBORG, with his greatcoat on and his hat in his hand, tears open the hall door. He looks somewhat confused and irritated.

LÖVBORG (*looking toward the hall*): And I tell you I must and will come in! There!

He closes the door, turns, sees HEDDA, at once regains his self-control, and bows.

HEDDA (*at the writing table*): Well, Mr. Lövborg, this is rather a late hour to call for Thea.

LÖVBORG: You mean rather an early hour to call on you. Pray pardon me.

HEDDA: How do you know that she is still here?

LÖVBORG: They told me at her lodgings that she had been out all night.

HEDDA (*going to the oval table*): Did you notice anything about the people of the house when they said that?

LÖVBORG (*looks inquiringly at her*): Notice anything about them?

HEDDA: I mean, did they seem to think it odd?

LÖVBORG (*suddenly understanding*): Oh yes, of course! I am dragging her down with me! However, I didn't notice any-thing.—I suppose Tesman is not up yet?

HEDDA: No—I think not—

LÖVBORG: When did he come home?

HEDDA: Very late.

LÖVBORG: Did he tell you anything?

HEDDA: Yes, I gathered that you had had an exceedingly jolly evening at Judge Brack's.

LÖVBORG: Nothing more?

HEDDA: I don't think so. However, I was so dreadfully sleepy—

MRS. ELVSTED *enters through the curtains of the middle doorway.*

MRS. ELVSTED (*going toward him*): Ah, Lövborg! At last—!

LÖVBORG: Yes, at last. And too late!

MRS. ELVSTED (*looks anxiously at him*): What is too late?

LÖVBORG: Everything is too late now. It is all over with me.

MRS. ELVSTED: Oh no, no—don't say that!

LÖVBORG: You will say the same when you hear—

MRS. ELVSTED: I won't hear anything!

HEDDA: Perhaps you would prefer to talk to her alone! If so, I will leave you.

LÖVBORG: No, stay—you too. I beg you to stay.

MRS. ELVSTED: Yes, but I won't hear anything, I tell you.

LÖVBORG: It is not last night's adventures that I want to talk about.

MRS. ELVSTED: What is it then—?

LÖVBORG: I want to say that now our ways must part.

MRS. ELVSTED: Part!

HEDDA (*involuntarily*): I knew it!

LÖVBORG: You can be of no more service to me, Thea.

MRS. ELVSTED: How can you stand there and say that! No

more service to you! Am I not to help you now, as before?
Are we not to go on working together?

LÖVBORG: Henceforward I shall do no work.

MRS. ELVSTED (*despairingly*): Then what am I to do with my
life?

LÖVBORG: You must try to live your life as if you had never
known me.

MRS. ELVSTED: But you know I cannot do that!

LÖVBORG: Try if you cannot, Thea. You must go home
again—

MRS. ELVSTED (*in vehement protest*): Never in this world!
Where you are, there will I be also! I will not let myself be
driven away like this! I will remain here! I will be with you
when the book appears.

HEDDA (*half aloud, in suspense*): Ah yes—the book!

LÖVBORG (*looks at her*): My book and Thea's; for that is what
it is.

MRS. ELVSTED: Yes, I feel that it is. And that is why I have a
right to be with you when it appears! I will see with my
own eyes how respect and honor pour in upon you afresh.
And the happiness—the happiness—oh, I must share it
with you!

LÖVBORG: Thea—our book will never appear.

HEDDA: Ah!

MRS. ELVSTED: Never appear!

LÖVBORG: Can never appear.

MRS. ELVSTED (*in agonized foreboding*): Lövborg—what
have you done with the manuscript?

HEDDA (*looks anxiously at him*): Yes, the manuscript—?

MRS. ELVSTED: Where is it?

LÖVBORG: Oh Thea—don't ask me about it!

MRS. ELVSTED: Yes, yes, I will know. I demand to be told at
once.

LÖVBORG: The manuscript— Well then—I have torn the
manuscript into a thousand pieces.

MRS. ELVSTED (*shrieks*): Oh no, no—!

HEDDA (*involuntarily*): But that's not—

LÖVBORG *(looks at her)*: Not true, you think?

HEDDA *(collecting herself)*: Oh well, of course—since you say so. But it sounded so improbable—

LÖVBORG: It is true, all the same.

MRS. ELVSTED *(wringing her hands)*: Oh God—oh God, Hedda—torn his own work to pieces!

LÖVBORG: I have torn my own life to pieces. So why should I not tear my life-work too—?

MRS. ELVSTED: And you did this last night?

LÖVBORG: Yes, I tell you! Tore it into a thousand pieces and scattered them on the fiord—far out. There there is cool seawater at any rate—let them drift upon it—drift with the current and the wind. And then presently they will sink—deeper and deeper—as I shall, Thea.

MRS. ELVSTED: Do you know, Lövborg, that what you have done with the book—I shall think of it to my dying day as though you had killed a little child.

LÖVBORG: Yes, you are right. It is a sort of child-murder.

MRS. ELVSTED: How could you, then—! Did not the child belong to me too?

HEDDA *(almost inaudibly)*: Ah, the child—

MRS. ELVSTED *(breathing heavily)*: It is all over then. Well, well, now I will go, Hedda.

HEDDA: But you are not going away from town?

MRS. ELVSTED: Oh, I don't know what I shall do. I see nothing but darkness before me. *(She goes out by the hall door.)*

HEDDA *(stands waiting for a moment)*: So you are not going to see her home, Mr. Lövborg?

LÖVBORG: I? Through the streets? Would you have people see her walking with me?

HEDDA: Of course I don't know what else may have happened last night. But is it so utterly irretrievable?

LÖVBORG: It will not end with last night—I know that perfectly well. And the thing is that now I have no taste for that sort of life either. I won't begin it anew. She has broken my courage and my power of braving life out.

HEDDA (*looking straight before her*): So that pretty little fool has had her fingers in a man's destiny. (*Looks at him.*) But all the same, how could you treat her so heartlessly.

LÖVBORG: Oh, don't say that it was heartless!

HEDDA: To go and destroy what has filled her whole soul for months and years! You do not call that heartless!

LÖVBORG: To you I can tell the truth, Hedda.

HEDDA: The truth?

LÖVBORG: First promise me—give me your word—that what I now confide to you Thea shall never know.

HEDDA: I give you my word.

LÖVBORG: Good. Then let me tell you that what I said just now was untrue.

HEDDA: About the manuscript?

LÖVBORG: Yes. I have not torn it to pieces—nor thrown it into the fiord.

HEDDA: No, n— But—where is it then?

LÖVBORG: I have destroyed it nonetheless—utterly destroyed it, Hedda!

HEDDA: I don't understand.

LÖVBORG: Thea said that what I had done seemed to her like a child-murder.

HEDDA: Yes, so she said.

LÖVBORG: But to kill this child—that is not the worst thing a father can do to it.

HEDDA: Not the worst?

LÖVBORG: No. I wanted to spare Thea from hearing the worst.

HEDDA: Then what is the worst?

LÖVBORG: Suppose now, Hedda, that a man—in the small hours of the morning—came home to his child's mother after a night of riot and debauchery, and said: "Listen—I have been here and there—in this place and in that. And I have taken our child with me—to this place and to that. And I have lost the child—utterly lost it. The devil knows into what hands it may have fallen—who may have had their clutches on it."

HEDDA: Well—but when all is said and done, you know—this was only a book—

LÖVBORG: Thea's pure soul was in that book.

HEDDA: Yes, so I understand.

LÖVBORG: And you can understand, too, that for her and me together no future is possible.

HEDDA: What path do you mean to take then?

LÖVBORG: None. I will only try to make an end of it all—the sooner the better.

HEDDA (*a step nearer him*): Eilert Lövborg—listen to me.— Will you not try to—to do it beautifully?

LÖVBORG: Beautifully? (*Smiling.*) With vine leaves in my hair, as you used to dream in the old days—?

HEDDA: No, no. I have lost my faith in the vine leaves. But beautifully nevertheless! For once in a way!—Good-bye! You must go now—and do not come here anymore.

LÖVBORG: Good-bye, Mrs. Tesman. And give George Tesman my love. (*He is on the point of going.*)

HEDDA: No, wait! I must give you a memento to take with you.

She goes to the writing table and opens the drawer and the pistol case; then returns to LÖVBORG *with one of the pistols.*

LÖVBORG (*looks at her*): This? Is this the memento?

HEDDA (*nodding slowly*): Do you recognize it? It was aimed at you once.

LÖVBORG: You should have used it then.

HEDDA: Take it—and do you use it now.

LÖVBORG (*puts the pistol in his breast pocket*): Thanks!

HEDDA: And beautifully, Eilert Lövborg. Promise me that!

LÖVBORG: Good-bye, Hedda Gabler. (*He goes out by the hall door.*)

HEDDA listens for a moment at the door. Then she goes up the writing table, takes out the packet of manuscript, peeps under the cover, draws a few of the sheets half out,

*and looks at them. Next she goes over and seats herself in
the armchair beside the stove, with the packet in her lap.
Presently she opens the stove door, and then the packet.*

HEDDA *(throws one of the quires*[9] *into the fire and whispers
to herself):* Now I am burning your child, Thea!—Burning
it, curly-locks! *(Throwing one or two more quires into the
stove.)* Your child and Eilert Lövborg's. *(Throws the rest
in.)* I am burning—I am burning your child.

ACT FOUR

The same rooms at the TESMANS'. *It is evening. The drawing room is in darkness. The back room is lighted by the hanging lamp over the table. The curtains over the glass door are drawn close.*

HEDDA, *dressed in black, walks to and fro in the dark room. Then she goes into the back room and disappears for a moment to the left. She is heard to strike a few chords on the piano. Presently she comes in sight again, and returns to the drawing room.*

BERTA *enters from the right, through the inner room, with a lighted lamp, which she places on the table in front of the corner settee in the drawing room. Her eyes are red with weeping, and she has black ribbons in her cap. She goes quietly and circumspectly out to the right.*

HEDDA *goes up to the glass door, lifts the curtain a little aside, and looks out into the darkness.*

Shortly afterward, MISS TESMAN, *in mourning, with a bonnet and veil on, comes in from the hall.* HEDDA *goes toward her and holds out her hand.*

MISS TESMAN: Yes, Hedda, here I am, in mourning and forlorn; for now my poor sister has at last found peace.

HEDDA: I have heard the news already, as you see. Tesman sent me a card.

MISS TESMAN: Yes, he promised me he would. But nevertheless I thought that to Hedda—here in the house of life—I ought myself to bring the tidings of death.

HEDDA: That was very kind of you.

MISS TESMAN: Ah, Rina ought not to have left us just now. This is not the time for Hedda's house to be a house of mourning.

HEDDA (changing the subject): She died quite peacefully, did she not, Miss Tesman?

MISS TESMAN: Oh, her end was so calm, so beautiful. And then she had the unspeakable happiness of seeing George once more—and bidding him good-bye.—Has he come home yet?

HEDDA: No. He wrote that he might be detained. But won't you sit down?

MISS TESMAN: No thank you, my dear, dear Hedda. I should like to, but I have so much to do. I must prepare my dear one for her rest as well as I can. She shall go to her grave looking her best.

HEDDA: Can I not help you in any way?

MISS TESMAN: Oh, you must not think of it! Hedda Tesman must have no hand in such mournful work. Nor let her thoughts dwell on it either—not at this time.

HEDDA: One is not always mistress of one's thoughts—

MISS TESMAN (continuing): Ah yes, it is the way of the world. At home we shall be sewing a shroud; and here there will soon be sewing too, I suppose—but of another sort, thank God!

GEORGE TESMAN enters by the hall door.

HEDDA: Ah, you have come at last!

TESMAN: You here, Aunt Julia? With Hedda? Fancy that!

MISS TESMAN: I was just going, my dear boy. Well, have you done all you promised?

TESMAN: No; I'm really afraid I have forgotten half of it. I must come to you again tomorrow. Today my brain is all in a whirl. I can't keep my thoughts together.

MISS TESMAN: Why, my dear George, you mustn't take it in this way.

TESMAN: Mustn't—? How do you mean?

MISS TESMAN: Even in your sorrow you must rejoice, as I do—rejoice that she is at rest.

TESMAN: Oh yes, yes—you are thinking of Aunt Rina.

HEDDA: You will feel lonely now, Miss Tesman.

MISS TESMAN: Just at first, yes. But that will not last very long, I hope. I daresay I shall soon find an occupant for poor Rina's little room.

TESMAN: Indeed? Who do you think will take it? Eh?

MISS TESMAN: Oh, there's always some poor invalid or other in want of nursing, unfortunately.

HEDDA: Would you really take such a burden upon you again?

MISS TESMAN: A burden! Heaven forgive you, child—it has been no burden to me.

HEDDA: But suppose you had a total stranger on your hands—

MISS TESMAN: Oh, one soon makes friends with sick folk; and it's such an absolute necessity for me to have someone to live for. Well, heaven be praised, there may soon be something in this house, too, to keep an old aunt busy.

HEDDA: Oh, don't trouble about anything here.

TESMAN: Yes, just fancy what a nice time we three might have together, if—?

HEDDA: If—?

TESMAN (uneasily): Oh, nothing. It will all come right. Let us hope so—eh?

MISS TESMAN: Well, well, I daresay you two want to talk to each other. (Smiling.) And perhaps Hedda may have something to tell you too, George. Good-bye! I must go home to Rina. (*Turning at the door.*) How strange it is to think that now Rina is with me and with my poor brother as well!

TESMAN: Yes, fancy that, Aunt Julia! Eh? (MISS TESMAN *goes out by the hall door.*)

HEDDA (*follows* TESMAN *coldly and searchingly with her eyes*): I almost believe your Aunt Rina's death affects you more than it does your Aunt Julia.

TESMAN: Oh, it's not that alone. It's Eilert I am so terribly uneasy about.

HEDDA (*quickly*): Is there anything new about him?

TESMAN: I looked in at his rooms this afternoon, intending to tell him the manuscript was in safekeeping.

HEDDA: Well, did you not find him?

TESMAN: No. He wasn't at home. But afterward I met Mrs. Elvsted, and she told me that he had been here early this morning.

HEDDA: Yes, directly after you had gone.

TESMAN: And he said that he had torn his manuscript to pieces—eh?

HEDDA: Yes, so he declared.

TESMAN: Why, good heavens, he must have been completely out of his mind! And I suppose you thought it best not to give it back to him, Hedda?

HEDDA: No, he did not get it.

TESMAN: But of course you told him that we had it?

HEDDA: No. (*Quickly.*) Did you tell Mrs. Elvsted?

TESMAN: No; I thought I had better not. But you ought to have told him. Fancy, if, in desperation, he should go and do himself some injury! Let me have the manuscript, Hedda! I will take it to him at once. Where is it?

HEDDA (*cold and immovable, leaning on the armchair*): I have not got it.

TESMAN: Have not got it? What in the world do you mean?

HEDDA: I have burned it—every line of it.

TESMAN (*with a violent movement of terror*): Burned! Burned Eilert's manuscript!

HEDDA: Don't scream so. The servant might hear you.

TESMAN: Burned! Why, good God—! No, no, no! It's impossible!

HEDDA: It is so, nevertheless.

TESMAN: Do you know what you have done, Hedda? It's unlawful appropriation of lost property. Fancy that! Just ask Judge Brack, and he'll tell you what it is.

HEDDA: I advise you not to speak of it—either to Judge Brack, or to anyone else.

TESMAN: But how could you do anything so unheard-of? What put it into your head? What possessed you? Answer me that—eh?

HEDDA (*suppressing an almost imperceptible smile*): I did it for your sake, George.

TESMAN: For my sake!

HEDDA: This morning, when you told me about what he had read to you—

TESMAN: Yes, yes—what then?

HEDDA: You acknowledged that you envied him his work.

TESMAN: Oh, of course I didn't mean that literally.

HEDDA: No matter—I could not bear the idea that anyone should throw you into the shade.

TESMAN (*in an outburst of mingled doubt and joy*): Hedda! Oh, is this true? But—but—I never knew you to show your love like that before. Fancy that!

HEDDA: Well, I may as well tell you that—just at this time— (*Impatiently, breaking off.*) No, no; you can ask Aunt Julia. She will tell you, fast enough.

TESMAN: Oh, I almost think I understand you, Hedda! (*Clasps his hands together.*) Great heavens! do you really mean it! Eh?

HEDDA: Don't shout so. The servant might hear.

TESMAN (*laughing in irrepressible glee*): The servant! Why, how absurd you are, Hedda. It's only my old Berta! Why, I'll tell Berta myself.

HEDDA (*clenching her hands together in desperation*): Oh, it is killing me,—it is killing me, all this!

TESMAN: What is, Hedda? Eh?

HEDDA (*coldly, controlling herself*): All this—absurdity—George.

TESMAN: Absurdity! Do you see anything absurd in my being overjoyed at the news! But after all—perhaps I had better not say anything to Berta.

HEDDA: Oh—why not that too?

TESMAN: No, no, not yet! But I must certainly tell Aunt Julia. And then that you have begun to call me George too! Fancy that! Oh, Aunt Julia will be so happy—so happy!

HEDDA: When she hears that I have burned Eilert Lövborg's manuscript—for your sake?

TESMAN: No, by-the-bye—that affair of the manuscript—of course nobody must know about that. But that you love me so much, Hedda—Aunt Julia must really share my joy in that! I wonder, now, whether this sort of thing is usual in young wives? Eh?

HEDDA: I think you had better ask Aunt Julia that question too.

TESMAN: I will indeed, some time or other. (*Looks uneasy and downcast again.*) And yet the manuscript—the manuscript! Good God! it is terrible to think what will become of poor Eilert now.

MRS. ELVSTED, *dressed as in the first Act, with hat and cloak, enters by the hall door.*

MRS. ELVSTED (*greets them hurriedly, and says in evident agitation*): Oh, dear Hedda, forgive my coming again.

HEDDA: What is the matter with you, Thea?

TESMAN: Something about Eilert Lövborg again—eh?

MRS. ELVSTED: Yes! I am dreadfully afraid some misfortune has happened to him.

HEDDA (*seizes her arm*): Ah,—do you think so?

TESMAN: Why, good Lord—what makes you think that, Mrs. Elvsted?

MRS. ELVSTED: I heard them talking of him at my boardinghouse—just as I came in. Oh, the most incredible rumors are afloat about him today.

TESMAN: Yes, fancy, so I heard too! And I can bear witness that he went straight home to bed last night. Fancy that!

HEDDA: Well, what did they say at the boardinghouse?

MRS. ELVSTED: Oh, I couldn't make out anything clearly. Either they knew nothing definite, or else— They stopped talking when they saw me; and I did not dare to ask.

TESMAN (*moving about uneasily*): We must hope—we must hope that you misunderstood them, Mrs. Elvsted.

MRS. ELVSTED: No, no; I am sure it was of him they were talking. And I heard something about the hospital or—

TESMAN: The hospital?

HEDDA: No—surely that cannot be!

MRS. ELVSTED: Oh, I was in such mortal terror! I went to his lodgings and asked for him there.

HEDDA: You could make up your mind to that, Thea!

MRS. ELVSTED: What else could I do? I really could bear the suspense no longer.

TESMAN: But you didn't find him either—eh?

MRS. ELVSTED: No. And the people knew nothing about him. He hadn't been home since yesterday afternoon, they said.

TESMAN: Yesterday! Fancy, how could they say that?

MRS. ELVSTED: Oh, I am sure something terrible must have happened to him.

TESMAN: Hedda dear—how would it be if I were to go and make inquiries—?

HEDDA: No, no—don't you mix yourself up in this affair.

JUDGE BRACK, *with his hat in his hand, enters by the hall door, which* BERTA *opens, and closes behind him. He looks grave and bows in silence.*

TESMAN: Oh, is that you, my dear Judge? Eh?

BRACK: Yes. It was imperative I should see you this evening.

TESMAN: I can see you have heard the news about Aunt Rina?

BRACK: Yes, that among other things.

TESMAN: Isn't it sad—eh?

BRACK: Well, my dear Tesman, that depends on how you look at it.

TESMAN (*looks doubtfully at him*): Has anything else happened?

BRACK: Yes.

HEDDA (*in suspense*): Anything sad, Judge Brack?

BRACK: That, too, depends on how you look at it, Mrs. Tesman.

MRS. ELVSTED (*unable to restrain her anxiety*): Oh! it is something about Eilert Lövborg!

BRACK (*with a glance at her*): What makes you think that, Madam? Perhaps you have already heard something—?

MRS. ELVSTED (*in confusion*): No, nothing at all, but—

TESMAN: Oh, for heaven's sake, tell us!

BRACK (*shrugging his shoulders*): Well, I regret to say Eilert Lövborg has been taken to the hospital. He is lying at the point of death.

MRS. ELVSTED (*shrieks*): Oh God! Oh God—!

TESMAN: To the hospital! And at the point of death.

HEDDA (*involuntarily*): So soon then—

MRS. ELVSTED (*wailing*): And we parted in anger, Hedda!

HEDDA (*whispers*): Thea—Thea—be careful!

MRS. ELVSTED (*not heeding her*): I must go to him! I must see him alive!

BRACK: It is useless, Madam. No one will be admitted.

MRS. ELVSTED: Oh, at least tell me what has happened to him? What is it?

TESMAN: You don't mean to say that he has himself—eh?

HEDDA: Yes, I am sure he has.

TESMAN: Hedda, how can you—?

BRACK (*keeping his eyes fixed upon her*): Unfortunately you have guessed quite correctly, Mrs. Tesman.

MRS. ELVSTED: Oh, how horrible!

TESMAN: Himself, then! Fancy that!

HEDDA: Shot himself!

BRACK: Rightly guessed again, Mrs. Tesman.

MRS. ELVSTED (*with an effort at self-control*): When did it happen, Mr. Brack?

BRACK: This afternoon—between three and four.

TESMAN: But, good Lord, where did he do it? Eh?

BRACK (*with some hesitation*): Where? Well—I suppose at his lodgings.

MRS. ELVSTED: No, that cannot be; for I was there between six and seven.

BRACK: Well, then, somewhere else. I don't know exactly. I only know that he was found—. He had shot himself—in the breast.

MRS. ELVSTED: Oh, how terrible! That he should die like that!

HEDDA (*to Brack*): Was it in the breast?

BRACK: Yes—as I told you.

HEDDA: Not in the temple?

BRACK: In the breast, Mrs. Tesman.

HEDDA: Well, well—the breast is a good place, too.

BRACK: How do you mean, Mrs. Tesman?

HEDDA (*evasively*): Oh, nothing—nothing.

TESMAN: And the wound is dangerous, you say—eh?

BRACK: Absolutely mortal. The end has probably come by this time.

MRS. ELVSTED: Yes, yes, I feel it. The end! The end! Oh, Hedda—!

TESMAN: But tell me, how have you learned all this?

BRACK (*curtly*): Through one of the police. A man I had some business with.

HEDDA (*in a clear voice*): At last a deed worth doing!

TESMAN (*terrified*): Good heavens, Hedda! what are you saying?

HEDDA: I say there is beauty in this.

BRACK: Hm, Mrs. Tesman—

TESMAN: Beauty! Fancy that!

MRS. ELVSTED: Oh, Hedda, how can you talk of beauty in such an act!

HEDDA: Eilert Lövborg has himself made up his account with life. He has had the courage to do—the one right thing.

MRS. ELVSTED: No, you must never think that was how it happened! It must have been in delirium that he did it.

TESMAN: In despair!

HEDDA: That he did not. I am certain of that.

MRS. ELVSTED: Yes, yes! In delirium! Just as when he tore up our manuscript.

BRACK (*starting*): The manuscript? Has he torn that up?

MRS. ELVSTED: Yes, last night.

TESMAN (*whispers softly*): Oh, Hedda, we shall never get over this.

BRACK: Hm, very extraordinary.

TESMAN (*moving about the room*): To think of Eilert going out of the world in this way! And not leaving behind him the book that would have immortalized his name—

MRS. ELVSTED: Oh, if only it could be put together again!

TESMAN: Yes, if it only could! I don't know what I would not give—

MRS. ELVSTED: Perhaps it can, Mr. Tesman.

TESMAN: What do you mean?

MRS. ELVSTED (*searches in the pocket of her dress*): Look here. I have kept all the loose notes he used to dictate from.

HEDDA (*a step forward*): Ah—!

TESMAN: You have kept them, Mrs. Elvsted! Eh?

MRS. ELVSTED: Yes, I have them here. I put them in my pocket when I left home. Here they still are—

TESMAN: Oh, do let me see them!

MRS. ELVSTED (*hands him a bundle of papers*): But they are in such disorder—all mixed up.

TESMAN: Fancy, if we could make something out of them, after all! Perhaps if we two put our heads together—

MRS. ELVSTED: Oh, yes, at least let us try—

TESMAN: We will manage it! We must! I will dedicate my life to this task.

HEDDA: You, George? Your life?

TESMAN: Yes, or rather all the time I can spare. My own collections must wait in the meantime. Hedda—you understand, eh? I owe this to Eilert's memory.

HEDDA: Perhaps.

TESMAN: And so, my dear Mrs. Elvsted, we will give our whole minds to it. There is no use in brooding over what can't be undone—eh? We must try to control our grief as much as possible, and—

MRS. ELVSTED: Yes, yes, Mr. Tesman, I will do the best I can.

TESMAN: Well then, come here. I can't rest until we have looked through the notes. Where shall we sit? Here? No, in there, in the back room. Excuse me, my dear Judge. Come with me, Mrs. Elvsted.

MRS. ELVSTED: Oh, if only it were possible!

TESMAN *and* MRS. ELVSTED *go into the back room. She takes off her hat and cloak. They both sit at the table under the hanging lamp, and are soon deep in an eager examination of the papers.* HEDDA *crosses to the stove and sits in the armchair. Presently* BRACK *goes up to her.*

HEDDA (*in a low voice*): Oh, what a sense of freedom it gives one, this act of Eilert Lövborg's.

BRACK: Freedom, Mrs. Hedda? Well, of course, it is a release for him—

HEDDA: I mean for me. It gives me a sense of freedom to know that a deed of deliberate courage is still possible in this world,—a deed of spontaneous beauty.

BRACK (*smiling*): Hm—my dear Mrs. Hedda—

HEDDA: Oh, I know what you are going to say. For you are a kind of specialist too, like—you know!

BRACK (*looking hard at her*): Eilert Lövborg was more to you than perhaps you are willing to admit to yourself. Am I wrong?

HEDDA: I don't answer such questions. I only know that Eilert Lövborg has had the courage to live his life after his own fashion. And then—the last great act, with its beauty!

Ah! that he should have the will and the strength to turn away from the banquet of life—so early.

BRACK: I am sorry, Mrs. Hedda,—but I fear I must dispel an amiable illusion.

HEDDA: Illusion?

BRACK: Which could not have lasted long in any case.

HEDDA: What do you mean?

BRACK: Eilert Lövborg did not shoot himself—voluntarily.

HEDDA: Not voluntarily?

BRACK: No. The thing did not happen exactly as I told it.

HEDDA (in suspense): Have you concealed something? What is it?

BRACK: For poor Mrs. Elvsted's sake I idealized the facts a little.

HEDDA: What are the facts?

BRACK: First, that he is already dead.

HEDDA: At the hospital?

BRACK: Yes—without regaining consciousness.

HEDDA: What more have you concealed?

BRACK: This—the event did not happen at his lodgings.

HEDDA: Oh, that can make no difference.

BRACK: Perhaps it may. For I must tell you—Eilert Lövborg was found shot in—in Mademoiselle Diana's boudoir.

HEDDA (makes a motion as if to rise, but sinks back again): That is impossible, Judge Brack! He cannot have been there again today.

BRACK: He was there this afternoon. He went there, he said, to demand the return of something which they had taken from him. Talked wildly about a lost child—

HEDDA: Ah—so that was why—

BRACK: I thought probably he meant his manuscript; but now I hear he destroyed that himself. So I suppose it must have been his pocketbook.

HEDDA: Yes, no doubt. And there—there he was found?

BRACK: Yes, there. With a pistol in his breast pocket, discharged. The ball had lodged in a vital part.

HEDDA: In the breast—yes.

BRACK: No—in the bowels.

HEDDA (*looks up at him with an expression of loathing*): That too! Oh, what curse is it that makes everything I touch turn ludicrous and mean?

BRACK: There is one point more, Mrs. Hedda—another disagreeable feature in the affair.

HEDDA: And what is that?

BRACK: The pistol he carried—

HEDDA (*breathless*): Well? What of it?

BRACK: He must have stolen it.

HEDDA (*leaps up*): Stolen it! That is not true! He did not steal it!

BRACK: No other explanation is possible. He must have stolen it— Hush!

TESMAN *and* MRS. ELVSTED *have risen from the table in the back room, and come into the drawing room.*

TESMAN (*with the papers in both his hands*): Hedda dear, it is almost impossible to see under that lamp. Think of that!

HEDDA: Yes, I am thinking.

TESMAN: Would you mind our sitting at your writing table—eh?

HEDDA: If you like. (*Quickly.*) No, wait! Let me clear it first!

TESMAN: Oh, you needn't trouble, Hedda. There is plenty of room.

HEDDA: No, no, let me clear it, I say! I will take these things in and put them on the piano. There! (*She has drawn out an object, covered with sheet music, from under the bookcase, places several other pieces of music upon it, and carries the whole into the inner room, to the left.* TESMAN *lays the scraps of paper on the writing table, and moves the lamp there from the corner table. He and* MRS. ELVSTED *sit down and proceed with their work.* HEDDA *returns.*)

HEDDA (*behind* MRS. ELVSTED'S *chair, gently ruffling her hair*): Well, my sweet Thea,—how goes it with Eilert Lövborg's monument?

MRS. ELVSTED (*looks dispiritedly up at her*): Oh, it will be terribly hard to put in order.

TESMAN: We must manage it. I am determined. And arranging other people's papers is just the work for me.

HEDDA *goes over to the stove, and seats herself on one of the footstools.* BRACK *stands over her, leaning on the armchair.*

HEDDA (*whispers*): What did you say about the pistol?

BRACK (*softly*): That he must have stolen it.

HEDDA: Why stolen it?

BRACK: Because every other explanation ought to be impossible, Mrs. Hedda.

HEDDA: Indeed?

BRACK (*glances at her*): Of course Eilert Lövborg was here this morning. Was he not?

HEDDA: Yes.

BRACK: Were you alone with him?

HEDDA: Part of the time.

BRACK: Did you not leave the room while he was here?

HEDDA: No.

BRACK: Try to recollect. Were you not out of the room a moment?

HEDDA: Yes, perhaps just a moment—out in the hall.

BRACK: And where was your pistol case during that time?

HEDDA: I had it locked up in—

BRACK: Well, Mrs. Hedda?

HEDDA: The case stood there on the writing table.

BRACK: Have you looked since, to see whether both the pistols are there?

HEDDA: No.

BRACK: Well, you need not. I saw the pistol found in Lövborg's pocket, and I knew it at once as the one I had seen yesterday—and before, too.

HEDDA: Have you it with you?

BRACK: No; the police have it.

HEDDA: What will the police do with it?

BRACK: Search till they find the owner.

HEDDA: Do you think they will succeed?

BRACK (*bends over her and whispers*): No, Hedda Gabler—not so long as I say nothing.

HEDDA (*looks frightened at him*): And if you do not say nothing,—what then?

BRACK (*shrugs his shoulders*): There is always the possibility that the pistol was stolen.

HEDDA (*firmly*): Death rather than that.

BRACK (*smiling*): People say such things—but they don't do them.

HEDDA (*without replying*): And supposing the pistol was not stolen, and the owner is discovered? What then?

BRACK: Well, Hedda—then comes the scandal.

HEDDA: The scandal!

BRACK: Yes, the scandal—of which you are mortally afraid. You will, of course, be brought before the court—both you and Mademoiselle Diana. She will have to explain how the thing happened—whether it was an accidental shot or murder. Did the pistol go off as he was trying to take it out of his pocket, to threaten her with? Or did she tear the pistol out of his hand, shoot him, and push it back into his pocket? That would be quite like her; for she is an able-bodied young person, this same Mademoiselle Diana.

HEDDA: But *I* have nothing to do with all this repulsive business.

BRACK: **No.** But you will have to answer the question: Why did you give Eilert Lövborg the pistol? And what conclusions will people draw from the fact that you did give it to him?

HEDDA (*lets her head sink*): That is true. I did not think of that.

BRACK: Well, fortunately, there is no danger, so long as I say nothing.

HEDDA (*looks up at him*): So I am in your power, Judge

Brack. You have me at your beck and call, from this time forward.

BRACK (*whispers softly*): Dearest Hedda—believe me—I shall not abuse my advantage.

HEDDA: I am in your power nonetheless. Subject to your will and your demands. A slave, a slave then! (*Rises impetuously.*) No, I cannot endure the thought of that! Never!

BRACK (*looks half mockingly at her*): People generally get used to the inevitable.

HEDDA (*returns his look*): Yes, perhaps. (*She crosses to the writing table. Suppressing an involuntary smile, she imitates* TESMAN'S *intonations.*) Well? Are you getting on, George? Eh?

TESMAN: Heaven knows, dear. In any case it will be the work of months.

HEDDA (*as before*): Fancy that! (*Passes her hands softly through* MRS. ELVSTED'S *hair.*) Doesn't it seem strange to you, Thea? Here are you sitting with Tesman—just as you used to sit with Eilert Lövborg?

MRS. ELVSTED: Ah, if I could only inspire your husband in the same way.

HEDDA: Oh, that will come too—in time.

TESMAN: Yes, do you know, Hedda—I really think I begin to feel something of the sort. But won't you go and sit with Brack again?

HEDDA: Is there nothing I can do to help you two?

TESMAN: No, nothing in the world. (*Turning his head.*) I trust to you to keep Hedda company, my dear Brack.

BRACK (*with a glance at* HEDDA): With the very greatest of pleasure.

HEDDA: Thanks. But I am tired this evening. I will go in and lie down a little on the sofa.

TESMAN: Yes, do dear—eh? (HEDDA *goes into the back room and draws the curtains. A short pause. Suddenly she is heard playing a wild dance on the piano.*)

MRS. ELVSTED *(starts from her chair)*: Oh—what is that?

TESMAN *(runs to the doorway)*: Why, my dearest Hedda— don't play dance music tonight! Just think of Aunt Rina! And of Eilert too!

HEDDA *(puts her head out between the curtains)*: And of Aunt Julia. And of all the rest of them.—After this, I will be quiet. *(Closes the curtains again.)*

TESMAN *(at the writing table)*: It's not good for her to see us at this distressing work. I'll tell you what, Mrs. Elvsted,— you shall take the empty room at Aunt Julia's, and then I will come over in the evenings, and we can sit and work there—eh?

HEDDA *(in the inner room)*: I hear what you are saying, Tesman. But how am *I* to get through the evenings out here?

TESMAN *(turning over the papers)*: Oh, I daresay Judge Brack will be so kind as to look in now and then, even though I am out.

BRACK *(in the armchair, calls out gaily)*: Every blessed evening, with all the pleasure in life, Mrs. Tesman! We shall get on capitally together, we two!

HEDDA *(speaking loud and clear)*: Yes, don't you flatter yourself we will, Judge Brack? Now that you are the one cock in the basket— *(A shot is heard from within.* TESMAN, MRS. ELVSTED, *and* BRACK *leap to their feet.)*

TESMAN: Oh, now she is playing with those pistols again. *(He throws back the curtains and runs in, followed by* MRS. ELVSTED. HEDDA *lies stretched on the sofa, lifeless. Confusion and cries.* BERTA *enters in alarm from the right.)*

TESMAN *(shrieks to* BRACK*)*: Shot herself! Shot herself in the temple! Fancy that!

BRACK *(half fainting in the armchair)*: Good God!—people don't do such things.

THE MASTER BUILDER

CHARACTERS

HALVARD SOLNESS, Master Builder

ALINE SOLNESS, his wife

DR. HERDAL, physician

KNUT BROVIK, formerly an architect, now in SOLNESS's
   employment

RAGNAR BROVIK, his son, draftsman

KAIA FOSLI, his niece, bookkeeper

MISS HILDA WANGEL

SOME LADIES

A CROWD IN THE STREET

The action passes in and about SOLNESS's house.

ACT ONE

A plainly furnished workroom in the house of HALVARD SOLNESS. Folding doors on the left lead out to the hall. On the right is the door leading to the inner rooms of the house. At the back is an open door into the draftsmen's office. In front, on the left, a desk with books, papers and writing materials. Further back than the folding door, a stove. In the right-hand corner, a sofa, a table and one or two chairs. On the table a water bottle and glass. A smaller table, with a rocking chair and armchair, in front on the right. Lighted lamps, with shades, on the table in the draftmen's office, on the table in the corner and on the desk.

In the draftsmen's office sit KNUT BROVIK and his son RAGNAR, occupied with plans and calculations. At the desk in the outer office stands KAIA FOSLI, writing in the ledger. KNUT BROVIK is a spare old man with white hair and beard. He wears a rather threadbare but well-brushed black coat, spectacles and a somewhat discolored white neckcloth. RAGNAR BROVIK is a well-dressed, light-haired man in his thirties, with a slight *stoop.* KAIA FOSLI *is a slightly built girl, a little over twenty, carefully dressed and delicate-looking. She has a green shade over her eyes.—All three go on working for some time in silence.*

KNUT BROVIK *(rises suddenly, as if in distress, from the table; breathes heavily and laboriously as he comes forward into the doorway)*: No, I can't bear it much longer!

KAIA *(going up to him)*: You are feeling very ill this evening, are you not, Uncle?

BROVIK: Oh, I seem to get worse every day.

RAGNAR *(has risen and advances)*: You ought to go home, Father. Try to get a little sleep—

BROVIK *(impatiently)*: Go to bed, I suppose? Would you have me stifled outright?

KAIA: Then take a little walk.

RAGNAR: Yes, do. I will come with you.

BROVIK *(with warmth)*: I will not go till he comes! I am determined to have it out this evening with—*(in a tone of suppressed bitterness)*—with him—with the chief.

KAIA *(anxiously)*: Oh no, Uncle—do wait awhile before doing that.

RAGNAR: Yes, better wait, Father!

BROVIK *(draws his breath laboriously)*: Ha—ha—! I haven't much time for waiting.

KAIA *(listening)*: Hush! I hear him on the stairs.

All three go back to their work. A short silence. HALVARD SOLNESS *comes in through the hall door. He is a man no longer young, but healthy and vigorous, with close-cut hair, dark mustache and dark thick eyebrows. He wears a grayish-green buttoned jacket with an upstanding collar and broad lapels. On his head he wears a soft gray felt hat, and he has one or two light portfolios under his arm.*

SOLNESS *(near the door, points toward the draftsmen's office, and asks in a whisper)*: Are they gone?

KAIA *(softly, shaking her head)*: No.

She takes the shade off her eyes. SOLNESS *crosses the room, throws his hat on a chair, places the portfolios on the table by the sofa and approaches the desk again.* KAIA *goes on writing without intermission, but seems nervous and uneasy.*

SOLNESS *(aloud)*: What is that you are entering, Miss Fosli?

KAIA *(starts)*: Oh, it is only something that—

SOLNESS: Let me look at it, Miss Fosli. *(Bends over her, pretends to be looking into the ledger, and whispers.)* Kaia!

KAIA *(softly, still writing)*: Well?

SOLNESS: Why do you always take that shade off when I come?

KAIA *(as before)*: I look so ugly with it on.

SOLNESS *(smiling)*: Then you don't like to look ugly, Kaia?

KAIA *(half glancing up at him)*: Not for all the world. Not in your eyes.

SOLNESS *(stroking her hair gently)*: Poor, poor little Kaia—

KAIA *(bending her head)*: Hush—they can hear you.

SOLNESS *strolls across the room to the right, turns and pauses at the door of the draftsmen's office.*

SOLNESS: Has anyone been here for me?

RAGNAR *(rising)*: Yes, the young couple who wants a villa built, out at Lövstrand.

SOLNESS *(growling)*: Oh, those two! They must wait. I am not quite clear about the plans yet.

RAGNAR *(advancing, with some hesitation)*: They were very anxious to have the drawing at once.

SOLNESS *(as before)*: Yes, of course—so they all are.

BROVIK *(looks up)*: They say they are longing so to get into a house of their own.

SOLNESS: Yes, yes—we know all that! And so they are content to take whatever is offered them. They get a—a roof over their heads—an address—but nothing to call a home. No, thank you! In that case, let them apply to somebody else. Tell them that, the next time they call.

BROVIK (*pushes his glasses up on to his forehead and looks in astonishment at him*): To somebody else? Are you prepared to give up the commission?

SOLNESS (*impatiently*): Yes, yes, yes, devil take it! If that is to be the way of it—. Rather that, than build away at random. (*Vehemently.*) Besides, I know very little about these people as yet.

BROVIK: The people are safe enough. Ragnar knows them. He is a friend of the family. Perfectly safe people.

SOLNESS: Oh, safe—safe enough! That is not at all what I mean. Good Lord—don't you understand me either? (*Angrily.*) I won't have anything to do with these strangers. They may apply to whom they please, so far as I am concerned.

BROVIK (*rising*): Do you really mean that?

SOLNESS (*sulkily*): Yes I do,—For once in a way.

He comes forward. BROVIK *exchanges a glance with* RAGNAR, *who makes a warning gesture. Then* BROVIK *comes into the front room.*

BROVIK: May I have a few words with you?

SOLNESS: Certainly.

BROVIK (*to* KAIA): Just go in there for a moment, Kaia.

KAIA (*uneasily*): Oh, but Uncle—

BROVIK: Do as I say, child. And shut the door after you.

KAIA *goes reluctantly into the draftsmen's office, glances anxiously and imploringly at* SOLNESS, *and shuts the door.*

BROVIK (*lowering his voice a little*): I don't want the poor children to know how ill I am.

SOLNESS: Yes, you have been looking very poorly of late.

BROVIK: It will soon be all over with me. My strength is ebbing—from day to day.

SOLNESS: Won't you sit down?

BROVIK: Thanks—may I?

SOLNESS (*placing the armchair more conveniently*): Here—take this chair.—And now?

BROVIK *(has seated himself with difficulty)*: Well, you see, it's about Ragnar. That is what weighs most upon me. What is to become of him?

SOLNESS: Of course your son will stay with me as long as ever he likes.

BROVIK: But that is just what he does not like. He feels that he cannot stay here any longer.

SOLNESS: Why, I should say he was very well off here. But if he wants more money, I should not mind—

BROVIK: No, no! It is not that. *(Impatiently.)* But sooner or later he, too, must have a chance of doing something on his own account.

SOLNESS *(without looking at him)*: Do you think that Ragnar has quite talent enough to stand alone?

BROVIK: No, that is just the heartbreaking part of it—I have begun to have my doubts about the boy. For you have never said so much as—as one encouraging word about him. And yet I cannot but think there must be something in him—he can't be without talent.

SOLNESS: Well, but he has learned nothing—nothing thoroughly, I mean. Except, of course, to draw.

BROVIK *(looks at him with covert hatred and says hoarsely)*: You had learned little enough of the business when you were in my employment. But that did not prevent you from setting to work—*(breathing with difficulty)*—and pushing your way up and taking the wind out of my sails— mine, and so many other people's.

SOLNESS: Yes, you see—circumstances favored me.

BROVIK: You are right there. Everything favored you. But then how can you have the heart to let me go to my grave—without having seen what Ragnar is fit for? And of course I am anxious to see them married, too—before I go.

SOLNESS *(sharply)*: Is it she who wishes it?

BROVIK: Not Kaia so much as Ragnar—he talks about it every day. *(Appealingly.)* You must—you must help him to get some independent work now! I must see something that the lad has done. Do you hear?

SOLNESS (*peevishly*): Hang it, man, you can't expect me to drag commissions down from the moon for him!

BROVIK: He has the chance of a capital commission at this very moment. A big bit of work.

SOLNESS (*uneasily, startled*): Has he?

BROVIK: If you would give your consent.

SOLNESS: What sort of work do you mean?

BROVIK (*with some hesitation*): He can have the building of that villa out at Lövstrand.

SOLNESS: That! Why, I am going to build that myself.

BROVIK: Oh, you don't much care about doing it.

SOLNESS (*flaring up*): Don't care! I? Who dares to say that?

BROVIK: You said so yourself just now.

SOLNESS: Oh, never mind what I say.—Would they give Ragnar the building of that villa?

BROVIK: Yes. You see, he knows the family. And then—just for the fun of the thing—he has made drawings and estimates and so forth—

SOLNESS: Are they pleased with the drawings? The people who will have to live in the house?

BROVIK: Yes. If you would only look through them and approve of them.

SOLNESS: Then they would let Ragnar build their home for them?

BROVIK: They were immensely pleased with his idea. They thought it exceedingly original, they said.

SOLNESS: Oho! Original! Not the old-fashioned stuff that *I* am in the habit of turning out!

BROVIK: It seemed to them different.

SOLNESS (*with suppressed irritation*): So it was to see Ragnar that they came here—while I was out!

BROVIK: They came to call upon you—and at the same time to ask whether you would mind retiring—

SOLNESS (*angrily*): Retire? I?

BROVIK: In case you thought that Ragnar's drawings—

SOLNESS: I? Retire in favor of your son!

BROVIK: Retire from the agreement, they meant.

SOLNESS: Oh, it comes to the same thing. (*Laughs angrily.*) So that is it, is it? Halvard Solness is to see about retiring now! To make room for younger men! For the very youngest, perhaps! He must make room! Room! Room!

BROVIK: Why, good heavens! there is surely room for more than one single man—

SOLNESS: Oh, there's not so very much room to spare either. But, be that as it may—I will never retire! I will never give way to anybody! Never of my own free will. Never in this world will I do that!

BROVIK (*rises with difficulty*): Then I am to pass out of life without any certainty? Without a gleam of happiness? Without any faith or trust in Ragnar? Without having seen a single piece of work of his doing? Is that to be the way of it?

SOLNESS (*turns half aside and mutters*): Hm—don't ask more just now.

BROVIK: I must have an answer to this one question. Am I to pass out of life in such utter poverty?

SOLNESS (*seems to struggle with himself; finally he says, in a low but firm voice*): You must pass out of life as best you can.

BROVIK: Then be it so.

He goes up the room.

SOLNESS (*following him, half in desperation*): Don't you understand that I cannot help it? I am what I am, and I cannot change my nature!

BROVIK: No, no; I suppose you can't. (*Reels and supports himself against the sofa table.*) May I have a glass of water?

SOLNESS: By all means.

Fills a glass and hands it to him.

BROVIK: Thanks.

Drinks and puts the glass down again. SOLNESS *goes up and opens the door of the draftsmen's office.*

SOLNESS: Ragnar—you must come and take your father home.

RAGNAR *rises quickly. He and* KAIA *come into the workroom.*

RAGNAR: What is the matter, Father?

BROVIK: Give me your arm. Now let us go.

RAGNAR: Very well. You had better put your things on, too, Kaia.

SOLNESS: Miss Fosli must stay—just for a moment. There is a letter I want written.

BROVIK (*looks at* SOLNESS): Good night. Sleep well—if you can.

SOLNESS: Good night.

BROVIK *and* RAGNAR *go out by the hall door.* KAIA *goes to the desk.* SOLNESS *stands with bent head, to the right, by the armchair.*

KAIA (*dubiously*): Is there any letter—?

SOLNESS (*curtly*): No, of course not. (*Looks sternly at her.*) Kaia!

KAIA (*anxiously, in a low voice*): Yes!

SOLNESS (*points imperatively to a spot on the floor*): Come here! At once!

KAIA (*hesitatingly*): Yes.

SOLNESS (*as before*): Nearer!

KAIA (*obeying*): What do you want with me?

SOLNESS (*looks at her for a while*): Is it you I have to thank for all this?

KAIA: No, no, don't think that!

SOLNESS: But confess now—you want to get married!

KAIA (*softly*): Ragnar and I have been engaged for four or five years, and so—

SOLNESS: And so you think it time there were an end to it. Is not that so?

KAIA: Ragnar and Uncle say I must. So I suppose I shall have to give in.

SOLNESS (*more gently*): Kaia, don't you really care a little bit for Ragnar, too?

KAIA: I cared very much for Ragnar once—before I came here to you.

SOLNESS: But you don't now? Not in the least?

KAIA (*passionately, clasping her hands and holding them out toward him*): Oh, you know very well there is only one person I care for now! One, and one only, in all the world! I shall never care for anyone else.

SOLNESS: Yes, you say that. And yet you go away from me—leave me alone here with everything on my hands.

KAIA: But could I not stay with you, even if Ragnar—?

SOLNESS (*repudiating the idea*): No, no, that is quite impossible. If Ragnar leaves me and starts work on his own account, then of course he will need you himself.

KAIA (*wringing her hands*): Oh, I feel as if I could not be separated from you! It's quite, quite impossible!

SOLNESS: Then be sure you get those foolish notions out of Ragnar's head. Marry him as much as you please—(*alters his tone*)—I mean—don't let him throw up his good situation with me. For then I can keep you, too, my dear Kaia.

KAIA: Oh yes, how lovely that would be, if it could only be managed!

SOLNESS (*clasps her head with his two hands and whispers*): For I cannot get on without you, you see. I must have you with me every single day.

KAIA (*in nervous exaltation*): My God! My God!

SOLNESS (*kisses her hair*): Kaia—Kaia!

KAIA (*sinks down before him*): Oh, how good you are to me! How unspeakably good you are!

SOLNESS (*vehemently*): Get up! For goodness' sake get up! I think I hear someone!

He helps her to rise. She staggers over to the desk. MRS. SOLNESS *enters by the door on the right. She looks thin and wasted with grief, but shows traces of bygone beauty.*

Blond ringlets. Dressed with good taste, wholly in black. Speaks somewhat slowly and in a plaintive voice.

MRS. SOLNESS *(in the doorway)*: Halvard!

SOLNESS *(turns)*: Oh, are you there, my dear—?

MRS. SOLNESS *(with a glance at KAIA)*: I am afraid I am disturbing you.

SOLNESS: Not in the least. Miss Fosli has only a short letter to write.

MRS. SOLNESS: Yes, so I see.

SOLNESS: What do you want with me, Aline?

MRS. SOLNESS: I merely wanted to tell you that Dr. Herdal is in the drawing room. Won't you come and see him, Halvard?

SOLNESS *(looks suspiciously at her)*: Hm—is the doctor so very anxious to talk to me?

MRS. SOLNESS: Well, not exactly anxious. He really came to see me; but he would like to say how-do-you-do to you at the same time.

SOLNESS *(laughs to himself)*: Yes, I daresay. Well, you must ask him to wait a little.

MRS. SOLNESS: Then you will come in presently?

SOLNESS: Perhaps I will. Presently, presently, dear. In a little while.

MRS. SOLNESS *(glancing again at KAIA)*: Well, now, don't forget, Halvard.

Withdraws and closes the door behind her.

KAIA *(softly)*: Oh dear, oh dear—I am sure Mrs. Solness thinks ill of me in some way!

SOLNESS: Oh, not in the least. Not more than usual, at any rate. But all the same, you had better go now, Kaia.

KAIA: Yes, yes, now I must go.

SOLNESS *(severely)*: And mind you get that matter settled for me. Do you hear?

KAIA: Oh, if it only depended on me—

SOLNESS: I will have it settled, I say! And tomorrow too—not a day later!

KAIA (*terrified*): If there's nothing else for it, I am quite willing to break off the engagement.

SOLNESS (*angrily*): Break it off? Are you mad? Would you think of breaking it off?

KAIA (*distracted*): Yes, if necessary. For I must—I must stay here with you! I can't leave you! That is utterly—utterly impossible!

SOLNESS (*with a sudden outburst*): But deuce take it—how about Ragnar then! It's Ragnar that I—

KAIA (*looks at him with terrified eyes*): It is chiefly on Ragnar's account, that—that you—

SOLNESS (*collecting himself*): No, no, of course not! You don't understand me either. (*Gently and softly.*) Of course it is you. I want to keep—you above everything, Kaia. But for that very reason, you must prevent Ragnar, too, from throwing up his situation. There, there,—now go home.

KAIA: Yes, yes—good night, then.

SOLNESS: Good night. (*As she is going.*) Oh, stop a moment! Are Ragnar's drawings in there?

KAIA: I did not see him take them with him.

SOLNESS: Then just go and find them for me. I might perhaps glance over them, after all.

KAIA (*happy*): Oh yes, please do!

SOLNESS: For your sake, Kaia dear. Now, let me have them at once, please.

> KAIA *hurries into the draftsmen's office, searches anxiously in the table drawer, finds a portfolio and brings it with her.*

KAIA: Here are all the drawings.

SOLNESS: Good. Put them down there on the table.

KAIA (*putting down the portfolio*): Good night, then. (*Beseechingly.*) And please, please think kindly of me.

SOLNESS: Oh, that I always do. Good night, my dear little Kaia. (*Glances to the right.*) Go, go now!

MRS. SOLNESS and DR. HERDAL enter by the door on the right. He is a stoutish, elderly man, with a round, good-humored face, clean shaven, with thin, light hair, and gold spectacles.

MRS. SOLNESS (*still in the doorway*): Halvard, I cannot keep the doctor any longer.

SOLNESS: Well then, come in here.

MRS. SOLNESS (*to KAIA, who is turning down the desk lamp*): Have you finished the letter already, Miss Fosli?

KAIA (*in confusion*): The letter—?

SOLNESS: Yes, it was quite a short one.

MRS. SOLNESS: It must have been very short.

SOLNESS: You may go now, Miss Fosli. And please come in good time tomorrow morning.

KAIA: I will be sure to. Good night, Mrs. Solness.

She goes out by the hall door.

MRS. SOLNESS: She must be quite an acquisition to you, Halvard, this Miss Fosli.

SOLNESS: Yes, indeed. She is useful in all sorts of ways.

MRS. SOLNESS: So it seems.

DR. HERDAL: Is she good at bookkeeping too?

SOLNESS: Well—of course she has had a good deal of practice during these two years. And then she is so nice and willing to do whatever one asks of her.

MRS. SOLNESS: Yes, that must be very delightful—

SOLNESS: It is. Especially when one is not too much accustomed to that sort of thing.

MRS. SOLNESS (*in a tone of gentle remonstrance*): Can you say that, Halvard?

SOLNESS: Oh, no, no, my dear Aline; I beg your pardon.

MRS. SOLNESS: There's no occasion.—Well then, Doctor, you will come back later on and have a cup of tea with us?

DR. HERDAL: I have only that one patient to see and then I'll come back.

MRS. SOLNESS: Thank you.

She goes out by the door on the right.

SOLNESS: Are you in a hurry, Doctor?

DR. HERDAL: No, not at all.

SOLNESS: May I have a little chat with you?

DR. HERDAL: With the greatest of pleasure.

SOLNESS: Then let us sit down. *(He motions the doctor to take the rocking chair and sits down himself in the arm-chair. Looks searchingly at him.)* Tell me—did you notice anything odd about Aline?

DR. HERDAL: Do you mean just now, when she was here?

SOLNESS: Yes, in her manner to me. Did you notice anything?

DR. HERDAL *(smiling)*: Well, I admit—one couldn't well avoid noticing that your wife—hm—

SOLNESS: Well?

DR. HERDAL: —that your wife is not particularly fond of this Miss Fosli.

SOLNESS: Is that all? I have noticed that myself.

DR. HERDAL: And I must say I am scarcely surprised at it.

SOLNESS: At what?

DR. HERDAL: That she should not exactly approve of your seeing so much of another woman, all day and every day.

SOLNESS: No, no, I suppose you are right there—and Aline too. But it's impossible to make any change.

DR. HERDAL: Could you not engage a clerk?

SOLNESS: The first man that came to hand? No, thank you—that would never do for me.

DR. HERDAL: But now, if your wife—? Suppose, with her delicate health, all this tries her too much?

SOLNESS: Even then—I might almost say—it can make no difference. I must keep Kaia Fosli. No one else could fill her place.

DR. HERDAL: No one else?

SOLNESS (*curtly*): No, no one.

DR. HERDAL (*drawing his chair closer*): Now listen to me, my dear Mr. Solness. May I ask you a question, quite between ourselves?

SOLNESS: By all means.

DR. HERDAL: Women, you see—in certain matters, they have a deucedly keen intuition—

SOLNESS: They have, indeed. There is not the least doubt of that. But—?

DR. HERDAL: Well, tell me now—if your wife can't endure this Kaia Fosli—?

SOLNESS: Well, what then?

DR. HERDAL: —may she not have just—just the least little bit of reason for this instinctive dislike?

SOLNESS (*looks at him and rises*): Oho!

DR. HERDAL: Now don't be offended—but hasn't she?

SOLNESS (*with curt decision*): No.

DR. HERDAL: No reason of any sort?

SOLNESS: No other reason than her own suspicious nature.

DR. HERDAL: I know you have known a good many women in your time.

SOLNESS: Yes, I have.

DR. HERDAL: And have been a good deal taken with some of them, too.

SOLNESS: Oh, yes, I don't deny it.

DR. HERDAL: But as regards Miss Fosli, then? There is nothing of that sort in the case?

SOLNESS: No; nothing at all—on my side.

DR. HERDAL: But on her side?

SOLNESS: I don't think you have any right to ask that question, Doctor.

DR. HERDAL: Well, you know, we were discussing your wife's intuition.

SOLNESS: So we were. And for that matter—(*lowers his voice*)—Aline's intuition, as you call it—in a certain sense, it has not been so far astray.

DR. HERDAL: Aha! there we have it!

SOLNESS *(sits down)*: Dr. Herdal—I am going to tell you a strange story—if you care to listen to it.

DR. HERDAL: I like listening to strange stories.

SOLNESS: Very well then. I daresay you recollect that I took Knut Brovik and his son into my employment—after the old man's business had gone to the dogs.

DR. HERDAL: Yes, so I have understood.

SOLNESS: You see, they really are clever fellows, these two. Each of them has talent in his own way. But then the son took it into his head to get engaged; and the next thing, of course, was that he wanted to get married—and begin to build on his own account. That is the way with all these young people.

DR. HERDAL *(laughing)*: Yes, they have a bad habit of wanting to marry.

SOLNESS: Just so. But of course that did not suit my plans; for I needed Ragnar myself—and the old man, too. He is exceedingly good at calculating bearing-strains and cubic contents—and all that sort of devilry, you know.

DR. HERDAL: Oh, yes, no doubt that's indispensable.

SOLNESS: Yes, it is. But Ragnar was absolutely bent on setting to work for himself. He would hear of nothing else.

DR. HERDAL: But he has stayed with you all the same.

SOLNESS: Yes, I'll tell you how that came about. One day this girl, Kaia Fosli, came to see them on some errand or other. She had never been here before. And when I saw how utterly infatuated they were with each other, the thought occurred to me: if I could only get her into the office here, then perhaps Ragnar, too, would stay where he is.

DR. HERDAL: That was not at all a bad idea.

SOLNESS: Yes, but at the time I did not breathe a word of what was in my mind. I merely stood and looked at her—and kept on wishing intently that I could have her here. Then I talked to her a little, in a friendly way—about one thing and another. And then she went away.

DR. HERDAL: Well?

SOLNESS: Well, then, next day, pretty late in the evening,

when old Brovik and Ragnar had gone home, she came here again and behaved as if I had made an arrangement with her.

DR. HERDAL: An arrangement? What about?

SOLNESS: About the very thing my mind had been fixed on. But I hadn't said one single word about it.

DR. HERDAL: That was most extraordinary.

SOLNESS: Yes, was it not? And now she wanted to know what she was to do here—whether she could begin the very next morning, and so forth.

DR. HERDAL: Don't you think she did it in order to be with her sweetheart?

SOLNESS: That was what occurred to me at first. But no, that was not it. She seemed to drift quite away from him— when once she had come here to me.

DR. HERDAL: She drifted over to you, then?

SOLNESS: Yes, entirely. If I happen to look at her when her back is turned, I can tell that she feels it. She quivers and trembles the moment I come near her. What do you think of that?

DR. HERDAL: Hm—that's not very hard to explain.

SOLNESS: Well, but what about the other thing? That she believed I had said to her what I had only wished and willed—silently—inwardly—to myself? What do you say to that? Can you explain that, Dr. Herdal?

DR. HERDAL: No, I won't undertake to do that.

SOLNESS: I felt sure you would not; and so I have never cared to talk about it till now. But it's a cursed nuisance to me in the long run, you understand. Here I have to go on day after day pretending—. And it's a shame to treat her so, too, poor girl. (Vehemently.) But I cannot do anything else. For if she runs away from me—then Ragnar will be off too.

DR. HERDAL: And you have not told your wife the rights of the story?

SOLNESS: No.

DR. HERDAL: Then why on earth don't you?

SOLNESS (*looks fixedly at him, and says in a low voice*): Because I seem to find a sort of—of salutary self-torture in allowing Aline to do me an injustice.

DR. HERDAL (*shakes his head*): I don't in the least understand what you mean.

SOLNESS: Well, you see—it is like paying off a little bit of a huge, immeasurable debt—

DR. HERDAL: To your wife?

SOLNESS: Yes; and that always helps to relieve one's mind a little. One can breathe more freely for a while, you understand.

DR. HERDAL: No, goodness knows, I don't understand at all—

SOLNESS (*breaking off, rises again*): Well, well, well—then we won't talk any more about it. (*He saunters across the room, returns and stops beside the table. Looks at the doctor with a sly smile.*) I suppose you think you have drawn me out nicely now, Doctor?

DR. HERDAL (*with some irritation*): Drawn you out? Again I have not the faintest notion what you mean, Mr. Solness.

SOLNESS: Oh come, out with it; I have seen it quite clearly, you know.

DR. HERDAL: What have you seen?

SOLNESS (*in a low voice, slowly*): That you have been quietly keeping an eye upon me.

DR. HERDAL: That *I* have! And why in all the world should I do that?

SOLNESS: Because you think that I—(*Passionately.*) Well, devil take it—you think the same of me as Aline does.

DR. HERDAL: And what does she think about you?

SOLNESS (*having recovered his self-control*): She has begun to think that I am—that I am—ill.

DR. HERDAL: Ill! You! She has never hinted such a thing to me. Why, what can she think is the matter with you?

SOLNESS (*leans over the back of the chair and whispers*): Aline has made up her mind that I am mad. That is what she thinks.

DR. HERDAL (*rising*): Why, my dear good fellow—!

SOLNESS: Yes, on my soul she does! I tell you it is so. And she has got you to think the same! Oh, I can assure you, Doctor, I see it in your face as clearly as possible. You don't take me in so easily, I can tell you.

DR. HERDAL (*looks at him in amazement*): Never, Mr. Solness—never has such a thought entered my mind.

SOLNESS (*with an incredulous smile*): Really? Has it not?

DR. HERDAL: No, never! Nor your wife's mind either, I am convinced. I could almost swear to that.

SOLNESS: Well, I wouldn't advise you to. For, in a certain sense, you see, perhaps—perhaps she is not so far wrong in thinking something of the kind.

DR. HERDAL: Come now, I really must say—

SOLNESS (*interrupting, with a sweep of his hand*): Well, well, my dear doctor—don't let us discuss this any further. We had better agree to differ. (*Changes to a tone of quiet amusement.*) But look here now, Doctor—hm—

DR. HERDAL: Well?

SOLNESS: Since you don't believe that I am—ill—and crazy, and mad, and so forth—

DR. HERDAL: What then?

SOLNESS: Then I daresay you fancy that I am an extremely happy man.

DR. HERDAL: Is that mere fancy?

SOLNESS (*laughs*): No, no—of course not! Heaven forbid! Only think—to be Solness the master builder! Halvard Solness! What could be more delightful?

DR. HERDAL: Yes, I must say it seems to me you have had the luck on your side to an astounding degree.

SOLNESS (*suppresses a gloomy smile*): So I have, I can't complain on that score.

DR. HERDAL: First of all that grim old robbers' castle was burned down for you. And that was certainly a great piece of luck.

SOLNESS (*seriously*): It was the home of Aline's family. Remember that.

DR. HERDAL: Yes, it must have been a great grief to her.

SOLNESS: She has not got over it to this day—not in all these twelve or thirteen years.

DR. HERDAL: Ah, but what followed must have been the worst blow for her.

SOLNESS: The one thing with the other.

DR. HERDAL: But you—yourself—you rose upon the ruins. You began as a poor boy from a country village—and now you are at the head of your profession. Ah, yes, Mr. Solness, you have undoubtedly had the luck on your side.

SOLNESS (*looking at him with embarrassment*): Yes, but that is just what makes me so horribly afraid.

DR. HERDAL: Afraid? Because you have the luck on your side!

SOLNESS: It terrifies me—terrifies me every hour of the day. For sooner or later the luck must turn, you see.

DR. HERDAL: Oh nonsense! What should make the luck turn?

SOLNESS (*with firm assurance*): The younger generation.

DR. HERDAL: Pooh! The younger generation! You are not laid on the shelf yet, I should hope. Oh no—your position here is probably firmer now than it has ever been.

SOLNESS: The luck will turn. I know it—I feel the day approaching. Someone or other will take it into his head to say: Give me a chance! And then all the rest will come clamoring after him, and shake their fists at me and shout: Make room—make room—make room! Yes, just you see, Doctor—presently the younger generation will come knock at my door—

DR. HERDAL (*laughing*): Well, and what if they do?

SOLNESS: What if they do? Then there's an end of Halvard Solness.

There is a knock at the door on the left.

SOLNESS (*starts*): What's that? Did you not hear something?

DR. HERDAL: Someone is knocking at the door.

SOLNESS (*loudly*): Come in.

HILDA WANGEL *enters by the hall door. She is of middle height, supple and delicately built. Somewhat sunburned.*

Dressed in a tourist costume, with skirt caught up for walking, a sailor's collar open at the throat and a small sailor hat on her head. Knapsack on back, plaid in strap, and alpenstock.[1]

HILDA *(goes straight up to* SOLNESS, *her eyes sparkling with happiness)*: Good evening!

SOLNESS *(looks doubtfully at her)*: Good evening—

HILDA *(laughs)*: I almost believe you don't recognize me!

SOLNESS: No—I must admit that—just for the moment—

DR. HERDAL *(approaching)*: But I recognize you, my dear young lady—

HILDA *(pleased)*: Oh, is it you that—

DR. HERDAL: Of course it is. *(To* SOLNESS.*)* We met at one of the mountain stations this summer. *(To* HILDA.*)* What became of the other ladies?

HILDA: Oh, they went westward.

DR. HERDAL: They didn't much like all the fun we used to have in the evenings.

HILDA: No, I believe they didn't.

DR. HERDAL *(holds up his finger at her)*: And I am afraid it can't be denied that you flirted a little with us.

HILDA: Well that was better fun than to sit there knitting stockings with all those old women.

DR. HERDAL *(laughs)*: There I entirely agree with you.

SOLNESS: Have you come to town this evening?

HILDA: Yes, I have just arrived.

DR. HERDAL: Quite alone, Miss Wangel?

HILDA: Oh, yes!

SOLNESS: Wangel? Is your name Wangel?

HILDA *(looks in amused surprise at him)*: Yes, of course it is.

SOLNESS: Then you must be a daughter of the district doctor up at Lysanger?

HILDA *(as before)*: Yes, who else's daughter should I be?

SOLNESS: Oh, then I suppose we met up there, that summer when I was building a tower on the old church.

HILDA *(more seriously)*: Yes, of course it was then we met.

SOLNESS: Well, that is a long time ago.

HILDA (*looks hard at him*): It is exactly ten years.

SOLNESS: You must have been a mere child then, I should think.

HILDA (*carelessly*): Well, I was twelve or thirteen.

DR. HERDAL: Is this the first time you have ever been up to town, Miss Wangel?

HILDA: Yes, it is indeed.

SOLNESS: And don't you know anyone here?

HILDA: Nobody but you. And of course, your wife.

SOLNESS: So you know her, too?

HILDA: Only a little. We spent a few days together at the sanatorium.

SOLNESS: Ah, up there?

HILDA: She said I might come and pay her a visit if ever I came up to town. (*Smiles.*) Not that that was necessary.

SOLNESS: Odd that she should never have mentioned it.

> HILDA *puts her stick down by the stove, takes off the knap-sack and lays it and the plaid on the sofa.* DR. HERDAL *offers to help her.* SOLNESS *stands and gazes at her.*

HILDA (*going toward him*): Well, now I must ask you to let me stay the night here.

SOLNESS: I am sure there will be no difficulty about that.

HILDA: For I have no other clothes than those I stand in, except a change of linen in my knapsack. And that has to go to the wash, for it's very dirty.

SOLNESS: Oh, yes, that can be managed. Now I'll just let my wife know—

DR. HERDAL: Meanwhile I will go and see my patient.

SOLNESS: Yes, do; and come again later on.

DR. HERDAL (*playfully, with a glance at* HILDA): Oh, that I will, you may be very certain! (*Laughs.*) So your prediction has come true, Mr. Solness!

SOLNESS: How so?

DR. HERDAL: The younger generation did come knocking at your door.

SOLNESS (*cheerfully*): Yes, but in a very different way from what I meant.

DR. HERDAL: Very different, yes. That's undeniable.

He goes out by the hall door. SOLNESS *opens the door on the right and speaks into the side room.*

SOLNESS: Aline! Will you come in here, please. Here is a friend of yours—Miss Wangel.

MRS. SOLNESS (*appears in the doorway*): Who do you say it is? (*Sees* HILDA.) Oh, is it you, Miss Wangel? (*Goes up to her and offers her hand.*) So you have come to town after all.

SOLNESS: Miss Wangel has this moment arrived; and she would like to stay the night here.

MRS. SOLNESS: Here with us? Oh yes, certainly.

SOLNESS: Till she can get her things a little in order, you know.

MRS. SOLNESS: I will do the best I can for you. It's no more than my duty. I suppose your trunk is coming on later?

HILDA: I have no trunk.

MRS. SOLNESS: Well, it will be all right, I daresay. In the meantime, you must excuse my leaving you here with my husband, until I can get a room made a little comfortable for you.

SOLNESS: Can we not give her one of the nurseries? They are all ready as it is.

MRS. SOLNESS: Oh, yes. There we have room and to spare. (*To* HILDA.) Sit down now, and rest a little.

She goes out to the right. HILDA, *with her hands behind her back, strolls about the room and looks at various objects.* SOLNESS *stands in front, beside the table, also with his hands behind his back, and follows her with his eyes.*

HILDA (*stops and looks at him*): Have you several nurseries?

SOLNESS: There are three nurseries in the house.

HILDA: That's a lot. Then I suppose you have a great many children?

SOLNESS: No. We have no child. But now you can be the child here, for the time being.

HILDA: For tonight, yes. I shall not cry. I mean to sleep as sound as a stone.

SOLNESS: Yes, you must be very tired I should think.

HILDA: Oh, no! But all the same— It's so delicious to lie and dream.

SOLNESS: Do you dream much of nights?

HILDA: Oh, yes! Almost always.

SOLNESS: What do you dream about most?

HILDA: I shan't tell you tonight. Another time, perhaps.

She again strolls about the room, stops at the desk and turns over the books and papers a little.

SOLNESS (*approaching*): Are you searching for anything?

HILDA: No, I am merely looking at all these things. (*Turns.*) Perhaps I mustn't?

SOLNESS: Oh, by all means.

HILDA: Is it you that write in this great ledger?

SOLNESS: No, it's my bookkeeper.

HILDA: Is it a woman?

SOLNESS (*smiles*): Yes.

HILDA: One you employ here, in your office?

SOLNESS: Yes.

HILDA: Is she married?

SOLNESS: No, she is single.

HILDA: Oh, indeed!

SOLNESS: But I believe she is soon going to be married.

HILDA: That's a good thing for her.

SOLNESS: But not such a good thing for me. For then I shall have nobody to help me.

HILDA: Can't you get hold of someone else who will do just as well?

SOLNESS: Perhaps you would stay here and write in the ledger?

HILDA (*measures him with a glance*): Yes, I daresay! No, thank you—nothing of that sort for me.

She again strolls across the room and sits down in the rocking chair. SOLNESS, *too, goes to the table.*

HILDA (*continuing*): For there must surely be plenty of other things to be done here. (*Looks smiling at him.*) Don't you think so, too?

SOLNESS: Of course. First of all, I suppose, you want to make a round of the shops and get yourself up in the height of fashion.

HILDA (*amused*): No, I think I shall let that alone!

SOLNESS: Indeed.

HILDA: For you must know I have run through all my money.

SOLNESS (*laughs*): Neither trunk nor money, then.

HILDA: Neither one nor the other. But never mind—it doesn't matter now.

SOLNESS: Come now, I like you for that.

HILDA: Only for that?

SOLNESS: For that among other things. (*Sits in the armchair.*) Is your father alive still?

HILDA: Yes, Father's alive.

SOLNESS: Perhaps you are thinking of studying here?

HILDA: No, that hadn't occurred to me.

SOLNESS: But I suppose you will be staying for some time?

HILDA: That must depend upon circumstances.

She sits awhile rocking herself and looking at him, half seriously, half with a suppressed smile. Then she takes off her hat and puts it on the table in front of her.

HILDA: Mr. Solness!

SOLNESS: Well?

HILDA: Have you a very bad memory?

SOLNESS: A bad memory? No, not that I am aware of.

HILDA: Then have you nothing to say to me about what happened up there?

SOLNESS (*in momentary surprise*): Up at Lysanger? (*Indifferently.*) Why, it was nothing much to talk about, it seems to me.

HILDA (*looks reproachfully at him*): How can you sit there and say such things?

SOLNESS: Well, then, you talk to me about it.

HILDA: When the tower was finished, we had grand doings in the town.

SOLNESS: Yes, I shall not easily forget that day.

HILDA (*smiles*): Will you not? That comes well from you.

SOLNESS: Comes well?

HILDA: There was music in the churchyard—and many, many hundreds of people. We schoolgirls were dressed in white; and we all carried flags.

SOLNESS: Ah yes, those flags—I can tell you I remember them!

HILDA: Then you climbed right up the scaffolding, straight to the very top; and you had a great wreath with you; and you hung that wreath right away up on the weather vane.[2]

SOLNESS (*curtly interrupting*): I always did that in those days. It was an old custom.

HILDA: It was so wonderfully thrilling to stand below and look up at you. Fancy, if he should fall over! He—the master builder himself!

SOLNESS (*as if to divert her from the subject*): Yes, yes, yes, that might very well have happened, too. For one of those white-frocked little devils,—she went on in such a way, and screamed up at me so—

HILDA (*sparkling with pleasure*): "Hurrah for Master Builder Solness!" Yes!

SOLNESS: —and waved and flourished with her flag, so that I—so that it almost made me giddy to look at it.

HILDA (*in a lower voice, seriously*): That little devil—that was *I*.

SOLNESS (*fixes his eyes steadily upon her*): I am sure of that now. It must have been you.

HILDA (*lively again*): Oh, it was so gloriously thrilling! I could not have believed there was a builder in the whole world that could build such a tremendously high tower. And then, that you yourself should stand at the very top of it, as

large as life! And that you should not be the least bit dizzy!
It was that above everything that made one—made one
dizzy to think of.

SOLNESS: How could you be so certain that I was not—?

HILDA (*scouting the idea*): No indeed! Oh, no! I knew that
instinctively. For if you had been, you could never have
stood up there and sung.

SOLNESS (*looks at her in astonishment*): Sung? Did *I* sing?

HILDA: Yes, I should think you did.

SOLNESS (*shakes his head*): I have never sung a note in my
life.

HILDA: Yes indeed, you sang then. It sounded like harps in
the air.

SOLNESS (*thoughtfully*): This is very strange—all this.

HILDA (*is silent awhile, looks at him and says in a low voice*):
But then,—it was after that—and the real thing happened.

SOLNESS: The real thing?

HILDA (*sparkling with vivacity*): Yes, I surely don't need to
remind you of that?

SOLNESS: Oh, yes, do remind me a little of that, too.

HILDA: Don't you remember that a great dinner was given in
your honor at the Club?

SOLNESS: Yes, to be sure. It must have been the same afternoon, for I left the place next morning.

HILDA: And from the Club you were invited to come round
to our house to supper.

SOLNESS: Quite right, Miss Wangel. It is wonderful how all
these trifles have impressed themselves on your mind.

HILDA: Trifles! I like that! Perhaps it was a trifle, too, that I
was alone in the room when you came in?

SOLNESS: Were you alone?

HILDA (*without answering him*): You didn't call me a little
devil then?

SOLNESS: No, I suppose I did not.

HILDA: You said I was lovely in my white dress, and that I
looked like a little princess.

SOLNESS: I have no doubt you did, Miss Wangel.—And besides—I was feeling so buoyant and free that day—

HILDA: And then you said that when I grew up I should be your princess.

SOLNESS (*laughing a little*): Dear, dear—did I say that, too?

HILDA: Yes, you did. And when I asked how long I should have to wait, you said that you would come again in ten years—like a troll and carry me off—to Spain or some such place. And you promised you would buy me a kingdom there.

SOLNESS (*as before*): Yes, after a good dinner one doesn't haggle about the halfpence. But did I really say all that?

HILDA (*laughs to herself*): Yes. And you told me, too, what the kingdom was to be called.

SOLNESS: Well, what was it?

HILDA: It was to be called the kingdom of Orangia, you said.

SOLNESS: Well, that was an appetizing name.

HILDA: No, I didn't like it a bit; for it seemed as though you wanted to make game of me.

SOLNESS: I am sure that cannot have been my intention.

HILDA: No, I should hope not—considering what you did next—

SOLNESS: What in the world did I do next?

HILDA: Well, that's the finishing touch, if you have forgotten that, too. I should have thought no one could help remembering such a thing as that.

SOLNESS: Yes, yes, just give me a hint, and then perhaps—Well—

HILDA (*looks fixedly at him*): You came and kissed me, Mr. Solness.

SOLNESS (*openmouthed, rising from his chair*): I did!

HILDA: Yes, indeed you did. You took me in both your arms, and bent my head back and kissed me—many times.

SOLNESS: Now really, my dear Miss Wangel—!

HILDA (*rises*): You surely cannot mean to deny it?

SOLNESS: Yes, I do. I deny it altogether!

HILDA (*looks scornfully at him*): Oh, indeed!

She turns and goes slowly close up to the stove, where she remains standing motionless, her face averted from him, her hands behind her back. Short pause.

SOLNESS (*goes cautiously up behind her*): Miss Wangel—!

HILDA (*is silent and does not move*).

SOLNESS: Don't stand there like a statue. You must have dreamt all this. (*Lays his hand on her arm.*) Now just listen—

HILDA (*makes an impatient movement with her arm*).

SOLNESS (*as a thought flashes upon him*): Or—! Wait a moment! There is something under all this, you may depend!

HILDA (*does not move*).

SOLNESS (*in a low voice, but with emphasis*): I must have thought all that. I must have wished it—have willed it—have longed to do it. And then—. May not that be the explanation?

HILDA (*is still silent*).

SOLNESS (*impatiently*): Oh very well, deuce take it all—then I did it, I suppose.

HILDA (*turns her head a little, but without looking at him*): Then you admit it now?

SOLNESS: Yes—whatever you like.

HILDA: You came and put your arms around me?

SOLNESS: Oh, yes!

HILDA: And bent my head back?

SOLNESS: Very far back.

HILDA: And kissed me?

SOLNESS: Yes, I did.

HILDA: Many times?

SOLNESS: As many as ever you like.

HILDA (*turns quickly toward him and has once more the sparkling expression of gladness in her eyes*): Well, you see, I got it out of you at last!

SOLNESS (*with a slight smile*): Yes—just think of my forgetting such a thing as that.

HILDA (*again a little sulky, retreats from him*): Oh, you have kissed so many people in your time, I suppose.

SOLNESS: No, you mustn't think that of me. (HILDA *seats herself in the armchair.* SOLNESS *stands and leans against the rocking chair. Looks observantly at her.*) Miss Wangel!

HILDA: Yes!

SOLNESS: How was it now? What came of all this—between us two?

HILDA: Why, nothing more came of it. You know that quite well. For then the other guests came in, and then—bah!

SOLNESS: Quite so! The others came in. To think of my forgetting that, too!

HILDA: Oh, you haven't really forgotten anything: you are only a little ashamed of it all. I am sure one doesn't forget things of that kind.

SOLNESS: No, one would suppose not.

HILDA (*lively again, looks at him*): Perhaps you have even forgotten what day it was?

SOLNESS: What day—?

HILDA: Yes, on what day did you hang the wreath on the tower? Well? Tell me at once!

SOLNESS: Hm—I confess I have forgotten the particular day. I only knew it was ten years ago. Sometime in the autumn.

HILDA (*nods her head slowly several times*): It was ten years ago—on the 19th of September.

SOLNESS: Yes, it must have been about that time. Fancy your remembering that, too! (*Stops.*) But wait a moment—! Yes—it's the 19th of September today.

HILDA: Yes, it is; and the ten years are gone. And you didn't come—as you promised me.

SOLNESS: Promised you? Threatened, I suppose you mean?

HILDA: I don't think there was any sort of threat in that.

SOLNESS: Well then, a little bit of fun.

HILDA: Was that all you wanted? To make fun of me?

SOLNESS: Well, or to have a little joke with you. Upon my

soul, I don't recollect. But it must have been something of that kind; for you were a mere child then.

HILDA: Oh, perhaps I wasn't quite such a child either. Not such a mere chit as you imagine.

SOLNESS *(looks searchingly at her)*: Did you really and seriously expect me to come again?

HILDA *(conceals a half-teasing smile)*: Yes, indeed; I did expect that of you.

SOLNESS: That I should come back to your home and take you away with me?

HILDA: Just like a troll—yes.

SOLNESS: And make a princess of you?

HILDA: That's what you promised.

SOLNESS: And give you a kingdom as well?

HILDA *(looks up at the ceiling)*: Why not? Of course it need not have been an actual, everyday sort of kingdom.

SOLNESS: But something else just as good?

HILDA: Yes, at least as good. *(Looks at him a moment.)* I thought, if you could build the highest church towers in the world, you could surely manage to raise a kingdom of one sort or another as well.

SOLNESS *(shakes his head)*: I can't quite make you out, Miss Wangel.

HILDA: Can you not? To me it seems all so simple.

SOLNESS: No, I can't make up my mind whether you mean all you say, or are simply having a joke with me.

HILDA *(smiles)*: Making fun of you, perhaps? I, too?

SOLNESS: Yes, exactly. Making fun—of both of us. *(Looks at her.)* Is it long since you found out that I was married?

HILDA: I have known it all along. Why do you ask me that?

SOLNESS *(lightly)*: Oh, well, it just occurred to me. *(Looks earnestly at her and says in a low voice.)* What have you come for?

HILDA: I want my kingdom. The time is up.

SOLNESS *(laughs involuntarily)*: What a girl you are!

HILDA *(gaily)*: Out with my kingdom, Mr. Solness! *(Raps with her fingers.)* The kingdom on the table!

SOLNESS (*pushing the rocking chair nearer and sitting down*): Now, seriously speaking—what have you come for? What do you really want to do here?

HILDA: Oh, first of all, I want to go around and look at all the things that you have built.

SOLNESS: That will give you plenty of exercise.

HILDA: Yes, I know you have built a tremendous lot.

SOLNESS: I have indeed—especially of late years.

HILDA: Many church towers among the rest? Immensely high ones?

SOLNESS: No. I build no more church towers now. Nor churches either.

HILDA: What do you build, then?

SOLNESS: Homes for human beings.

HILDA (*reflectively*): Couldn't you build a little—a little bit of a church tower over these homes as well?

SOLNESS (*starting*): What do you mean by that?

HILDA: I mean—something that points—points up into the free air. With the vane at a dizzy height.

SOLNESS (*pondering a little*): Strange that you should say that—for that is just what I am most anxious to do.

HILDA (*impatiently*): Why don't you do it, then?

SOLNESS (*shakes his head*): No, the people will not have it.

HILDA: Fancy their not wanting it!

SOLNESS (*more lightly*): But now I am building a new home for myself—just opposite here.

HILDA: For yourself?

SOLNESS: Yes. It is almost finished. And on that there is a tower.

HILDA: A high tower?

SOLNESS: Yes.

HILDA: Very high?

SOLNESS: No doubt people will say it is too high—too high for a dwelling house.

HILDA: I'll go out and look at that tower the first thing tomorrow morning.

SOLNESS (*sits resting his cheek on his hand and gazes at her*):

Tell me, Miss Wangel—what is your name? Your Christian name, I mean?

HILDA: Why, Hilda, of course.

SOLNESS (*as before*): Hilda? Indeed?

HILDA: Don't you remember that? You called me Hilda yourself—that day when you misbehaved.

SOLNESS: Did I really?

HILDA: But then you said "little Hilda"; and I didn't like that.

SOLNESS: Oh, you don't like that, Miss Hilda?

HILDA: No, not at such a time as that. But—"Princess Hilda"—that will sound very well, I think.

SOLNESS: Very well indeed. Princess Hilda of—of—what was to be the name of the kingdom?

HILDA: Pooh! I won't have anything to do with that stupid kingdom. I have set my heart upon quite a different one!

SOLNESS (*has leaned back in the chair, still gazing at her*): Isn't it strange—? The more I think of it now, the more it seems to me as though I had gone about all these years torturing myself with—hm—

HILDA: With what?

SOLNESS: With the effort to recover something—some experience, which I seemed to have forgotten. But I never had the least inkling of what it could be.

HILDA: You should have tied a knot in your pocket handkerchief, Mr. Solness.

SOLNESS: In that case, I should simply have had to go racking my brains to discover what the knot could mean.

HILDA: Oh, yes, I suppose there are trolls of that kind in the world, too.

SOLNESS (*rises slowly*): What a good thing it is that you have come to me now.

HILDA (*looks deeply into his eyes*): Is it a good thing?

SOLNESS: For I have been so lonely here. I have been gazing so helplessly at it all. (*In a lower voice.*) I must tell you—I have begun to be so afraid—so terribly afraid of the younger generation.

HILDA *(with a little snort of contempt)*: Pooh—is the younger generation a thing to be afraid of?

SOLNESS: It is indeed. And that is why I have locked and barred myself in. *(Mysteriously.)* I tell you the younger generation will one day come and thunder at my door! They will break in upon me!

HILDA: Then I should say you ought to go out and open the door to the younger generation.

SOLNESS: Open the door?

HILDA: Yes. Let them come in to you on friendly terms, as it were.

SOLNESS: No, no, no! The younger generation—it means retribution, you see. It comes, as if under a new banner, heralding the turn of fortune.

HILDA *(rises, looks at him and says with a quivering twitch of her lips)*: Can I be of any use to you, Mr. Solness?

SOLNESS: Yes, you can indeed! For you, too, come—under a new banner, it seems to me. Youth marshaled against youth—!

DR. HERDAL *comes in by the hall door.*

DR. HERDAL: What—you and Miss Wangel here still?

SOLNESS: Yes. We have had no end of things to talk about.

HILDA: Both old and new.

DR. HERDAL: Have you really?

HILDA: Oh, it has been the greatest fun. For Mr. Solness—he has such a miraculous memory. All the least little details he remembers instantly.

MRS. SOLNESS *enters by the door on the right.*

MRS. SOLNESS: Well, Miss Wangel, your room is quite ready for you now.

HILDA: Oh, how kind you are to me!

SOLNESS *(to MRS. SOLNESS)*: The nursery?

MRS. SOLNESS: Yes, the middle one. But first let us go in to supper.

SOLNESS *(nods to* HILDA*)*: Hilda shall sleep in the nursery, she shall.

MRS. SOLNESS *(looks at him)*: Hilda?

SOLNESS: Yes, Miss Wangel's name is Hilda. I knew her when she was a child.

MRS. SOLNESS: Did you really, Halvard? Well, shall we go? Supper is on the table.

She takes DR. HERDAL'S *arm and goes out with him to the right.* HILDA *has meanwhile been collecting her traveling things.*

HILDA *(softly and rapidly to* SOLNESS*)*: Is it true, what you said? Can I be of use to you?

SOLNESS *(takes the things from her)*: You are the very being I have needed most.

HILDA *(looks at him with happy, wondering eyes and clasps her hands)*: But then, great heavens—!

SOLNESS *(eagerly)*: What—?

HILDA: Then I have my kingdom!

SOLNESS *(involuntarily)*: Hilda—!

HILDA *(again with the quivering twitch of her lips)*: Almost—I was going to say.

She goes out to the right, SOLNESS *follows her.*

ACT TWO

A prettily furnished small drawing room in SOLNESS's *house. In the back, a glass door leading out to the verandah and garden. The right-hand corner is cut off transversely by a large bay window, in which are flower stands. The left-hand corner is similarly cut off by a transverse wall, in which is a small door papered like the wall. On each side, an ordinary door. In front, on the right, a console table with a large mirror over it. Well-filled stands of plants and flowers. In front, on the left, a sofa with a table and chairs. Further back, a bookcase. Well forward in the room, before the bay window, a small table and some chairs. It is early in the day.*

SOLNESS *sits by the little table with* RAGNAR BROVIK's *portfolio open in front of him. He is turning the drawings over and closely examining some of them.* MRS. SOLNESS *moves about noiselessly with a small watering pot, attending to her flowers. She is dressed in black as before. Her hat, cloak and parasol lie on a chair near the mirror. Unobserved by her,* SOLNESS *now and again follows her with his eyes. Neither of them speaks.*

343

KAIA FOSLI *enters quietly by the door on the left.*

SOLNESS (*turns his head, and says in an off-hand tone of indifference*): Well, is that you?

KAIA: I merely wished to let you know that I have come.

SOLNESS: Yes, yes, that's all right. Hasn't Ragnar come, too?

KAIA: No, not yet. He had to wait a little while to see the doctor. But he is coming presently to hear—

SOLNESS: How is the old man today?

KAIA: Not well. He begs you to excuse him; he is obliged to keep his bed today.

SOLNESS: Why, of course; by all means let him rest. But now, get to work.

KAIA: Yes. (*Pauses at the door.*) Do you wish to speak to Ragnar when he comes?

SOLNESS: No—I don't know that I have anything particular to say to him.

KAIA *goes out again to the left.* SOLNESS *remains seated, turning over the drawings.*

MRS. SOLNESS (*over beside the plants*): I wonder if he isn't going to die now, as well?

SOLNESS (*looks up to her*): As well as who?

MRS. SOLNESS (*without answering*): Yes, yes—depend upon it, Halvard, old Brovik is going to die, too. You'll see that he will.

SOLNESS: My dear Aline, ought you not to go out for a little walk?

MRS. SOLNESS: Yes, I suppose I ought to.

She continues to attend to the flowers.

SOLNESS (*bending over the drawings*): Is she still asleep?

MRS. SOLNESS (*looking at him*): Is it Miss Wangel you are sitting there thinking about?

SOLNESS (*indifferently*): I just happened to recollect her.

MRS. SOLNESS: Miss Wangel was up long ago.

SOLNESS: Oh, was she?

MRS. SOLNESS: When I went in to see her, she was busy putting her things in order.

She goes in front of the mirror and slowly begins to put on her hat.

SOLNESS *(after a short pause)*: So we have found a use for one of our nurseries after all, Aline.

MRS. SOLNESS: Yes, we have.

SOLNESS: That seems to me better than to have them all standing empty.

MRS. SOLNESS: That emptiness is dreadful; you are right there.

SOLNESS *(closes the portfolio, rises and approaches her)*: You will find that we shall get on far better after this, Aline. Things will be more comfortable. Life will be easier—especially for you.

MRS. SOLNESS *(looks at him)*: After this?

SOLNESS: Yes, believe me, Aline—

MRS. SOLNESS: Do you mean—because she has come here?

SOLNESS *(checking himself)*: I mean, of course—when once we have moved into the new house.

MRS. SOLNESS *(takes her cloak)*: Ah, do you think so, Halvard? Will it be better then?

SOLNESS: I can't think otherwise. And surely you think so, too?

MRS. SOLNESS: I think nothing at all about the new house.

SOLNESS *(cast down)*: It's hard for me to hear you say that; for you know it is mainly for your sake that I have built it.

He offers to help her on with her cloak.

MRS. SOLNESS *(evades him)*: The fact is, you do far too much for my sake.

SOLNESS *(with a certain vehemence)*: No, no, you really mustn't say that, Aline! I cannot bear to hear you say such things!

MRS. SOLNESS: Very well, then I won't say it, Halvard.

SOLNESS: But I stick to what *I* said. You'll see that things will be easier for you in the new place.

MRS. SOLNESS: O heavens—easier for me—!

SOLNESS (*eagerly*): Yes, indeed they will! You may be quite sure of that! For you see—there will be so very, very much there that will remind you of your own home—

MRS. SOLNESS: The home that used to be Father's and Mother's—and that was burned to the ground—

SOLNESS (*in a low voice*): Yes, yes, my poor Aline. That was a terrible blow for you.

MRS. SOLNESS (*breaking out in lamentation*): You may build as much as ever you like, Halvard—you can never build up again a real home for me!

SOLNESS (*crosses the room*): Well, in heaven's name, let us talk no more about it, then.

MRS. SOLNESS: Oh, yes, Halvard, I understand you very well. You are so anxious to spare me—and to find excuses for me, too—as much as ever you can.

SOLNESS (*with astonishment in his eyes*): You! Is it you—yourself, that you are talking about, Aline?

MRS. SOLNESS: Yes, who else should it be but myself?

SOLNESS (*involuntarily to himself*): That, too!

MRS. SOLNESS: As for the old house, I wouldn't mind so much about that. When once misfortune was in the air—why—

SOLNESS: Ah, you are right there. Misfortune will have its way—as the saying goes.

MRS. SOLNESS: But it's what came of the fire—the dreadful thing that followed—! That is the thing! That, that, that!

SOLNESS (*vehemently*): Don't think about that, Aline!

MRS. SOLNESS: Ah, that is exactly what I cannot help thinking about. And now, at last, I must speak about it, too; for I don't seem able to bear it any longer. And then never to be able to forgive myself—

SOLNESS (*exclaiming*): Yourself—!

MRS. SOLNESS: Yes, for I had duties on both sides—both

toward you and toward the little ones. I ought to have hardened myself—not to have let the horror take such hold upon me—nor the grief for the burning of my old home. *(Wrings her hands.)* Oh, Halvard, if I had only had the strength!

SOLNESS *(softly, much moved, comes closer)*: Aline—you must promise me never to think these thoughts anymore.—Promise me that, dear!

MRS. SOLNESS: Oh, promise, promise! One can promise anything.

SOLNESS *(clenches his hands and crosses the room)*: Oh, but this is hopeless, hopeless! Never a ray of sunlight! Not so much as a gleam of brightness to light up our home!

MRS. SOLNESS: This is no home, Halvard.

SOLNESS: Oh no, you may well say that. *(Gloomily.)* And God knows whether you are not right in saying that it will be no better for us in the new house, either.

MRS. SOLNESS: It will never be any better. Just as empty—just as desolate—there as here.

SOLNESS *(vehemently)*: Why in all the world have we built it then? Can you tell me that?

MRS. SOLNESS: No; you must answer the question for yourself.

SOLNESS *(glances suspiciously at her)*: What do you mean by that, Aline?

MRS. SOLNESS: What do I mean?

SOLNESS: Yes, in the devil's name! You said it so strangely—as if you had hidden some meaning in it.

MRS. SOLNESS: No, indeed, I assure you—

SOLNESS *(comes closer)*: Oh, come now—I know what I know. I have both my eyes and my ears about me, Aline—you may depend upon that!

MRS. SOLNESS: Why, what are you talking about? What is it?

SOLNESS *(places himself in front of her)*: Do you mean to say you don't find a kind of lurking, hidden meaning in the most innocent word I happen to say?

MRS. SOLNESS: *I*, do you say? *I* do that?

SOLNESS (*laughs*): Ho-ho-ho! It's natural enough, Aline! When you have a sick man on your hands—

MRS. SOLNESS (*anxiously*): Sick? Are you ill, Halvard?

SOLNESS (*violently*): A half-mad man then! A crazy man! Call me what you will.

MRS. SOLNESS (*feels blindly for a chair and sits down*): Halvard—for God's sake—

SOLNESS: But you are wrong, both you and the doctor. I am not in the state you imagine.

He walks up and down the room. MRS. SOLNESS *follows him anxiously with her eyes. Finally he goes up to her.*

SOLNESS (*calmly*): In reality there is nothing whatever the matter with me.

MRS. SOLNESS: No, there isn't, is there? But then what is it that troubles you so?

SOLNESS: Why this, that I often feel ready to sink under this terrible burden of debt—

MRS. SOLNESS: Debt, do you say? But you owe no one anything, Halvard!

SOLNESS (*softly, with emotion*): I owe a boundless debt to you—to you—to you, Aline.

MRS. SOLNESS (*rises slowly*): What is behind all this? You may just as well tell me at once.

SOLNESS: But there is nothing behind it; I have never done you any wrong—not wittingly and willfully, at any rate. And yet—and yet it seems as though a crushing debt rested upon me and weighed me down.

MRS. SOLNESS: A debt to me?

SOLNESS: Chiefly to you.

MRS. SOLNESS: Then you are—ill after all, Halvard.

SOLNESS (*gloomily*): I suppose I must be—or not far from it. (*Looks toward the door to the right, which is opened at this moment.*) Ah! now it grows lighter.

HILDA WANGEL *comes in. She has made some alteration in her dress and let down her skirt.*

HILDA: Good morning, Mr. Solness!

SOLNESS (*nods*): Slept well?

HILDA: Quite deliciously! Like a child in a cradle. Oh—I lay and stretched myself like—like a princess!

SOLNESS (*smiles a little*): You were thoroughly comfortable then?

HILDA: I should think so.

SOLNESS: And no doubt you dreamed, too.

HILDA: Yes, I did. But that was horrid.

SOLNESS: Was it?

HILDA: Yes, for I dreamed I was falling over a frightfully high, sheer precipice. Do you never have that kind of dream?

SOLNESS: Oh yes—now and then—

HILDA: It's tremendously thrilling—when you fall and fall—

SOLNESS: It seems to make one's blood run cold.

HILDA: Do you draw your legs up under you while you are falling?

SOLNESS: Yes, as high as ever I can.

HILDA: So do I.

MRS. SOLNESS (*takes her parasol*): I must go into town now, Halvard. (*To* HILDA.) And I'll try to get one or two things that you may require.

HILDA (*making a motion to throw her arms around her neck*): Oh, you dear, sweet Mrs. Solness! You are really much too kind to me! Frightfully kind—

MRS. SOLNESS (*deprecatingly, freeing herself*): Oh, not at all. It's only my duty, so I am very glad to do it.

HILDA (*offended, pouts*): But really, I think I am quite fit to be seen in the streets—now that I've put my dress to rights. Or do you think I am not?

MRS. SOLNESS: To tell you the truth, I think people would stare at you a little.

HILDA (*contemptuously*): Pooh! Is that all? That only amuses me.

SOLNESS (*with suppressed ill humor*): Yes, but people might take it into their heads that you were mad, too, you see.

HILDA: Mad? Are there so many mad people here in town, then?

SOLNESS (*points to his own forehead*): Here you see one, at all events.

HILDA: You—Mr. Solness!

MRS. SOLNESS: Oh, don't talk like that, my dear Halvard!

SOLNESS: Have you not noticed that yet?

HILDA: No, I certainly have not. (*Reflects and laughs a little.*) And yet—perhaps in one single thing.

SOLNESS: Ah, do you hear that, Aline?

MRS. SOLNESS: What is that one single thing, Miss Wangel?

HILDA: No, I won't say.

SOLNESS: Oh, yes, do!

HILDA: No, thank you—I am not so mad as that.

MRS. SOLNESS: When you and Miss Wangel are alone, I daresay she will tell you, Halvard.

SOLNESS: Ah—you think she will?

MRS. SOLNESS: Oh, yes, certainly. For you have known her so well in the past. Ever since she was a child—you tell me.

She goes out by the door on the left.

HILDA (*after a little while*): Does your wife dislike me very much?

SOLNESS: Did you think you noticed anything of the kind?

HILDA: Did you not notice it yourself?

SOLNESS (*evasively*): Aline has become exceedingly shy with strangers of late years.

HILDA: Has she really?

SOLNESS: But if only you could get to know her thoroughly—! Ah! she is so good—so kind—so excellent a creature—

HILDA (*impatiently*): But if she is all that—what made her say that about her duty?

SOLNESS: Her duty?

HILDA: She said that she would go out and buy something for me, because it was her duty. Oh, I can't bear that ugly, horrid word!

SOLNESS: Why not?

HILDA: It sounds so cold and sharp and stinging. Duty—duty—duty. Don't you think so, too? Doesn't it seem to sting you?

SOLNESS: Hm—haven't thought much about it.

HILDA: Yes, it does. And if she is so good—as you say she is—why should she talk in that way?

SOLNESS: But, good Lord, what would you have had her say, then?

HILDA: She might have said she would do it because she had taken a tremendous fancy to me. She might have said something like that—something really warm and cordial, you understand.

SOLNESS *(looks at her)*: Is that how you would like to have it?

HILDA: Yes, precisely. *(She wanders about the room, stops at the bookcase and looks at the books.)* What a lot of books you have.

SOLNESS: Yes, I have got together a good many.

HILDA: Do you read them all, too?

SOLNESS: I used to try to. Do you read much?

HILDA: No, never! I have given it up. For it all seems so irrelevant.

SOLNESS: That is just my feeling.

HILDA *wanders about a little, stops at the small table, opens the portfolio and turns over the contents.*

HILDA: Are all these drawings yours?

SOLNESS: No, they are drawn by a young man whom I employ to help me.

HILDA: Someone you have taught?

SOLNESS: Oh, yes, no doubt he has learned something from one, too.

HILDA *(sits down)*: Then I suppose he is very clever. *(Looks at a drawing.)* Isn't he?

SOLNESS: Oh, he might be worse. For my purpose—

HILDA: Oh, yes—I'm sure he is frightfully clever.

SOLNESS: Do you think you can see that in the drawings?

HILDA: Pooh—these scrawlings! But if he has been learning from you—

SOLNESS: Oh, so far as that goes—there are plenty of people that have learned from me and have come to little enough for all that.

HILDA (*looks at him and shakes her head*): No, I can't for the life of me understand how you can be so stupid.

SOLNESS: Stupid? Do you think I am so very stupid?

HILDA: Yes, I do indeed. If you are content to go about here teaching all these people—

SOLNESS (*with a slight start*): Well, and why not?

HILDA (*rises, half serious, half laughing*): No indeed, Mr. Solness! What can be the good of that? No one but you should be allowed to build. You should stand quite alone—do it all yourself. Now you know it.

SOLNESS (*involuntarily*): Hilda—!

HILDA: Well!

SOLNESS: How in the world did that come into your head?

HILDA: Do you think I am so very far wrong, then?

SOLNESS: No, that's not what I mean. But now I'll tell you something.

HILDA: Well?

SOLNESS: I keep on—incessantly—in silence and alone— brooding on that very thought.

HILDA: Yes, that seems to me perfectly natural.

SOLNESS (*looks somewhat searchingly at her*): Perhaps you have noticed it already?

HILDA: No, indeed I haven't.

SOLNESS: But just now—when you said you thought I was— off my balance? In one thing, you said—

HILDA: Oh, I was thinking of something quite different.

SOLNESS: What was it?

HILDA: I am not going to tell you.

SOLNESS (*crosses the room*): Well, well—as you please. (*Stops at the bow window.*) Come here, and I will show you something.

HILDA (*approaching*): What is it?

SOLNESS: Do you see—over there in the garden—?

HILDA: Yes?

SOLNESS (*points*): Right above the great quarry—?

HILDA: That new house, you mean?

SOLNESS: The one that is being built, yes. Almost finished.

HILDA: It seems to have a very high tower.

SOLNESS: The scaffolding is still up.

HILDA: Is that your new house?

SOLNESS: Yes.

HILDA: The house you are soon going to move into?

SOLNESS: Yes.

HILDA (*looks at him*): Are there nurseries in that house, too?

SOLNESS: Three, as there are here.

HILDA: And no child.

SOLNESS: And there never will be one.

HILDA (*with a half smile*): Well, isn't it just as I said—?

SOLNESS: That—?

HILDA: That you are a little—a little mad after all.

SOLNESS: Was that what you were thinking of?

HILDA: Yes, of all the empty nurseries I slept in.

SOLNESS (*lowers his voice*): We have had children—Aline and I.

HILDA (*looks eagerly at him*): Have you—?

SOLNESS: Two little boys. They were of the same age.

HILDA: Twins, then.

SOLNESS: Yes, twins. It's eleven or twelve years ago now.

HILDA (*cautiously*): And so both of them—? You have lost both the twins, then?

SOLNESS (*with quiet emotion*): We kept them only about three weeks. Or scarcely so much. (*Bursts forth.*) Oh, Hilda, I can't tell you what a good thing it is for me that you have come! For now at last I have someone I can talk to!

HILDA: Can you not talk to—her, too?

SOLNESS: Not about this. Not as I want to talk and must talk. (*Gloomily.*) And not about so many other things, either.

HILDA *(in a subdued voice)*: Was that all you meant when you said you needed me?

SOLNESS: That was mainly what I meant—at all events, yesterday. For today I am not so sure—*(Breaking off.)* Come here and let us sit down, Hilda. Sit there on the sofa—so that you can look into the garden. (HILDA *seats herself in the corner of the sofa.* SOLNESS *brings a chair closer.*) Should you like to hear about it?

HILDA: Yes, I shall love to sit and listen to you.

SOLNESS *(sits down)*: Then I will tell you all about it.

HILDA: Now I can see both the garden and you, Mr. Solness. So now, tell away! Begin!

SOLNESS *(points toward the bow window)*: Out there on the rising ground—where you see the new house—

HILDA: Yes?

SOLNESS: Aline and I lived there in the first years of our married life. There was an old house up there that had belonged to her mother; and we inherited it, and the whole of the great garden with it.

HILDA: Was there a tower on that house, too?

SOLNESS: No, nothing of the kind. From the outside it looked like a great, dark, ugly wooden box; but all the same, it was snug and comfortable enough inside.

HILDA: Then did you pull down the ramshackle old place?

SOLNESS: No, it burned down.

HILDA: The whole of it?

SOLNESS: Yes.

HILDA: Was that a great misfortune for you?

SOLNESS: That depends on how you look at it. As a builder, the fire was the making of me—

HILDA: Well, but—?

SOLNESS: It was just after the birth of the two little boys—

HILDA: The poor little twins, yes.

SOLNESS: They came healthy and bonny into the world. And they were growing too—you could see the difference from day to day.

HILDA: Little children do grow quickly at first.

SOLNESS: It was the prettiest sight in the world to see Aline lying with the two of them in her arms.—But then came the night of the fire—

HILDA (*excitedly*): What happened? Do tell me! Was anyone burned?

SOLNESS: No, not that. Everyone got safe and sound out of the house—

HILDA: Well, and what then—?

SOLNESS: The fright had shaken Aline terribly. The alarm—the escape—the breakneck hurry—and then the ice-cold night air—for they had to be carried out just as they lay—both she and the little ones.

HILDA: Was it too much for them?

SOLNESS: Oh no, they stood it well enough. But Aline fell into a fever, and it affected her milk. She would insist on nursing them herself; because it was her duty, she said. And both our little boys, they—(*clenching his hands*)—they—oh!

HILDA: They did not get over that?

SOLNESS: No, that they did not get over. That was how we lost them.

HILDA: It must have been terribly hard for you.

SOLNESS: Hard enough for me; but ten times harder for Aline. (*Clenching his hands in suppressed fury.*) Oh, that such things should be allowed to happen here in the world! (*Shortly and firmly.*) From the day I lost them, I had no heart for building churches.

HILDA: Did you not like the church tower in our town?

SOLNESS: I didn't like it. I know how free and happy I felt when the tower was finished.

HILDA: *I* know that, too.

SOLNESS: And now I shall never—never build anything of that sort again. Neither churches nor church towers.

HILDA (*nods slowly*): Nothing but houses for people to live in.

SOLNESS: Homes for human beings, Hilda.

HILDA: But homes with high towers and pinnacles upon them.

SOLNESS: If possible. *(Adopts a lighter tone.)* But, as I said before, that fire was the making of me—as a builder, I mean.

HILDA: Why don't you call yourself an architect, like the others?

SOLNESS: I have not been systematically enough taught for that. Most of what I know, I have found out for myself.

HILDA: But you succeeded all the same.

SOLNESS: Yes, thanks to the fire. I laid out almost the whole of the garden in villa lots; and there I was able to build after my own heart. So I came to the front with a rush.

HILDA *(looks keenly at him)*: You must surely be a very happy man, as matters stand with you.

SOLNESS *(gloomily)*: Happy? Do you say that, too—like all the rest of them?

HILDA: Yes, I should say you must be. If you could only cease thinking about the two little children—

SOLNESS *(slowly)*: The two little children—they are not so easy to forget, Hilda.

HILDA *(somewhat uncertainly)*: Do you still feel their loss so much—after all these years?

SOLNESS *(looks fixedly at her, without replying)*: A happy man you said—

HILDA: Well, now, are you not happy—in other respects?

SOLNESS *(continues to look at her)*: When I told you all this about the fire—hm—

HILDA: Well?

SOLNESS: Was there not one special thought that you—that you seized upon?

HILDA *(reflects in vain)*: No. What thought should that be?

SOLNESS *(with subdued emphasis)*: It was simply and solely by that fire that I was enabled to build homes for human beings. Cosy, comfortable, bright homes, where father and mother and the whole troop of children can live in safety and gladness, feeling what a happy thing it is to be alive in the world—and most of all to belong to each other—in great things and in small.

HILDA *(ardently)*: Well, and is it not a great happiness for you to be able to build such beautiful homes?

SOLNESS: The price, Hilda! The terrible price I had to pay for the opportunity!

HILDA: But can you never get over that?

SOLNESS: No. That I might build homes for others, I had to forgo—to forgo for all time—the home that might have been my own. I mean a home for a troop of children—and for father and mother, too.

HILDA *(cautiously)*: But need you have done that? For all time, you say?

SOLNESS *(nods slowly)*: That was the price of this happiness that people talk about. *(Breathes heavily.)* This happiness—hm—this happiness was not to be bought any cheaper, Hilda.

HILDA *(as before)*: But may it not come right even yet?

SOLNESS: Never in this world—never. That is another consequence of the fire—and of Aline's illness afterward.

HILDA *(looks at him with an indefinable expression)*: And yet you build all these nurseries?

SOLNESS *(seriously)*: Have you never noticed, Hilda, how the impossible—how it seems to beckon and cry aloud to one?

HILDA *(reflecting)*: The impossible? *(With animation.)* Yes, indeed! Is that how you feel too?

SOLNESS: Yes, I do.

HILDA: There must be—a little of the troll in you, too.

SOLNESS: Why of the troll?

HILDA: What would you call it, then?

SOLNESS *(rises)*: Well, well, perhaps you are right. *(Vehemently.)* But how can I help turning into a troll, when this is how it always goes with me in everything—in everything!

HILDA: How do you mean?

SOLNESS (*speaking low, with inward emotion*): Mark what I say to you, Hilda. All that I have succeeded in doing, building, creating—all the beauty, security, cheerful comfort—ay, and magnificence, too— (*Clenches his hands.*) Oh, is it not terrible even to think of—!

HILDA: What is so terrible?

SOLNESS: That all this I have to make up for, to pay for— not in money, but in human happiness. And not with my own happiness only, but with other people's, too. Yes, yes, do you see that, Hilda? That is the price which my position as an artist has cost me—and others. And every single day I have to look on while the price is paid for me anew. Over again, and over again—and over again forever!

HILDA (*rises and looks steadily at him*): Now I can see that you are thinking of—of her.

SOLNESS: Yes, mainly of Aline. For Aline—she, too, had her vocation in life, just as much as I had mine. (*His voice quivers.*) But her vocation has had to be stunted, and crushed and shattered—in order that mine might force its way to—to a sort of great victory. For you must know that Aline—she, too, had a talent for building.

HILDA: She! For building?

SOLNESS (*shakes her head*): Not houses and towers, and spires—not such things as I work away at—

HILDA: Well, but what then?

SOLNESS (*softly, with emotion*): For building up the souls of little children, Hilda. For building up children's souls in perfect balance, and in noble and beautiful forms. For enabling them to soar up into erect and full-grown human souls. That was Aline's talent. And there it all lies now— unused and unusable forever—of no earthly service to anyone—just like the ruins left by a fire.

HILDA: Yes, but even if this were so—?

SOLNESS: It is so! It is so! I know it!

HILDA: Well, but in any case it is not your fault.

SOLNESS (*fixes his eyes on her and nods slowly*): Ah, that is the great, terrible question. That is the doubt that is gnawing me—night and day.

HILDA: That?

SOLNESS: Yes. Suppose the fault was mine—in a certain sense.

HILDA: Your fault! The fire!

SOLNESS: All of it; the whole thing. And yet, perhaps—I may not have had anything to do with it.

HILDA (*looks at him with a troubled expression*): Oh, Mr. Solness—if you can talk like that, I am afraid you must be—ill, after all.

SOLNESS: Hm—I don't think I shall ever be of quite sound mind on that point.

RAGNAR BROVIK *cautiously opens the little door in the left-hand corner.* HILDA *comes forward.*

RAGNAR (*when he sees* HILDA): Oh. I beg pardon, Mr. Solness— (*He makes a movement to withdraw.*)

SOLNESS: No, no, don't go. Let us get it over.

RAGNAR: Oh, yes—if only we could.

SOLNESS: I hear your father is no better?

RAGNAR: Father is fast growing weaker—and therefore I beg and implore you to write a few kind words for me on one of the plans! Something for Father to read before he—

SOLNESS (*vehemently*): I won't hear anything more about those drawings of yours!

RAGNAR: Have you looked at them?

SOLNESS: Yes—I have.

RAGNAR: And they are good for nothing? And *I* am good for nothing, too?

SOLNESS (*evasively*): Stay here with me, Ragnar. You shall have everything your own way. And then you can marry Kaia and live at your ease—and happily, too, who knows? Only don't think of building on your own account.

RAGNAR: Well, well, then I must go home and tell Father what you say—I promised I would.—Is this what I am to tell Father—before he dies?

SOLNESS *(with a groan)*: Oh tell him—tell him what you will, for me. Best to say nothing at all to him! *(With a sudden outburst).* I cannot do anything else, Ragnar!

RAGNAR: May I have the drawings to take with me?

SOLNESS: Yes, take them—take them by all means! They are lying there on the table.

RAGNAR *(goes to the table)*: Thanks.

HILDA *(puts her hand on the portfolio)*: No, no; leave them here.

SOLNESS: Why?

HILDA: Because I want to look at them, too.

SOLNESS: But you have been— *(To RAGNAR)*. Well, leave them here, then.

RAGNAR: Very well.

SOLNESS: And go home at once to your father.

RAGNAR: Yes. I suppose I must.

SOLNESS *(as if in desperation)*: Ragnar—you must not ask me to do what is beyond my power! Do you hear, Ragnar? You must not!

RAGNAR: No, no. I beg your pardon—

He bows and goes out by the corner door. HILDA *goes over and sits down on a chair near the mirror.*

HILDA *(looks angrily at SOLNESS)*: That was a very ugly thing to do.

SOLNESS: Do you think so, too?

HILDA: Yes, it was horrible ugly—and hard and bad and cruel as well.

SOLNESS: Oh, you don't understand my position.

HILDA: No matter—. I say you ought not to be like that.

SOLNESS: You said yourself, only just now, that no one but *I* ought to be allowed to build.

HILDA: *I* may say such things—but you must not.

SOLNESS: I most of all, surely, who have paid so dear for my position.

HILDA: Oh yes—with what you call domestic comfort—and that sort of thing.

SOLNESS: And with my peace of soul into the bargain.

HILDA (*rising*): Peace of soul! (*With feeling.*) Yes, yes, you are right in that! Poor Mr. Solness—you fancy that—

SOLNESS (*with a quiet, chuckling laugh*): Just sit down again, Hilda, and I'll tell you something funny.

HILDA (*sits down; with intent interest*): Well?

SOLNESS: It sounds such a ludicrous little thing; for, you see, the whole story turns upon nothing but a crack in a chimney.

HILDA: No more than that?

SOLNESS: No, not to begin with.

He moves a chair nearer to HILDA *and sits down.*

HILDA (*impatiently, taps on her knee*): Well, now for the crack in the chimney!

SOLNESS: I had noticed the split in the flue long, long before the fire. Every time I went up into the attic, I looked to see if it was still there.

HILDA: And it was?

SOLNESS: Yes; for no one else knew about it.

HILDA: And you said nothing?

SOLNESS: Nothing.

HILDA: And did not think of repairing the flue either?

SOLNESS: Oh, yes, I thought about it—but never got any further. Every time I intended to set to work, it seemed just as if a hand held me back. Not today, I thought—tomorrow; and nothing ever came of it.

HILDA: But why did you keep putting it off like that?

SOLNESS: Because I was revolving something in my mind. (*Slowly, and in a low voice.*) Through that little black crack in the chimney, I might, perhaps, force my way upward—as a builder.

HILDA (*looking straight in front of her*): That must have been thrilling.

SOLNESS: Almost irresistible—quite irresistible. For at that time it appeared to me a perfectly simple and straight-forward matter. I would have had it happen in the winter-

time—a little before midday. I was to be out driving Aline
in the sleigh. The servants at home would have made huge
fires in the stoves.

HILDA: For, of course, it was to be bitterly cold that day?

SOLNESS: Rather biting, yes—and they would want Aline
to find it thoroughly snug and warm when she came
home.

HILDA: I suppose she is very chilly by nature?

SOLNESS: She is. And as we drove home, we were to see the
smoke.

HILDA: Only the smoke?

SOLNESS: The smoke first. But when we came up to the garden gate, the whole of the old timber-box was to be
a rolling mass of flames.—That is how I wanted it to be,
you see.

HILDA: Oh why, why could it not have happened so!

SOLNESS: You may well say that, Hilda.

HILDA: Well, but now listen, Mr. Solness. Are you perfectly
certain that the fire was caused by that little crack in the
chimney?

SOLNESS: No, on the contrary—I am perfectly certain that
the crack in the chimney had nothing whatever to do with
the fire.

HILDA: What?

SOLNESS: It has been clearly ascertained that the fire broke
out in a clothes cupboard—in a totally different part of
the house.

HILDA: Then what is all this nonsense you are talking about
the crack in the chimney?

SOLNESS: May I go on talking to you a little, Hilda?

HILDA: Yes, if you'll only talk sensibly—

SOLNESS: I will try.

He moves his chair nearer.

HILDA: Out with it, then, Mr. Solness.

SOLNESS *(confidentially)*: Don't you agree with me, Hilda,
that there exist special, chosen people who have been

endowed with the power and faculty of desiring a thing, craving for a thing, willing a thing—so persistently and so—so inexorably—that at last it has to happen? Don't you believe that?

HILDA (*with an indefinable expression in her eyes*): If that is so, we shall see, one of these days, whether *I* am one of the chosen.

SOLNESS: It is not one's self alone that can do such great things. Oh, no—the helpers and the servers—they must do their part, too, if it is to be of any good. But they never come of themselves. One has to call upon them very persistently—inwardly, you understand.

HILDA: What are these helpers and servers?

SOLNESS: Oh, we can talk about that some other time. For the present, let us keep to this business of the fire.

HILDA: Don't you think that fire would have happened all the same—even without your wishing for it?

SOLNESS: If the house had been old Knut Brovik's, it would never have burned down so conveniently for him. I am sure of that; for he does not know how to call for the helpers—no, nor for the servers, either. (*Rises in unrest.*) So you see, Hilda—it is my fault, after all, that the lives of the two little boys had to be sacrificed. And do you think it is not my fault, too, that Aline has never been the woman she should and might have been—and that she most longed to be?

HILDA: Yes, but if it is all the work of those helpers and servers—?

SOLNESS: Who called for the helpers and servers? It was I! And they came and obeyed my will. (*In increasing excitement.*) That is what people call having the luck on your side; but I must tell you what this sort of luck feels like! It feels like a great raw place here on my breast. And the helpers and servers keep on flaying pieces of skin off other people in order to close my sore!—But still the sore is not healed—never, never! Oh, if you knew how it can sometimes gnaw and burn.

HILDA (*looks attentively at him*): You are ill, Mr. Solness. Very ill, I almost think.

SOLNESS: Say mad; for that is what you mean.

HILDA: No, I don't think there is much amiss with your intellect.

SOLNESS: With what then? Out with it!

HILDA: I wonder whether you were not sent into the world with a sickly conscience.

SOLNESS: A sickly conscience? What devilry is that?

HILDA: I mean that your conscience is feeble—too delicately built, as it were—hasn't strength to take a grip of things— to lift and bear what is heavy.

SOLNESS (*growls*): Hm! May I ask, then, what sort of conscience one ought to have?

HILDA: I should like your conscience to be—to be thoroughly robust.

SOLNESS: Indeed? Robust, eh? Is your own conscience robust, may I ask?

HILDA: Yes, I think it is. I have never noticed that it wasn't.

SOLNESS: It has not been put very severely to the test, I should think.

HILDA (*with a quivering of the lips*): Oh, it was no such simple matter to leave Father—I am so awfully fond of him.

SOLNESS: Dear me! for a month or two—

HILDA: I think I shall never go home again.

SOLNESS: Never? Then why did you leave him?

HILDA (*half seriously, half banteringly*): Have you forgotten that the ten years are up?

SOLNESS: Oh nonsense. Was anything wrong at home? Eh?

HILDA (*quite seriously*): It was this impulse within me that urged and goaded me to come—and lured and drew me on, as well.

SOLNESS (*eagerly*): There we have it! There we have it, Hilda! There is a troll in you, too, as in me. For it's the troll in one, you see—it is that that calls to the powers outside us. And then you must give in—whether you will or no.

HILDA: I almost think you are right, Mr. Solness.

SOLNESS (*walks about the room*): Oh, there are devils innumerable abroad in the world, Hilda, that one never sees!

HILDA: Devils, too?

SOLNESS (*stops*): Good devils and bad devils; light-haired devils and black-haired devils. If only you could always tell whether it is the light or dark ones that have got hold of you! (*Paces about.*) Ho-ho! Then it would be simple enough.

HILDA (*follows him with her eyes*): Or if one had a really vigorous, radiantly healthy conscience—so that one dared to do what one would.

SOLNESS (*stops beside the console table*): I believe, now, that most people are just as puny creatures as I am in that respect.

HILDA: I shouldn't wonder.

SOLNESS (*leaning against the table*): In the sagas[3]— Have you read any of the old sagas?

HILDA: Oh, yes! When I used to read books, I—

SOLNESS: In the sagas you read about Vikings, who sailed to foreign lands,[4] and plundered and burned and killed men—

HILDA: And carried off women—

SOLNESS: —and kept them in captivity—

HILDA: —took them home in their ships—

SOLNESS: —and behaved to them like—like the very worst of trolls.

HILDA (*looks straight before her, with a half-veiled look*): I think that must have been thrilling.

SOLNESS (*with a short, deep laugh*): To carry off women?

HILDA: To be carried off.

SOLNESS (*looks at her a moment*): Oh, indeed.

HILDA (*as if breaking the thread of the conversation*): But what made you speak of these Vikings, Mr. Solness?

SOLNESS: Why, those fellows must have had robust consciences, if you like! When they got home again, they could eat, and drink and be as happy as children. And the women, too! They often would not leave them on any account. Can you understand that, Hilda?

HILDA: Those women I can understand exceedingly well.

SOLNESS: Oho! Perhaps you could do the same yourself?

HILDA: Why not?

SOLNESS: Live—of your own free will—with a ruffian like that?

HILDA: If it was a ruffian I had come to love—

SOLNESS: Could you come to love a man like that?

HILDA: Good heavens, you know very well one can't choose whom one is going to love.

SOLNESS (looks meditatively at her): Oh, no, I suppose it is the troll within one that's responsible for that.

HILDA (half laughing): And all those blessed devils, that you know so well—both the light-haired and the dark-haired ones.

SOLNESS (quietly and warmly): Then I hope with all my heart that the devils will choose carefully for you, Hilda.

HILDA: For me they have chosen already—once and for all.

SOLNESS (looks earnestly at her): Hilda—you are like a wild bird of the woods.

HILDA: Far from it. I don't hide myself away under the bushes.

SOLNESS: No, no. There is rather something of the bird of prey in you.

HILDA: That is nearer it—perhaps. (Very earnestly.) And why not a bird of prey? Why should not I go a-hunting—I, as well as the rest. Carry off the prey I want—if only I can get my claws into it and do with it as I will.

SOLNESS: Hilda—do you know what you are?

HILDA: Yes, I suppose I am a strange sort of bird.

SOLNESS: No. You are like a dawning day. When I look at you—I seem to be looking toward the sunrise.

HILDA: Tell me, Mr. Solness—are you certain that you have never called me to you? Inwardly, you know?

SOLNESS (softly and slowly): I almost think I must have.

HILDA: What did you want with me?

SOLNESS: You are the younger generation, Hilda.

HILDA (*smiles*): That younger generation that you are so afraid of?

SOLNESS (*nods slowly*): And which, in my heart, I yearn toward so deeply.

HILDA *rises, goes to the little table and fetches* RAGNAR BROVIK's *portfolio.*

HILDA (*holds out the portfolio to him*): We were talking of these drawings—

SOLNESS (*shortly, waving them away*): Put those things away! I have seen enough of them.

HILDA: Yes, but you have to write your approval on them.

SOLNESS: Write my approval on them? Never!

HILDA: But the poor old man is lying at death's door! Can't you give him and his son this pleasure before they are parted? And perhaps he might get the commission to carry them out, too.

SOLNESS: Yes, that is just what he would get. He has made sure of that—has my fine gentleman!

HILDA: Then, good heavens—if that is so—can't you tell the least little bit of a lie for once in a way?

SOLNESS: A lie? (*Raging.*) Hilda—take those devil's drawings out of my sight!

HILDA (*draws the portfolio a little nearer to herself*): Well, well, well—don't bite me.—You talk of trolls—but I think you go on like a troll yourself. (*Looks around.*) Where do you keep your pen and ink?

SOLNESS: There is nothing of the sort in here.

HILDA (*goes toward the door*): But in the office where that young lady is—

SOLNESS: Stay where you are, Hilda!—I ought to tell a lie, you say. Oh, yes, for the sake of his old father I might well do that—for in my time I have crushed him, trodden him under foot—

HILDA: Him, too?

SOLNESS: I needed room for myself. But this Ragnar—he must on no account be allowed to come to the front.

HILDA: Poor fellow, there is surely no fear of that. If he has nothing in him—

SOLNESS (*comes closer, looks at her and whispers*): If Ragnar Brovik gets his chance, he will strike me to the earth. Crush me—as I crushed his father.

HILDA: Crush you? Has he the ability for that?

SOLNESS: Yes, you may depend upon it he has the ability! He is the younger generation that stands ready to knock at my door—to make an end of Halvard Solness.

HILDA (*looks at him with quiet reproach*): And yet you would bar him out. Fie, Mr. Solness!

SOLNESS: The fight I have been fighting has cost heart's blood enough.—And I am afraid, too, that the helpers and servers will not obey me any longer.

HILDA: Then you must go ahead without them. There is nothing else for it.

SOLNESS: It is hopeless, Hilda. The luck is bound to turn. A little sooner or a little later. Retribution is inexorable.

HILDA (*in distress, putting her hands over her ears*): Don't talk like that! Do you want to kill me? To take from me what is more than my life?

SOLNESS: And what is that?

HILDA: The longing to see you great. To see you, with a wreath in your hand, high, high up upon a church tower. (*Calm again.*) Come, out with your pencil now. You must have a pencil about you?

SOLNESS (*takes out his pocketbook*): I have one here.

HILDA (*lays the portfolio on the sofa table*): Very well. Now let us two sit down here, Mr. Solness. (SOLNESS *seats himself at the table.* HILDA *stands behind him, leaning over the back of the chair.*) And now we will write on the drawings. We must write very, very nicely and cordially—for this horrid Ruar—or whatever his name is.

SOLNESS (*writes a few words, turns his head and looks at her*): Tell me one thing, Hilda.

HILDA: Yes!

SOLNESS: If you have been waiting for me all these ten years—

HILDA: What then?

SOLNESS: Why have you never written to me? Then I could have answered you.

HILDA *(hastily)*: No, no, no! That was just what I did not want.

SOLNESS: Why not?

HILDA: I was afraid the whole thing might fall to pieces.— But we were going to write on the drawings, Mr. Solness.

SOLNESS: So we were.

HILDA *(bends forward and looks over his shoulder while he writes)*: Mind now, kindly and cordially! Oh how I hate— how I hate this Ruald—

SOLNESS *(writing)*: Have you never really cared for anyone, Hilda?

HILDA *(harshly)*: What do you say?

SOLNESS: Have you never cared for anyone?

HILDA: For anyone else, I suppose you mean?

SOLNESS *(looks up at her)*: For anyone else, yes. Have you never? In all these ten years? Never?

HILDA: Oh, yes, now and then. When I was perfectly furious with you for not coming.

SOLNESS: Then you did take an interest in other people, too?

HILDA: A little bit—for a week or so. Good heavens, Mr. Solness, you surely know how such things come about.

SOLNESS: Hilda—what is it you have come for?

HILDA: Don't waste time talking. The poor old man might go and die in the meantime.

SOLNESS: Answer me, Hilda. What do you want of me?

HILDA: I want my kingdom.

SOLNESS: Hm—

He gives a rapid glance toward the door on the left and then goes on writing on the drawings. At the same moment MRS. SOLNESS *enters; she has some packages in her hand.*

MRS. SOLNESS: Here are a few things I have got for you, Miss Wangel. The large parcels will be sent later on.

HILDA: Oh, how very, very kind of you!

MRS. SOLNESS: Only my simple duty. Nothing more than that.

SOLNESS (*reading over what he has written*): Aline!

MRS. SOLNESS: Yes?

SOLNESS: Did you notice whether the—the bookkeeper was out there?

MRS. SOLNESS: Yes, of course, she was out there.

SOLNESS (*puts the drawings in the portfolio*): Hm—

MRS. SOLNESS: She was standing at the desk, as she always is—when *I* go through the room.

SOLNESS (*rises*): Then I'll give this to her and tell her that—

HILDA (*takes the portfolio from him*): Oh, no, let me have the pleasure of doing that! (*Goes to the door, but turns.*) What is her name?

SOLNESS: Her name is Miss Fosli.

HILDA: Pooh, that sounds too cold! Her Christian name, I mean?

SOLNESS: Kaia—I believe.

HILDA (*opens the door and calls out*): Kaia, come in here! Make haste! Mr. Solness wants to speak to you.

KAIA FOSLI *appears at the door.*

KAIA (*looking at him in alarm*): Here I am—?

HILDA (*handing her the portfolio*): See here, Kaia! You can take this home; Mr. Solness has written on them now.

KAIA: Oh, at last!

SOLNESS: Give them to the old man as soon as you can.

KAIA: I will go straight home with them.

SOLNESS: Yes, do. Now Ragnar will have a chance of building for himself.

KAIA: Oh, may he come and thank you for all—?

SOLNESS (*harshly*): I won't have any thanks! Tell him that from me.

KAIA: Yes, I will—

SOLNESS: And tell him at the same time that henceforward I do not require his services—nor yours either.

KAIA (*softly and quiveringly*): Not mine either?

SOLNESS: You will have other things to think of now and to attend to; and that is a very good thing for you. Well, go home with the drawings now, Miss Fosli. At once! Do you hear?

KAIA (*as before*): Yes, Mr. Solness.

She goes out.

MRS. SOLNESS: Heavens! what deceitful eyes she has.

SOLNESS: She? That poor little creature?

MRS. SOLNESS: Oh—I can see what I can see, Halvard.—Are you really dismissing them?

SOLNESS: Yes.

MRS. SOLNESS: Her as well?

SOLNESS: Was not that what you wished?

MRS. SOLNESS: But how can you get on without her—? Oh, well, no doubt you have someone else in reserve, Halvard.

HILDA (*playfully*): Well, I for one am not the person to stand at that desk.

SOLNESS: Never mind, never mind—it will be all right, Aline. Now all you have to do is to think about moving into our new home—as quickly as you can. This evening we will hang up the wreath—(*Turns to* HILDA.)—right on the very pinnacle of the tower. What do you say to that, Miss Hilda?

HILDA (*looks at him with sparkling eyes*): It will be splendid to see you so high up once more.

SOLNESS: Me!

MRS. SOLNESS: For heaven's sake, Miss Wangel, don't imagine such a thing! My husband!—when he always gets so dizzy!

HILDA: He gets dizzy! No, I know quite well he does not!

MRS. SOLNESS: Oh, yes, indeed he does.

HILDA: But I have seen him with my own eyes right up at the top of a high church tower!

MRS. SOLNESS: Yes, I hear people talk of that; but it is utterly impossible—

SOLNESS (*vehemently*): Impossible—impossible, yes! But there I stood all the same!

MRS. SOLNESS: Oh, how can you say so, Halvard? Why, you can't even bear to go out on the second-story balcony here. You have always been like that.

SOLNESS: You may perhaps see something different this evening.

MRS. SOLNESS (*in alarm*): No, no, no! Please God I shall never see that. I will write at once to the doctor—and I am sure he won't let you do it.

SOLNESS: Why, Aline—!

MRS. SOLNESS: Oh, you know you're ill, Halvard. This proves it! Oh God—Oh God!

She goes hastily out to the right.

HILDA (*looks intently at him*): Is it so, or is it not?

SOLNESS: That I turn dizzy?

HILDA: That my master builder dares not—cannot—climb as high as he builds?

SOLNESS: Is that the way you look at it?

HILDA: Yes.

SOLNESS: I believe there is scarcely a corner in me that is safe from you.

HILDA (*looks toward the bow window*): Up there, then. Right up there—

SOLNESS (*approaches her*): You might have the topmost room in the tower, Hilda—there you might live like a princess.

HILDA (*indefinably, between earnest and jest*): Yes, that is what you promised me.

SOLNESS: Did I really?

HILDA: Fie, Mr. Solness! You said I should be a princess, and

that you would give me a kingdom. And then you went
and— Well!

SOLNESS (*cautiously*): Are you quite certain that this is not a
dream—a fancy, that has fixed itself in your mind?

HILDA (*sharply*): Do you mean that you did not do it?

SOLNESS: I scarcely know myself. (*More softly.*) But now I
know so much for certain, that I—

HILDA: That you—? Say it at once!

SOLNESS: —that I ought to have done it.

HILDA (*exclaims with animation*): Don't tell me you can ever
be dizzy!

SOLNESS: This evening, then, we will hang up the wreath—
Princess Hilda.

HILDA (*with a bitter curve of the lips*): Over your new
home, yes.

SOLNESS: Over the new house, which will never be a home
for me.

He goes out through the garden door.

HILDA (*looks straight in front of her with a faraway expression and whispers to herself. The only words audible are*):
—frightfully thrilling—

ACT THREE

The large, broad verandah of SOLNESS's dwelling house. Part
of the house, with outer door leading to the verandah, is seen
to the left. A railing along the verandah to the right. At the
back, from the end of the verandah, a flight of steps leads
down to the garden below. Tall old trees in the garden spread
their branches over the verandah and toward the house. Far
to the right, in among the trees, a glimpse is caught of the
lower part of the new villa, with scaffolding round so much
as is seen of the tower. In the background the garden is
bounded by an old wooden fence. Outside the fence, a street
with low, tumble-down cottages.

Evening sky with sunlit clouds.

On the verandah, a garden bench stands along the wall of
the house, and in front of the bench a long table. On the other
side of the table, an armchair and some stools. All the furniture is of wickerwork.

MRS. SOLNESS, wrapped in a large white crape shawl, sits
resting in the armchair and gazes over to the right. Shortly
after, HILDA WANGEL comes up the flight of steps from
the garden. She is dressed as in the last act and wears her

hat. She has in her bodice a little nosegay of small common flowers.

MRS. SOLNESS *(turning her head a little)*: Have you been round the garden, Miss Wangel?

HILDA: Yes, I have been taking a look at it.

MRS. SOLNESS: And found some flowers, too, I see.

HILDA: Yes, indeed! There are such heaps of them in among the bushes.

MRS. SOLNESS: Are there really? Still? You see I scarcely ever go there.

HILDA *(closer)*: What! Don't you take a run down into the garden every day, then?

MRS. SOLNESS *(with a faint smile)*: I don't "run" anywhere, nowadays.

HILDA: Well, but do you not go down now and then to look at all the lovely things there?

MRS. SOLNESS: It has all become so strange to me. I am almost afraid to see it again.

HILDA: Your own garden!

MRS. SOLNESS: I don't feel that it is mine any longer.

HILDA: What do you mean—?

MRS. SOLNESS: No, no, it is not—not—not as it was in my mother's and father's time. They have taken away so much—so much of the garden, Miss Wangel. Fancy—they have parceled it out—and built houses for strangers—people that I don't know. And they can sit and look in upon me from their windows.

HILDA *(with a bright expression)*: Mrs. Solness!

MRS. SOLNESS: Yes!

HILDA: May I stay here with you a little?

MRS. SOLNESS: Yes, by all means, if you care to.

HILDA *moves a stool close to the armchair and sits down.*

HILDA: Ah—here one can sit and sun oneself like a cat.

MRS. SOLNESS *(lays her hand softly on* HILDA's *neck)*: It is nice of you to be willing to sit with me. I thought you wanted to go in to my husband.

HILDA: What should I want with him?

MRS. SOLNESS: To help him, I thought.

HILDA: No, thank you. And besides, he is not in. He is over there with the workmen. But he looked so fierce that I did not care to talk to him.

MRS. SOLNESS: He is so kind and gentle in reality.

HILDA: He!

MRS. SOLNESS: You do not really know him yet, Miss Wangel.

HILDA (*looks affectionately at her*): Are you pleased at the thought of moving over to the new house?

MRS. SOLNESS: I ought to be pleased; for it is what Halvard wants—

HILDA: Oh, not just on that account, surely.

MRS. SOLNESS: Yes, yes, Miss Wangel; for it is only my duty to submit myself to him. But very often it is dreadfully difficult to force one's mind to obedience.

HILDA: Yes, that must be difficult indeed.

MRS. SOLNESS: I can tell you it is—when one has so many faults as I have—

HILDA: When one has gone through so much trouble as you have—

MRS. SOLNESS: How do you know about that?

HILDA: Your husband told me.

MRS. SOLNESS: To me he very seldom mentions these things.—Yes, I can tell you I have gone through more than enough trouble in my life, Miss Wangel.

HILDA (*looks sympathetically at her and nods slowly*): Poor Mrs. Solness. First of all there was the fire—

MRS. SOLNESS (*with a sigh*): Yes, everything that was mine was burned.

HILDA: And then came what was worse.

MRS. SOLNESS (*looking inquiringly at her*): Worse?

HILDA: The worst of all.

MRS. SOLNESS: What do you mean?

HILDA (*softly*): You lost the two little boys.

MRS. SOLNESS: Oh, yes, the boys. But, you see, that was a thing apart. That was a dispensation of Providence; and in such things one can only bow in submission—yes, and be thankful, too.

HILDA: Then you are so?

MRS. SOLNESS: Not always, I am sorry to say. I know well enough that it is my duty—but all the same I cannot.

HILDA: No, no, I think that is only natural.

MRS. SOLNESS: And often and often I have to remind myself that it was a righteous punishment for me—

HILDA: Why?

MRS. SOLNESS: Because I had not fortitude enough in misfortune.

HILDA: But I don't see that—

MRS. SOLNESS: Oh, no, no, Miss Wangel—do not talk to me anymore about the two little boys. We ought to feel nothing but joy in thinking of them; for they are so happy—so happy now. No, it is the small losses in life that cut one to the heart—the loss of all that other people look upon as almost nothing.

HILDA (*lays her arms on* MRS. SOLNESS's *knees and looks up at her affectionately*): Dear Mrs. Solness—tell me what things you mean!

MRS. SOLNESS: As I say, only little things. All the old portraits were burned on the walls. And all the old silk dresses were burned, that had belonged to the family for generations and generations. And all Mother's and Grandmother's lace—that was burned, too. And only think—the jewels, too! (*Sadly.*) And then all the dolls.

HILDA: The dolls?

MRS. SOLNESS (*choking with tears*): I had nine lovely dolls.

HILDA: And they were burned, too?

MRS. SOLNESS: All of them. Oh, it was hard—so hard for me.

HILDA: Had you put by all these dolls, then? Ever since you were little?

MRS. SOLNESS: I had not put them by. The dolls and I had gone on living together.

HILDA: After you were grown up?

MRS. SOLNESS: Yes, long after that.

HILDA: After you were married, too?

MRS. SOLNESS: Oh, yes, indeed. So long as he did not see it—. But they were all burned up, poor things. No one thought of saving them. Oh, it is so miserable to think of. You mustn't laugh at me, Miss Wangel.

HILDA: I am not laughing at the least.

MRS. SOLNESS: For you see, in a certain sense, there was life in them, too. I carried them under my heart—like little unborn children.

DR. HERDAL, *with his hat in his hand, comes out through the door and observes* MRS. SOLNESS *and* HILDA.

DR. HERDAL: Well, Mrs. Solness, so you are sitting out here catching cold?

MRS. SOLNESS: I find it so pleasant and warm here today.

DR. HERDAL: Yes, yes. But is there anything going on here? I got a note from you.

MRS. SOLNESS (*rises*): Yes, there is something I must talk to you about.

DR. HERDAL: Very well; then perhaps we had better go in. (*To* HILDA.) Still in your mountaineering dress, Miss Wangel?

HILDA (*gaily, rising*): Yes—in full uniform! But today I am not going climbing and breaking my neck. We two will stop quietly below and look on, Doctor.

DR. HERDAL: What are we to look on at?

MRS. SOLNESS (*softly, in alarm, to* HILDA): Hush, hush—for God's sake! He is coming. Try to get that idea out of his head. And let us be friends, Miss Wangel. Don't you think we can?

HILDA (*throws her arms impetuously round* MRS. SOLNESS's *neck*): Oh, if we only could!

MRS. SOLNESS (*gently disengages herself*): There, there, there! There he comes, Doctor. Let me have a word with you.

DR. HERDAL: Is it about him?

MRS. SOLNESS: Yes, to be sure it's about him. Do come in.

She and the doctor enter the house. Next moment SOL-
NESS *comes up from the garden by the flight of steps. A
serious look comes over* HILDA'S *face.*

SOLNESS (*glances at the house door, which is closed cautiously from within*): Have you noticed, Hilda, that as
soon as I come, she goes?

HILDA: I have noticed that as soon as you come, you make
her go.

SOLNESS: Perhaps so. But I cannot help it. (*Looks observantly at her.*) Are you cold, Hilda? I think you look cold.

HILDA: I have just come up out of a tomb.

SOLNESS: What do you mean by that?

HILDA: That I have got chilled through and through, Mr.
Solness.

SOLNESS (*slowly*): I believe I understand—

HILDA: What brings you up here just now?

SOLNESS: I caught sight of you from over there.

HILDA: But then you must have seen her too?

SOLNESS: I knew she would go at once if I came.

HILDA: Is it very painful for you that she should avoid you in
this way?

SOLNESS: In one sense, it's a relief as well.

HILDA: Not to have her before your eyes?

SOLNESS: Yes.

HILDA: Not to be always seeing how heavily the loss of the
little boys weighs upon her?

SOLNESS: Yes. Chiefly that.

HILDA *drifts across the verandah with her hands behind her back, stops at the railing and looks out over the
garden.*

SOLNESS (*after a short pause*): Did you have a long talk
with her?

HILDA *stands motionless and does not answer.*

SOLNESS: Had you a long talk, I asked?

HILDA *is silent as before.*

SOLNESS: What was she talking about, Hilda?

HILDA *continues silent.*

SOLNESS: Poor Aline! I suppose it was about the little boys.

HILDA (*a nervous shudder runs through her; then she nods hurriedly once or twice*).

SOLNESS: She will never get over it—never in this world. (*Approaches her.*) Now you are standing there again like a statue; just as you stood last night.

HILDA (*turns and looks at him, with great serious eyes*): I am going away.

SOLNESS (*sharply*): Going away!

HILDA: Yes.

SOLNESS: But I won't allow you to!

HILDA: What am I to do here now?

SOLNESS: Simply to be here, Hilda!

HILDA (*measures him with a look*): Oh, thank you. You know it wouldn't end there.

SOLNESS (*heedlessly*): So much the better!

HILDA (*vehemently*): I cannot do any harm to one whom I know! I can't take away anything that belongs to her.

SOLNESS: Who wants you to do that?

HILDA (*continuing*): A stranger, yes! for that is quite a different thing! A person I have never set eyes on. But one that I have come into close contact with—! Oh, no! Oh, no! Ugh!

SOLNESS: Yes, but I never proposed you should.

HILDA: Oh, Mr. Solness, you know quite well what the end of it would be. And that is why I am going away.

SOLNESS: And what is to become of me when you are gone? What shall I have to live for then?—After that?

HILDA (*with the indefinable look in her eyes*): It is surely not so hard for you. You have your duties to her. Live for those duties.

SOLNESS: Too late. These powers—these—these—

HILDA: —devils—

SOLNESS: Yes, these devils! And the troll within me as well—they have drawn all the lifeblood out of her. (*Laughs in desperation.*) They did it for my happiness! Yes, yes! (*Sadly.*) And now she is dead—for my sake. And I am chained alive to a dead woman. (*In wild anguish.*) I—I who cannot live without joy in life!

HILDA moves round the table and seats herself on the bench, with her elbows on the table, and her head supported by her hands.

HILDA (*sits and looks at him awhile*): What will you build next?

SOLNESS (*shakes his head*): I don't believe I shall build much more.

HILDA: Not those cosy, happy homes for mother and father, and for the troop of children?

SOLNESS: I wonder whether there will be any use for such homes in the coming time.

HILDA: Poor Mr. Solness! And you have gone all these ten years—and staked your whole life—on that alone.

SOLNESS: Yes, you may well say so, Hilda.

HILDA (*with an outburst*): Oh, it all seems to me so foolish—so foolish!

SOLNESS: All what?

HILDA: Not to be able to grasp at your own happiness—at your own life! Merely because someone you know happens to stand in the way!

SOLNESS: One whom you have no right to set aside.

HILDA: I wonder whether one really has not the right! And yet, and yet—. Oh, if one could only sleep the whole thing away!

She lays her arms flat on the table, rests the left side of her head on her hands and shuts her eyes.

SOLNESS (*turns the armchair and sits down at the table*): Had you a cosy, happy home—up there with your father, Hilda?

HILDA (*without stirring, answers as if half asleep*): I had only a cage.

SOLNESS: And you are determined not to go back to it?

HILDA (*as before*): The wild bird never wants to go into the cage.

SOLNESS: Rather range through the free air—

HILDA (*still as before*): The bird of prey loves to range—

SOLNESS (*lets his eyes rest on her*): If only one had the viking spirit in life—

HILDA (*in her usual voice; opens her eyes but does not move*): And the other thing? Say what that was!

SOLNESS: A robust conscience.

HILDA *sits erect on the bench, with animation. Her eyes have once more the sparkling expression of gladness.*

HILDA (*nods to him*): I know what you are going to build next!

SOLNESS: Then you know more than I do, Hilda.

HILDA: Yes, builders are such stupid people.

SOLNESS: What is it to be then?

HILDA (*nods again*): The castle.

SOLNESS: What castle?

HILDA: My castle, of course.

SOLNESS: Do you want a castle now?

HILDA: Don't you owe me a kingdom, I should like to know?

SOLNESS: You say I do.

HILDA: Well—you admit you owe me this kingdom. And you can't have a kingdom without a royal castle, I should think!

SOLNESS (*more and more animated*): Yes, they usually go together.

HILDA: Good! Then build it for me! This moment!

SOLNESS (*laughing*): Must you have that on the instant, too?

HILDA: Yes, to be sure! For the ten years are up now, and I am not going to wait any longer. So—out with the castle, Mr. Solness!

SOLNESS: It's no light matter to owe you anything, Hilda.

HILDA: You should have thought of that before. It is too late now. So—*(tapping the table)*—the castle on the table! It is my castle! I will have it at once!

SOLNESS *(more seriously, leans over toward her, with his arms on the table)*: What sort of castle have you imagined, Hilda?

Her expression becomes more and more veiled. She seems gazing inward at herself.

HILDA *(slowly)*: My castle shall stand on a height—on a very great height—with a clear outlook on all sides, so that I can see far—far around.

SOLNESS: And no doubt it is to have a high tower!

HILDA: A tremendously high tower. And at the very top of the tower there shall be a balcony. And I will stand out upon it—

SOLNESS *(involuntarily clutches at his forehead)*: How can you like to stand at such a dizzy height—?

HILDA: Yes, I will, right up there will I stand and look down on the other people—on those that are building churches, and homes for mother and father and the troop of children. And you may come up and look on at it, too.

SOLNESS *(in a low tone)*: Is the builder to be allowed to come up beside the princess?

HILDA: If the builder will.

SOLNESS *(more softly)*: Then I think the builder will come.

HILDA *(nods)*: The builder—he will come.

SOLNESS: But he will never be able to build anymore. Poor builder!

HILDA *(animated)*: Oh yes, he will! We two will set to work together. And then we will build the loveliest—the very loveliest—thing in all the world.

SOLNESS *(intently)*: Hilda—tell me what that is!

HILDA *(looks smilingly at him, shakes her head a little, pouts and speaks as if to a child)*: Builders—they are such very—very stupid people.

SOLNESS: Yes, no doubt they are stupid. But now tell me

what it is—the loveliest thing in the world—that we two
are to build together?

HILDA *(is silent a little while, then says with an indefinable
expression in her eyes)*: Castles in the air.

SOLNESS: Castles in the air?

HILDA *(nods)*: Castles in the air, yes! Do you know what sort
of thing a castle in the air is?

SOLNESS: It is the loveliest thing in the world, you say.

HILDA *(rises with vehemence and makes a gesture of repulsion with her hand)*: Yes, to be sure it is! Castles in the
air—they are so easy to take refuge in. And so easy to
build, too—*(looks scornfully at him)*—especially for the
builders who have a—a dizzy conscience.

SOLNESS *(rises)*: After this day we two will build together,
Hilda.

HILDA *(with a half-dubious smile)*: A real castle in the air?

SOLNESS: Yes. One with a firm foundation under it.

RAGNAR BROVIK *comes out from the house. He is carrying
a large green wreath with flowers and silk ribbons.*

HILDA *(with an outburst of pleasure)*: The wreath! Oh, that
will be glorious!

SOLNESS *(in surprise)*: Have you brought the wreath,
Ragnar?

RAGNAR: I promised the foreman I would.

SOLNESS *(relieved)*: Ah, then I suppose your father is better?

RAGNAR: No.

SOLNESS: Was he not cheered by what I wrote?

RAGNAR: It came too late.

SOLNESS: Too late!

RAGNAR: When she came with it he was unconscious. He had
had a stroke.

SOLNESS: Why, then, you must go home to him! You must
attend to your father!

RAGNAR: He does not need me anymore.

SOLNESS: But surely you ought to be with him.

RAGNAR: She is sitting by his bed.

SOLNESS (*rather uncertainly*): Kaia?

RAGNAR (*looking darkly at him*): Yes—Kaia.

SOLNESS: Go home, Ragnar—both to him and to her. Give me the wreath.

RAGNAR (*suppresses a mocking smile*): You don't mean that you yourself—?

SOLNESS: I will take it down to them myself. (*Takes the wreath from him.*) And now you go home; we don't require you today.

RAGNAR: I know you do not require me anymore; but today I shall remain.

SOLNESS: Well, remain then, since you are bent upon it.

HILDA (*at the railing*): Mr. Solness, I will stand here and look on at you.

SOLNESS: At me!

HILDA: It will be fearfully thrilling.

SOLNESS (*in a low tone*): We will talk about that presently, Hilda.

He goes down the flight of steps with the wreath and away through the garden.

HILDA (*looks after him, then turns to* RAGNAR): I think you might at least have thanked him.

RAGNAR: Thanked him? Ought I to have thanked him?

HILDA: Yes, of course you ought!

RAGNAR: I think it is rather you I ought to thank.

HILDA: How can you say such a thing?

RAGNAR (*without answering her*): But I advise you to take care, Miss Wangel! For you don't know him rightly yet.

HILDA (*ardently*): Oh, no one knows him as I do!

RAGNAR (*laughs in exasperation*): Thank him, when he has held me down year after year! When he made Father disbelieve in me—made me disbelieve in myself! And all merely that he might—!

HILDA (*as if divining something*): That he might—? Tell me at once!

RAGNAR: That he might keep her with him.

HILDA (*with a start toward him*): The girl at the desk.

RAGNAR: Yes.

HILDA (*threateningly, clenching her hands*): That is not true! You are telling falsehoods about him!

RAGNAR: I would not believe it either until today—when she said so herself.

HILDA (*as if beside herself*): What did she say? I will know! At once! at once!

RAGNAR: She said that he had taken possession of her mind— her whole mind—centered all her thoughts upon himself alone. She says that she can never leave him—that she will remain here, where he is—

HILDA (*with flashing eyes*): She will not be allowed to!

RAGNAR (*as if feeling his way*): Who will not allow her?

HILDA (*rapidly*): He will not either!

RAGNAR: Oh no—I understand the whole thing now. After this, she would merely be—in the way.

HILDA: You understand nothing—since you can talk like that! No, *I* will tell you why he kept hold of her.

RAGNAR: Well then, why?

HILDA: In order to keep hold of you.

RAGNAR: Has he told you so?

HILDA: No, but it is so. It must be so! (*Wildly.*) I will—I will have it so!

RAGNAR: And at the very moment when you came—he let her go.

HILDA: It was you—you that he let go. What do you suppose he cares about strange women like her?

RAGNAR (*reflects*): Is it possible that all this time he has been afraid of me?

HILDA: He afraid! I would not be so conceited if I were you.

RAGNAR: Oh, he must have seen long ago that I had something in me, too. Besides—cowardly—that is just what he is, you see.

HILDA: He! Oh, yes, I am likely to believe that!

RAGNAR: In a certain sense he is cowardly—he, the great master builder. He is not afraid of robbing others of their life's happiness—as he has done both for my father and for me. But when it comes to climbing up a paltry bit of scaffolding—he will do anything rather than that.

HILDA: Oh, you should just have seen him high, high up—at the dizzy height where I once saw him.

RAGNAR: Did you see that?

HILDA: Yes, indeed I did. How free and great he looked as he stood and fastened the wreath to the church vane!

RAGNAR: I know that he ventured that, once in his life—one solitary time. It is a legend among us younger men. But no power on earth would induce him to do it again.

HILDA: Today he will do it again!

RAGNAR (scornfully): Yes, I daresay!

HILDA: We shall see it!

RAGNAR: That neither you nor I will see.

HILDA (with uncontrollable vehemence): I will see it! I will and must see it!

RAGNAR: But he will not do it. He simply dare not do it. For you see he cannot get over his infirmity—master builder though he be.

MRS. SOLNESS comes from the house on to the verandah.

MRS. SOLNESS (looks around): Is he not here? Where has he gone to?

RAGNAR: Mr. Solness is down with the men.

HILDA: He took the wreath with him.

MRS. SOLNESS (terrified): Took the wreath with him! Oh, God! oh, God! Brovik—you must go down to him! Get him to come back here!

RAGNAR: Shall I say you want to speak to him, Mrs. Solness?

MRS. SOLNESS: Oh, yes, do!—No, no—don't say that I want anything! You can say that somebody is here, and that he must come at once.

RAGNAR: Good. I will do so, Mrs. Solness.

He goes down the flight of steps and away through the garden.

MRS. SOLNESS: Oh, Miss Wangel, you can't think how anxious I feel about him.

HILDA: Is there anything in this to be so terribly frightened about?

MRS. SOLNESS: Oh, yes; surely you can understand. Just think, if he were really to do it! If he should take it into his head to climb up the scaffolding!

HILDA (*eagerly*): Do you think he will?

MRS. SOLNESS: Oh, one can never tell what he might take into his head. I am afraid there is nothing he mightn't think of doing.

HILDA: Aha! Perhaps you too think that he is—well—?

MRS. SOLNESS: Oh, I don't know what to think about him now. The doctor has been telling me all sorts of things; and putting it all together with several things I have heard him say—

DR. HERDAL *looks out, at the door.*

DR. HERDAL: Is he not coming soon?

MRS. SOLNESS: Yes, I think so. I have sent for him at any rate.

DR. HERDAL (*advancing*): I am afraid you will have to go in, my dear lady—

MRS. SOLNESS: Oh, no! Oh, no! I shall stay out here and wait for Halvard.

DR. HERDAL: But some ladies have just come to call on you—

MRS. SOLNESS: Good heavens, that too! And just at this moment!

DR. HERDAL: They say they positively must see the ceremony.

MRS. SOLNESS: Well, well, I suppose I must go to them after all. It is my duty.

HILDA: Can't you ask the ladies to go away?

MRS. SOLNESS: No, that would never do. Now that they are here, it is my duty to see them. But do you stay out here in the meantime—and receive him when he comes.

DR. HERDAL: And try to occupy his attention as long as possible—

MRS. SOLNESS: Yes, do, dear Miss Wangel. Keep a firm hold of him as ever you can.

HILDA: Would it not be best for you to do that?

MRS. SOLNESS: Yes; God knows that is my duty. But when one has duties in so many directions—

DR. HERDAL (*looks toward the garden*): There he is coming.

MRS. SOLNESS: And I have to go in!

DR. HERDAL (*to* HILDA): Don't say anything about my being here.

HILDA: Oh, no! I daresay I shall find something else to talk to Mr. Solness about.

MRS. SOLNESS: And be sure you keep firm hold of him. I believe you can do it best.

MRS. SOLNESS *and* DR. HERDAL *go into the house.* HILDA *remains standing on the verandah.* SOLNESS *comes from the garden, up the flight of steps.*

SOLNESS: Somebody wants me, I hear.

HILDA: Yes; it is I, Mr. Solness.

SOLNESS: Oh, is it you, Hilda? I was afraid it might be Aline or the doctor.

HILDA: You are very easily frightened, it seems!

SOLNESS: Do you think so?

HILDA: Yes; people say that you are afraid to climb about— on the scaffoldings, you know.

SOLNESS: Well, that is quite a special thing.

HILDA: Then it is true that you are afraid to do it?

SOLNESS: Yes, I am.

HILDA: Afraid of falling down and killing yourself?

SOLNESS: No, not of that.

HILDA: Of what, then?

SOLNESS: I am afraid of retribution, Hilda.

HILDA: Of retribution? (*Shakes her head.*) I don't understand that.

SOLNESS: Sit down and I will tell you something.

HILDA: Yes, do! At once!

She sits on a stool by the railing and looks expectantly at him.

SOLNESS *(throws his hat on the table)*: You know that I began by building churches.

HILDA *(nods)*: I know that well.

SOLNESS: For, you see, I came as a boy from a pious home in the country; and so it seemed to me that this church building was the noblest task I could set myself.

HILDA: Yes, yes.

SOLNESS: And I venture to say that I built those poor little churches with such honest and warm and heartfelt devotion that—that—

HILDA: That—? Well?

SOLNESS: Well, that I think that he ought to have been pleased with me.

HILDA: He? What he?

SOLNESS: He who was to have the churches, of course! He to whose honor and glory they were dedicated.

HILDA: Oh, indeed! But are you certain, then, that—that he was not—pleased with you?

SOLNESS *(scornfully)*: He pleased with me! How can you talk so, Hilda? He who gave the troll in me leave to lord it just as it pleased. He who bade them be at hand to serve me, both day and night—all these—all these—

HILDA: Devils—

SOLNESS: Yes, of both kinds. Oh, no, he made me feel clearly enough that he was not pleased with me. *(Mysteriously.)* You see, that was really the reason why he made the old house burn down.

HILDA: Was that why?

SOLNESS: Yes, don't you understand? He wanted to give me the chance of becoming an accomplished master in my own sphere—so that I might build all the more glorious churches for him. At first I did not understand what he was driving at; but all of a sudden it flashed upon me.

HILDA: When was that?

SOLNESS: It was when I was building the church tower up at Lysanger.

HILDA: I thought so.

SOLNESS: For you see, Hilda—up there, amid those new surroundings, I used to go about musing and pondering within myself. Then I saw plainly why he had taken my little children from me. It was that I should have nothing else to attach myself to. No such thing as love and happiness, you understand. I was to be only a master builder—nothing else. And all my life long I was to go on building for him. *(Laughs.)* But I can tell you nothing came of that!

HILDA: What did you do, then?

SOLNESS: First of all, I searched and tried my own heart—

HILDA: And then?

SOLNESS: Then I did the impossible—I no less than he.

HILDA: The impossible?

SOLNESS: I had never before been able to climb up to a great, free height. But that day I did it.

HILDA *(leaping up)*: Yes, yes, you did!

SOLNESS: And when I stood there, high over everything, and was hanging the wreath over the vane, I said to him: Hear me now, thou Mighty One! From this day forward I will be a free builder—I, too, in my sphere—just as thou in thine. I will never more build churches for thee—only homes for human beings.

HILDA *(with great sparkling eyes)*: That was the song that I heard through the air!

SOLNESS: But afterward his turn came.

HILDA: What do you mean by that?

SOLNESS *(looks despondently at her)*: Building homes for human beings—is not worth a rap, Hilda.

HILDA: Do you say that now?

SOLNESS: Yes, for now I see it. Men have no use for these homes of theirs—to be happy in. And I should not have had any use for such a home, if I had had one. *(With a quiet, bitter laugh.)* See, that is the upshot of the whole affair, however far back I look. Nothing really built; nor anything sacrificed for the chance of building. Nothing, nothing! the whole is nothing.

HILDA: Then you will never build anything more?

SOLNESS (*with animation*): On the contrary, I am just going to begin!

HILDA: What, then? What will you build? Tell me at once!

SOLNESS: I believe there is only one possible dwelling place for human happiness—and that is what I am going to build now.

HILDA (*looks fixedly at him*): Mr. Solness—you mean our castle?

SOLNESS: The castles in the air—yes.

HILDA: I am afraid you would turn dizzy before we got halfway up.

SOLNESS: Not if I can mount hand in hand with you, Hilda.

HILDA (*with an expression of suppressed resentment*): Only with me? Will there be no others of the party?

SOLNESS: Who else should there be?

HILDA: Oh—that girl—that Kaia at the desk. Poor thing—don't you want to take her with you, too?

SOLNESS: Oho! Was it about her that Aline was talking to you?

HILDA: Is it so—or is it not?

SOLNESS (*vehemently*): I will not answer such a question. You must believe in me, wholly and entirely!

HILDA: All these ten years I have believed in you so utterly—so utterly.

SOLNESS: You must go on believing in me!

HILDA: Then let me see you stand free and high up!

SOLNESS (*sadly*): Oh Hilda—it is not every day that I can do that.

HILDA (*passionately*): I will have you do it! I will have it! (*Imploringly.*) Just once more, Mr. Solness! Do the impossible once again!

SOLNESS (*stands and looks deep into her eyes*): If I try it, Hilda, I will stand up there and talk to him as I did that time before.

HILDA (*in rising excitement*): What will you say to him?

SOLNESS: I will say to him: Hear me, Mighty Lord—thou may'st judge me as seems best to thee. But hereafter I will build nothing but the loveliest thing in the world—

HILDA (*carried away*): Yes—yes—yes!

SOLNESS: —build it together with a princess, whom I love—

HILDA: Yes, tell him that! Tell him that!

SOLNESS: Yes. And then I will say to him: Now I shall go down and throw my arms round her and kiss her—

HILDA: —many times! Say that!

SOLNESS: —many, many times, I will say.

HILDA: And then—?

SOLNESS: Then I will wave my hat—and come down to the earth—and do as I said to him.

HILDA (*with outstretched arms*): Now I see you again as I did when there was song in the air.

SOLNESS (*looks at her with his head bowed*): How have you become what you are, Hilda?

HILDA: How have you made me what I am?

SOLNESS (*shortly and firmly*): The princess shall have her castle.

HILDA (*jubilant, clapping her hands*): Oh, Mr. Solness—! My lovely, lovely castle. Our castle in the air!

SOLNESS: On a firm foundation.

In the street a crowd of people has assembled, vaguely seen through the trees. Music of wind instruments is heard far away behind the new house. MRS. SOLNESS, with a fur collar round her neck, DR. HERDAL with her white shawl on his arm, and some ladies, come out on the verandah. RAGNAR BROVIK comes at the same time up from the garden.

MRS. SOLNESS (*to RAGNAR*): Are we to have music, too?

RAGNAR: Yes. It's the band of the Mason's Union. (*To SOLNESS.*) The foreman asked me to tell you that he is ready now to go up with the wreath.

HOLNESS (*takes his hat*): Good. I will go down to him myself.

MRS. SOLNESS (*anxiously*): What have you to down there, Halvard?

SOLNESS (*curtly*): I must be down below with the men.

MRS. SOLNESS: Yes, down below—only down below.

HOLNESS: That is where I always stand—on everyday occasions.

He goes down the flight of steps and away through the garden.

MRS. SOLNESS (*calls after him over the railing*): But do beg the man to be careful when he goes up? Promise me that, Halvard!

DR. HERDAL (*to* MRS. SOLNESS): Don't you see that I was right? He has given up all thought of that folly.

MRS. SOLNESS: Oh, what a relief! Twice workmen have fallen, and each time they were killed on the spot. (*Turns to* HILDA.) Thank you, Miss Wangel, for having kept such a firm hold upon him. I should never have been able to manage him.

DR. HERDAL (*playfully*): Yes, yes, Miss Wangel, you know how to keep firm hold on a man, when you give your mind to it.

MRS. SOLNESS and DR. HERDAL go up to the ladies, who are standing nearer to the steps and looking over the garden. HILDA *remains standing beside the railing in the foreground.* RAGNAR *goes up to her.*

RAGNAR (*with suppressed laughter, half whispering*): Miss Wangel—do you see all those young fellows down in the street?

HILDA: Yes.

RAGNAR: They are my fellow students, come to look at the master.

HILDA: What do they want to look at him for?

RAGNAR: They want to see how he daren't climb to the top of his own house.

HILDA: Oh, that is what those boys want, is it?

RAGNAR (*spitefully and scornfully*): He has kept us down so long—now we are going to see him keep quietly down below himself.

HILDA: You will not see that—not this time.

RAGNAR (*smiles*): Indeed! Then where shall we see him?

HILDA: High—high up by the vane! That is where you will see him!

RAGNAR (*laughs*): Him! Oh, yes, I daresay!

HILDA: His will is to reach the top—so at the top you shall see him.

RAGNAR: His will, yes; that I can easily believe. But he simply cannot do it. His head would swim round, long, long before he got halfway. He would have to crawl down again on his hands and knees.

DR. HERDAL (*points across*): Look! There goes the foreman up the ladders.

MRS. SOLNESS: And of course he has the wreath to carry, too. Oh, I do hope he will be careful!

RAGNAR (*stares incredulously and shouts*): Why, but it's—

HILDA (*breaking out in jubilation*): It is the master builder himself!

MRS. SOLNESS (*screams with terror*): Yes, it is Halvard! Oh, my great God—! Halvard! Halvard!

DR. HERDAL: Hush! Don't shout to him!

MRS. SOLNESS (*half beside herself*): I must go to him! I must get him to come down again!

DR. HERDAL (*holds her*): Don't move, any of you! Not a sound!

HILDA (*immovable, follows* SOLNESS *with her eyes*): He climbs and climbs. Higher and higher! Higher and higher! Look! Just look!

RAGNAR (*breathless*): He must turn now. He can't possibly help it.

HILDA: He climbs and climbs. He will soon be at the top now.

MRS. SOLNESS: Oh, I shall die of terror. I cannot bear to see it.

DR. HERDAL: Then don't look up at him.

HILDA: There he is standing on the topmost planks. Right at the top!

DR. HERDAL: Nobody must move! Do you hear?

HILDA (*exulting, with quiet intensity*): At last! At last! Now I see him great and free again!

RAGNAR (*almost voiceless*): But this is im—

HILDA: So I have seen him all through these ten years. How secure he stands! Frightfully thrilling all the same. Look at him! Now he is hanging the wreath round the vane.

RAGNAR: I feel as if I were looking at something utterly impossible.

HILDA: Yes, it is the impossible that he is doing now! (*With the indefinable expression in her eyes.*) Can you see anyone else up there with him?

RAGNAR: There is no one else.

HILDA: Yes, there is one he is striving with.

RAGNAR: You are mistaken.

HILDA: Then do you hear no song in the air, either?

RAGNAR: It must be the wind in the treetops.

HILDA: *I* hear a song—a mighty song! (*Shouts in wild jubilation and glee.*) Look, look! Now he is waving his hat! He is waving it to us down here! Oh, wave, wave back to him. For now it is finished! (*Snatches the white shawl from the doctor, waves it and shouts up to* SOLNESS.) Hurrah for Master Builder Solness!

DR. HERDAL: Stop! Stop! For God's sake—!

The ladies on the verandah wave their pocket handkerchiefs, and the shouts of "Hurrah" are taken up in the street below. Then they are suddenly silenced, and the crowd bursts out into a shriek of horror. A human body, with planks and fragments of wood, is vaguely perceived crashing down behind the trees.

MRS. SOLNESS AND THE LADIES (*at the same time*): He is falling! He is falling!

MRS. SOLNESS *totters, falls backward, swooning, and is caught, amid cries and confusion, by the ladies. The crowd in the street breaks down the fence and storms into the garden. At the same time* DR. HERDAL, *too, rushes down thither. A short pause.*

HILDA *(stares fixedly upward and says, as if petrified)*: My Master Builder.

RAGNAR *(supports himself, trembling, against the railing)*: He must be dashed to pieces—killed on the spot.

ONE OF THE LADIES *(while* MRS. SOLNESS *is carried into the house)*: Run down for the doctor—

RAGNAR: I can't stir a foot—

ANOTHER LADY: Then call to someone!

RAGNAR *(tries to call out)*: How is it? Is he alive?

A VOICE *(below in the garden)*: Mr. Solness is dead!

OTHER VOICES *(nearer)*: The head is all crushed.—He fell right into the quarry.

HILDA *(turns to* RAGNAR *and says quietly)*: I can't see him up there now.

RAGNAR: This is terrible. So, after all, he could not do it.

HILDA *(as if in quiet spellbound triumph)*: But he mounted right to the top. And I heard harps in the air. *(Waves her shawl in the air, and shrieks with wild intensity.)* My—my Master Builder!

NOTES

A Doll's House

1. **Title:** Many translators have argued that the title should be *A Doll House*. The possessive apostrophe emphasizes Nora's role. Its absence emphasizes Ibsen's dissection of the middle-class home and family as a whole.
2. **steamer:** Steamship.
3. **tarantella:** A dance from southern Italy. The dancer moves in rapid whirling movements that, according to folk wisdom, either drive out the poison of the tarantula bite, or (in other versions) are the frenzied results of the bite.
4. **my father's youthful amusements:** His father's mistresses, from whom he contracted syphilis. Rank is suffering from its inherited effects (presumably his mother contracted it from his father). Both Nora and the doctor skirt around a bald statement on this taboo subject. It lay at the heart of Ibsen's *Ghosts* (1881), causing an enormous scandal.
5. **a black domino:** A cloak with a half mask covering the

upper half of the face. Used as an alternative to costume dress at masked balls.

6. **Capri maiden:** An island off the coast of southern Italy. The reference is to Nora's tarantella dance.

The Wild Duck

1. **lively customer in his day:** I.e., a young man of spirits. Possibly a good lover, with the concurrent implication of frequenting houses of prostitution.
2. **works:** Ironworks: a place where iron is smelted and iron goods are made.
3. **maraschino:** A liqueur made from macerated cherries. It is strong and sweet, traditionally drunk after dinner, as a dessert.
4. **to retouch:** It was a common practice to improve and sometimes color photographs by painting on the original print.
5. **sunshine:** I.e., court favor.
6. **blindman's-buff:** A game in which the "blind man" is blindfolded and tries to catch hold and guess the identity of the other players.
7. **garret:** The uppermost apartment in a house, similar to an attic, directly under the roof. The Ekdals' garret appears to run the length of the house and to be very high.
8. **roof-tree:** The main beam of a roof.
9. **tumblers and a pair of pouters:** Species of show pigeons.
10. **hutch:** Rabbit housing.
11. **Muscovy:** A breed of duck originating in Brazil, not derived from the more common mallard.
12. **"Harrison's History of London":** *New and Universal History of the Cities of London and Westminster* by Walter Harrison, London, 1775.
13. **Death with an hourglass and a woman:** Allegorical figures—death, time, and (possibly) Eve, and therefore original sin.

14. **"The Flying Dutchman":** The legend of the Flying Dutchman concerns a ship captain who, upon running into a storm off the southern tip of Africa, vowed to sail around the Cape of Good Hope if he had to keep trying until doomsday, thus cursing himself to forever sail after his death.

15. **engrave:** An ancient printing technique in which the reverse image is carved into a material such as a copper plate or wood block that is then covered with ink and pressed into paper, creating both color blocks and a raised edge of paper.

16. **the gray clothes:** Prison uniform.

17. **allowed to wear his uniform again:** As a criminal, he has been disbarred from the military and its concurrent honors.

18. **that claim:** Usually a debt, such as an insurance claim. The doctor's pun is satirical.

19. **share in the property:** Norwegian law dictated that before remarrying, a widower must settle a portion of his property on any children from the previous marriage.

Hedda Gabler

1. **west end of Christiania:** The capital, cultural center, and largest city of Norway. Renamed Oslo in 1925.

2. **long black habit:** A woman's horse-riding costume. A long loose skirt paired with a tight, double-breasted jacket.

3. **mortgage on our annuity:** The aunts have taken out a loan based on their annual income (probably from inherited land), with the understanding that it will only be used for "security,"—that is, if their nephew cannot pay his bills.

4. **du:** The informal version of *you*. English has no contemporary equivalent, but many languages, including Spanish, French, and Italian, use a formal and informal second person.

5. **De?:** Mrs. Elvsted has reverted to the formal second person.
6. **a parley through?:** I.e., is there no way we can find a way across our differences and talk? Literally, a chink (hole) in the wall through which to chat.
7. **stirrup cup:** I.e., one for the road. A last glass before riding away. "Cold punch" is usually a champagne punch made with juices, and sometimes other alcohol and sweet cream.
8. **Tyrol:** A western province of Austria with magnificent mountains. The place names that follow all refer to various groups of mountains or vistas.
9. **quires:** Packets or stacks of paper.

The Master Builder

1. **tourist costume . . . alpenstock:** I.e., an outfit typical for the Scandinavian summer pastime of walking in the mountainous countryside from town to town. An alpenstock is a long wooden walking staff tipped with a point of iron, originally used for climbing in the Alps.
2. **on the weather vane:** Church towers are traditionally topped by a weather vane. To crown the vane with a wreath, the master builder would have to climb to the very top of the church and reach out to the vane with the wreath while standing on the scaffolding.
3. **sagas:** Epic cycles of the Scandinavian peoples whose heroes are often the great Norwegian kings of the fourth to eighth centuries. They also feature Norse gods and goddesses and, later, fantastical stories about the coming of Christianity, often written by monks. Many of these stories (save the latter) were censored or repressed after the establishment of Christianity, but they were preserved in more remote areas, particularly Iceland. Ibsen spent several years collecting folktales and songs for the Norwegian government and used material from the

sagas in his early works. The "trolls" and "helpers" to
which Solness refers are also from this cosmology.

4. **Vikings, who sailed to foreign lands:** In the ninth
   century these Scandinavian marauders were among the
   most skilled seaman and feared warriors in the Western
   world. Traveling in huge wooden ships, they conquered
   the coastal peoples from Lapland and Finland to as far
   south as Britain and northern France and invaded as far
   south as Sicily and northern Africa. In Scandinavia the
   time of the Vikings is sometimes looked upon nostalgi-
   cally as a time when Scandinavia ruled the world.

INTERPRETIVE NOTES

A DOLL'S HOUSE

The Plot

An exploration of the dark side of middle-class marriage and family life. Nora, the beautiful young wife of Torvald Helmer, a bank official, has borrowed money fraudulently in order to provide him with a lifesaving trip to Italy. Helmer does not know about the money, or the threat to his life. When Helmer is promoted at the bank, an old school friend of Nora's comes to visit just before Christmas, hoping for a job. The series of confrontations that follow reveal truths and secrets that undo the perfect "doll's house" of Helmer and Nora's world.

Characters

Nora Helmer. A beautiful young woman whose manners typify the ideal of middle-class femininity, taste, and talents. Her intelligence is well hidden behind her "chirping" cheerfulness. She is the daughter of a public official of doubtful ethics, wife of a rising banking official, mother of three young children, and head of a bustling middle-class household.

Torvald Helmer. Nora's loving but authoritative and condescending husband. An ambitious banker, he is a man who believes in rules and reputation above all else.

Dr. Rank. A prosperous, well-educated, dying doctor with a mordant sense of humor and generously cynical view of the world. Helmer's friend and Nora's admirer.

Christine. A school friend of Nora's who has since fallen on difficult times. A quiet, hardworking woman of hard-won integrity.

Nils Krogstad. A minor bank official, part-time loan shark and blackmailer, and Christine's former suitor. He is more merciful and flexible in his views than Helmer.

THE WILD DUCK

The Plot

An exploration of the subtle nature of truth and the possible values of illusion. Gregers Werle, the son of a wealthy and influential businessman, returns to town and, in the name of truth and high ideals, reveals what he believes are his father's dirty dealings with a former business partner, Old Ekdal, Ekdal's son, Hialmar, and his wife, Gina. His "mission" for truth plunges the family into tragedy.

Characters

Gregers Werle. A young man of wealth and education whose high ideals about truth, integrity, and marriage have little grounding in life experience. He has, nonetheless, rejected his father and his father's money.

Håkon Werle. A wealthy, aging, influential businessman and widow. He craves company in his old age and believes his son, like his former wife, is a neurotic.

Old Ekdal. Formerly a respected lieutenant and dashing sportsman, Old Ekdal is now a wreck, and an impoverished and doddering alcoholic, after spending time in prison for an illegal business deal in which Werle senior was also involved.

Hialmar Ekdal. A dreamy man, given to self-exaggeration, Hialmar is, at his best, a loving father and husband. Ostensibly a photographer, he spends most of his days playing in the garret with his father and dreaming of his mythical invention. He is an old school friend of Gregers.

Gina Ekdal. Older than her husband, practical and uneducated, with little tolerance for flights of fancy, Gina is the true manager of the family business. A former housekeeper of the Werles.

Hedvig Ekdal. A bright, imaginative, loving fourteen-year-old girl who adores reading and drawing in spite of her weak eyes. One of her most prized possessions is a wounded wild duck given to her by Håkon Werle.

Mrs. Sörby. Werle senior's housekeeper and good-time girl. An affable hostess with a checkered past, she is honest and unashamed.

Relling. A strangely dissolute doctor who boards at the Ekdals'. He calls himself a manufacturer of "life-lies." An old suitor of Mrs. Sörby.

Molvik. An equally dissolute and drunken theology student.

HEDDA GABLER
The Plot

In spite of its many dramatic events, *Hedda Gabler* is essentially a portrait of its protagonist. Powerful Hedda is woefully mismatched with the affable scholar George Tesman, whom she does not love. With cold precision, she manipulates those around her—Tesman, Eilert Lövborg (a rival scholar who was once her "comrade"), and a beautiful younger woman she has known since her school days—while the equally sardonic Judge Brack watches and comments from the sidelines, waiting for his chance to control her. Hedda's motives are complex, but her actions—including those against herself—are fierce and destructive.

Characters

Hedda Gabler. A twenty-nine-year-old woman of cold, composed beauty whose father was a wealthy and respected general. She is manipulative, cynical, aloof, and appears pitiless but also shows deep frustration and boredom. She wishes "to mold a human destiny."

George Tesman. A genial, befuddled "specialist" and "collector" whose scholarly research is on a satirically narrow subject. He was spoiled by the two aunts who brought him up and has a weakness for good food and drink.

Thea Elvsted. A beautiful young woman trapped in a loveless marriage, she is paradoxically frail and courageous, naive and intelligent. In their school days together, Hedda threatened to burn off her abundant blond hair.

Eilert Lövborg. An alcoholic and a brilliant scholar who, inspired by Mrs. Elvsted to temperance, has written a book on "the march of human civilization" and another, as yet unpublished, on "the future of civilization." A former admirer of Hedda's.

Judge Brack. Full of knowing innuendo, the judge is Hedda's evil equal and wishes to be her controlling admirer. He is Tesman's supposed friend.

Miss Juliana Tesman. A generous, down-to-earth old woman who believes her nephew can do no wrong. She has a keen eye and a loving heart.

Berta. The longtime servant at the Tesmans' villa. She expresses pity for Hedda.

THE MASTER BUILDER

The Plot

A tale of ambition, genius, defiance, and loss of faith. Halvard Solness, a master builder in the prime of his professional life, is terrified of losing his place to the upcoming generation, and specifically to Ragnar Brovik, a young man who works for him (and whose father, another builder, is dying). Solness is haunted by the actions he has taken to further his ambition, and the uncanny way in which some of his wishes—evil, but unacted upon—have come true. He believes he may be mad. His frail wife mourns the loss of her childhood home and possessions more than the loss of her two children. The uncanny young Hilda Wangel arrives, as though from a folktale, exactly ten years after she last witnessed the master builder at his freest and most defiant. Insisting that, at that time, he kissed her and promised her he would return and make her a princess, she urges him on to dangerous heights.

Characters

Halvard Solness. A proud individualist and man of great talent, Solness was never formally trained as an architect. He began life with humble faith in God but grew to challenge and cease serving him.

Miss Hilda Wangel. A strange but rosily healthy young woman who arrives at the Solness residence with nothing but the clothes on her back and a change of linen. She demands a "kingdom" from Solness, whom she reveres with an intensity bordering on madness.

Aline Solness. A frail, oddly selfish woman of upper-middle-class background. She keeps a jealous eye on her husband but can barely stand to be in the same room with him.

Knut Brovik. An ill and elderly man who was once a renowned architect. A former employer of Solness driven out of business by Solness's ambitions, he now works for Solness.

Ragnar Brovik. Knut's son, who also works for Solness. A talented, angry, ambitious young man who longs to be recognized by, or made independent from, Solness.

Kaia Fosli. A timid but passionate young woman in love with Solness. She is Knut's niece and Ragnar's fiancée and works as Solness's bookkeeper.

Dr. Herdal. Ostensibly Aline's doctor for her many vague ailments, he is also a family friend who is increasingly concerned about Solness.

Ibsen's Themes and Symbols

Keeping Up Appearances: Tradition, Morality, Hypocrisy, and Reputation. Many of Ibsen's characters are all concerned—and some are nearly obsessed—with the problem of keeping their reputations intact. The male protagonists of *A Doll's House*, *Hedda Gabler*, and *The Master Builder* all prize and protect their professional reputations. In *The Wild Duck*, lost reputation and social standing have driven Old Ekdal into madness and decrepitude. Werle senior, like the Master Builder, is willing to commit ruthless acts to protect his standing, while his son commits equally ruthless acts in the hypocritical and merciless service of a supposedly higher morality.

Money and Control of Money. Under the cover of Ibsen's characters' obsession with keeping up appearances runs their taboo obsession with the getting and spending of money. In *A Doll's House*, Nora needs money desperately but can't ask for it or even borrow it on her own terms, though she takes pleasure in working for it, as does Christine. Nora's husband, Helmer, is a banker, and he continues his putative control over money at home, where he doles it out to Nora after she wheedles and charms him into doing so. In *The Wild Duck*, Gregers rejects his father's money, but Ibsen raises questions about the morality, or even possibility, of rejecting the control that goes along with it. In *Hedda Gabler*, Hedda *must* have money in order to maintain the narrow realm of social power allowed to her.

The Roles of Women. Though the debates about whether or not he can be called "feminist" continue to rage, the Ibsen represented in this collection is clearly a creator of complex female characters who finds women a useful subject for his explorations of human bondage. He exposes the limitations of women's lives and the selfishness, egoism, cruelty, and simple obliviousness of the men that surround them, if only through his dissection of middle-class marriage itself. In all four of the plays collected here, we are presented with middle-class women raised to please first their fathers, and then their husbands, and to sacrifice themselves in the name of family. In *A Doll's House*, we have not only Nora's example, but also that of Christine, who marries herself off for money to support her family. Hedda Gabler reacts to these limitations by identifying with her father and with his guns. In *The Master Builder*, Aline lives a kind of death-in-life, while the uncanny Hilda escapes into amoral fantasy. It seems that when Ibsen's female characters have little to say, they are most often treated with dignity and respect. In *The Wild Duck*, the hardworking Gina Ekdal is the only person keeping her family afloat. Her lack of imagination and education pale beside her forthright love for her daughter and husband. And gentle Hedvig, poised on the edge of womanhood, epitomizes both the demand for female self-sacrifice and squandered potential of women as humans.

Truth, Illusion, and Imagination. Ibsen's attitude toward truth, illusion, and imagination is complex, but they are always among his themes. He is most often characterized as a dour truth teller and exposer of hypocrisy, a role he certainly plays in *A Doll's House*. However, as we can see in *The Wild Duck*, Ibsen leaves open the possibility that imaginative acts—which are, after all, necessary in order to write a play—might make life bearable, and even allow for its improvement, at the same time that they conceal corruption. The "truths" revealed by Gregers cause only tragic unhappiness, destroying even the most youthful and innocent of illusions. We remain unsure, in fact, whether Gregers fully understands the complexity of the truth. In *The Master Builder*, it is the struggle for a higher truth, the ability to envision a life beyond the ordinary, that both exalts and destroys the play's characters. In *Hedda Gabler*, Lövborg's visionary triumph is linked to his destructive alcoholism, while the narrow vision and self-protecting delusions of Tesman allow him to flourish.

Ibsen's Symbolism. It is easy, perhaps too easy, to name the magical resonant objects and spaces that are symbolic in each of Ibsen's plays. Some objects obviously imbued with symbolic meaning are: Hedvig's wild duck, the Ekdals' garret and their photography studio, General Gabler's guns and Lövborg's manuscript, the doll Nora buys for her daughter, Solness's towers and wreath. All of them are rich in meaning and deeply important to the unfolding of their respective plays. Indeed, they are so rich that they resist any easy, allegorical interpretations of what they "symbolize." As many contemporary critics have noted, the history of Ibsen criticism stands as a warning against expecting to resolve the puzzles they pose. Instead, it invites Ibsen readers to allow them to accrue layers of meaning, standing, as they would on the set of a stage, as both actual objects and conduits for stories, memories, and dreams.

CRITICAL EXCERPTS

Biographies and Biographical Studies

Meyer, Michael. *Ibsen: A Biography,* New York: Doubleday & Company, Inc., 1971.

Meyer is a world-renowned expert on Ibsen. This mammoth (865-page) scholarly work has been celebrated not only as the definitive Ibsen biography but also as one of the definitive works of its genre. Though exhaustive, it remains clear and engaging and is filled with concrete details of Ibsen's world.

> So explosive was the message of *A Doll's House*—that a marriage was not sacrosanct, that a man's authority in his home should not go unchallenged, and that the prime duty of anyone was to find out who he or she really was and to become that person—that the technical originality of the play is often forgotten. It achieved the most powerful and moving effect by the highly untraditional methods of extreme simplicity and economy of language—a kind of literary Cubism.

Ferguson, Robert. *Henrik Ibsen: A New Biography,* London: Richard Cohen Books, 1996.

Ferguson draws on newly available materials illuminating Ibsen's intimate life, provides a more detailed portrait of the phases of his personality, and champions his early works. Here he describes Ibsen's life at sixteen as a pharmacist's apprentice in Grimstad.

Being a sea-faring town there were customers requiring attention night and day, and when the night-bell rang it was Ibsen's job to pull on his dressing-gown and, passing through the maids' room, climb the precipitous staircase to the dispensary. For the next six years he had to live "in the open" like this, never alone, always observed, powerless to control any aspect of his immediate environment. The effect on his personality was profound, and when success and money finally made it possible for him he would indulge his need for privacy until it bordered on the pathological.

Early Reviews and Interpretations

Gosse, Edmund. "Ibsen's Social Dramas," *Fortnightly Review,* January 1, 1889.

Gosse was one of Ibsen's earliest English-speaking champions. After visiting Norway, he campaigned tirelessly for Ibsen's works to be translated and produced in England. It was this article that first drew the interest of Ibsen's later important champions, dramatist George Bernard Shaw and novelist Henry James.

Ibsen, be it admitted, for the sake of the gentle reader, is not a poet to the taste of every one. The school of critics now flourishing amongst us, to whom what is serious in literature is eminently distasteful, and who claim of modern writing that it should be light, amusing, romantic, and unreal, will find Ibsen much too imposing.

Scott, Clement. "A Doll's House," *Theatre,* July 1889.

Scott's essay, published in the midst of the intense scandal over *A Doll's House,* was the first of many in his tireless campaign against Ibsen. Though he initially praised the play's craft in a review, here he castigates Ibsen for both unreal and shameful ideas. The theme of Nora as an unfeeling, unnatural mother became a common one. Note also, the blow against socialism.

> She [Nora] a loving affectionate woman, forgets all about the eight years' happy married life, forgets the nest of the little bird, forgets her duty, her very instinct as a mother, forgets the three innocent children who are asleep in the next room, forgets her responsibilities, and does a thing that one of the lower animals would not do. A cat or dog would tear apart any one who separated it from its offspring, but the socialistic Nora, the apostle of the new creed of humanity, leaves her children almost without a pang. . . . It is all self, self, self!

Archer, William. "Ghosts and Gibberings," *Pall Mall Gazette,* April 8, 1891.

Archer, along with Gosse, was Ibsen's staunch champion as well as his translator and producer. In this famous article, a turning point in Ibsen's reception, he collected the invective with which English critics greeted Ibsen's *Ghosts.* Presented with their own hysteria (one critic notoriously called the play "A loathsome sore unbandaged; a dirty act done publicly; a lazar house with all its doors and windows open"), the literary community modified their tone thereafter.

> This article, I shall be told, is purely negative, and contains no rational discussion of the merits and demerits of *Ghosts.* True; but who can carry on a rational discussion with men whose first argument is a howl for the police?

James, Henry. "On the Occasion of *Hedda Gabler*," *New Review*, June 1891.

James was, at first, baffled by Ibsen's technical innovations. However, after several years of reading and attending Ibsen's works, he became a fervent supporter of Ibsen's social realism, which he illuminates here. This essay was another turning point in Ibsen's acceptance.

Illusions are sweet to the dreamer, but not so to the observer, who has a horror of a fool's paradise. Henrik Ibsen will have led him inexorably into the rougher road. Such recording and illuminating agents are precious; they tell us where we are in the thickening fog of life, and we feel for them much of the grateful respect excited in us at sea, in dim weather, by the exhibition of the mysterious instrument with which the captain takes an observation. We have held *Ghosts*, or *Rosmersholm*, or *Hedda Gabler* in our hand, and *they* have been our little instrument.

Shaw, George Bernand. *The Quintessence of Ibsenism*, New York: Hill and Wang, 1913.

Many scholars now argue that Shaw's "quintessence" is mostly of Shaw, rather than of Ibsen, and that his importance as an Ibsen critic has been overrated. However, his place in the Ibsen canon is undeniable, and his book, revised and printed three times to include further writings, is a fascinating catalog of a major playwright's working out of his most powerful influence. The below is from "Hedda Gabler, 1890."

Hedda Gabler has no ethical ideals at all, only romantic ones. She is a typical nineteenth century figure falling into the abyss between the ideals which do not impose on her and the realities she has not yet discovered. The result is that though she has imagination, and an intense appetite for beauty, she has no conscience, no conviction: with plenty of cleverness, energy, and personal fascination she

remains mean, envious, insolent, cruel in protest against
others' happiness, fiendish in her dislike of inartistic people and things, a bully in reaction from her own cowardice.

Critical Interpretations:
1920s–1950s

Forster, E. M. "Ibsen the Romantic," *Abinger Harvest*, London: Edward Arnold, 1936. (First published 1928.)
  In this influential essay, novelist and essayist Forster
traces the continued presence of the romanticism of Ibsen's
early fantastical verse plays in his later realist social dramas.
The quote below references *The Wild Duck*.

> The trees in old Ekdal's aviary are as numerous as the
> forest because they are countless, the water in the chick-
> ens' trough includes all the waves on which the Vikings
> could sail. To his impassioned vision dead and damaged
> things, however contemptible socially, dwell for ever in
> the land of romance, and this is the secret of his so-called
> symbolism: a connection is found between objects that
> lead different types of existence; they reinforce one an-
> other and each lives more intensely than before. Conse-
> quently his stage throbs with a mysteriousness for which
> no obvious preparation has been made, with beckonings,
> tremblings, sudden compressions of air, and his charac-
> ters as they wrangle among the oval tables and stoves
> are watched by an unseen power which slips between
> their words.

Koht, Halvdan. "Shakespeare and Ibsen," *Journal of English
and Germanic Philology* 44:1, January 1945.
  Koht's early biography of Ibsen, first translated in the
early 1930s, is still cited. Here he argues that Shakespeare
"liberated" Ibsen from classicism, but that Ibsen pushed his
character development even further.

Ibsen developed and deepened the psychology he found in Shakespeare's dramas. He never placed before us a complete self-confessed villain such as we can meet with in Shakespeare. . . . Ibsen never allowed his persons to be mere villains; they are always thoroughly human, complex by nature and in motive, studied and pictured down to their deepest aspirations and qualities.

Le Gallienne, Eva. *Preface to Ibsen's "Hedda Gabler" with a New Translation of the Play,* London: Faber and Faber Limited, 1953.

Le Gallienne was an American actress, educated in France, who founded and directed the first successful American theater company, the Civic Repertory Theatre in New York City. She produced and performed many of Ibsen's works and provided stage directions along with an actress's point of view.

The play is so modern in essence, and always will be, that when I first played it in 1927–8, I thought it would bring the play closer to modern audiences if one dressed it in modern clothes. . . . I have felt for the past few years that I was mistaken in this. Modern audiences are so literal-minded [lists audience objections ending with] ". . . A woman of our emancipated age would never have found herself in Hedda's position, or if she had, she would have easily been able to escape from it, etc." This last objection is of course sheer nonsense since, in spite of the plodding wage-earning millions of "emancipated" women, the Hedda type persists—the inevitable parasite. She could never have earned her own living; she would have been lost, unless she became a great demimondaine; but her fastidious and conventional nature would never have allowed her to be that. She is, above everything else, a "great lady"; there still exist many women of this sort; it is the nonsense of ignorance to deny it.

Critical Interpretations: 1960s–1980s

McFarlane, James. *Ibsen and the Temper of Norwegian Literature,* London: Oxford University Press, 1960.

McFarlane is a major Ibsen scholar and the editor of several volumes of Ibsen criticism and documents. In the comments from which the selection below is drawn, he discusses the paradoxical nature of Ibsen's work and how it defeats easy classification.

> One thing inevitably emerges from any closer study of Ibsen, something rather unsettling to critical orthodoxy; and this is the realization that he does not seem to react very satisfactorily to any of the standard laboratory tests of criticism; further, that any account of his work that limits itself to what is positive and obtrusive in it seems destined to end in triteness; or else—something which is strange and astonishing in this seemingly so straightforward author—it turns out that any generalization once made seems to demand reservation and qualification so drastic that the end result is little short of flat contradiction.

Egan, Michael, ed. *Ibsen: the Critical Heritage,* London: Routledge and Kegan Paul Ltd., 1972.

Egan has collected a wide variety of famous and infamous early responses to Ibsen's work in England and America. In his vivid and funny introduction, he traces the scandal of Ibsen's reception and outlines the cultural currents behind it.

> That major innovating talents are frequently received with hostility is a commonplace in literary history; yet to point this out is only partly to account for the uniquely bitter and vicious antagonisms which characterized Ibsen's contemporary reception in Europe and the United States. It was almost as if the future of civilization itself was felt to be at stake.

Templeton, Joan. "The Doll House Backlash: Criticism, Feminism, and Ibsen," *PMLA* 104:1, January 1989.

Templeton reviews the still ongoing controversy over whether *A Doll's House* can or should be read as an early feminist play, and sharply critiques the methods and motives of critics seeking to "save Ibsen from feminism."

> Anyone who claims that Ibsen thought of Nora as a silly, hysterical, or a selfish woman is either ignoring or misrepresenting the plain truth, present from the earliest to the most recent biographies, that Ibsen admired, even adored, Nora Helmer. Among all his characters, she was the one he liked best and found most real.

Critical Interpretations: 1990s and Beyond

Johnston, Brian. *The Ibsen Cycle,* revised edition, University Park, Penn.: The Pennsylvania State University Press, 1992.

Originally published in 1975, Johnston's book helped raise Ibsen to the status he enjoys today after the relative neglect of the 1950s and 1960s. His argument, that the twelve plays, from *Pillars of Society* to *When We Dead Awaken,* are "a single, Hegelian, cyclical, and evolutionary structure that might well come to be seen as the greatest single art work of the nineteenth century," was radical when published, and currently influential.

> Serious interpretation of *The Master Builder* is a somewhat formidable task from the extreme complexity of Ibsen's total intention, and we had better begin with first impressions. We are aware of an extraordinary regression into childhood on the part of the two major characters and, furthermore, on the part of another middle-aged character, Aline Solness. . . . The theme of childhood obviously is an important part of the play's meaning: childhood as a lost condition to be returned to by sickly adults; childhood as the victim of sick maturity; and childhood as

a terrifying challenge to the older generation clinging to life and power.

Goldman, Michael. *Ibsen: The Dramaturgy of Fear*, New York: Columbia University Press, 1999.

Goldman argues that "Ibsen's characters are killers," literally and metaphorically, drawing on Freudian theory to paint a picture of characters driven by childhood traumas. Here he comments on the metaphor of seeing and of retouching photographs in *The Wild Duck*.

> "[M]aking the picture come out right" is not only a matter of hypocrisy or convenient self-deception. It rises from the cloudiest springs of human disposition. . . . Just as the play, for all its humor, is not simply comic, so the drive to retouch is located by Ibsen not simply in the human comedy of saving appearances or in the relatively conscious motors of self-interest but in deep and deeply deformed sources of imagination and desire. A child is at the center of *The Wild Duck* because the adult efforts at retouching that shape its action are all linked to the volatile and distorted psychic life we bring with us from childhood.

Moi, Toril. " 'It was as if he meant something different from what he said—all the time': Language, Metaphysics and the Everyday in *The Wild Duck*," *New Literary History: A Journal of Theory and Interpretation*, Autumn 2002.

Using the philosophy of Ludwig Wittgenstein and Stanley Cavell, Moi traces the way Ibsen juxtaposes ordinary daily life and its language with Gregers Werle's tragic insistence on things meaning more (or much less) than they seem.

> Ibsen's turn towards the everyday in *The Wild Duck* takes the form of a rejection of all the usual theatrical forms: comedy, melodrama, and tragedy. Turning towards the everyday means trying to treat all his characters (not just

the high, as in tragedy, and not just the low, as in comedy) with equal respect and attention. . . .

Ibsen placed no mouthpiece for himself in *The Wild Duck*. Perhaps he really did set out to write a play about language, metaphysics, and the everyday, even if he would not have used precisely those terms to describe his project. Perhaps he saw that modernity was becoming increasingly characterized by the skeptical crisis of language and trust. But he never said so. Instead he made us look at the child. At the center of *The Wild Duck* there is a frightened, loving child struggling and failing to make sense of words and the world.

Bentley, Eric. "What Ibsen Has Meant," *Southwest Review* 88:4, September 1, 2003.
    Originally a keynote address to the 2003 International Ibsen Society Conference, Bentley argues for the importance of seeing Ibsen in performance, his connection to the "well-made plays" of shock and melodrama, and closes with a conservative call to continue the legacy of Ibsen as a "hero" in the tradition of the "Master Builder."

In our time, the twentieth and now the twenty-first century, civilization—specifically, our Western civilization—has come under attack. And it has been an attack not just politically from the East but also culturally from would-be radical scholars here at home in the West. A foundation stone of Western civilization is the great individual, the great poet, composer, painter. The would-be radical critic denies his existence, affirming that the master builders of the West were all Halvard Solnesses or worse, rotten with guilt and hideously inadequate. It is true of course, that Ibsen took the hero down a peg or two.

QUESTIONS FOR DISCUSSION

Nora's decision to leave her husband and children was beyond shocking when *A Doll's House* was first staged. How do you feel about Nora's decision? Do you think it is more likely that a woman would behave this way today than when Ibsen wrote his play? Why or why not? How are women who leave their children behind viewed by society today?

Ibsen is often portrayed as a courageous truth teller. How is truth telling portrayed in *The Wild Duck*? How are imagination and illusion portrayed?

Plays are meant to be performed. Which of Ibsen's plays do you think would change the most for you if you saw it performed instead of reading it? What scenes or sets do you think would present a challenge? For example, how do you imagine the garret in *The Wild Duck* would appear onstage? How would you stage the end of *The Master Builder,* or of *Hedda Gabler*? Do you think any of the plays would be better as a movie?

423

Hedda Gabler has been labeled as everything from an evil, unfeeling femme fatale to a cruelly thwarted woman with power, intelligence, and ambition. Why do you think Hedda Gabler behaves the way that she does? Does she have any contemporary counterparts?

Ibsen is celebrated for his realism, yet many readers have noted the fairy-tale aspects of *The Master Builder*. Which fairy tales does it remind you of? Which parts of the play seem more real than others? Why do you think Ibsen employs this technique? Does he use it in any of the other plays?

In his day, Ibsen revolutionized the theater and rocked the social foundations of his middle-class audiences. Is it possible for art or literature to have a similar impact today? Can you think of any contemporary books, plays, or movies that have shocked their audiences and challenged or changed their worldview?

Suggestions for the
Interested Reader

If you enjoyed *Four Great Plays of Henrik Ibsen*, you might also be interested in the following:

Through a Glass Darkly and *Scenes from a Marriage* (VHS, DVD). These are two of the finest films crafted by pioneering Swedish filmmaker Ingmar Bergman, whom many critics consider as important to cinematic arts as Ibsen was to the theatrical arts. Both films— *Through a Glass Darkly* came out in 1961 and *Scenes from a Marriage* in 1973—share a certain Scandinavian dourness with Ibsen's work, and both examine hidden tragedies and repression in middle-class families.

The Hours by Michael Cunningham. This much-praised novel about three very different women struggling to come to terms with their lives was made into an Academy Award–nominated film starring Nicole Kidman, Meryl Streep, and Julianne Moore.

The Awakening by Kate Chopin. This short novel, set among the Creole elite of Louisiana at the turn of the twentieth century, was extremely controversial when it was published in 1899. It is a sensuous story of a woman's reactions to the constraints of marriage and motherhood.

Death of a Salesman by Arthur Miller. This classic 1949 play by Arthur Miller is one of the best-known plays in all of American literature. Miller's debt to Ibsen is clear in this realistic, ultimately tragic story of self-aggrandizing salesman Willy Loman and his family. A terrific 1966 television adaptation starring Lee J. Cobb as Loman is available on DVD and VHS. Dustin Hoffman and John Malkovich star in an excellent 1985 production of the play, also available on DVD.

BESTSELLING ENRICHED CLASSICS

JANE EYRE
Charlotte Brontë
0-671-01479-X
$5.99

WUTHERING HEIGHTS
Emily Brontë
0-7434-8764-8
$4.95

THE GOOD EARTH
Pearl S. Buck
0-671-51012-6
$6.99

THE AWAKENING AND SELECTED STORIES
Kate Chopin
0-7434-8767-2
$4.95

HEART OF DARKNESS AND *THE SECRET SHARER*
Joseph Conrad
0-7434-8765-6
$4.95

GREAT EXPECTATIONS
Charles Dickens
0-7434-8761-3
$4.95

A TALE OF TWO CITIES
Charles Dickens
0-7434-8760-5
$4.95

THE COUNT OF MONTE CRISTO
Alexandre Dumas
0-7434-8755-9
$6.50

FROM
POCKET BOOKS